Dance Hall

A Novel of
Sing Sing

DAVID PIETRUSZA

Church & Reid Books

Dance Hall
A Novel of
Sing Sing

For information email: dap@davidpietrusza.com.

ISBN: 1440494053
ISBN-13: 978-1440494055

Dance Hall (definition):

1. A place of dance business.

2. The area of prison cells adjacent to the electric chair at Sing Sing Prison, where the condemned inmate spent his last day before execution.

The Crime

Each detail, likely and unlikely, one following upon another, had come tumbling out at the trial, a mercifully brief, though, nevertheless, desultory proceeding, attended by none save those whose presence was absolutely required—coppers and lawyers and court officers and witnesses, and, most reluctantly of all, by a brace of silent, patently guilty, defendants.

And, as a matter of course, for a very long time, those tumbling details had all returned like tenement roof homing pigeons to the alphabetically first of those defendants, to Mr. Edward Marek—as the clearest and the most vivid, and yet the blackest and most suffocating of memories, gallingly flavored by rancid, roughly-equal quadrants of despair, of rage, of regret, and yes, of guilt. Memories wended their way back to him like said homing pigeons each and every night. Only now, he, not they, was caged.

One plan was how he recalled it.

Two .38 caliber revolvers.

One pal.

One twenty-year-old Filipina.

No. The twenty-year-old Filipina never came out at the trial—for even convicted thieves have their standards.

His current difficulties, Eddie Marek noted, commenced with talk—big talk, desperate talk, stupid talk. It required a mere two weeks for stupid talk to give way to stupid action.

It was, he also recalled, his great pal "Foxy" who had first heard about the gin joint on East Fourteenth Street—Knocko Monahan's by name. That was where they obtained the two Colt .38s—illegal guns for illegal purposes bought in an illegal place.

No use doing things halfway.

Or, as Foxy used to say, why go to Purgatory when you can go to straight to Hell?

Knocko Monahan's was neither the best nor the meanest of Manhattan speakeasies, though by the rather wide-open standards of October 1930, it operated with admirable discretion, entered only through a side alley that in retrospect was a little too neat and down a creaky staircase where one rapped loudly upon a heavy wooden door—clad in iron thick enough to discourage police and business rivals—and uttered the properly mysterious password.

Such circumspect measures were necessitated because once safely inside, a patron could secure far more than innocent, illegal hootch.

You could, it seemed, get just about anything you desired at Knocko Monahan's.

A hard-looking redhead, clad in a frock two years removed from the newest fashion, had opened the peephole. She listened for the requisite password, inspected the two jokers—Eddie and Foxy—standing before her, and, between snaps of Wrigley Spearmint, tersely bade them enter.

"Five apiece," said a man in a brown felt hat, sizing up his two prospective customers as distinctly small-time, so amateurish and young and callow, that they could not possibly be the law.

"Four!" protested tall, lanky, muscular, and towheaded Eddie Marek. His courage fortified by liquid means, Marek wanted to pay four bucks apiece for a pair of hot guns and not a penny more, for on this October evening he didn't have very many pennies remaining. His pale blue eyes stole a glance at his pal, the weasel-faced, John "Foxy" Renard. Eddie Marek needed to know Foxy Renard was on board.

Taking all this in, of course, was The Redhead—who happened to be not only the keeper of the door, but The Man in the Brown Felt Hat's girlfriend. They were quite the couple. She had driven the getaway car on their first date. Or, at least, that was one of the stories folks told on that stretch of Fourteenth Street.

Some of those stories were even true.

The Man in the Brown Felt Hat kept talking, kept selling. He knew how to sell.

"Four? You kidding? These are Colt .38 'Detective Specials.' Not some piece of dime store junk. Quality merchandise. Genuine walnut stock. All the detectives and half the best crooks carry these. You want some two-bit piece of crap that blows up in your damn face? Four clams? Look, if you pikers ain't serious . . ."

"We're serious," averred Foxy Renard, his voice rising in pitch from a serious case of rapidly-fraying nerves, "Serious about paying four bucks."

"Four bucks? Gentleman, this is the very same model firearm that placed the illustrious Arnold Rothstein into the veritable wooden kimono. I would be spitting on his grave to let these babies go for less than a fin apiece."

Renard pondered that. The gun that killed Rothstein with a single shot that ripped through a multiplicity of vital organs, including some better left unreferenced in mixed company? Mr. Big? The Big Bankroll himself? Those were swell guns indeed. *This* was big time incarnate.

"We'll take 'em!" said Foxy Renard.

Five bucks. Some negotiator, fumed Marek, who now wanted to use his new gun first upon Renard. Giving Eddie pause was the uncertainty of having enough dough left over for bullets.

The deal was, nonetheless, done. And, despite going twenty percent over budget, Renard and Marek had obtained marvelous little firearms—small, shiny, deadly. They had, in fact, not overpaid.

"The most powerful arm that can be carried conveniently in a coat side pocket," is how the Colt Company advertised them. People were pretty straightforward about such things back then.

But not straightforward enough to say, "Powerful enough to kill a man."

Not that Edward Marek wanted to throw lead at anyone. He didn't hate anybody that much. He merely wanted to scare the hell out of whatever poor bastard worked behind the counter of whichever grocery or confectionary he was going to rob the next night—scare him more than he himself was scared.

Eddie and Foxy *did* have enough money for bullets, and they *did* rob some poor bastard that night, and they *kept* on robbing. "Crime does not pay," people said. Well, it did pay, though not particularly well at entry level.

If it did, more people might apply.

Tonight—six weeks later—they were at it yet again. Eddie reached into his pocket, delicately sliding his finger onto the

Colt's exceedingly delicate trigger. He nodded to Renard. Bundled against the damp Manhattan air in their threadbare overcoats, these two boys—and Marek was barely short of his twentieth birthday, Renard just a year older—had pushed their gray, well-worn fedoras tight upon their heads, damn near screwing them into their crania, as if that might offer significant disguise.

They were, after all, *not* sophisticated operators.

They shivered within sight of their current target, a sad little outpost of the Daniel Reeves grocery chain, located precisely at 113 Amsterdam Avenue, just below West Sixty-Fifth Street— where a poet might say Hell's Kitchen kisses the Upper West Side goodnight, but which Messrs. Marek and Renard merely found to be a semi-slum not any warmer or drier this evening than any of the better neighborhoods. Hundreds of these little cash-and-carry Daniel Reeves joints dotted the city streets. And above each "Daniel Reeves" sign, was another placard visible only to the desperate, the shiftless, the violent, of which there were so many more each day. Neon and flashing, it proclaimed: "ROB ME"—and each year desperate men read such signs and acted on them.

Tonight, Wednesday, November 19, 1930, two kids from Brooklyn stood a ways off from the store entrance, glancing toward their prey as casually as possible, hoping not to be noticed. Inside, a couple lingered, older people jabbering to the man with Vitalis-slick auburn hair behind the counter. They took, it seemed, forever.

"Flatfoot coming by again?" Marek asked, his eyes narrowing nervously.

"He does and we call it a night, Polack."

The counterman, John Finnegan by name, hit the magic key. Sale! Thirty-three cents. His customers, their brown paper bag cradled in the old man's arms, departed. Eddie and Foxy watched them head up the street, not so much to make sure they had departed, but for fear of what they themselves would have to do once they entered the store and did what they had to do.

"Hey, ma'am!" Eddie shouted.

Foxy Renard couldn't believe what his partner was doing.

"You dropped your scarf!"

"Whadda you auditioning for? The boy scouts?" said Renard.

"Aw, pipe down, pal!"

The little brass bell above the door heralded Marek and Renard's entrance.

"Help you gents?"

"You bet," said Marek, trying to be as friendly, as sanguine, as possible, though he was not in the least sanguine. And though he had robbed before he was not experienced enough to be anywhere *near* sanguine. Inside his coat pocket, his hand shook slightly. He prayed he wouldn't blow his foot off.

"Nice cash register you got there," said Foxy Renard.

"Yeah," Finnegan answered, "I like it." Daniel Reeves managers did not normally relish conversations of this nature.

"What's in it?"

"What?"

"Hand it over!"

"What?"

"Hand it over!"

John Finnegan was a smart man. Not smart enough to own the joint, but possessing wisdom enough to manage it when jobs were tight. Wise enough to hand over the cash.

Nobody got hurt.

Walk in. Help yourself to some working capital. Walk out. Edward Stanley Marek liked it that way.

Circumstances remained likable for only part of the way down the block.

"Hey, you! You two! Stop!" boomed the big, rasping voice behind them, slashing Manhattan's night air like the beam of a squad-car searchlight. Marek and Renard broke and ran—no use looking back.

BANG!!! A shot sundered whatever peace resided on Amsterdam Avenue—then—BANG!!!—another. Foxy Renard felt his left arm sting. He knew he'd been hit but didn't know whether the bullet had grazed him or hit bone, how much he was bleeding or even whether or not he bled at all. He didn't have much experience being a clay pigeon. Maybe, he thought, it was just a flesh wound, like in the movies or the radio or the detective magazines or the dime novels. Nothing to really worry about, except there never is such thing as *just* a flesh wound when it's *your* flesh.

He had no time to think. He and Eddie kept running—faster, faster—rounding West Sixty-Fourth Street, hailing a cab, hopping in, and barking, though labored breaths to head for Foxy's Greenpoint apartment—and to make it snappy.

"You OK?" Eddie Marek whispered, as he tied his own necktie, tourniquet-style round his partner's bleeding arm. He was scared, more scared than he had even been in his entire twenty-two years, but he didn't show it.

"I think so," answered Foxy Renard ". . . I don't know, Eddie . . . I just don't know."

Mr. & Mrs. Marek

Edward Stanley Marek Jr. did not like most things about his life. He did not like robbing stores or sticking guns in people's faces. He particularly did like seeing his partner oozing frighteningly bright red globs of blood and evidence onto the dirty backseat of a Yellow Cab.

Eddie Marek had not been raised to rob. But he was not sure what he was raised for. His uncles worked like dogs three hundred feet underground in the Scranton coal mines. His father pushed a broom at the elementary school down the block, but at home he acted like he was king of the universe—a mad, drunken, broken-English king of the universe. Edward Marek Sr. screamed at his only son, beat him with his thick leather belt and beat his mother and his three younger sisters with his fists, and even tied Eddie onto a stiff-back kitchen chair and shoved him into a darkened closet until he was good-and-ready to let him out. By sixteen, Eddie had more than enough. He dreamed of getting as far away as possible from his old man and from the black hell of the mines, and the United States Marines Corps looked like it could do just that for him. The leatherneck recruiter who stared suspiciously at Eddie from beneath his furrowed beetle brow wasn't particularly choosy. In some ways he was just as desperate as Eddie was, and he took just about whoever showed up and could lie with a straight face about their record and/or their age. Eddie kept his face plenty straight and before he knew it he was wearing Marine khakis and steaming across the Equator and toward for the Philippines. At twenty, he gratefully became an ex-Marine—discharged at the Brooklyn Navy Yard and ready for life on his own.

He had not planned on robbery or on gunplay, but times were tough for a kid scarcely out of the Marines. Jobs? Forget about them. It was a miracle to keep one, let alone find one. So Foxy Renard had hatched up a scheme. Hike down to the foot of Greenpoint Avenue, sneak aboard the ferry to Twenty-Third Street, snag a couple of hot guns, and go into business for themselves. The capital outlay was small—and there they were.

Foxy Renard claimed he needed the cash to stay off the streets and out of the flophouses and convinced Eddie that armed robbery in the first degree afforded more dignity than panhandling, though, in his more reflective moments, he did concede that it somewhat diminished the dignity of those being robbed.

Eddie wasn't buying it.

"What do you know about holdups?" he demanded.

"I know what I hear. What do I need to know?" said Renard, lowering his eyes and his voice and his already low level of truth, for Foxy Renard knew a great deal more about armed robbery than he cared to admit: where, for example, to get guns to go into business, and where, along the East River docks to toss them when the heat was on. And he recognized the importance of keeping new recruits in the dark about anything that wasn't their, or anyone else's, beeswax—and, most importantly of all, Foxy Renard knew that if you kept your loot close at hand and divvied it up only after your own private inventory, the traditional fifty-fifty split need not always be what it appeared to be.

Eddie Marek remained unconvinced. At least at first, he did, but Foxy kept after him, because Foxy knew enough about holdups to know he needed a partner, and it wasn't that he couldn't trust his old partners any longer, but that they no longer trusted him very much.

Eddie weakened. He needed the dough, and not just for himself, but for his recently-acquired wife. Mr. & Mrs. Marek resided in a dingy, third-floor walk-up above a tailor shop, not far from the Brooklyn docks, in Greenpoint, a rough-and-tumble place, and growing more tumble down by the day. For a while Eddie had found work as a stevedore, unloading lumber on the waterfront, but you had to get called for those jobs, picked out of the shapeup. The Stock Market crashed. Things got tough. Then they got tougher. He got picked less and less, and then not at all.

None of the other places in the neighborhood, neither the refineries, nor the still more malodorous varnish factories and soap plants, nor even the lumber yards themselves, were hiring either. Yet, Eddie was strong enough to work at any of these joints—six feet tall, 170 pounds of sinewy muscle, possessing a certain small town intelligence, one might say even a shrewdness. And he thought the shrewdest thing he had ever done was to have married Carissa Queveda.

"Carrie" was a year and five months younger than Eddie—and Filipino. They had met when Eddie was in the Marines, aboard the *USS Bulmer* and stationed at Manila between patrols up the China coast.

Her English was decent, her parents having worked at the American naval base since before her birth. But it was not her diction or vocabulary that attracted Eddie to her, though he indeed found the gentle lilt of her Tagalog accent charming. It was her flashing smile, her dark brown eyes, set in a face that to him seemed faintly Chinese, her midnight black hair that fell far well below her shoulders, her lithe body, and the gentleness of her manner, a very real beauty combined with a certain vulnerability that together translated into an irresistible charm.

Even if she was one of *them*.

He had first caught notice of her late one evening as he chanced to walk past the pink stuccoed officer's club hall. Inside was an officer's soiree, the men in their gleaming dress whites and their women in their satins and lace, with the sounds of the club's small orchestra tinnily floating through the moonlit tropical air. The only way either Eddie or the creature standing before him might attend the festivities inside was as servants—and both of them knew that. Eddie was merely passing though on his way to his barracks. But she stood there transfixed, listening to the melodies of a far-off nation and wanted so badly to be inside—wanting to be even further away from her home, located a block from the city's largest *matadero*—a far nicer term, at least in English, than *slaughterhouse*—in the humanity-filled slums of the city's teeming, poverty-stricken *Tondo* district.

And he knew, right from the start, that he wanted to be with her. Not just strolling along Manila's barge-clogged Pasig River or along its miles of canals or dodging its horse-drawn *caramatos* and trolleys or meandering under its blessedly shaded colonial arcades—or not even merely in her embrace—but *forever*. Not long afterward, the *Bulmer* sailed for Shandong Province, but when he returned, they were married, in her ancient parish church, *Sto. Niño de Tondo*, he in his starched corporal's dress blue uniform, she in her gloriously long handmade *mantilla* and white butterfly-sleeved *terno*. And when he returned to Brooklyn, unlike any Lieutenant Pinkerton, he sent for her, and, after they had first adjourned to his modest apartment, he took her to the grandest dance hall he could think of, to Coney Island's Oriental Danceland. Carrie had never seen anything like the Oriental, nothing at all like the great white-tuxedoed orchestras, the onrushing waves of swirling dancers, the roar of youth and energy, nothing like strolling upon the boardwalk in the moonlight to the clattering serenade of The Cyclone and The Thunderbolt and The Tornado and the squeals and screams of each contraption's tempest-tossed, bilious, white-knuckled patrons—nights of music and roller-coasters and dreams.

"May I have this dance, Corporal Marek?" Eddie Marek asked his newly-American bride, with less hesitation and delay than even he had thought possible. They would dance that night and not all the officers and all their ladies in the world would be able to stop them.

Their American honeymoon—and a lot more—ended when Wall Street nosedived and took the country down with it, and one day, after Carrie had gotten the fish-eye from the butcher one time too many, she screwed up the courage to tell Eddie what was on her mind: she was going to get a job. A pal of hers two floors down the hallway had said she could get her one, at a dancehall down the trolley line. A dime a dance from the customers, with each girl keeping a nickel of that, and maybe there's enough nickels to pay the butcher and the rent, so her Eddie would not have to worry so much about all the dimes he no longer had.

That was *her* plan.

And, that was when Eddie started listening *seriously* to Foxy's plan. No wife of his was going to nickel hop in one of those dives. He knew those joints from near the Navy Yard.

Liquored-up bums with their hands all over the girls. Snot-nosed punks. Mumbling losers from the boardinghouses. Chinks and spicks just waiting to get their mitts on any woman they could . . .

. . . and worse . . . much worse.

Hell, no. A man has principles, after all. A husband has even more.

At first, though, Eddie had protested Foxy's idea.

"Can't we just be bootleggers, Foxy, why robbers?"

"For the same reason we can't be in Herbert Hoover's cabinet," Renard shot back, "Them jobs are filled, and even if there was a vacancy, we don't have the resumes. And besides— the last time I looked neither one of us was a Dago or a Yid—or even a Mick!"

Foxy Renard had clearly given the question prior reflection.

Soon, Eddie had enough dough in his wallet to tell Carrie to stay home, dry the dishes, and listen to *Amos 'n' Andy* on the radio. He didn't tell her where the money was coming from— and she was afraid to ask.

"Going out for a paper," said Mr. Marek one morning as if he was merely preparing to depart for a *Daily News* or a *Daily Mirror.*

He was really going to see Foxy—Foxy was OK now, a little sore from the gunshot, but healing well. It really was "just" a flesh wound—and they were thinking up another job. Thinking up another job took time, they told themselves. You just didn't walk into some West Side grocery store and stick a gun in some clerk's scared-silly kisser. They even considered branching out. Auto theft seemed promising, and, at the very least, would provide them with a getaway car for their original line of work.

Carrie, still in her frayed satin dressing gown, busied herself, removing cracked dishes and mismatched silverware from their porcelain-topped kitchen table. Eddie retrieved his overcoat from a chair back. He checked for the five-dollar Colt .38 in his right pocket.

"I see you later," Carrie called to him.

He advanced a single step. The hallway door came crashing, splintering, forward. Men, big burly, hard-looking lugs, harder than any he had seen on the docks or the Marines or the breadlines, came hurtling through it. It happened all too fast. They rushed him and grabbed him and pinned him to the kitchen floor, slamming his chin against the worn linoleum, so hard they bloodied it, so hard he bit his tongue, and more blood oozed from his lips.

He still had his hand on his gun, but they had their hands all over him, and there was no use blowing a hole in your coat pocket and maybe yourself and making things worse. No use getting yourself killed. No use getting Carrie killed.

"Edward Marek, you're under arrest."

And then someone kicked Eddie in the head.

No use taking chances with a man with his right hand in his overcoat pocket.

Up the River

Pure morning light, miraculously untainted by Manhattan's soot-tinged air, streamed in luminous shafts through windows twelve stories high. Past waves of businessmen and clerks, mothers and daughters, redcaps and shoeshine boys, three men trekked across Grand Central Station's gleaming, teaming vastness. Two of the men, one bulky and florid and mature, the other, angular and still young but with burdens of anxiety and regret already pressing upon him, walked very close together across acres of scuffed Tennessee pink marble, walked together, in fact, entirely too proximate each other. The trio's third member, sandy-haired and jowly, slid a ten-dollar gold certificate across the New York Central ticket counter.

"Three for Ossining. Two round-trip—one one-way."

They re-crossed the great concourse, past more waves of businessmen and clerks, mothers and daughters, redcaps and shoeshine boys, descending the stairs to Track 41, where they found a train and two rows of seats facing each other, beginning a lurching four-mile ride underground, not emerging into daylight until East Ninety-Sixth Street—East Harlem.

As they rode, the same thoughts cascaded through Eddie Marek's mind, again and again, submerging every normal idea and emotion. Cascading now were unkind notions regarding one John "Foxy" Renard. Eddie Marek had believed his partner would never sell him out. He had been proven unduly optimistic. Young Mr. Renard had made his own deal, ratting out Eddie, implicating him in everything but the teaching of evolution in Tennessee. Between Foxy's squealing and the pull his mother's brother-in-law Mike had down at Borough Hall, shirt-tail relative that their clan was with the McCooeys and the McQuades, Foxy got himself one sweet deal—a year and a day in The Tombs.

Eddie got more—a lot more. He was not amused.

"Scarborough! Next stop Ossining!"

"That's us," said Detective Sgt. George Thomas O'Brien, his first communication since asking to stop at the men's room at Grand Central.

Firmly handcuffed to O'Brien, Eddie Marek had been the model of decorum—even in that rest room. There was no need for anyone to wrestle him to the floor, to bloody his chin. No escape attempts. No lip. Not even a dirty look. Prisoners became remarkably well behaved and levelheaded when shackled to lawmen. Why add to your sentence before even starting it?

The New York Central line's tracks ran right through Sing Sing, cutting it in half. The station lay a little northward, but a special stop just before that permitted cons and their traveling companions to exit more conveniently, and that is where this trio exited, near enough to the main gate to save cab fare. For Eddie Marek, Sing Sing's heavy, wide metal gates clanked open in a downright welcoming gesture, though he did not quite see it that way.

This pile of rocks and walls and searchlights and peak-roofed guard towers would be his home for the next eight to eighteen years. Shackled to a New York City police detective, he did not relish the thought of those gates closing *behind* him. He did not like being caught. He did not like being so stupid. He did not like being so shamed, and a more than a small part of him did not like being so *wrong*. But above all, he did not want to be *here*, with heavy iron gates rolling shut behind him, in the company of detectives O'Brien and Merklinger. But even they were links to a life he was leaving. They would—could—return to New York. So could he—in eight to eighteen years—if he didn't do something equally stupid.

He wasn't betting on it.

"Yankees look good this year," said a pudgy, fifty-ish man with plain, round, black-framed glasses, the slightest remnants of County Kilkenny brogue, and a stiff, white Roman collar.

The spectacles, collar, and accent all belonged to Father Gelasius Eugene Bryant. Some priests you expected to see in the archdiocesan Chancery, some to teach in a seminary or toil in a local parish. Some to be prison chaplains, Father Gelasius fit neatly into the latter category. Nothing lace-curtain Irish about him. Yes, he had, of course, attended seminary—done well there, studied Latin and theology and even some basic psychology—

but he retained the traces and mannerisms of the workingman, the kid from the family of six brothers and two sisters, the eighth-grade dropout he had once been.

He had once been assigned to a very decent parish, on Second Avenue, on Murray Hill—but not for long. There had been an indiscretion—its details by chance overheard by his pastor, a man not incapable of reading between carefully-worded lines. Father Gelasius was summoned to the Chancery, where an auxiliary bishop barely controlling his anger and disgust curtly informed him he could stay a priest, that Holy Mother Church believed in forgiveness and redemption, but he would have his own penance. He was going to where there were no young women, no temptations, only time to reflect on what he had done to wound the Mystical Body of Christ. He was going to Sing Sing—and he was never coming out.

Not all the lifers wore stripes.

Sing Sing Warden Stewart Beck, middle-aged, steely-eyed, deliberate in motion, had not paid substantial attention to Father Gelasius's ponderings regarding the Yankees. Stewart Beck was a stocky man—in fact, he was distinctly overweight—his bulky frame capped with the white brushy, distinctly unmanageable, remainder of what several decades previously had indeed once been a fine blond head of hair. Today—as was invariably his habit—he was attired in one of his closet full of gray woolen, three-piece, pin-striped suits, each pockmarked and cratered by the torrent of red-hot cinders that invariably flew from his curved silver-and-wood Dunhill pipe—the solitary concession Warden Beck extended to either fashion or to luxury, but a luxury that left the rest of him resembling the results of a night on the Bowery.

Beck had something more substantial than baseball on his mind as he stared down at the little drama transpiring just inside his prison's main gate, a tragedy featuring a tall, thin young man in a rumpled suit, a loosened tie, and a not particularly snappy snap-brim hat, a tragedy starring Eddie Marek.

Beck knew the script by heart. It was a very old one. But he never got used to it. To Stewart Beck, each man entering through that gate was unique, was as significant and tragic a character as if conceived by Shakespeare, instead of having merely been sentenced here by some Magistrate's Court hack who paid Tammany ten grand for his position and might just as easily be behind bars himself.

"Another one."

"Say something, Stewart?"

"No, not really," said Beck, watching Eddie Marek disappear through a doorway to the prison intake room.

But Father Gelasius had indeed heard what Stewart Beck had muttered and he knew *precisely* what he had meant and why he had said it so quietly—and quite so sadly.

Welcoming Committee

While Cell 314, Gallery 13, lay vacant, awaiting the momentary arrival of its next occupant, Edward Stanley Marek Jr., Cell 315 sheltered a man of much less introspective inclination. Nick Strecker crouched behind latticed iron prison bars, glaring at the stone and steel that marked his new world's cramped boundaries.

Nick Strecker was in his early thirties, still young, but far older, and far, far more cynical and tougher than Marek—exceedingly far more than most people, or, more significantly, than even the great majority of convicted felons. He was also a remarkably sturdy man, the sort of figure a prudent individual would be wise to fear not only in a darkened alley but also upon a crowded boulevard in bright sunlight.

Strecker's old man had died or disappeared—nobody knew which—when Nick was barely more than a toddler. His mother was sickly, always weak, and always ill, always coughing up whatever she was coughing up, barely able to work and of little value to any employer when she did. Which is why she held so many jobs, each one, it seemed, for progressively shorter periods and even more meager pay. When she died, broke and worn out, she left behind a dirty Ludlow Street fourth-floor walk-up filled with tattered and broken furniture, a mangy white cat, two months of unpaid rent, and a nine-year old boy too scared to cry or even to follow his mothers' cheap wicker coffin down the stairs and out onto the street.

Mrs. Larrabee across the hall took Nick in—providing him with a roof over his head but not much more. It might be said that Mr. Larrabee was a mean drunk, but it was exceedingly difficult to ascertain if he was any meaner drunk than sober for he never seemed sober at all. For safety and sanity, young Nick wandered the streets. He hired out for errands of dubious legality. He rolled drunks in stinking, rat-filled alleyways—there was, after all, no shortage of inebriates on Ludlow Street. He pinched what he could from pushcart vendors and shopkeepers and ran like hell. He was an Artful Dodger without a Fagin, on the road to becoming a Bill Sikes without a Nancy.

Nick grew up to be powerfully built, with shaved head, and cold gray eyes—damned intimidating when he wanted to be, which was most of the time. To Strecker a gun or knife were desirable tools—but not completely necessary. He could rob or beat or even kill you with his bare hands. Stewart Beck liked telling visitors that only about twenty-five percent of his wards were actually a menace to society.

Nick Strecker would soon be counted among Stewart Beck's sinister twenty-five percent.

Strecker interrupted Gallery 13's silence. "Hey, Rossi!" he shouted, in a voice deepened by ten thousand Lucky Strikes, "What day is it?"

Salvatore Rossi, a short, dark-haired Sicilian from Greenwich Village's Bleecker Street, occupied Cell 316. Unlike Nick Strecker, Sal was not so much into robbing people; he preferred strong-arming them, though, on occasion, he had been known to simultaneously do both. Basically, if you desired someone to see reason, Salvatore Rossi could rapidly accelerate that process, being particularly effective regarding those involved in labor disputes—though when they saw that light it was most often from the intensive-care ward of St. Vincent's Hospital. While effective, however, he was not particularly connected in the ranks of his profession or with Tammany Hall or the police. In fact, he was downright expendable. During the course of one exceptionally vicious strike, when he and his associates had pistol-whipped and crippled a 42-year old coat-maker named Jonah Glaser to within three-quarters of an inch of his life, the newspapers—and, following them, the District Attorney— became, shall we say, upset. And with no one significantly interested in protecting Sal, not his fellow goons, nor their union employers, nor anyone at Tammany, justice was done . . .

. . . twenty-years-to-life.

And thus, twenty-five year-old Salvatore Rossi currently resided in Cell 316. Lying calmly upon his bunk, he paused from leafing through a well-worn copy of *Saturday Evening Post*, an issue so old, Rossi figured Ben Franklin himself must have edited it.

He pondered Strecker's question before responding, "St. Anthony's Day—Friday the Thirteenth."

The answer puzzled Strecker, who had known Rossi from time spent together in The Tombs. "How long you been religious?" Nick wanted to know.

"Since I saw the type of people you get to meet in hell."

The answer touched a nerve in Strecker, but not a very big one. Eternity in hell didn't bother him as much as someone swiping one of his cigarettes or watering his whiskey. "Ah, dry up!" he ordered Rossi, but being nearly as much an agitator as he was a thug, he shouted down past him: "Hey! Myers, he must be talking about you!"

Sanford "Sandy" Myers, a.k.a. Sanford Milstein, Sheldon Myerson, and Stephen Morgan, newly arrived in Cell 317, remained intent on his game of solitaire, barely listening to the burly hoodlum two cells down. Myers differed markedly from Strecker and Rossi. Tall and trim, not even his prison grays could disguise his air of Upper West Side culture and education and, yes, of money easily obtained and then expended with style. Strecker or Rossi robbed with muscle and fists and cold, shiny steel. Myers robbed with brains and words, but mostly thanks to the gullibility and avarice of his victims. He was a swindler, a scam artist, a flim-flam man, who had fleeced the boob-oisie in any number of venues, in backroom midnight card rooms, on small town main streets, in the finer salons, and in the most lucrative operation yet devised by the hand of man for scamming suckers, on Wall Street itself. For most of his career he had been successful, that is, he had not been caught. No longer successful, he faced the prospect of not being successful again for ten-to-fifteen years.

"You say something?" asked Myers, seemingly without much interest before adding, ". . . *worth hearing.*" With that, Sandy Myers discretely craned his long neck, checking to see if anyone was looking in—and proceeded to cheat himself at solitaire.

It was, thought Sanford Myers, good to keep in practice.

In Sing Sing's library, a man with a wispy white moustache—about sixty, damned old for a con—toiled silently and alone. Not merely old, he was small, barely 150 pounds, but when it moved him, which was not uncommon, he could display a look that gave pause to the most muscular of toughs. Nick Strecker had nothing on him.

Today—and every day—he sported a modest, black bow tie, and a glistening silk shirt, the uniform not of an inmate or a guard or a civilian employee like the clerk in the intake center, but of a trustee. Trustees occupied a slightly elevated rung on Sing Sing's social ladder. They enjoyed greater freedom to move about and the joint's better jobs. They might on occasion be dispatched to the warden's residence, allowed to stroll through the main gates and escape—pardon the expression—however temporarily into the great world that existed beyond cell checks and machine guard towers. Nonetheless, their income tax bracket remained low. Library work still earned only a cent-and-a-half per day.

This trustee now shelved books and magazines, glancing briefly at each. Occasionally, however, he found some quality literature, even a classic or two. He noticed the spine of one heavy, well-worn volume that read "Crime and Punishment" and gave Messrs. Dostoevsky and Raskolnikov a knowing smirk. His outside career had specialized in knowing smirks.

The door opened. In walked not another trustee or inmate, nor even a guard, but an auburn-haired, green-eyed woman in her mid-forties, of medium build and height and of decidedly pale complexion, attired in a plain, but not too plain blue dress—alone and not particularly afraid to be among twenty-six hundred inmates.

"Anything you need, Mr. Graham?"

"Tell your husband," said Mr. Percy Graham, "that I need about fifteen-hundred more books here—some of which hopefully were published after the War of 1812." He paused for effect, "We'd like to know who won."

"He's just the warden, Mr. Graham," she responded, placing a manicured finger before her lips, stifling a tiny laugh, "not Governor Roosevelt." Others might fear this Mr. Graham. She did not. She did not really fear anyone. Not because Kathryn

Sumner Beck's husband was warden of all Sing Sing, nor because she terrorized people as did Mr. Graham's querulous persona, but rather because something inside her had long ago largely banished fear and hate and resentment.

"Well, then tell him I need some mucilage. He ought to be able to swing that."

***

They shaved the sides of Eddie Marek's head, stripped him, and ordered him to shower, confiscated his valuables and his cash, though in his particular case, there was hardly much to surrender: three dollars and eighty-five cents in coin and two crumpled one-dollar bills and two actual valuables—an Elgin 7-jewel wristwatch and his ten-carat gold wedding band. He tugged the ring from his left hand and dropped it upon the counter. He could have his jewelry back, along with his three dollars and eighty-five cents, in eight-to-eighteen years. Nobody mentioned whether or not his money would draw interest.

In return, they issued Eddie his new wardrobe. Gray was in fashion that season at Sing Sing—every season, in fact—so Marek now reposed in gray trousers, gray jacket, gray hickory shirt, and gray cap, along with rough, high-topped brogan work shoes. No black bow tie for Eddie Marek. Nothing that fit either. Not his jacket, nor his shirt, nothing. His jacket was too tight, his sleeves too long. His pants legs terminated three inches above each ankle. Fortuitously, his socks—his *gray* socks—bridged the gap.

A guard escorted him to the prison photographer's studio, shoved him down onto a metal stool, hung upon his neck a small black plate featuring two lines of white letters—"62896" on the top and "June 13" on the bottom—and shoved him straight forward.

A magnesium flashbulb exploded in his eyes. Marek blinked. The photographer ordered him to swing left. He obeyed. Flash!

"Swing right."

Flash!!

Next stop: Gallery 13, Cell 314. Home Sweet Home.

Gallery 13, six stories high and a century old, lacked charm, it being the oldest, dreariest, most depressing region in Sing Sing's depressing kingdom. A jug-eared gallery officer led Marek up a spiral staircase, opened Cell 314's steel-plate door, let Marek in— and left.

A forty-watt bulb hanging overhead emitted a strange yellowish light unlike any other luminosity Eddie Marek had ever seen. It must have been like what passed for light in the deepest recesses of coalmines or when the doctor shined that little flashlight in your ear. He seated himself on his lumpy, creaking, inhospitable bunk, alone in this sparse stone tomb, wondering how his life had come to this. *If my mother could see her little Eddie now.* He almost punched the wall, he was so angry, but he wasn't *that* angry, and he knew that one more stupid move wasn't going to make his life any better.

He heard a voice, the first friendly one since Detective Merklinger waved goodbye. He kind of missed Merklinger.

"Welcome to Sing Sing, kid. Got a name?"

And so, Eddie Marek met Nick Strecker. Strecker was turning on the charm. It was a rough charm, but in these circumstances, it, nonetheless, had its points.

"Marek. Edward Marek."

"How long am I going to be looking at *you*?"

"Eight-to-eighteen."

Strecker exhaled a slow, low whistle.

"What'd ya do—shoot the mayor's girlfriend?"

Marek didn't answer. He'd already undergone one stupid interrogation too many that day.

"I suppose you was framed."

"Held up some stores. Got caught on the last one. Seventy-six dollars and twenty-five cents! That's what I got—that's what *we* got. Thirty-eight dollars and twelve-and-a-half cents apiece. That's eight bucks a year here if I'm lucky." Eddie didn't even bother to tell Strecker what he had discovered at the trial—that the Amsterdam Avenue job was the only job Foxy hadn't shorted him on. He felt like a big enough sap as it were.

Man, if I only got $76.25 and had to split it with anyone, I'd just as soon get a job, Strecker thought—but kept it to himself.

"Yeah?" he continued.

". . . and a buck twelve a year if I ain't."

Strecker silently admired Marek's mathematical calculations. Math was never Nick's strong point—nor, for that matter, was spelling nor geography nor history nor science nor grammar . . .

Hidden from Nick Strecker or any other human being, Marek cradled his head in his hands. He was not taking it well. Strecker, as insensitive as he was, nonetheless, recognized the tremor in Marek's voice, the weariness, the hopelessness, the defeat. Marek had hoped to hide all that, to appear tough.

He was not succeeding.

Strecker remembered his own introduction to a real prison. He was a tough egg even then, even for a punk kid in for a second story job, but not so tough it didn't hurt.

"Who says the dollar doesn't go as far as it used to. By the way, kid, my name's Strecker. Nick Strecker. Along the way I've been charged and convicted of robbing a coal yard—that's my current sentence—assault, resisting arrest, burglary, gambling, bootlegging . . . and truancy—though my attendance has been very good of late."

Marek let go a little laugh. "I bet it has! I bet it has."

"How'd they get you, kid?"

"Sold out. My partner. Bastard named Foxy Renard. No good son of a bitch." Eddie thought back to how Renard had ratted him out when everything had unraveled, how the cabbie had spotted Foxy's blood in the back of his cab, read the papers about a robbery on Amsterdam Avenue, thought about it for awhile, and figured that if he put two and two together, he might earn a reward from the Daniel Reeves Corporation—or, at least, a favor from the cops if he ever needed one.

Renard, Strecker thought to himself, *No, the Renard I knew had to be somebody else—Jim Renard, yes, Jim Renard from the East 30s. He was a son of a bitch, too, come to think of it. Must be something about those Renards.*

Strecker was not so preoccupied regarding the moral failings of the Renard clan that he failed to sense footfalls upon the catwalk. He lowered his voice to little more than a whisper: "Oh, and, by the way, I'm completely innocent of all charges—including the ones I confessed to."

This is a Prison

"Hey, Nick!"

"Yeah, Marek?"

"How long they gonna keep us here? Don't they ever let us out?"

"Eventually," answered Strecker, simultaneously scratching his head and his butt. It was his one ambidextrous skill. "They want us to know who's in charge. And you know them questions they asked you yesterday?"

"Not the ones when I first got here?"

"Nah, not those. The ones *yesterday*—you got bars on your ears? They was to see what kind of work we'd be suited for. They got to make up their minds about that—analyze it. Penology. Very scientific."

Nick was very proud to know the meaning of "penology." He thought it placed him above the common herd.

"I wonder if they'll make me a doctor," Eddie answered, "Or a lawyer."

"I'm holding out for chaplain myself—," declared Strecker, "though I'm flexible regarding the denomination." Nick gave the whole idea of vocational training some thought, swiveled and called out, "Hey, Rossi, what do you want to be?"

"I want to conduct the joint's symphony orchestra!"

Myers, looking out at nothing particular through his cell door grate, took a long drag on his Old Gold. He found Rossi's cultural ambitions too precious to ignore.

"Signore Organ Grinder! Too bad your monkey got sentenced to Dannemora."

Rossi sprang to his feet. He was very sensitive about both monkeys *and* Dannemora.

"One more word, you bastard!"

Myers could have cared less.

"Pipe down, you birds!" bellowed Strecker, louder than both Rossi and Myers put together, "Hey, Marek, what's the big hurry? Somebody you want to meet here?"

Before Marek answered, Myers started serenading Rossi, "How are things in Dannemora?"

"I said, 'Somebody you want to meet here?'" repeated Strecker.

"Yeah," said Marek, glancing downward toward his ill-fitting new trousers, "I want to meet the guy who's got my pants."

Two men trudged past this fractious quartet early each morning and late each afternoon. A ruddy-faced young prisoner, Gaelic to his County Cork brogue, struggled with a heavy, tin water bucket. "Gunga Tim" everybody called him both behind his broad back and to his rosy features. A guard, Gallery Officer Smithson, concurrently spied not very discretely into each cell. *I haven't been anywhere in three days except to take some stupid test,* Marek thought, *except to answer more stupid questions, and dump crap out of my damn bucket. I don't know anybody here except this jamoke, Strecker, and Sherlock Holmes here thinks I've got something in my cell.*

He thought again: *Maybe he knows something I don't.*

"Want some?" inquired Gallery Officer Smithson, "Ossining 1931." Smithson was clearly not cut out to be a gallery officer.

"A fine vintage," interrupted Strecker, looking up from his own libation, "I recommend it heartily, Monsieur Edouard. Far superior to Gowanus Canal 1926."

Marek extended his own battered tin cup through the door.

"Got a treat for you boys tomorrow," said Smithson, "You get to meet a celebrity. The warden."

"If I'm having company," said Marek, I'll need *two* tin cups, sir."

The next morning, expectation, indeed, rustled through Gallery 13, or, at least, it did in comparison to previous days which saw nothing transpire at all. Nonetheless, each prisoner still lugged his heavy iron bucket teaming with his own excrement across the steel catwalk and awkwardly down the spiral staircase—*very* carefully not to spill any of his bucket's contents on the con below him. "This isn't what I thought they meant by indoor plumbing," Eddie mumbled as he struggled with his own bucket. It was an odiferous walk through the yard to dump each bucket into a trench connecting with the still scenic but increasingly less sanitary Hudson. "First, the indoor part," Strecker whispered to Marek, "now the outdoor part. I don't know which part I like best."

The cons planned on a prompt return to Gallery 13—at least after breakfast—but Gallery Officer Smithson had indeed told the truth. They *were* to meet a celebrity. "OK," shouted another guard, a decidedly more fearsome specimen going by the name of George Mowbridge Tannahill, "you guys, hurry up. You got an appointment with Warden Beck! Just don't expect him to shake hands with you!"

Sing Sing wasn't exactly spacious, but it contained its quotient of open spaces, a ballfield, its yards, the nooks and crannies and walkways between buildings. On a good-sized patch of scruffy lawn tucked between the Administration Building and the Laundry, Marek, Strecker, Rossi, Myers, and sixteen other new cons, formed themselves into four rows, three feet between each row, as straight as they could be, awaiting Warden Stewart E. Beck.

Marek vaguely knew who Stewart Beck was and just how important and famous he had become. He'd first heard of Beck in The Tombs. He'd learned more from Strecker and Myers and Rossi. Sing Sing was the nation's most famous penitentiary, close enough to Manhattan to house the city's most notorious criminals and to attract the nation's most widely-read journalists when Gotham's most notorious criminals entered its gates, departed through its gates, escaped over or under its walls—or—most spectacularly—when they found themselves strapped into "Old Sparky" and dispatched to their final reward. When people wrote about Sing Sing, they invariably also wrote about its warden.

Reporters stopped by Sing Sing. Celebrities stopped by as well: Babe Ruth, Lou Gehrig, Jack Dempsey, Harry Houdini, Sir Thomas Lipton, the great Russian bass Feodor Chaliapin, actors like Charlie Chaplin and Paul Muni. Everyone wanted to see what it was like behind bars—and still be able to leave as soon as possible. Stewart Beck greeted each high-profile guest and inevitably later read about it in the *News* or the *Mirror* or the *Journal-American*. It could not be said which he enjoyed more: the actual visits or reading about them later.

Beck was The Nation's Warden. He was caring. He was efficient. He was also the best press agent a jail ever had. He knew all about the press. As a kid growing up far upstate, he had worked on the local paper and fell in love with the power of the written word, set in cold type, dropped each day on lawns and front porches and hawked on street corners—and able to make or break public careers, often simply for the fun of it.

Stewart Beck was determined not merely to escape being broken by any newspaper. Indeed, he determined to use the press to advance not merely himself, but also his rather progressive—and often decidedly controversial—agenda. What Stewart Beck stood for was fair dealing with his inmates and, hopefully, rehabilitation. Not every warden in the nation did. Few dared stand for it in the ways Beck did, stretching his bare-bones budget by instituting educational and recreational programs, extending the prison's self-government and being unusually generous with individual leaves. If a trusted prisoner had a sick relative to visit on the outside, it was not unusual he be given an unescorted leave to visit his loved one. Beck had not lost a man on such a trip yet.

No, ash-flecked Stewart Beck was no ordinary warden.

Now, he addressed not Ruth nor Dempsey and Houdini and Chaplin. He addressed Marek, Strecker, Rossi, and Myers. At exactly 7:30 AM, he strode down his administration building's broad white steps. Only a solitary guard accompanied him, but Principal Keeper Joe McKaig, Beck's chief assistant, was the toughest looking screw Marek had ever seen. McKaig stood just behind his boss, far enough for deference, near enough if anyone was crazy enough to try anything. Principal Keeper McKaig possessed and exhibited far less faith in mere convicts than did his superior.

Beck's eyes narrowed, squinting in the morning sun, as he scanned the front row of cons. "Good morning, gentlemen," he began in an even, vaguely welcoming tone. He might have been greeting old friends, restaurant patrons, or miscreant schoolboys. It was all very disarming.

"Welcome to Sing Sing. I am your warden, Stewart E. Beck. I have been in correctional work since 1905. I have been warden here since New Year's Day 1920."

He paused, walking the length of the front row, before speaking again. His tone changed.

"Orders will be obeyed . . ."

In what he, for some reason, thought was the safety of the back row, Strecker whispered, "I think I've heard this one before." Marek couldn't believe Nick could be so stupid.

". . . infractions will not be ignored."

Strecker thought to himself, "*I have heard it.*"

"This is a prison."

Strecker whispered *again*, "I knew I heard it somewhere." Marek saw himself serving the full eighteen years—just for starters. "*Shut up, just shut up,*" he prayed.

Beck nodded to McKaig, a feint, discreet little nod, barely more than a twitch. McKaig nodded to his subordinate George Tannahill, then moved forward. His face assumed an odd little grin aimed directly at Strecker. Strecker's pupils expanded. He grew edgier as Beck advanced past Rossi, then Myers, then Marek, finally halting right before him. For a brief while, the warden of Sing Sing said . . . nothing.

"I am the warden." Beck continued long seconds later, "You are the inmates. You are here for good reasons. One, you were depraved enough to commit crimes against your fellow citizens. Two, you were dumb enough to get caught. It's simply amazing how often these two points intersect. You might wish to ponder that. Three, society has decided you will be punished for your deeds. This is not a hotel. Not a summer camp. None of this may be news to you. I trust it is not. Point four, may indeed be news to you, however—and it is good news. Society also wishes to treat you fairly—firmly—but fairly. That is one reason the State of New York has appointed me to serve as your warden.

"I will not tolerate cruelty inflicted upon you. You will not be starved or frozen or worked to death or beaten on a guard's whim. We represent *civilization*, and we *will* be civilized."

"*You* will too. You are children of God, and we love you dearly. That having been said, when you leave these gates at the end of your term I never want to see you again. I certainly don't want to see you back *here* again."

"I want you to be productive members of society—law-abiding, family men who made a mistake once—*or maybe more than once*—and paid for it, learned from it."

"If you have trades we want to know about them. I want you to practice them. I don't want your skills to atrophy." He noticed some puzzlement in the ranks and repeated "atrophy," as if repeating a word to people who didn't understand its meaning somehow caused them to understand it—a technique usually used on foreigners. There were variants on it, however: speaking louder or speaking more slowly. All usually worked about as well.

Beck employed a new tack. He noticed an older trustee walking toward the Administration Building.

"Hey, Graham, explain 'atrophy' to these gentlemen!"

"Atrophy," the old timer answered, combining perfect diction and projection with a stately, albeit diminutive, bearing, "Noun. Any weakening or degeneration—especially through lack of use. Verb. To undergo atrophy, i.e., 'muscles that are not used will atrophy.'" *There*, thought Stewart Beck, was a man who knew the English language.

Beck whirled around quickly, almost gracefully for a big man, then continued his homily, "If you do not have trades, I want to teach you. Times are tough out there. I want you to be able to support yourself—and your families—when you go free. That's all. Play by the rules!"

At which point, Nick Strecker merely snorted, not a loud snort, but though it was still discernable enough if one were paying attention. Eddie Marek was paying attention, and he knew both he and Nick were asking for more trouble than they needed. As for Nick, over the years, he'd heard enough guff from cops and guards, to take any promise he heard from anyone like a cop or a guard at less than face value. He wasn't buying what Beck was selling.

Beck noticed. He shot McKaig another glance. McKaig, in turn again nodded slightly to George Tannahill, the guard who had escorted the men to their meeting with Beck.

"Orders will be obeyed . . ." said Beck. He did not need to say more—and that was it.

Tannahill escorted twenty newly-minted inmates back to Gallery 13. As he turned a corner, he swung his wooden billy club in a controlled, measured, but highly painful, arc, slamming Eddie Marek from behind square in the kidneys.

"I didn't do anything!" Eddie grunted.

"I know that. That other goon did," said Tannahill, pointing his club at Strecker, "He gets two demerits—warden's order. You get a reminder not to be as stupid as your friend." And as Nick Strecker congratulated himself that a demerit would be the worst thing he would get, he too received a quick shot from behind to *his* kidneys.

Tannahill's blow had sent Eddie to the ground, as much from surprise as from pain. Nick remained standing.

"Is that the best you can do?" he asked Tannahill.

"Anyone care to find out?" Tannahill responded.

Nobody, not even Nick Strecker, dared respond.

That night, after Marek had finished recriminating against Strecker's stupidity, he asked Nick, "You think he meant all that?"

"The old guy?"

"Nah! That warden feller."

"Sure kid," said Nick, "that's why you got whacked. Why don't you just send Beck a telegram about what happened to you."

"No, I mean it, Nick. Despite everything, I think maybe he really did mean it. *He* seemed OK."

"Sure, kid, sure. Believe exactly what you want."

The Trustee

Sing Sing, for all its huddled masses, its car thieves and second story men and outright thugs, boasted its quota of public luminaries, exceeding it by great bounds, actually. There was, after all, more scratch in New York City than anywhere in the country, more to pinch and more people to pinch it from. More victims to murder or swindle or kidnap, and more reporters and columnists with bigger morning and evening circulations to sensationalize it all, and when these celebrity perpetrators, no matter how great their fame or how large their haul, were at last apprehended, tried by their peers, and convicted, they were more often than not transported in cuffs to Sing Sing—to share grease-encrusted cellblocks with mere nickel-and-dimers like Eddie Marek.

Warden Beck's establishment thus boasted a veritable Miscreants Who's Who, a Rogue's Gallery of Rogues, but despite intense—some might say cutthroat competition—its most distinguished resident, aside from the honorable Mr. Beck himself, was no mobster or gonif or bullyboy but the old guy in the yard with the big vocabulary—Percy Graham.

Beck allowed Graham the virtual run of the joint. Yes, the possibilities of rehabilitation fascinated Stewart Beck. But the power and glory and glamour and tinsel of the daily press fixated him still more. Percy Graham embodying the allure of Gotham's daily press. He drew Stewart Beck to him like a fluttering moth to a burning flame. Graham—Mighty Flame of the Press, even here—saw his opportunities and took them, seizing full advantage of the privileges Beck had conferred on him, high-hatting his fellow cons—and half the guards too.

And yes, there was another reason, Stewart Beck extended such unusual privileges to Percy Graham, and it had nothing to do editors or newspapers or celebrity. Beck believed there might yet be a remnant of a soul left somewhere within the wizened, yet still bitterly arrogant, husk of Percy Graham, a soul that had darkened and shriveled long before Graham had entered Sing Sing or even pulled a trigger.

Stewart Beck was determined to find that soul—and to cleanse it.

***

Cons are an even more curious bunch than wardens. They want to know everything, particularly what goes on about them. Their world is small, and they want to count and analyze every molecule in it because at some point they might be able to use one of those molecules—or, worse, it might be used against them. So, Sanford Myers turned on his considerable charm and inquired of a guard—not George Tannahill; Myers did not believe he had *that* much charm—who the old fart with the black bow tie and the big vocabulary was. When he found out, the wheels of his prodigious memory commenced to rotate.

"Let me tell you about Percy Graham," he announced during dinner—stew, an unfortunate harbinger of seventy-five percent of evenings to come.

Marek could only respond, "Who?" But Graham's name rang a vague bell with Nick Strecker. "Murder?" he asked.

"Very good, Nick," Myers continued, "but that's only the punch line to the story."

"What story?" Marek demanded.

"The old guy. 'Atrophy.'"

"Ah," said Salvatore Rossi.

"Ah," said Sanford Myers, annoying Salvatore Rossi, but not any more than was already the norm, "Percy Graham was one *big* big shot, gentlemen. Newspaper editor. The gold-domed tower of the *New York World.* Top of the heap. Would do anything for a story. Drove his reporters like dogs. Big man. Big suite in the Plaza. Big yacht. Racehorses. The world was his oyster—with mustard on top."

Suddenly, Myers recognized how mixed his gastronomical metaphor was. Mixed and unappetizing.

"Graham gets into money trouble," Myers continued, pushing away from the idea of mustard covered oysters, "and he thought he might dig his way out of it when his uncle, John Carl Hovey . . ."

"John Carl Hovey!" Rossi interrupted, "The 'Money King'?"

"None other. Percy Graham thought his rich uncle John would leave him a bundle. All he really left our acquaintance was his best wishes and, when the bills started coming due and Percy Graham's own stocks started tumbling into the tank, he hit the panic button. He figured he'd be ruined, so he'd kill himself, but then he figured his wife wouldn't be able to handle the disgrace—and the poverty."

"A thoughtful soul," observed Strecker, gnawing on a substance that might have once been a living organism.

"So thoughtful," Sandy continued, "that he decided that before he offed himself, he'd off her. When they retired for the evening, he waited for her to nod off. Then he went to the top shelf of his closet—pulled down a .32, put the gun under her ear and BAM!!"

"Sad story," said Eddie Marek, shaking his head and thinking of how he too had disgraced someone he had loved, but also recoiling at the thought of killing Carrie like that.

"Sadder still, my lad," said Myers. "She wasn't dead."

"Always hire a professional if you want a job done right," said Strecker.

"He had to wait, all crouched by her bedside," Myers, a more compassionate, or, at least, a less bloodthirsty, sort, continued, "another half hour for her to die. *And nobody heard the shot.* The walls are truly great at the Plaza. They really are. He had to wait a half hour for her to die. Then he went out, rode around the city for a couple days—and never had the guts to pull the trigger on himself."

"Where'd they catch him?" Rossi wanted to know.

"Didn't catch him."

Rossi gave Myers the fish eye.

"He turned himself in at the station house. And, you know what? After they sentenced him to this joint, they tried to figure out where all those big debts were. They placed ads in the papers and everything, and all they could find was the back rent he owed at the Plaza. The whole thing didn't make much sense at all. I guess a lot of things in Sing Sing don't make all that much sense."

"No," said Eddie Marek, "I guess they don't. . . . Pass the pepper, please."

***

Marek and Strecker and Rossi and Myers awaited assignment. Five days passed. Then, five days more. They took their places, in the good old summertime, in the good old prison laundry, Dante's ninth circle of hell—only hotter and with more Boraxo. All new prisoners, not the elderly or the infirm, mind you, but those of good health and sturdy constitution, invariably initiated—or resumed—their prison careers either in the laundry or in the nearby stone quarry, breaking rocks. Such initial assignments tended to make their next jobs look desirable.

This quartet of newcomers drew the laundry.

"Scientific!" fumed Myers about the charade of aptitude tests he had been subjected to, "is that what you call them? Administered by charlatans!"

"What are you bitching about?" Salvatore Rossi answered. "My conducting career is in tatters," he said, his turn of phrase inspired by the well-worn undershirt he held before him, "Five years at the reformatory—er, conservatory—own the drain." Myers slammed down a soaking-wet pair of trousers he'd been holding, spraying Rossi and Strecker's faces in the process.

Nearby, Marek squatted in a corner of this inferno, hidden away, but not for long. A supervisor, an older convict, noticed his absence, went looking for him and found him. There were a limited number of places to hide in a prison laundry. "Hey, you!" his supervisor roared above the noise, "Rookie! Yeah, you!"

Marek glanced upward. He had malingered aboard some of the finer ships the United States Navy had afloat and wasn't about to get excited over this little incident. He arose, slowly and with barely disguised contempt.

"Break's at ten, punk!"

"I joined the garment washers union," Marek snorted, though joining a union here was a privilege not even Sal Rossi could facilitate.

***

Of the many privileges Warden Beck dispensed or denied—visitors were among the most prized. Letters were important, magazines and books and recreation were fine, but real live human contact with the people left behind—and who they hoped to dwell amongst again one day—that was quite another matter. That was what the men hungered for.

They met their loved ones, their friends, their associates, their lawyers, in a long room, with three rows of stations, under a big framed sign that contained no greetings (or, for that matter, punctuation), merely a block-lettered warning: "NO SMOKING EATING READING WRITING." The room contained no metal booths, no shatterproof glass, or microphones. Visitors and cons alike sat upon heavy wooden, prison-made stools, separated merely by low counters.

It was all very informal, in some ways sloppy and dangerous. It was easy to envision items being easily slipped from visitors to prisoners—and they were. Some were harmless; some not.

The most dangerous contraband of all, however, was the creation—and dashing—of hopes.

This morning witnessed Carrie Quevada Marek's first visit to Sing Sing. She had, of course, visited Eddie at Brooklyn's decrepit gray stone Raymond Street Jail before his trial, but she had not seen him since. He had forbade her present in the courtroom, wanting to spare her the pain of watching her husband in the dock, not being able to do anything about it, aching to spare her from the very public shame of it all. That is how he might have explained it to her, but in his agony, he did not, merely grunting a few terse orders to stay away. She might have interpreted his instructions as he had so inarticulately meant them, and, on occasion she did. But at other times, as her heart raced crazily about, goaded by the constantly unfolding nightmare that had engulfed them, she could only ponder other, less pleasant scenarios—of rejection, and, yes, even of resentment.

She had put two and two and two and two together—their financial problems, her suggestion that she might take work of which he had so vehemently disapproved, his sudden, unexplained prosperity, and his more sudden arrest. Had she caused it all? Had she pushed her Eddie into this hell? Was she in her naïveté somehow more responsible than he? The questions spun over and over in her mind, and when she arrived at Sing Sing on this Saturday morning, her anxieties were perhaps even greater than that of the normal first-time visitor.

She said she missed him. He said he missed her. But there was little news of comfort from the world beyond Ossining that she might bring. No words of support from her family on Luzon or from the neighbors, who had never relished the idea of a white man and a Filipina living together, though some never quite grasped what she indeed was—the "China woman" they called her. Certainly none from his best pal Foxy Renard. Eddie tried his best to convince her that things were not so bad at Sing Sing, and in comparison to the squalid Raymond Street lockup, that was true—but not very true.

They parted, more awkwardly, more painfully, than when they met. An hour in the Visitor's Room is both very short—and very long.

***

Within the prison library, Percy Graham shelved books, checked records and, shushed readers. It was not his first job at Sing Sing. His first job had been curling up and dying.

It had not been easy for a man as big and powerful and puffed-up as Percy Graham to enter prison. And harder still for one who had pumped a 32-caliber slug into the skull of a woman he'd lived with and loved for three decades and who now comprehended the grotesque magnitude of his act. Graham had arrived at Sing Sing, lay down upon a rickety cot in its hospital and waited—and wanted—to die.

A woman, not a nurse, but a civilian, saw him there, and he saw her. She wore a blue dress, its bottom trimmed in red, neither a good nor a bad dress for its time and place, a hat with a wide brim and a hint of a veil, and black cloth gloves. He had seen worse, both in regard to wardrobes and to women. Graham couldn't decipher who she was or why she was there, but in his condition—his physical and, particularly, his extremely ragged emotional state—he figured it wasn't any of his business anyway. He no longer possessed much of any business.

The woman, on the other hand, still made other person's business her business, their troubles, hers. Someone else might have only have noticed merely an unshaven, decrepit old con, laying upon an equally seedy cot, his face twisted by decades of superciliousness and hatred and now despoiled further by despair and self-pity . . . and walked right by.

She didn't.

"Oh," you are such a nice-looking man," she chirped, "What are you doing here?"

The fatuousness of her remark startled not only him—but oddly enough also her.

Graham did not answer. She did not press him to. He fixed his gaze toward her and turned her query back upon her. Enough still survived in him for that. What, he asked, was *she* doing *here*?

She had no great reason not to answer, so she did: "My husband may be the next warden."

Graham pondered that. "I hope to God he is," he replied, though he did not often speak of God—nor, at this juncture, or of hope.

Kathryn Beck remained at his side, chatting about this and that. Stewart Beck soon joined her. He inquired how Beck was doing. He wished a sick, old man well.

"Are you the new warden?" Graham rasped.

Beck hadn't decided. A lot of men had tried and failed to rule Sing Sing. He didn't like to fail.

"I'm praying you take it," Graham responded, though he did not often pray, "You're the first man who gave me a kindly nod since I got here."

Beck took the job. Graham continued to waste away, willing himself oblivion—though not succeeding even in that. A week later, Beck visited Graham. "I thought you'd given me up, you faker." Graham summoned enough bile to complain, "You've been here a full week, and you haven't been back to see me."

Beck explained he'd been settling into his new job. "I've been thinking about you, though," he said, "Percy, how would you like to get out of bed?"

Percy, the old editor thought, *Mr. Graham to you, turnkey!* He did not answer.

"You're going to have to, Percy. I'm putting you to work. Something that I think you will like. We've got a newspaper here at Sing Sing called the *Star-Bulletin*. It's not very good. In fact, they barely ever get it out, and when they do even a birdcage wouldn't take a subscription. I want you to run it. Put some zip into it!"

Graham stared upward to Beck's eyes, struggling to believe that the words he heard were true. He hedged. Life had not been good to Percy Graham lately. Perhaps, Beck's offer merely ranked as another of heartless fate's mordant jests.

"Get well quickly, Percy. Otherwise, it's no dice. We can't wait too long. The news waits for no man."

Percy Graham was on his feet in days.

And when he was he turned the *Star-Bulletin* into something worth reading. But he also transformed it into a forceful advocate for prison reform, and, above all, into an outlet for his own talents, opinions, and still towering egotism. Soon Graham had jettisoned the paper's other writers and was authoring every last syllable himself, including massive installments of his own autobiography.

Prison authorities in Albany did not like his memoirs. Neither did they appreciate his crusading. They failed to relish the idea of inmates complaining about food poisoning outbreaks or revealing any of the system's figurative dirty laundry. They especially resented the concept of a convicted murderer railing against the death penalty at taxpayer expense. They were convinced Graham was out of control, and the more they thought about it they thought Stewart Beck himself had similarly spun beyond their control. Sing Sing's new warden was already generating far too much publicity for himself. It was Beck this and Beck this. Stewart Beck knew everything there was to know about prisons and prisoners and crime and punishment and rehabilitation. Why, one would have thought Beck was the Superintendent of Prisons himself and not merely a solitary warden—one among the many.

Such dyspeptic thoughts agitated New York State's actual superintendent of prisons, one Charles F. MacFarlane. MacFarlane was by no means a bad man, but he was no firebrand. He had encouraged Beck's appointment. Yet, it is one thing to appoint a man and quite another to have him outshine you. Beck outshone MacFarlane as the sun outshone a lump of coal.

And so, Charles MacFarlane inexorably grew to resent Beck, then to hate him, to hamstring his programs, and to slowly ponder his downfall.

He began by censoring the *Star-Bulletin*, ordering Graham to submit all copy to Albany, there to be joyfully shredded into the pale confetti of government-approved journalism. Beck circumvented MacFarlane, approaching the governor directly—a dangerous game because MacFarlane enjoyed his own political connections. MacFarlane retreated—temporarily. Citing budget restraints, he slashed the *Star-Bulletin*'s appropriation for newsprint and ink to little more than cab fare. Graham surrendered. He abandoned his editorship, taking a job in the prison library. Shelving books from a beat-up little wooden cart and replacing them on crowded, silverfish-infested shelves, however, failed to challenge Percy Graham. His interest quickly flagged. He seemed headed for a one-way ticket to his old cot

Father Gelasius developed a theory. He was never short of theories. They kept *him* going in this forlorn establishment.

This one was not about the Philadelphia Athletics

"Father, you startled me," said Graham, as the chaplain entered the library.

"You look like you've just seen a priest, Percy. You're white as a sheet."

Percy Graham *did* look like he had just seen a priest. Even Protestants look like that occasionally.

"I'm OK."

Father Gelasius never knew how receptive Percy Graham might be to his advice, though he often could unfortunately guess correctly. Nonetheless, today he decided to press forward with an exceedingly unlikely suggestion.

"You ought to get out more, Percy."

"There's a thought."

"I mean in the yard. Maybe if you dig a little garden, Percy, you would feel better."

Percy Graham rarely hesitated—particularly when it involved saying "no" to something or someone. This time, he fiddled with a dog-eared index card before responding.

"The hell I would."

***

The intercom on Stewart Beck's desk buzzed but once.

"Superintendent MacFarlane for you, Warden."

Beck nodded to Principal Keeper McKaig. Beck would take the call. Of course, he'd take the call. Long distance calls were expensive and were usually harbingers of bad news.

"Yes, Superintendent?"

"Beck, I see in your budget a $3,000 request for 'landscaping.' Care to explain?"

Beck had prayed MacFarlane wouldn't notice that little line item.

"Sing Sing is simply not an attractive place," he quickly countered, "It's just no Attica. Its grounds, as you well know, need work. Some tidying up might perk up the men, build morale, decrease tensions. And it would provide some of our inmates with meaningful work out-of-doors."

"Meaningful?" MacFarlane countered, "It's not easy squeezing even *essential* appropriations out of those upstate hardheads in the legislature, let alone another of your pie-in-the-sky reform ideas. Three thousand dollars is a lot of money these days."

"Yes, but the program is also excellent vocational training, Superintendent."

MacFarlane's normally baritone voice rose in both pitch and volume: "And what might Mr. Graham's qualifications be to train gardeners, Warden?"

Damn! Who had told MacFarlane that Graham was involved? His name was the kiss of death. Worse, MacFarlane was indeed right: what *were* Percy Graham's qualifications for this job? Beck needed to regroup quickly.

"Graham possesses excellent management skills. He proved that at the *World.* And I have two very skilled landscaping men who will assist him. In point of fact, Warden Beck only *hoped* he had two skilled landscaping men to assist Percy Graham—and if he didn't he would certainly transfer two men who would—even if he had to transfer them from Dannemora.

"And," Beck added, "he's less likely to write anything as a gardener."

"Need I remind you, Mr. Beck, that he can write all he wants but we don't have to publish it. That mistake is not about to be repeated!"

"He has friends who own bigger printing presses than ours. This might turn his mind from such things. I think it might be well worth it, Superintendent," Beck continued.

"I can't get $3,000 past the governor, let alone past the legislature," MacFarlane countered. He paused before adding, "I'll put in for $250."

"Thank you sir," Beck responded, feigning enthusiasm. Hanging up, he gazed up at his Principal Keeper, and, as he did, he heard Father Gelasius, and Gelasius's Protestant counterpart, the Rt. Rev. J. Stone Bowers, arriving outside, scheduled as they were to discuss overdue chapel repairs—yet another expenditure requiring Superintendent MacFarlane's grudging acquiescence. *"The things I let that priest talk me into,"* Beck silently fumed, *"Gardens! Graham! MacFarlane!"*

Gelasius could not but sense Beck's anger and could not but fear its cause. He stared down at his spit-shined black shoes. His discomfort—and it erupted whenever Beck's temper flew or when he merely seemed out of sorts—was entirely natural. In time, it lessened but never quite vanished.

"I take it His Excellency did not react positively," asked Principal Keeper McKaig.

"No," Beck answered, "His Excellency did not respond positively."

"A very beautiful name"

Percy Graham was, however, hardly the most significant individual the Becks had met in their introduction to Sing Sing.

Not by a longshot.

Stewart Beck met him first. He thought nothing of his introduction, nor of the person to whom he found himself introduced. True, this new acquaintance seemed pleasant enough. Competent. Intelligent. Decent. But there was nothing about him that triggered any strong interest or emotion—or, in the hustle and bustle of settling in to a new job, to even cause Beck to mention his name to his wife.

And, so it was that when Kathryn Beck herself met him a full week later, she was indeed totally unprepared for the event.

As she approached her husband's new office, Stewart heard her arrival and advanced into his anteroom to greet her. "I want you meet someone, Kathryn," he said, referring to the man still inside his office, "our prison chaplain, Father Gelasius Bryant."

She blanched. No breath escaped her lips. Her heart stopped—and splintered into sharp, jagged shards. Her respectable universe, so carefully and painfully reconstructed, so very long before, stood poised to rip itself asunder.

She stood immobile, her mind racing, wanting to flee, wanting to die.

Gelasius Bryant stepped forward from her husband's office to meet her.

And now he knew who *she* was. He could not help but recognize her. Even now.

Kathryn Beck was the young woman he had impregnated decades before.

Kathryn Beck was the young woman he had *loved* decades before.

In the wreckage of their young lives, neither had ever been able—even discreetly—to inquire as to the other's whereabouts. Gelasius had never learned what had happened to Kathryn. To where had she been sent? Was she alive or dead? What had become of their child? Had she married? And, if she had, to whom?

Now he knew at least some of the answers.

And, for her part, she had not been able to ask much about him. She had made passing inquiries to her family—a long time ago. But they were necessarily guarded in the extreme, and no one knew anything about anything. She could not ask more without risking more, without jeopardizing far too much.

The hour for risk—stupid, pointless, selfish risk—in her life had long since passed.

And Stewart Beck? He knew what he knew. A young girl. A miscarriage. And that was all, and, in truth, that was enough—at least, it was until this moment. He stood there and repeated, "Kathryn, Father Gelasius Bryant."

"Father Bryant, my wife Kathryn."

"Pleased to meet you, Father," Kathryn Beck managed to utter—and with some aplomb, all things considered.

"Did you say 'Catherine?'" asked the priest.

"'Kathryn'—K-A-T-H-R-Y-N," explained her husband.

"It's very unusual," said his wife.

"I knew someone with that name once," said the priest, "It's a very beautiful name."

***

And there they were.

When Kathryn and Gelasius could talk privately, and it seemed like years before that moment, though it was but a week, Kathryn explained that while her husband knew of her baby, he did not, however, know the identity of its father. She explained how she had lost her child. She explained how Stewart Beck had taken her in and loved her and married her and given her his name, when most respectable men would have either rightly fled from her—or been less than respectable.

She said she loved her husband, and the great silence that followed punctuated that declaration as gravely as distant thunder threatening an otherwise placid summer sky.

It also signified that it was Gelasius' turn.

The archdiocese, he informed her, certainly knew of her identity. They knew quite a bit. That was why he was in Sing Sing and remained there so long—and would remain there longer still. They probably were not, however, cognizant of *her* current identity. A change in last name leaves one's tracks very covered. He seriously doubted they *were* completely covered, He seriously *prayed* they were.

He expressed his regret about the child (he drew back from saying "their" child)—and remorse for what had preceded it. And said he too was married—to the Church—and, unlike earlier days, he had now been keeping his vows for some time and, with God's grace, intended to continue to keep them— intended to as strongly as he had once intended to violate them.

Another silence followed; this one shorter. Kathryn's voice was sharp, as he had never heard it. She was no nineteen year-old any more.

"Well, here we are."

"Here we are," he answered, and he sensed that as she was no longer nineteen she might also no longer be the secret, determined jezebel she had once so successfully had been—and that was a relief. She also seemed more determined in tone and bearing that even he had ever witnessed.

"What is our relationship?" she asked. It was no more a question, than those posed long ago in parochial school: "Gelasius, would you like to clap the erasers for me and wash off the blackboard?" *Of course*, he wanted to. He was no fool then, and he was no fool today.

"Priest—and warden's wife?" he answered.

"Priest and warden's wife exactly, Father," Kathryn responded, coldly in control. But inside, she knew not control, only fear. Yes, *only* fear. Love—and lust—had long since vanished. Somewhere between Auburn and Sing Sing her senses had returned. She wanted no part of grand adventures. No illicit romances. No defiling of Holy Church or holy men.

No more sin—or the near occasion of sin. No more folly.

And she certainly did not tolerate the idea—still looming immensely, hideously large—of her husband's career ruined, nor his life turned inside-out, nor his great heart broken. And to avoid this new disaster, she required not merely chastity, but virtues yet even more precious, and often rarer: silence, and discretion, and forbearance.

"Penitent and confessor?" she continued ever so curtly— and knew precisely what answer she wanted.

"No." he answered. He knew the pitfalls of what she asking. They had been there before.

"No?" she tested him once more. She wanted to make sure, and she wanted *him* sure as well.

"Only if in danger of death."

"That is the correct answer Father." And for the first time she allowed herself a hint of a smile. She *sensed*—or, at least, now was able to *hope*—that he too might have moved beyond what had once been and should never *have* been. Then she quickly added, "The second part of your answer is correct by the Baltimore Catechism, the first part by mine."

"Now, it is time to rejoin my husband," she said as she edged away from him, toward the door and back out toward the administration building.

"You must, however," she said as the distances between them grew, "join us for dinner some evening."

"Dig—a grave!"

In Brooklyn, Carrie Marek's luck had finally changed, and she found work at the big Abraham & Strauss department store downtown on Livingston Street. Nothing special, forty hours a week as a stock girl in the women's shoe department, but she was indeed fortunate to obtain it. The Depression was only worsening. Jobs grew scarcer, breadlines longer. More and more desperate men and women took to the streets, serenading passersby on the accordion or the violin for spare change, selling apples and pencils, or just plain panhandling.

Some women sold more than pencils.

Working at Abraham & Strauss was a woman named Winifred Starrett. She was a few years older than Carrie, blond, brassy, always out for laughs. Somebody must have forgotten to tell Winnie that the '20s were over. Most women at Abraham & Strauss loathed her and treated her as though she possessed some disease that could be spread not only on toilet seats but contracted merely by saying hello to her without sufficient sneering. And though Miss Starrett was indeed a bit boisterous even for Carrie's quiet tastes, Carrie cut her some slack, traded small talk with her, ran with her to the trolley, and, yes, even dared to sit across from her in the lunchroom—even brought some food from home to share with her. And, in truth, Winnie Starrett was one of the few humble shopgirls humble enough to break bread with a Filipina.

One Friday lunchtime, Winnie invited Carrie to accompany her after work to the Strand Danceland. Carrie had never heard of the joint but it seemed to her to be a reasonable plan, a good place to blow off stock room steam, to kick up her heels and, for a least a couple of hours, to pretend that she was indeed a little something more than an A & S shopgirl.

Four stops down the BMT, they scampered down the elevated line's cold steel stairway and onto Fulton Street. Two doors to their left, in all its tawdry glory, stood the Strand.

"What is—??" Carrie exclaimed, catching herself before she said anything further—or her current opinion of Winnie Starrett, which was that her companion was a complete five-star edition, stop-the-presses idiot. Just because someone was an American didn't mean they weren't.

The Strand was no Oriental Danceland.

It wasn't even close.

"Hey, ladies! Enjoying a night out?" came a sharply-Brooklyn accented voice.

Attached to that voice was one of the least attractive males Carrie Queveda Marek had seen in quite some time. Oh, not that he was hideously obese, with rolls of fat welling up over his collar, so immense that buttons popped off his shirtfront in cartoon-like fashion. Or down-in-the-gutter drunk, stinking, and bug-infested. Or toothless and gumming—or anything like that. It was something in his leer, the upturned curl of his obscene grin, the greasy blackness of his pomaded coiffure, and the slimy lilt of each syllable that rendered him so instantly hideous.

And, hideous as well, was the illuminated red-white-and-blue sheet-metal sign bolted above the tiny Strand ticket booth, proclaiming, "Dancing Tonight! Fifty Beautiful Lady Instructors."

Yes, The Strand was no Oriental Danceland. It was of the species of taxi-dance-palace dive that admitted only males. The only females permitted entrance toiled there for each buffalo nickel they wrung out of each dime-a-dance dance. It was, in short, the sort of establishment that Carrie Marek had once so desperately and naively thought to be a good idea for her own employment.

This place did not look like a good idea.

"Is this the Strand?" Winnie Starrett asked in confused innocence. It was not unknown to Carrie that Winnie might on occasion confuse key details—say, theoretically, as which dance halls admitted which ladies. This instance, evidently, was to be recorded among such misapprehensions.

"Why yes it is, Miss," Mr. Greasy Pomade responded, though Winnie's question was addressed not to him in particular, but rather merely to her own confused brain, "Of course, you know, ladies are not admitted to the premises unless they are employed here." And with that, he provided both Winnie and

Carrie with a look that, if it did not entirely undress them, reduced them to their Abraham & Strauss house brand unmentionables.

"Are you ladies here to apply for a position?" he continued, suddenly mulling over all sorts of possibilities.

"Why—" Miss Starrett began, but Carrie, not confident at all in regards to what the rest of Winnie's reply might contain, did not allow her the opportunity to complete, or, perhaps, even to begin, her thoughts. Gripping Winnie by the arm, she fairly pulled her back up the steps toward the El platform.

"You know," Mr. Greasy Pomade shouted after them, "we're always looking for the right kind of 'instructors.' You know, not just dames, but ladies with a certain class—like yourselves!"

"He took us for one of those, what do you call them, nickel hoppers!" Carrie hissed as she hustled Winnie across the El's station.

"Uh . . . maybe it was The Paramount Danceland I was thinking of," Winnie protested. Carrie just glared.

Upon the sidewalk below great laughter erupted. A great booming evil laugh followed by a rising chorus of more mockery that threatened to swallow up even the roar of the oncoming BMT. Two five-cent pieces rattled through the turnstiles. Four legs that would not be dancing tonight passed through them and ran toward the arriving train.

It could not pull away fast enough.

***

Kathryn Beck entered Sing Sing's gymnasium, gently pushing her way through the heavy, steel doorway.

A guard—a new, young guard, beefy rather than paunchy— took notice of her entrance. Puzzled, he advanced quickly toward what to him was an unexpected and quite unlikely visitor.

"Pardon me, ma'am," he said with more deference than authority, "But could I ask what you're doing here? You really should be escorted by a guard."

"Are you new here?" Kathryn responded, assuming an air more of authority than deference. She thought it might prove useful.

The guard, John Weeks, by name, again hesitated. He realized he'd misstepped, though, he could not explain to himself exactly why.

"I am," he admitted.

"Yes, I thought so. I didn't recognize you. I'm Kathryn Beck. My husband is Warden Beck, and I've worked among prisoners for as long as my husband has been a warden or superintendent. If my husband has been entrusted to care for these men, I will care for them as well. To do that, I must meet them and meet them on a basis of trust. My husband and I take care of these men, and they take care of me. I don't fret about it. You shouldn't either."

She nodded, smiling but firmly, as if to signal the end of the discussion, turning toward the bleachers, ascending them in a slow, huffing, but, nonetheless, decidedly determined manner. Guard Weeks still wasn't sure what to make of it all. Neither did the oddly disparate quartet of Gallery 13 inmates who presently found themselves ensconced very self-consciously adjacent to the warden's wife. Nicholas Strecker, Salvatore Rossi, Sanford Myers, and Eddie Marek *wanted* to say something. They were rarely at a loss of words. Now, they said nothing—and said it awkwardly, though Nick Strecker's ungainly, unuttered thoughts were more sinister than most.

He had plans.

***

Percy Graham strolled very deliberately across the prison yard. He reflected on Father Gelasius's latest plans and how he had somehow signed on to them. He was, he admitted, at least, to himself, just drifting. He needed a purpose, and this marble and rock-strewn piece of ground might serve some. On the other hand, however, he knew almost nothing about gardening or plants or growing living things. He poked along, kicking pebbles, staring down at what passed for soil.

"Dig a garden!" he snorted, "Dig—a grave!"

***

In truth, Kathryn Beck merely projected fearlessness.

She was indeed cognizant that any given foray into cellblock or workhouse might be her last. That any former murderer or rapist might murder or rape yet again. And, yes, she took these risks, as she quietly professed, because both she and her husband did care for the men in their trust. But she was afraid, nonetheless, often trembling violently before she ventured forth from her comfortable official quarters or from the insulated confines of the Administration Building. She might have resorted to drink to calm her fraying nerves, but she knew no prisoner—or guard or anyone—could ever be allowed to smell alcohol upon her breath or spy a wobble in her walk as she made her rounds.

Kathryn Beck assumed these risks—and had for years—not merely from charity but from the immense weight of her guilt. She had defiled her Church—*recklessly* defiled her Church—and herself. What *had* she thought—or not thought?—she interrogated herself over and over again, all without ever discovering a compelling answer. A madness had once passed over her, and into her, the devil himself, toiling overtime on one seemingly demure young lady who should have known better—and now, at great cost, did.

And worse than what she had done to Church or herself, she had ruined Gelasius Bryant's career. He might have been a pastor and a monsignor by now, maybe even an auxiliary bishop, not a mere priest, growing gray and worn, eternally sentenced to Sing Sing's earth-bound purgatory.

Yes, she *had* loved him once and might yet still love him. It was not, in truth, something she could rule out entirely. Old feelings never entirely die. Old memories never let them.

Yes, Kathryn Beck often shook before making her rounds—and, not always, from fear.

***

Salvatore Rossi no longer worked in the laundry. He worked in the tailor shop. Sewing was sort of a family occupation. He sister Marie was a seamstress. His mother had been one. This morning, he trudged down a long and cheerless corridor and saw what— or, rather, who—he did not want to see coming straight at him. George Mowbridge Tannahill was roughly the same height and build as Nick Strecker and why one was behind bars and one wasn't remained an enduring mystery to Salvatore Rossi, and, indeed, to virtually every prisoner in Sing Sing. Stewart Beck may have been progressive, but he was neither perfect nor omniscient, and the continued presence of George Tannahill at Sing Sing was ready proof of that. He had not hired Tannahill but he had not gotten rid of him either.

Rossi and Tannahill drew nearer and nearer to each other. The normally fearless Rossi grew nervous. Tannahill had something to ask. Rossi knew what it, and, worse, knew he did not have the right answer. Two other cons walked past. They disappeared around a corner, and Rossi knew his moment of truth was at hand.

"Rossi . . . c'mon," Tannahill spoke in a low voice.

"Yeah?" Rossi responded.

"Yeah," said Tannahill.

"I couldn't do it."

"I told you. I want those shirts you guys make. I got buyers on the outside."

And, indeed, George Tannahill did have buyers on the outside, local vendors who trafficked in prison-made goods that found their way by hook-or-crook—but always by prison guard—out of their shops. Some guards used favors to obtain merchandise, cigarettes or special privileges. Some used threats. Tannahill used threats, not always physical threats, but a guard could make it tough on a con, and Tannahill had the temperament for such malice even without an excuse.

"I ain't got 'em, Tannahill!" Rossi spat out, with a touch of panic entering his voice, "I couldn't sneak 'em out. You want too many of 'em! Be reasonable!"

A slight smile played upon Tannahill's slit-like mouth. "OK," he replied almost pleasantly, betraying no hint of rancor.

"Sorry," Sal muttered, hoping this would end things—at least, temporarily.

Tannahill slammed Rossi hard in the stomach. There had been no warning. He hit him again and then again. Rossi fell to the floor. Tannahill delivered a kick to his side.

"Don't worry. You won't get it in the mug."

His boot slammed into Rossi again. Marek and Myers came round the corner. Marek grabbed Tannahill, shoving him hard against the brick corridor wall. He stood ready to smash his cruel and corrupt face.

"Don't do it!" Myers ordered Marek.

"Yeah! Marek!" Rossi gasped, echoing Myers, "It's OK! It's OK!"

Tannahill edged backward.

"See you guys later," was all he had to say.

They did not like the sound of it—but they were glad he was gone.

That night in the mess hall, Myers, Marek, Rossi, and Strecker moved along the chow line. Rossi advanced particularly slowly.

"Look," Myers advised Marek, "I wouldn't con you."

"That's a first," Rossi interrupted, "What're you in for? Confidence games! Stock fraud! Forgery! Wouldn't con me!"

Even in his pain and in their mutual aversion to scum like Tannahill, Rossi still could not disguise his hostility for Myers. Part of it was a sheer clash of personalities. Some of it was ideological, though Gallery 13 was the last place one thought to find ideology.

"Union goon!" Myers shot back.

"Wall Street manipulator!"

"I said I'd get that screw!" Marek interjected, "Nobody does that to a pal of mine."

"Gentlemen!" Strecker interrupted, assuming an unlikely peacemaker's role.

"Succotash?" asked a con behind the steam table, daintily holding a ladle full of some indefinable substance.

"The slop du jour!" Rossi snapped. The sight of succotash, which he hated nearly as much as he hated Myers and nearly as much as he hated Tannahill, seemed to rejuvenate him.

"Look," Myers asked Marek *soto voce* as they shuffled past what was billed as roast pork, beyond the chalk-white bread and the cherry Jell-O that shimmered like a squad car's flashing roof light, "Look, what's your sentence?"

"Eight-to-eighteen."

"Think, moron! Stay clean. You're out in eight. Fight for justice—fight the screws—do eighteen. Do the math. You're the one always talking how you got bupkis for that robbery. You'll get less than bupkis for this stunt! What kind of suicidal stunt are you up to? Pickett's Charge? Pickett ended up dead."

Actually, General Pickett didn't end up dead. He ended up an insurance agent—but neither Myers nor Marek knew that.

"Let it go, Marek." Rossi added, "LET IT GO! You're not going to nail him anywhere in some corridor and get away with it. You're not going to snitch to the Warden. You do that and both of us will be marked men!"

Marek did let it go. Not easily, but he did, which is what you do when you have no real choice.

That night Eddie Marek marked another "X" on his calendar—which is another thing you do when you have no options, except to wait . . . and wait . . . and wait.

And to hate every second of that waiting.

Payback

In Brooklyn's Raymond Street Jail, surrounded by peeling paint
and woebegone furnishings, artifacts merely antiquated without
being antiques, John Renard straightened his garish tie, shook the
lapels on his double-breasted suit, and readied himself for his
release. He had been sentenced to one full year in the slammer,
but authorities had not only factored in the time he had served
before his trial, they had chopped off a little more for good, or,
at least, tolerable, behavior. Now, a mere seven months, three
weeks, and two days later, Foxy Renard was going home—
wherever that was.

"You're the most pissed off looking free man I've ever
seen," a scar-faced turnkey said as Renard headed out on to the
street. Renard's expression indeed betrayed the contents of his
angry mind, and, on a day that should have been filled with
sunshine and thoughts of a woefully overdue free lunch at J. P.
Hogan's Fulton Street Bar & Grill, his mind had found itself
trespassed once more by thoughts regarding his former associate
Edward Stanley Marek, Jr. Never mind that Marek remained
locked up doing eight-to-eighteen. Never mind that Foxy Renard
was going free. Never mind that Foxy had ratted Eddie out to
secure his own little sweetheart deal. Never mind that it was
Foxy's idea to team up in the first place.

No, never mind any of those things. In Foxy Renard's
corkscrew mind it was Eddie Marek who had caused all of this,
Eddie who got him behind bars—because Foxy Renard was
never much for blaming himself for much of anything at all, let
alone the huge disasters that periodically befell him.

No, Eddie Marek was to blame. Eddie Marek should have
hustled a little faster that night on Amsterdam Avenue. If he had,
they both would have been done and gone by the time that
flatfoot appeared. And Foxy Renard would have been just fine,
thank you.

It didn't make much sense, but it didn't have to, but it was
an excuse, and excuses were about all Foxy Renard had right
about now.

Yes, Foxy Renard was the most pissed off looking free man Raymond Street had seen for quite some time.

***

As George Tannahill skulked though the empty Sing Sing mailroom in the course of one desultory lunch hour, his ever-suspicious glance spied one particular envelope, nestled atop the tottering, heart-breaking piles of that day's incoming mail.

It was not the envelope itself—that was of mere dime-store quality—but the name inscribed upon it in fine feminine script that captured his professionally always curious attention. He ripped it open. The message inside was of no great import, the usual litany from the outside of dull recent events and reports on the weather and ailing relatives, but included in it was one piece of news that by its mere withholding might bring to George Tannahill a cloyingly sweet taste of revenge. And though Tannahill preferred to exact his vengeance in direct ways that would serve to reinforce the fear he held over his prisoners, he was not, on occasion, above—or below—a far different approach.

And this instance was one of them.

He returned the letter to its envelope, placing it carefully inside his inside breast pocket—before ripping it to tiny pieces a half hour later.

***

Eddie Marek sat apprehensively in his cell that Saturday, awaiting word of his wife's arrival. It was Saturday and she normally caught a very early train and arrived early, usually around 8 AM. But that hour came and went and so did the next and ultimately so did the whole morning and the very day itself. And still no Carrie and no visit. And it felt like the longest day Eddie Marek had spent in his entire life. And he wondered why. Had something happened to her? Some harm? Some accident? Or was it something far worse than that? Did she no longer care to visit him? She was, after all, an attractive woman, alone in a big city . . . His mind raced. And the day only grew longer and ran into the next day and the next and the next . . .

A week passed. At 8 AM Saturday morning, Eddie Marek, his heart welling with fear and hope and anger and joy was indeed summoned, as normal, to the Visitors Room. And Carrie behaved as normal as ever, completely unprepared for the agitated reception she would receive.

"Where *were* you last week?"

"I wrote to you."

"You never did! I sat waiting the whole lousy day for you."

"I wrote to you!"

"Well, I never got it!"

The unexpected stridency of Eddie's tone shocked her. She might have interpreted it as a reflection of how much he missed her, how very much her presence meant to him, and how angry and crazy men grew in confinement. She *tried* to think that way. But the implications that she had lied hurt. Tears welled up within her eyes and flowed down her cheeks. The sight of her tears calmed Eddie down, made him realize he was wrong. He apologized, but the damage had been done, and the remainder of the hour was immeasurably more tense and awkward than usual.

And when Carrie rose to leave and walked out the big steel door to the corridor, a burly guard happened to speak to her. "I couldn't help but hear him raise his voice to you ma'am," he said, "There's simply no excuse for such behavior."

She stopped momentarily. "No . . . I guess there is not," she sighed, dropping her tear-stained handkerchief.

George Tannahill bent down and picked it up. He could be a very gracious man when things had gone his way.

Death Row

Some people did not scratch days off their calendars. For them the passage of time brought not relief but terror.

They lived on death row.

Tonight, they numbered seven.

These seven, in no particular order, neither in order of arrival or departure or magnitude of offense, were, by name and crime:

Raymon Vergez, a pudgy little Mexican who had strangled his girlfriend—your basic domestic disagreement.

Vinnie Amerigo, who had knifed a guard at Dannemora through the heart and two more screws through the gut. Vinnie liked knives. They'd sent him to Dannemora for cutting a fellow con at Auburn. Old habits, it seems, are tough to break.

Gus Ludwig, who slammed a man over the head with a wrench. The deceased suspected Ludwig of making moves on his wife. Gus begged to differ.

Steve Higgins, an upholsterer, who lusted after a customer, returned to her apartment, bound her with cord, raped her, and when he realized his behavior might result in serious repercussions, murdered her.

Gentro Akiyama, a Japanese butler in Poughkeepsie—probably the only Japanese butler in Poughkeepsie. When he became, through no choice of his own, the first Japanese ex-butler in Poughkeepsie, he snuck back into his former employer's house, slugged him with a bottle of mineral water, dragged him into the basement, and damn near severed his head with a butcher knife.

John "Old Doc Voodoo" Smith, a one-legged Harlem restaurateur, who had killed a man bold enough to be sitting on a bench in Macombs Dam Park with Old Doc Voodoo's not-so-true true love. For good measure, Old Doc killed her too.

Bad guys all, one might deign to say. But add their misdeeds together and multiply them by a hundred, no, a thousand, and you would not equal the evil committed by—no, embodied by—occupant number seven: a sixty-six-year-old demon with sunken blue eyes named Albert Fish who had murdered a ten-year old little angel of a girl named Grace Budd. He had also killed at least four boys, a four-year old, a five-year old, a mentally retarded boy, and a black boy down in Washington. Upon them—and upon himself—he had committed every perversion, perversions that would have shocked not only the gentlemen of Park Avenue and the ladies of the Women's Christian Temperance Union but the ladies of Eighth Avenue and the gentlemen who picked up sailors in Riverside Park and frolicked together at the Everard Baths. He had even eaten his victims' flesh. He loved pain, inflicting it and receiving it, and in prison he had somehow jabbed his flesh full of needles and left them there to fester and cause more pain. He boasted that he anticipated the chair as the "supreme thrill." Albert Fish probably meant it.

An eighth prisoner was absent.

He was segregated not for bad behavior, nor for illness, but because, for him, existence was now measured in hours.

Years before—before Stewart Beck had arrived—condemned prisoners remained on death row, alongside the Raymon Vergezes and the Albert Fishes, until the very moment their number was up and they would be directly escorted to the chair. The condemned might be distraught or at peace, but witnessing this macabre march only worsened the already edgy dispositions of their fellow inmates.

They not only saw their comrade led to his death, they were also close enough to *hear* the execution, to overhear Father Gelasius Bryant intone his Our Fathers and Hail Marys, to later hear—almost feel—the alternating current BUZZ-BUZZZZZ-BUZZ through the condemned's body.

Worst of all, when the voltage had finished coursing through the condemned and he had been cut loose, his autopsy was performed right there, virtually next to those men about to follow him. They heard the coroner's saw hack through their pal's skull. They heard the deceased's brain plop into a pan.

It was more humane now—equally fatal—but more humane.

To make it more humane, they had built a place that came to be known as the "Dance Hall." Death row prisoners never saw it, never entered its confines until their own date with the chair had been scheduled, but they knew all about it. They heard talk. Its wide-open middle section was the "dance hall," with six cells encircling it. Why so many cells had been built nobody knew. They must have expected to round up the gang that shot Lincoln once more. From the Dance Hall itself a little corridor led to the chair. A new autopsy room lay beyond the chair, properly distant from everybody.

It was all very considerate.

Two guards—accompanied by Warden Beck and Father Gelasius and a bearded Armenian Catholic Rite priest, Father Yeprem—escorted thirty-eight year old Alexandr Nazarbekian . . .

. . . from the Dance Hall.

Executions hung suspended like dark clouds over Sing Sing, thickening and blackened, as each appointment with the chair approached. On death row or in the cellblocks they prayed some gust from Albany would blow that cloud away.

It rarely did.

In his cell, Strecker whispered, "Just about time."

"Don't remind me," Eddie Marek responded.

"Like you're not thinking about it."

"Everybody's thinking about it."

Percy Graham rarely thought of anyone else and never of a fellow convict. But he thought about this event this night, focusing his sight through his barred window, toward the execution chamber.

"You know," Marek whispered to Strecker, "if that gun goes off when I'm holding up that store, I'm there. Right there in that chair, same as him."

"But you're not, kiddo."

The thought did not reassure him.

Father Yeprem held a crucifix to Nazarbekian's lips. The condemned man kissed it.

"Any last words?" asked Beck.

Nazarbekian did indeed have them, delivered evenly and without emotion, for he was now drained of all emotion, save for weariness and sadness. Nazarbekian was ready to go.

"Proverbs 24:11," he said to Warden Beck and to the world at large, "Rescue those who are unjustly sentenced to death; do not stand back and let them die."

He knew he would not be rescued.

"I heard he was innocent," Marek whispered.

"I heard that too," Strecker responded, for once without cynicism or sarcasm. Nobody joked on execution nights.

Nick Strecker had his limits. Percy Graham had yet to learn his. He looked out at the night sky, a moonless blackness punctuated by the dozens of stars that shone like pearls of fire and at a death house that shone before him like the portal to either heaven or hell. His face remained cold. He smirked and turned away.

"Stupid bastard," he muttered, though no one was there to hear him, "Had it coming."

Beck didn't think so. He wasn't sure about Nazarbekian, but he was sure about the death penalty. He hated it from any standpoint, but the part he hated most was his participation in it.

Stewart Beck never pulled the lever down. He merely gave the signal. The hand on the lever belonged to a professional executioner, a gaunt, grim, pipe-puffing Queens father of two named Robert Greene Elliot.

Robert Elliot's hand snapped downward, in one quick, chopping, deadly motion. Two-thousand-four-hundred volts of electricity flashed through Nazarbekian's body.

It all took about thirty seconds, and when it was over Alexandr Nazarbekian was bright red. His eyeballs had popped out of his head. His bodily fluids had left him, and the jolt had shocked his body so mightily that he had dislocated his right shoulder.

But a dislocated shoulder was of little import to Alexandr Nazarbekian because he was now dead.

The guards, the warden, the chaplain looked on. "Rescue those who are unjustly sentenced to death;" Warden Beck repeated ever so quietly, as quietly as he had spoken words, "do not stand back and let them die."

Father Gelasius heard him and said, only a little louder, "That's not your job, Stewart."

Sing Sing's doctor, Arnold Osborne Garrow, also stood nearby. If anyone looked like a country doctor it was Arnold Garrow. One might picture Garrow in his proper starched white collar and heavy tweed suit delivering babies, making house calls, doling out little yellow pills to the sick and those merely thinking they were sick. Dr. Garrow hated the chair as much as Beck did. He took his friend, his boss, by the arm.

Stewart Beck gazed down at the floor. He did not want to look up and see the smoldering remains of Alexandr Nazarbekian.

But he did.

It was his job.

Cherries

In the great world beyond Sing Sing's bleak parapets, life only got harder. A Depression that had caused two men to rob a grocery store on a November evening grew even worse in their enforced absence.

Carrie Marek's job at Abraham & Strauss vanished nearly as quickly as it appeared. One afternoon the ax fell on half her shift. She was, however, still young and pretty and able to foxtrot and learn the rumba and the continental. When her friend Winnie Starrett had been let go a few weeks previously, Winnie had, in her exuberant innocence and her less exuberant desperation, recalled the proposition she had heard shouted after her a few months previously: "You know, we're always looking for the right kind of 'instructors.' *You know, not just dames, but ladies with a certain class—like yourselves!*'

And so she took employment at the place she and Carrie had once fled so ingloriously, the unfortunate Strand Danceland. "C'mon, Carrie," Winnie now cajoled her pal, "The money's good, and you don't have to do nuthin' you don't want to. You got a better plan?"

Carrie didn't. The world wasn't exactly in the market for Filipinas.

She now, however, possessed data she had not possessed on her unfortunate previous journey to the Strand: that the hideous Mr. Greasy Pomade was, in fact, Mr. Al Brown (nee Alfredo Bruno), manager of the aforesaid dance hall.

She applied for the job anyway.

And she got it.

It was all very simple. A patron would sidle up to the Strand ticket booth, plunk down a dollar ten cents, an expenditure which entitled him to walk past the suspicious eyes of the joint's wiry but vicious bouncer, up the stairs to the dance hall itself, clutching a strip of ten pink tickets, each worth a single dance with an "instructor" or "hostess."

If he wanted additional dances, no problem. It was, as they said, a dime-a-dance—the sky being the limit.

It was also all very sad.

The Oriental Danceland and every other real dance hall was a place of, at least, some joy, with either the hope of meeting someone or hopes for whoever you had already met. People talked. People laughed. People even loved each other.

It would be too much to say that an eerie silence pervaded the Strand's red-and-green crepe-paper-festooned confines. After all, its four-piece band had strict orders to keep the music—and the dimes—coming. But there was no great undercurrent of conversation. Dancers rarely spoke to one another, their Terpsichore, being strictly business. Most of the men possessed few conversational skills—at least in English. And few of the girls wanted any of their conversation.

. . . or their stares. A dime-a-dance was a pretty steep price when the music stopped after ninety seconds tops—and just after a minute in a lot of cases. Most of males spent their time not dancing but just loitering on the sidelines . . . just silently staring . . . staring . . . staring . . . at the unobtainable (save for ninety seconds per ten cent piece) young women before them.

A dime a dance, and all the drunks and losers and punks Carrie could handle. "No Improper Dancing Permitted," a sign upon the Strand's fly-specked wall piously warned. What a joke. The job was all wandering hands and uninviting and uninvited propositions. All maneuvering into darkened corners and the grinding of their flesh onto your flesh. All the hectoring by the floor bosses to hustle up more business. On your feet until two or three in the morning. Stuffing half of each ticket into your top of your stocking because you couldn't trust management not to cheat you.

Yes, it was sad more than it was anything else—save for profitable. A girl could earn good money there. The nickels added up. A good week could put $35, or even $40, in her purse.

And, no, she did *not* tell Eddie.

Because profitable though it was, it was also just another step downward on a ladder that only went one way once you were perched on it, another lurch away from roots and family and respectability.

One night, about 10:30, having just completed his own year and a day in The Tombs, who breezed in but Mr. John Renard—*that* Foxy Renard, the Foxy Renard she knew had sold out her husband down the Hudson River, the East River, the Harlem River and any other river he could—and with a nerve Carrie never knew anyone had, he handed his dance tickets to the attendant and sidled up to her to hand to her the torn remaining halves of each. These she did not cram into her stocking. These she kept uncomfortably within a tightly-clenched fist.

She would soon discover what she did not previously know—though she should have suspected it—how very attractive she had always been to the young Mr. Renard. Somewhere about their third dance, Foxy's voice assumed an unpleasant mixture of lust and venom. His hands reached down past his dance partner's long silken hair down toward places his still-jailed friend would have killed him for reaching.

"I can't get over seeing you here, Carrie!"

"You said that to me before."

"No, no, I mean it, Dollface! You know why?"

Carrie didn't answer. Renard continued anyway.

"Because Eddie always hated the idea of you even *thinking* of working these taxi-dance joints! That's why he went into business with me."

That's why he went into business with me.

And that information coursed through Carrie's weary, disgusted frame like a bolt of electric current. She froze, unable to continue shuffling her feet to the music. Unable to bear the thought that it was her who had caused her Eddie to fall from grace, into this beast's clutches, to Sing Sing itself.

"Life's rich," cackled Foxy, "ain't it, Carrie?"

She wanted to spit in his eye. But all Mrs. Edward Stanley Marek Jr. responded—through gritted teeth—as she dodged his immobile feet and his too mobile hands, was, "Yes . . . life's . . . a . . . bowl . . . of . . . " And here her pause became excruciatingly long, and Foxy thought he might hear a word he had never heard escape from Mrs. Marek's chaste lips. But all he heard was ". . . cherries."

She broke loose from Foxy Renard's grip and beheld him with such unrelieved hatred that now it was he stood there transfixed. She flung his lousy dance tickets in his face, and stormed away.

"Hey! Hey! Where ya going?" Al Brown demanded as Carrie stormed past him and down the stairs and onto the street.

"Hey you!" Brown now demanded of Renard, "What did you do to my girl? You think you can just—"

"I didn't do nothing!"

"Barney!" Al Brown motioned to the Strand's bouncer, who had hastened to his side on the dance floor, "show this gentleman out. Show him out right now!"

"I didn't—"

"Show him out, Barney. Show him out! Nobody mistreats our instructors."

It was, however, an act of chivalry which provided precious little consolation to Carrie Marek, who quit the Strand Danceland that very evening.

And, no, she did *not* tell Eddie.

Rock Garden

"Got to be 120 degrees in here," Eddie Marek complained as he strained to pull a load of heavy, wet laundry out of a huge hamper.

"Stop reminding me," Strecker glared. He was not speaking rhetorically. He didn't want to be reminded of it, and by his look and by his tone, he reminded Eddie of that.

"Just making conversation."

"Make some cooler conversation."

Sandy Myers entered, bearing a proposition, "You guys looking for a change of climate?"

"What tipped you off?" Strecker answered.

"If you don't mind a little hard work . . ."

"Like this isn't," said Marek.

"A little pick-and-shovel work," Myers explained, "we might be able to get you into the cool, fresh air of Sing Sing."

"Oh, no!" Marek begged off, "I don't want any of that rock-breaking stuff. What are trying to do, Myers, volunteer me for the chain gang? You get a commission? Ten percent of each rock?"

"So, don't listen to me! What do I care what happens to you?"

"You're just blowing smoke up my ass anyway!" Strecker challenged Myers, "What do you know?"

"I hear plenty. I repeat half of it. Keep your ears open, and you can say goodbye to this racket—unless, of course, you want to be re-incarnated as a Chinaman."

Marek and Strecker responded with silence—and skepticism.

The next morning, however, after Marek, Myers, Strecker, and Rossi had taken their usual breakfast of lumpy oatmeal and brackish java, and as they walked through the yard toward their respective assignments, they stopped to hear over the prison loudspeaker system:

Attention! Warden Beck has requested the following announcement be made. Volunteers are requested to assist in landscaping of the prison grounds. Two dozen men will be selected for this task. It will be full-time duty. Volunteers will work under the supervision of trustee Percy Graham. To be considered leave your name with your gallery officer this evening. That is all.

Marek and Strecker exchanged glances. Myers responded with a mischievous wiggle of his eyebrows. It would take more than a wiggle, however, to transform Sing Sing's pathetic, rock-strewn landscape into anything approaching a garden or even a scruffy lawn. Marek remained skeptical. This was just plain loony.

Myers unleashed his full persuasive powers.

He spoke one word: "Laundry."

"Hold the starch," said Strecker to Marek. He was on board.

The next morning, several dozen men, Marek, Myers, and Strecker among them, far too many to all be assigned to the job in question, stood at strict attention before Percy Graham hoping to be chosen for this mysterious and perhaps bizarre assignment. Rossi was among them. He thought it might improve his health, though in a way not usually associated with outdoor work. Graham seemed transfigured, as if back at the *World*, terrorizing cringing reporters, goading them to produce yet another edition flawlessly, eloquently (yet *not* eloquently, yet *not* flawlessly, because only the great Graham could supply such attributes to their pathetic copy) and with a scoop on every line.

And so this gray, little man stood before these beefy cons, doing his best—which was very good—at projecting intelligence, leadership, initiative—and also arrogance, egotism, and a palpable, damn near evil, coldness of heart and soul.

"Gentlemen," he began, "you hope to be among the chosen. You see that little patch of ground over there?"

"Over by Administration?" Strecker answered.

Graham didn't expect anyone to dare speak. "Exactly," he shot back, "Our humble prototype. A little patch of green to be wrestled from the rock and ruin of Sing Sing will be our starting point."

The idea was pathetic. Each man thought that, but each wanted to stay outside at least for awhile. They held his tongues.

Graham continued orating, as much to convince himself as to convince them, because, after all, he did not really give a damn what they thought. "I'm going to turn this yard into one giant, lush garden. I don't know anything about gardens. I don't have any plants or seeds. I don't have any topsoil. But I have you—and you're going to help me transform this rock pile into a garden. Any questions?"

Rossi spoke: "Yes, sir. Why, sir?"

"Why what?" Graham sputtered, barely controlling himself.

"Why are we doing this?"

Graham did not know the answer to Sal's question. Didn't have a clue as to his own behavior, save that, at this point of his life, he could think of no other course of action. "'Why?' he responded, with a modicum of restraint, "is the question you should never ask here. You might answer it."

At lunch, the men discussed what they had seen and what they had heard.

"Well?" Myers asked, "What do think of his idea?"

"Insanity defense," Marek deadpanned.

"Know what I think?" asked Strecker.

"What?" Myers responded.

"We take them shovels and dig our way out of here."

"Insanity defense." Marek and Myers deadpanned in unison.

"Insanity defense," echoed Rossi.

"You gotta be faster," Marek and Myers, again in unison, advised—and felt good about it.

As it transpired, Marek, Strecker, Rossi, and Myers, despite their pitiful lack of relevant expertise, were each selected, for the inmates who actually did know anything about gardening knew enough to stay away both from this project and from trustee Percy Graham.

And so Graham's unlikely project lurched forward, possessing no real plan, no expertise, hardly any real tools or money, and a crew that, thinking him at best mad, was only along for what promised to be a bumpy ride. It was not a formula for success.

Yet, his makeshift crew worked, digging and shoveling, hauling dirt and rocks, making but tiny progress for the amount of work expended. And while they worked, Stewart Beck looked down from his office window and wondered how long he might allow Percy Graham to continue.

***

Stewart Beck lived not at Sing Sing but near to it. He liked the men well enough but not enough to relish all twenty-six hundred of them parading past his parlor window six times daily. He lived up the hill, not far beyond the gates, a comfortable home, possessing a great fireplace in its ornately wood-paneled parlor, decently furnished, staffed more than adequately, even exquisitely, by a dozen trustees. Beck spent this night at home but knew less peace than the men he had left behind.

"Something wrong?" Kathryn asked.

She had met her husband half-a-dozen prisons ago, long enough ago to know when something was merely wrong with him and when something was *very* wrong.

Tonight, something was *very* wrong.

So wrong he didn't answer. He didn't have to.

"It's Graham, isn't it?" she asked.

"Some days you wonder about everything you do," he said, "Do I give the men too much slack? Not enough? Graham! I know what they say about him—and me—that I coddle him. That he's my pet."

"Then why do you let him run loose like that?"

"Half the time even *I* can't say why. I know he's a supercilious bastard. Even here. Selfish. Hasn't learned a thing. But I think he can. And if he can—that sends a powerful message too."

Beck thought some more, about Graham and about all the men, the robbers and murderers and swindlers and whether they'd ever be able to go back out, earn a living, be trusted.

"Sometime," he continued, wearier than Kathryn had seen him in a long time, "you plant something, and it just doesn't grow."

"But what kind of a message are you sending to the rest of the men?"

He knew she was still talking about Graham. Kathryn Beck believed in rehabilitation as much as anyone, in—or out—of the prison. She also believed in something more powerful. She believed in redemption, but even she wondered about Percy Graham.

Her husband wondered too.

"But what kind of a message,' she asked one more, "are you sending to the rest of the men?"

They had had this conversation before, but this time, he didn't have an answer.

***

After supper each night Eddie Marek traversed the yard, and this he did one early evening, looking, without much success, for a place to sit.

He spied two—and only two—such places. Neither would have been counted among his first choices. They lay upon either side of an older, small, slight, blind prisoner, Lemuel Dunbar. You could easily tell he was blind by his darkened glasses and long white cane. You could also easily tell he was black. Filipinos was one thing. Blacks were something else. That's just the way it was—but the seats next to Dunbar were not only available, they were in the shade. Shade was not such a bad thing. Eddie Marek swallowed his pride and edged over.

"Mind if I sit down."

"I see no objection," Dunbar responded. Marek wondered if he was trying to be funny. He did not like funny black people.

He sat anyway. Across the yard, Rossi and Strecker exchanged knowing glances. They wanted to see how *this* played out.

"What you in for?" Marek asked.

"Murder."

Marek mulled that information, pondering that "Armed robbery." THOU SHALT NOT STEAL didn't seem like much compared to THOU SHALT NOT KILL.

Dunbar *had* killed. He'd been able to see back then. The murder was the usual story: a woman. Lemuel wasn't a criminal, merely another jealous guy with a cheating girlfriend, a temper worsened by cheap gin, and an equally cheap .22.

Dunbar's life had been spared at a very high price. Normally, he would have gone to the chair, but one day before he got there, a particular sadistic guard had found his progress toward the showers insufficiently energetic and responded by beating Dunbar across the face with his truncheon so brutally that the convict, lucky to even survive, never saw again. There were too many witnesses, and when the story got to the governor a deal was struck: your life for your silence. Dunbar took it, and now he lived in not only a prison of stone and steel but of darkness and helplessness.

"What you in for?" he now asked Eddie Marek.

"Armed robbery."

"Mmmm," Dunbar pondered out loud, "Where you from?"

Eddie thought he'd give the short form reply. He sat there for shade not conversation—and was about to learn that it did not pay to lie to a blind man regarding what he could *hear*. Blind men took what they heard *very* seriously.

"Brooklyn," he answered.

"You ain't from Brooklyn!"

Dunbar's response startled Eddie.

"Actually, I am" he responded, "—sort of."

"Sort of?"

"I'm from Scranton. You ever hear of that?"

"Yeah? Scranton, hell, yes! I'm from North Philly originally. But I used to travel all over hell. You don't get to be a Pullman porter by standing in one place. A Redcap maybe—but not a porter! Sure, I know all about Scranton. When you Scranton guys come up out of them mines, you're blacker than me!"

Eddie couldn't help but laugh. Then he thought for a moment.

"Yeah, Scranton," said Marek, "should have stayed there."

A visitor arrived, expected by one of them, though not at all by the other.

"How are you today, Lemuel?" asked Kathryn Beck.

"I'se fine, Mrs. Beck. And you?"

"I'se fine, Lemuel. I *am* fine, Lemuel. Are you ready for today's lesson? I brought along something for you to read."

She carefully opened a manila folder, removing a sheaf of stiff papers dotted with Braille. Marek wasn't sure exactly what was going on with the Braille, and he certainly wasn't sure what was transpiring with a white woman sitting herself down next to a black man. Neither were Nick Strecker and Sal Rossi, though the more Nick thought about Kathryn Beck, the more he pondered the many possibilities she presented.

Dunbar, at first with Kathryn's assistance, then alone, moved his long fingers along the dots.

"When," Dunbar started haltingly and continued more haltingly, "in the course of human events, it becomes necessary for one people to dissolve the political bands which have connected them with another." He paused and turned toward Kathryn, "I'd do better if I could have read better in the first place—you know—regular style."

"That may be the case, Lemuel, but you're doing fine, very, very good, actually. Don't worry about it. Keep going."

". . . and to assume among the powers of the earth, the separate and equal station to which the Laws of Nature and of Nature's God entitle them."

"That's the Declaration of Independence, Lemuel."

"1776," Marek interrupted, trying to display his own slim educational qualifications, "July 4."

"That's right," Kathryn responded.

"Oh, I'm sorry," she apologized, "I'm Mrs. Kathryn Beck."

Marek wasn't sure how to respond, though Kathryn's look indicated a response was in order. A dull stare didn't seem to qualify, so he jumped to his feet, respectfully saying, "Edward S. Marek, Block 13, ma'am. My friends sometimes call me Eddie, though."

"Pleased to meet you, Eddie."

His face betrayed the bit of pleasure he felt on hearing that.

"Should I go on, Mrs. Beck?" Dunbar asked.

She nodded, then quickly realizing the futility of her gesture, answered, "Yes, please."

". . . a decent respect to the opinions of mankind requires that they should declare the causes which impel them to the separation. We hold these truths to be self-evident, that all men are created equal . . ."

Marek smirked. Mrs. Beck noticed.

". . . that they are endowed by their Creator with certain unalienable Rights . . ."

"Yes, Lemuel," Kathryn responded quietly, though while she spoke she looked half at him and half at Marek "the rights to trial by jury, to confront your accusers, to be treated the same no matter who your family was, or where you're from—or what you did. Excuse me for interrupting. Please continue."

Her answer embarrassed Marek, and it showed. She had spoken quietly, without inflection, without rancor, but he was smart enough to know whom she really lectured. He did not like it, but, upon further reflection, he did not like his smirk very much either.

". . . that among these are Life, Liberty and the pursuit of Happiness . . ."

***

For Percy Graham the pursuit of happiness involved riding his crew to exhaustion, goading them, insulting them, as they hacked away each day at creating little bits of greenery from much larger bits of brown dirt and gray rocks. The summer sun remained in its ascendant power, and Sanford Myers, neither bred for the outdoors or for manual labor, worked along with the rest, his hands rough and blistered, hauling heavy wheelbarrows of dirt and debris. Salty sweat poured down his face in great droplets, as never before—even on this lousy job—stinging his eyes, nearly blinding him. He dropped the wheelbarrow down to wipe his glistening brow and burning eyes with his bare arm. It wasn't doing much good.

Graham saw him.

"Hey, what is this? Coney Island? A seaside vacation? There are no wheelbarrows in the *laundry*, Jewboy, none in the *coal yard*."

Marek heard him. A threat from Graham, he thought—of all people to threaten another human being. Myers might indeed be a *zhid*—and certainly a crook—but what did that have to do with anything? He had always treated Eddie square.

"Lay off, you miserable, old bastard!" Eddie shouted.

"What?"

"You heard me."

"And you heard me."

"I heard a con acting like a screw. That's what I heard. We get a cent-and-a-half a day. We're building your little pet project here. You're lucky the warden lets you have it. You ain't going to work Sandy to death for your damn imaginary rosebuds."

Not many people talked to Percy Graham like that.

"But *he's* going to work," Graham answered, "—and so are *you*—you white trash son of a whore!"

Eddie snapped. He dropped his shovel and rushed the old man. If Eddie reached him he'd strangle him, but he never did. Sandy flung himself at his pal, grabbing him from behind, dragging him down, landing both men on the rock-strewn ground, lacerating Eddie's bare arms, tearing his rough trousers.

Percy Graham merely grinned downward at the two prisoners, the sickly self-satisfied smirk of Satan himself, then calmly reached over, picked up a shovel and extended it toward the two men still lying on the hard ground before him. "Here," he goaded Marek and Meyers, "why don't one of you brave boys just take this shovel and send me to kingdom come?"

Marek reached for the shovel, ready to grab it and swing it in one great killing arc across his tormentor's head, to wipe that smirk off Graham's face, to forever silence his evil laugh.

Graham now lifted the shovel above his head, out of Marek's reach. Then he gracefully lowered it, as if it to hand it to his potential murderer. His steely courage unnerved Marek.

"He's going to work," Graham repeated to Eddie, "—and so are you—you white trash son of a whore!"

And that's exactly what they did.

Time and Distance

"Doing anything special over the weekend?" Stewart Beck, looking more rumpled and ash-strewn than usual, idly inquired of Principal Keeper Joe McKaig as another workweek mercifully tumbled toward conclusion.

"Well," McKaig responded, "It's my birthday. St. Joseph's Day. And that—aside from being the son of a Joseph Patrick and the grandson of a Patrick Joseph—is the true story of how Joseph Patrick McKaig Jr. got his Christian name. So today—and tonight—is my birthday. I expect a fine dinner, a present or two—and to be a year closer to my pension!"

Yes, it would be St. Joseph's Day, thought Beck. March 19. Yes, it would.

"A happy birthday—and nameday!—to you," Warden Beck responded, and when McKaig had departed Beck pondered not so much about birthdays or Joe McKaig, but about saints, or, at least, about one particular saint, who took a chance on a young girl with child. Beck thought himself no saint, and knew his bride was no virgin, but he had loved her and wed her anyway, and, indeed, he now cherished her all the more. Joseph—the saint, not the Principal Keeper—must have thought himself a fool, and, such thoughts had neither quite escaped Stewart Beck, at least, not in those early days. Love is blind. It is rarely deaf to the whispers haunting each human soul.

Yes, thoughts of playing the fool, had stalked Beck, as had equally sharp doses of fear—a fear that Kathryn had never forgotten her one-time lover, nor he her, and that someday, somewhere, embers of old love might flare yet again. Such apprehensions were nowhere as strong as they once had been. They were, in fact, most nearly extinguished. Kathryn had proven herself, had provided her spouse no cause for worry. She had moved with him from prison to prison, from town to town, and while she gave him no children, she gave him no worries, save for when she ventured behind prison walls, down cellblock corridors and through workshops and hospital wards. There had been words between them on that point—all along the way, from Elmira to Auburn to Hart's Island to New Hampton and to Sing Sing. But no words, no matter how firmly and loudly uttered, nor how often, might ever dissuade Kathryn Sumner Beck. And no title of warden's wife might protect her, or anyone, from harm, if harm was meant to be, if men who had not managed to control themselves on the outside might do no better inside.

But such possibilities, though real and dangerous and vexatious enough, were another worry. What was past was, indeed, past, what was done was, indeed, done. Time, it seemed, was a marvelous balm.

. . . as was distance.

"Come in," said Stewart Beck, as he heard a muffled knock rap thrice upon his office door, expecting it to be Joe McKaig, with yet one more question or request before he trundled off toward an evening of candles, cake, and frosting—and, if he were lucky, a plate, or, perhaps, even two, of his Friday favorite, Lobster Newburg.

"Are you busy, Warden?"

"No," answered Stewart Beck, "come right in, Father Gelasius."

Hearts and Flowers

Sanford Myers had a visitor: a successful-looking businessman of roughly forty, pencil-thin mustache, elegantly, but not flashily, dressed, fastidious down to the fine linen handkerchief tucked into his charcoal gray suit and the red geranium securely fastened to his lapel. The man in charcoal gray was Ben Miller, Sandy's one-time partner in the Spencer-Philips Holding Company, Iroquois Financial Services, the Boca Raton Realty Co., the La Paz Mining Co., and Exchange Place Diversified Enterprises.

Most remarkable about their conversation was not what they said, but that Ben Miller had ventured into the very heart of New York's penal system to hold it, for Ben Miller remained wanted by authorities for his association in the Spencer-Philips Holding Company, Iroquois Financial Services, the Boca Raton Realty Co., the La Paz Mining Co., and Exchange Place Diversified Enterprises.

Ben Miller was a man of *great* nerve.

They had made each other's acquaintance a dozen years previously, when both were young and impecunious but even then very bold. It was at Aqueduct on a Memorial Day. They had met at the rail and caught wind of a "sure thing," made all the surer by all the considerations that make "sure things" surer. They profited from their knowledge and from the friendship that instantly developed. They had a lot in common—a taste for gambling and speakeasies and Broadway and Times Square and petty frauds. They would soon have far larger frauds in common for they also possessed a mutual appetite for adventure and invention and daring.

Ben Miller traveled to Sing Sing not only to recall those good times but because he also remembered a certain card game in a Seventh Avenue hotel suite and a certain .32 caliber bullet— deflected by a platinum cigarette case—meant for him that Sandy Myers had stopped with his own flesh.

Ben Miller also traveled to Sing Sing because doing so was, in fact, the ultimate con. Men like Miller lived for such cons as much as they lived for their financial rewards.

Mr. Miller (for this visit known as Mr. Salinger) and Mr. Myers's conversation, intriguing as it was, was of little import compared to the one three stools down—between Mr. & Mrs. Edward Stanley Marek.

Said reunion started awkwardly. It went downhill from there.

"You haven't been here in three weeks," Marek complained.

"It's not easy to get away. I got to work Saturdays."

Her excuse was merely technically true—but only if one counted the hours after midnight on Friday as Saturday. Quitting the Strand Danceland had solved nothing. There was no shopgirl's job at Abraham & Strauss, or at Macy's or Gimbel's or S. Klein's or anywhere else. She possessed few skills besides a pretty face, a pleasant smile, a shapely figure, and the ability to stay on her feet on a dance floor for hours on end. A dancer from the Strand recommended her to the Luxor, a grotesquely tough joint on Sands Street near the Navy Yard. It wasn't much of a favor. The Luxor was jammed with sailors and underage hostesses and runaways from who knew where. These girls' eyes had once shone at the thought of New York. Those same eyes now were blank or hard or both—but these girls weren't going home any time soon.

Carrie Marek possessed money once more to cover rent and groceries, and even to regularly mail a five- or ten-spot home to the Philippines. There was, of course, more money available if she wanted it, but she didn't need it or want it that badly. The Luxor, however, stayed open an hour later for business than did the Strand, and she was in no position to hang up her dancing shoes early.

Not at all.

But this morning, with barely two hours of sleep, she dragged herself on to the train at Grand Central and saw in her husband's face not any pleasure at seeing her again but rather his suspicions of why she no longer visited him so regularly. He could not only see her absence, he could see the late hours in her face . . . when she did visit.

And suspicions flame all too brightly within the human soul—and burn as if gasoline were doused upon them in an inmate's heart.

"Easier than for me to get away," said Eddie.

"I didn't rob no store."

"I had to get the damn dough," said Marek, face flushing, gripping the rough wooden counter before him as hard he could, "You knew that. You sure didn't have any trouble spending it."

It was her turn for anger: "I didn't know how you got it. I didn't ask for it. I didn't drag myself all the way up here from Brooklyn to get this!"

"Don't come!" Marek countered, trying to keep his voice from rising, "Maybe you've got something better to do!"

Carrie grabbed her purse, rising to her feet stiffly and slowly. She struggled with competing emotions—with rage and anger and, yes, with guilt. "Damn you, Eddie Marek," she thought, "Damn you to hell forever. Damn you to this place forever!" Like an animal poised to strike, eyes glaring, cheeks flushed with shame, and nostrils flared, she glared down at Eddie, turned sharply—and simply left, so angry she left her purse behind her, a purse that contained a snapshot of her and her husband—and her pay envelope from the Luxor Dance Hall. A guard noticed her purse and called after her, "Miss! Miss!" She kept going. He retrieved it and galloped off after her.

Eddie Marek was left to ponder the consequences of what he had done, and thinking about a long, even lonelier procession back to his cell and, perhaps, never receiving another visitor again for the remainder of eight to eighteen years.

"Eddie," Sandy Myers said as he walked by, "what are you doing sitting there all by yourself?"

***

Time passed. The prisoners worked. The prisoners dined—if one may call it that. They took their modest turns about the yard and retired for the night. Tonight was mail call. "Salvatore Rossi?" bellowed the prisoner toting the big leather mail pouch, as if he were the mailman going from door to door back home, avoiding overly territorial beagles and terriers.

"That's me," said Rossi, extending his hand for a letter postmarked Manhattan.

"Nicholas Strecker?"

"Nicholas Strecker."

"Two for you today."

"Must be bills."

"Hey!" Marek pled as the man with the pouch slid past his cell, "You forget me?"

"Sorry, buddy, nothing today."

Marek plopped back onto his bunk, picked up an open book, and let it slip to the floor.

"Nothing any day," he muttered. It wasn't quite true, but it was true enough.

***

Life went on.

Carrie's letters grew even rarer, the visits rarer still, but there were amusements. Eddie Marek may not have been good at much beyond shoveling dirt for an ungrateful Percy Graham, but he was very good athletically, at nearly any sport, but particularly at baseball. He drifted into pickup games and competitions. He could run and throw and hit, and despite his spare frame, hit with some power.

He was young. He was strong. He was good. He was *very* good.

A con's self-respect requires constant reinforcement. Marek's athletic skills provided him a merciful path to psychological survival. Locked within his cell, Eddie Marek remained a con, a loser, an abysmally unsuccessful hold-up artist. He had wanted to be somebody. He had become a number. But on the baseball field, he was more than a con, more than a misplaced Pennsylvania Polack washed up upon a New York shore. He was a star. It felt good.

Not much else did.

Sing Sing's ball diamond lay near the Hudson, next to its workshops, not far removed from its coal-devouring, smoke-belching power plant. It was a beautiful Sunday afternoon, the kind where despite your circumstances, the air brimmed with hope and freshness and cleanliness—even if you were not far removed from a coal-devouring, smoke-belching power plant. A high brick wall surrounded the deep outfield. No balls were leaving the park. Nor were any of the outfielders.

A pickup game progressed, bottom of the third, home team at bat, though by necessity both teams were, in fact, the home team and never went on the road. Today's "home" contingent wore prison grays; the other, their only marginally less gray undershirts. Marek numbered himself among the undershirts, batting third, playing center. A hundred or so spectators ensconced themselves in the shabby wooden first base grandstand. Strecker roamed among them, too nervous to sit. Always on the prowl for something, he never knew what.

Occasionally, though, when he bumped into it, he knew what it was. "Hey, Whitetree" he bellowed, before swaggering toward a con he vaguely knew from the outside, Angus Whitetree, a thirty-ish inmate approximately a third of the way through ten-to-fifteen. It was always difficult to estimate such things precisely. You might estimate it one way. The Parole Board might figure it the other.

Whitetree hailed from Kahnawake, just outside of Montreal, a Mohawk Indian who had drifted stateside to toil on the girders of the new skyscrapers sprouting up along the Jazz Age Manhattan skyline. The jobs dried up after the Crash, but a high altitude ironworker's skill set proved easily transferable—to second story work—and Whitetree plied the rooftops and fire escapes of the better neighborhoods' apartments and townhouses with the same dexterity he used traversing the city's unfinished skyscrapers, concentrating now not on rivets and girders and I-beams but on cash and silverware and jewelry, particularly jewelry. Along the way—like Eddie Marek—he moved to Brooklyn, in his case to North Gowanus, where the bulk of the city's Kahnawake and the Caughnawaga Mohawk dwelt. Along the way—like Eddie Marek—he bought a gun. At the end of the day—like Eddie Marek—he got caught with it.

All the stories in Sing Sing included "he got caught."

"Hey, Whitetree, gotta smoke?" Strecker asked in a manner less a question, than a very strongly advised suggestion. Cigarettes were precious to Angus. They didn't grow on tobacco stalks at Sing Sing, but he still thought it advisable to share them with Nick.

"Sure. Anything for you, boss," said Angus, reluctantly fishing a Lucky Strike—LSMFT—"Lucky Strike Means Fine Tobacco"—from his jacket breast pocket. His right ring finger missed its last two joints.

"Got a match?"

"Boy," thought Angus, this guy beat all, what's he going to want next: An ashtray? A smoking jacket? A mother-of-pearl cigarette holder—to look like FDR? Yeah, Franklin Delano Strecker—that's the ticket. "Vote Strecker-Rossi: A Blackjack in Every Pot."

"Sure, Nick."

"Thanks," said Strecker. There was something about even saying thanks that made it sound menacing.

"Don't mention it," Angus Whitetree answered, "Anytime at all," as he pondered giving up smoking, rather than make good on that vague and insincere promise.

Near home plate sat Sanford Myers. He had a modest bet on the game's outcome and a couple of side bets on its more arcane points. Kathryn Beck sat with Lemuel Dunbar near first. Dunbar liked sitting in the sun and feeling the breeze and excitement. This afternoon, the warden's wife was his play-by-play announcer, a veritable female Ted Husing. In the bottom of the sixth, Lemuel heard the sudden heavy crack of bat on ball and exclaimed, "That's hit solid, Mrs. Beck! I say to center!"

"You've got 20-20 ears, Lemuel."

The ball was indeed hit like a rocket to center—right-center—and deep. Marek raced away from home plate and to his right, dove, making a shoe-string grab. Like everyone else present, the runner on second, a car thief named Coyne, thought the ball would land safely and sprinted for third—only to see his coach frantically urging him to retreat. Coyne raced back to second, though Marek's catch had been so spectacular, his dive to the turf so precipitous, no one expected more. Instead, he unleashed a bullet toward second. Coyne slid, his spikeless prison brogans kicking up a thick spray of dirt. The black-clad umpire jerked his right arm.

"Y'er out!!!"

The umpire looked down at Coyne and said, "He's got you boys out twice like that today."

"Yes, Father," the embarrassed Coyne admitted to the umpire—Father Gelasius Bryant, "and he'll probably get a third if we're stupid enough to run on him."

That was the day people began suspecting Eddie Marek was quite improbably something very special.

***

Father Gelasius and Percy Graham sat languidly upon a rough wooden bench in Sing Sing's upper yard, not far from the prison chapel, soaking in the rays of the midday sun, not particularly doing anything, nor, seemingly, about to do anything anytime soon.

Graham roused himself from his torpor. "We're both in the faith business, Father," he said. Gelasius hovered precipitously near the boundaries of mid-afternoon napdom. He had brought a lunch to Sing Sing that day, and it had been a good and large one.

"You think so?"

Gelasius Bryant did not know where Percy Graham was going with his line of reasoning, but he knew there wasn't any easy connection between the concept of faith and the concept of Percy Graham. He did, however, know there were times that, Christian charity aside he could barely stand Mr. Graham. He possessed a strong hunch this moment might eventually be numbered among them.

"Well, I was *formerly* in the faith business," Graham continued, holding up his eyeglasses to the sky to peruse them for whatever smudges and smears they might contain.

"I see, Percy," Father Gelasius responded calmly, convinced, though, that he was about to *really* not stand Graham.

"Yes, *you* build up faith. It's your stock-in-trade. I tore it down. Good news is never news. Bad news is always news—larceny, hypocrisy, corruption, infidelity, incompetence, disaster, pestilence—and, yes . . ." Here he took a long pause, not really wanting to say what he had to say, but knowing that having gone this far . . .

". . . murder."

Graham unbuttoned a single button of his white silk shirt, so as to employ the garment to meticulously wipe his invariably-smudged steel-rimmed bifocals clean. Father Gelasius considered offering him his handkerchief, then thought better of it. Cleanliness is next to godliness, but the handkerchief in question was currently closer to godliness than to cleanliness.

"Bad news tears down faith," Graham continued, warming up to his topic, "makes the reader doubt Man and doubt God. And those poor souls we call up and interview? All the quotes we wrench out of context, or make up out of the thinnest air? With them we destroy the faith of the public servant or the businessman or the simple man on the street who we call up at four o'clock in the afternoon, interrogate with loaded questions, and artfully transform into a fool or knave in the next morning's bulldog edition.

"We make men fear the truth even when it's on their side.

"Sometimes—just for fun—we fashion heroes out of whole cloth. Human interest we call it, and when we—or our public—has grown weary of our creations, we smash our idols, drag them through the mud, and hang them out to dry. Flattery and calumny are two sides of the same five dollar gold piece.

"Some profession."

Graham's last four syllables tossed Father Gelasius off balance. He was quite prepared to loathe Graham, but maybe,

maybe just a little, there remained hope for the old boy yet, some flickering spark of decency buried within him . . .

"Yes, some profession, Percy. I'm glad you recognize it. What made you think of it?"

Graham didn't answer. He was, after all, in the habit of posing questions, not answering them—so his eventually answer was naturally . . . a question.

"How come we never tore down your faith, padre?"

"Ah," thought the Father, "he's back to normal—the son of a bitch."

"I only read the box scores, Percy," he said very deliberately, knowing that he knew far more faith-shaking things about himself, than he could ever read in Percy Graham's evening editions, "Your boys couldn't do much with those."

"No," Percy Graham responded and began pondering how they could.

***

Percy Graham grew increasingly aware of the immensity—and the impossibility—of his underfunded, undermanned, unlikely mission and grew, even by his standards, alternately testier and more despondent by the day, sometimes by the hour.

He, of course, wasn't unique. Despair grew on trees in Sing Sing. It sprang from sodden gutters and stared back at you with slitted eyes through iron bars. It took its place on the mess line and lay between the lines of each page of every tattered library book. It lurked as night fell, darkening each grimy cell with heavier, sootier blackness. At daybreak it loomed as large and blinding as the sun.

Men snapped at Sing Sing. Some mornings a steel cell door would creak and groan and slide open, but no one exited. A guard would peer in; a lifeless body would be cut down.

More often, men merely turned mad. If they failed to snap out of it in the prison hospital, if the raving or the shaking or the screaming or the blank, motionless stupor wouldn't stop, Dr. Garrow would ship them three hundred miles north to

Dannemora's State Hospital for the Criminally Insane. Poor bastards.

Of course, many of Sing Sing's inhabitants arrived not quite right anyway. Father Gelasius Bryant's vocation included pondering the frailties of the human race—including his own—and he certainly contemplated those of Sing Sing's sorry inhabitants. Original Sin was a good starting point, and he had no problem with it—too great a body of evidence, particularly here, pointed towards its existence—but along the way he'd developed a few theories of his own.

Face to the wind, one gusty, overcast Friday evening Gelasius and Stewart Beck departed Sing Sing for the Warden's Residence to dine on plates of creamed tuna and toast personally prepared by Mrs. Beck. Such invitations never ceased to be uncomfortable, but they had significantly diminished in awkwardness. If all parties—or, at least, two of them—kept on their guard, all would go well.

But such a session remained in his future. Face to the wind, the Father struggled to keep his black homburg fixed upon his head. A chaplain's stipend did not allow for too many dinners paid for by himself or too many lost homburgs.

"A few years ago I started to notice something, Stewart," said Father Gelasius. Beck was not much for guessing games. If Gelasius was going to share this discovery, he'd do so without Beck having to guess or ask. If not—

"Among the insane, among the mentally unstable, it often starts with self-absorption. The deranged abandon all sense of perspective. Everything turns inward, on themselves, and the more their mind turns inward there's less room for anyone else in there or for tolerating another individual's needs or opinions."

Father Gelasius paused.

"That's it?" Beck asked. He had no idea where this monologue had originated—and hoped he had not personally inspired it.

"Not all of it, Stewart, no. For some of these unfortunates it may be physical—perhaps some chemical let loose in the bloodstream or a misshapen fragment of the skull jarring a particularly sensitive area of the brain, agitating some key nerve or tendril. Maybe it was something they ate—or smoked. There are many possible reasons, and I'm talking about just one.

"And, of course, sin may—and does—drive self-absorption. Man possesses free will. He may exercise it for good or for evil."

"I figured you'd get around to that, Father."

Large raindrops started falling, splattering the ground, the warden, and the priest. Beck wished he had ordered a car to drive to him home.

"But . . ." the chaplain continued, "the mentally ill, whether they be caged or free, whether blasphemous or pious, far too often have a common thread—*it's all about themselves*, Stewart."

Beck didn't reply, but Gelasius's theory *sounded* right. It even applied to more than a few non-prisoners he knew. Beck figured he'd let Gelasius roll on. Let the words tumble out—as long as he kept hiking as fast as he could.

"So the unhinged arrive here not caring who they robbed, who they beat up, who they killed, who they swindled, because somebody else had something they wanted, and *they* wanted it *now*. The *self* had to be satisfied. But here's the joke. As much as they care about themselves, even *they* still need other people. We're made in the image and likeness of God, and even God—who is love itself—requires love. That's why he made us—to love him. There existed the whole universe—the heavens and the earth—all creation. But the firmament can't love God or love anything at all—neither can planets nor moons nor stars nor galaxies. Oceans and mountains don't love. *People* love. And people *need* love.

"*That's the secret that everybody knows.*

"So when we put one of these really disturbed cases in a cell, padded or barred, logically, he should be happy. He's all by himself, with his favorite person. But when he looks around that cell and stares into a world containing only himself, he looks deep into his own eyes—and nobody stares back at him. He's entered the great void of selfishness, and because there is no value to anything beyond himself, no greater goal, no higher power, there exists no purpose to his life, and when there is no purpose, there is no hope. And where hope vanishes, only despair remains, crushing all things, and all men, as do the tons of gold or silver ore let loose in a collapsing mineshaft— wonderful shiny, glamorous stuff now worth less than nothing to those suffocating under its weight, glistening like cheap tinsel, rumbling loud with the dull, hollow roar of Satan's laughter."

Father Gelasius paused. Beck remained still. The flow and force of the priest's words had taken the Warden by surprise. He had just been counting on a brisk walk home, creamed tuna, and perhaps an hour of the Philharmonic on the radio.

"Might that be your homily for Sunday, Father?"

"No, Stewart, think I'll keep it lighter. I think I'll just tell them about Hell."

Opportunities

Even in Sing Sing, that dismal land of woefully constricted opportunities, many possibilities, nonetheless, presented themselves to those inclined to take them. Some, the authorities dutifully presented: for an education, to learn a trade, for recreation, for a better assignment, for an earlier parole. Far more numerous, and often more interesting, were Sing Sing's illicit opportunities, some of a nature best left unmentioned in polite company, but mostly they sorted themselves out into realms of less carnal contraband: a favor bartered from guards by a package of smokes or a sawbuck; a little hootch or some far harder stuff. Then again, one might seize the opportunity to fashion a crude but still potentially deadly shiv from some discarded or pilfered shard of machine shop metal—or, if one were less mechanically talented or inclined, to barter one from an enterprising con with one to spare.

It was in this latter manner, one rainy afternoon that Nick Strecker obtained for himself a fine little blade, six inches in length, sharpened to perfection, deadly as a forty-five minute lecture from the Civic Betterment League. Nick might have obtained said shiv merely on general principles, simply because he was not supposed to possess one, but, in fact, he had a very specific purpose in mind, one he dared not share with Eddie Marek or, at first, even Sal Rossi.

It was not a particularly well conceived purpose, though it possessed a certain straightforward logic. Sooner or later, Nick Strecker would, by chance or some semblance of design, come upon Kathryn Beck, not out in the open, mind you, nor in the yard or the gymnasium. No, fate would fling them together in some remote hall or passageway, some little, out-of-the-way room. She would be unguarded, as always. He would produce his shiv, press it menacingly upon her little neck, perhaps even hard even to draw a little blood, to convince her, her husband, and everyone else that he meant business, and to employ her as the ultimate barter: her virtuous life for his unvirtuous freedom, a getaway car, a full tank of high-octane fuel, an equally full revolver, and a change of clothes, in exchange for a promise of her release.

It made perfect sense to Nick Strecker when he first thought of it, and it made a lot more sense now that he had a wonderfully-fashioned steel shiv—and Sal Rossi in on it.

Peonies

Late one afternoon Percy Graham supervised his crew. A guard approached to announce, "Graham, man here to see you."

It didn't take much to set him off.

"Yeah, come see the murderer! Twenty-five cents! A mere two bits! The human monster! He writes! He edits! He kills! Sure."

Graham proceeded toward the Administration Building, where a man in a dark brown suit—not a particularly good one—a loosened tie, battered, dusty shoes, and a rumpled fedora, approached quite hesitantly. "Mr. Graham?" he asked.

Graham merely stared, exuding even more hostility than normally.

"I'm Frank Halifax. Halifax Nurseries. Tarrytown."

Graham softened, for if there is one thing overbearing newsmen can always summon is charm—when it suits their purpose.

"Oh, yes, I ordered some bulbs and bushes from you."

"You won't be able to do much with what you've ordered."

"I know," Graham responded, absent-mindedly kicking at the ground, "I had to dip into my tobacco money to even afford that."

"I heard about what you're trying to do. I think I can help."

Two days later—Graham could barely stand the wait—a large, open Chevy truck, bearing the inscription "Frank R. Halifax Nurseries Tarrytown, N.Y." rolled through Sing Sing's gates, loaded with rose bushes and shrubs, fertilizers and plants of every description. Percy Graham flashed the biggest and most genuine smile anyone in Sing Sing had seen him flash.

"I've been expecting you."

"We're gonna need some help. The truck's full. Roses. Peonies. Shrubs. Irises. Spruces."

Graham didn't answer. He no longer smiled. He marveled.

"Did you hear me?"

"Yes! Yes!" he shouted, roused from his wonder, "Marek! Marek! Get me three or four men! We're in business!"

They indeed were. Graham's little project became a big project. He had the material and when the outside world heard of the "Rose Man of Sing Sing's" accomplishments, he had truckload after truckload of supplies, so much that he ran short of men. Beck allowed him more.

Of course, Beck did not have a blank check. He still had to clear everything with Albany, through Superintendent MacFarlane.

"So nice to learn about your little projects in the newspapers, Warden," said MacFarlane, in one of their little phone calls.

Beck grasped MacFarlane's point. He acted as if he didn't.

"You are referring to?"

"The landscaping," the Superintendent answered quite tersely.

"That was in the budget sir. We discussed that over the phone, as I recall."

"I'm so glad to read of Trustee Graham."

"He's done a fine job, Superintendent."

"I'm so glad to read of Trustee Graham," MacFarlane repeated, slowly tapping his free hand on his heavy oak desk.

"He's done a fine job, Superintendent. That's all we can ask."

Beck *could* ask for more—more funding—and he would. With all the positive publicity surrounding Graham's efforts, he got it. The project accelerated. Percy Graham's disposition improved. His crew connected the two unlikely events—the success of the endeavor and his miraculously better attitude, but Graham himself found the metamorphosis more puzzling. Yes, things were going better—but compared to the success he had enjoyed on newspaper row, this was nothing new at all—and he had been irascible as hell throughout his editorial career. No, something far different was transpiring. Was it the open air? The sheer beauty of his creation? The lush grass? The verdant roses? The rows of peonies—red peonies, purple peonies, yellow peonies, white peonies, pink peonies—and petunias—red and pink and purple in their glory too—and shrubs of all heights and shades, all flowering beyond what he had any right to expect?

Or, was this metamorphosis something far, far different? Was it creation with no thought of greater compensation and precious little desire for greater glory? Had it resulted from the kindness of Frank Halifax—and the dozens of other strangers who provided him with plants and shrubbery and cash and tools and cash?

Whatever the cause, Graham *was* different—and the more he pondered why, he realized that maybe what he had told Salvatore Rossi, "'Why?' is the question you should never ask here" was the worst sort of advice to give a man in prison.

If you didn't have time to think about why *here*, where *would* you ponder it?

Summer turned to fall, and while it was good not to have the sun beating down on your brow, the sting of cold pick on hard rock smarted Marek's calloused hands. Without much warning, for Percy Graham had a habit of silently sneaking up on people, Eddie Marek found himself with a visitor.

"It's coming along." said Graham.

"What?"

"Oh. I was talking to myself. I guess I'm getting old. I guess I *am* old."

"It's *more* than coming along." Marek responded, surveying a long row of roses framed with every sort of plant that could flourish north of the Bronx-Westchester line.

"There's a lot more to do," Graham demurred.

"There's limits, Mr. Graham."

"Only if you put them on yourself. You know, I used to be an actor. Pretty good one too."

That surprised Marek.

"I thought you was an editor."

"Before that. Lousy tours. Stock companies and fire-trap vaudeville houses. Missed trains. Fleabag hotels. Half the time you get stiffed on your pay and have to ride the rails back to New York. A great life! I could have remained on the stage. But I became a reporter. Nobody came up to me and said: 'You're a reporter.' Hell! Nobody came up to me and said, 'You're an actor!' Nobody makes you anything. You make yourself what you are."

"I made myself a convict." Marek interrupted.

"So did I. Make yourself something new. Or make yourself a *better* convict. Look, you helped a bastard like me turn a damn rock pile into a garden."

Marek dared to open up. He wasn't sure why he was revealing himself to Percy Graham of all people, but he wasn't sure why Percy Graham was revealing himself to him, either.

"I dunno. I'm trying to stay out of trouble, but I'll never be anything. I'm doing eight-to-eighteen. I blew it. Big time."

"You know when you blow it? When you say, 'I blew it'— and give up. I gave up. I gave up when I killed my wife. Sure, I had financial troubles. I had legal troubles. I could have got past them. I know that now. Some consolation. But I gave up! On myself. I gave up on what little was left of myself when I got here. Just flopped down in the prison hospital waiting to die. Giving up is easy. Life after you give up is hard. My life's a lot easier now with these flowers, these roses, these peonies, these gladioli, these geraniums—and with you guys. You know, it wasn't too long ago I wouldn't have spit on you cons. I was still a big shot. A smart guy. Intelligent. Boy, was that the wrong attitude! Always was. Always had it. That's what I really had to get over—that I was better than everybody. You know what *you* got to get over? That everybody's *better* than *you*. They ain't. Make something of yourself."

"I wouldn't even know how to do that."

"There's more people in life willing to help you than you ever know."

Graham paused. He considered mentioning something else to Marek. What he was about to say was not his normal method of conversation, but he continued anyway, "By the way, Marek, I haven't said this to you guys, but you've done a hell of job. . . . Thanks."

That, as it is for many people, not just Percy Graham, was profoundly exhausting. For Percy Graham, it was an effort beyond his own comprehension and definitely *not* the way to end a conversation.

So he didn't.

"Get to work!" he snarled, hoping Marek wouldn't recall his fleeting burst of civility—or if he did—that he would at least dismiss it as some sort of aberration, perhaps something as transitory as a head cold or merely contradictory, but without meaning, like a sun shower.

Marek turned a shovelful of dirt. Graham walked away.

"Mr. Graham?"

Graham looked back. He did not walk back.

"Mr. Graham, you know why we get along?"

Graham stared.

"Cause we're the only two guilty men here."

Marek flashed a grin. Only then did Graham return.

"Can I show you something?" he asked.

"Sure," Marek answered, unsure of what Graham meant, but for once he was not afraid of him.

"Follow me."

He led Marek to his quarters, the little room chock full of his personal possessions, books and foodstuffs and even the small Atwater-Kent radio, that Beck permitted him. Eddie would have been less surprised if Graham led him to the train station and provided him a one-way sleeping-car ticket to Little Rock.

"You read blueprints?"

Marek indicated he did, but not very convincingly. Graham unrolled a print and placed it against a wall.

"See here," he started, "I drew this myself—and it's all to scale. Look. This part of the yard will all be filled in—69 x 124 feet of new topsoil. One great garden. Peonies. Irises. More roses than you ever saw in your life. A greenhouse—next to the wall by the old death house. And in the center—a 24-foot diameter concrete fountain. Look. Right there. Surrounded by a crushed gravel path. No, no. Forget gravel. Why think small? Marble chips!"

It was all very grand, too grand. Within a minute Eddie Marek went from being comfortable around Percy Graham to not knowing what to think at all. Everything being equal, he just wanted to get back to swinging a pick.

Unlike Percy Graham, Eddie Marek still feared to dream.

Scram!

It was not merely for Mr. Foxy Renard that the goons who ran taxi dance palaces employed bouncers.

Put a hundred or more lonely males adjacent to a couple of dozen attractive, slinkily-attired females, their hips swaying, the bodices sufficiently low-cut, and something was bound to happen—and usually did.

Somebody might get lippy with the help or with the other patrons. Somebody might give somebody else a dirty look or a shove, and before you knew it, one or both somebodies were getting hustled down the stairs. It was best, after all, for management to settle these matters privately, before a third somebody called the cops and before you knew it your business was in the papers—and you were out of business.

So it was one desultory Wednesday evening at the Luxor, when the usual trouble broke out, the usual trouble in this circumstance not being between a customer and any of the girls, but on the smoky sidelines where men loitered with a strip of tickets in their pocket, just killing time and ogling the action on the dance floor.

Business was slow, and Carrie Marek was taking both a break and the load off her feet, when she thought she heard something near the door. She saw two men, first getting in each other's faces, then pushing and shoving at each other before the Luxor's manager, a gent named Oscar "Oyster" Hoffman and its bouncer, a lug named Buster Green, arrived to break things up. Green would break your legs just for amusement—his, yours, anybody's. It didn't matter for whose enjoyment. Oyster Hoffman and Buster Green confronted the two troublemakers. The taller of the pair departed without much prodding, but the other guy didn't want to go. He gave Hoffman and Green some chatter, and before he knew it, Green had grabbed him by the left arm and swung it behind his back so quick and so hard that he was indeed lucky that his shoulder was not ripped from its socket. Green manhandled him down the stairs, and that seemed to be that.

A man about forty, mumbling a few syllables in what seemed to be an Eastern Mediterranean accent—maybe Greek, maybe Syrian or something—handed in his tickets for a dance with Carrie and then another and then one more. Ten dances in all, and, in the middle of the last, Carrie caught something out of the corner of her eye.

Such awareness was not unusual. A girl tried her best to avoid eye contact with her partners, and that left her either staring down into his chest or scanning the rest of the room. Having grown bored with this individual's chest somewhere about the fourth dance, Carrie now pursued her other option: sightseeing. Which others girls were dancing? Which were sitting? How many men were arriving, leaving, waiting? What were the boys in the band up to? They usually had a wink or nod for you. Was that busty new blonde wearing that *same* horrible satin dress again?

At the Luxor's entrance, Buster Green had spotted someone. It was the man he had ejected so forcefully minutes previously. Now, he was back.

"I thought I told you to scram."

The man didn't answer.

"I thought I told you to scram! You sure don't listen do you?"

Buster Green also possessed excellent powers of observation, particularly in situations such as these. So that when he saw the man ten feet before him reach into his jacket pocket, he instantly calculated what dangers he faced and what he might do to minimize them.

A hand emerged.

A .22 fired.

And even before its muzzle flashed fire and its deafening roar enveloped the room, Buster Green had thrown himself behind an adjacent table. A slug flew above him—and into the upper back of Carrie's dance partner, passing through his heart. As it exited, it smashed into his front ribcage, slowing it down enough so that when it finally plowed into the thick billfold he kept in his inside jacket breast pocket, it finally halted.

No more than an inch from Carrie Marek.

He fell to the floor, almost pulling Carrie down with him. But again it was her fortune that he was sufficiently deceased so that his grip loosened as he dropped straight downward. Specked now with his blood, Carrie screamed, and stood over him screaming ever more hysterically until one of the other girls, the busty new blonde in the horrible dress, put her arms gently around her and moved her away from the body.

The police never did find the man with the .22. Nobody, it seemed, could quite remember what he looked like. At the Strand or the Luxor or any taxi dance palace, everybody sort of looked alike anyway, just another stranger with an arm's length of tickets. As for the deceased, he was, in fact, Syrian. No next of kin. No headlines in the papers. No need to put anyone on the force on overtime to solve this one. No further bad publicity for the Luxor Danceland.

Buster Green, however, did find the man with the .22. There was no next of kin. There were no headlines in the papers. No body was ever found. The Luxor, after all, stood very near to the East River.

This time Carrie Marek did not quit the establishment in question. Compared to Foxy Renard, after all, a little murder in your arms was by now just a walk in the park.

Quinquagesima Sunday

Father Gelasius Bryant bent low to gently kiss his red, leather-bound, three-inch thick *Missale Romanum*, concluding his reading of that Sunday's Gospel.

"*Laus tibe, Christe!*" his two altar servers intoned in rough, but still acceptable, unison.

"Praise be to thee, O Christ!"

The pair of men serving as Father Gelasius's assistants—one, jowly and pockmarked and in his late fifties, the other, in his thirties with skin the color of a cup of coffee, one cream, no sugar—would not normally enjoy so equal a social footing. The first—the pockmarked, graying one—was an old-time guard, Leo Hodges by name. As a young corrections officer Hodges had been a hard-ass, cocky, and unpleasant. He admitted it. And as he looked back upon himself he admitted further that it was a miracle no harm ever befell him as he walked the cell blocks and corridors alone, for he had made no friends and precious few neutrals among the men he oversaw. But, in due course, as his years had served to teach him wisdom and forbearance, a form of gentleness grew in him—or at least as much of a gentleness as one might dare display as a corrections officer—and, now, the inmates generally liked and respected him, and even a hardened case like Nick Strecker sort of—*sort of*—liked Leo Hodges.

Even guards may achieve redemption at Sing Sing.

Hodges did not normally serve the Sunday Mass, but the con who usually did had taken ill, and Leo dusted off his "*Et cum spiritu tuos*" and "*Deo gratiases*" and pulled on a long black cassock and then a shorter, white cotton surplice. They were unfashionably snug, but even had they been more tailored, they were hardly standard issue garb in the New York State Department of Prisons.

Except when Father Gelasius asked you . . .

His fellow altar server was Angus Whitetree, erstwhile second story man and unwilling accessory to Nick Strecker's smoking habit. Whitetree unpinned the maniple from Father

Gelasius's left arm, carefully folded the violet silken cloth and laid it upon the altar as gently as if it were a robin's egg.

Gentler.

Angus Whitetree possessed few mechanisms to turn back the clock, to run the film of his life through the sprockets of time and regret to prior to his being a thief—and many other things— but this was one of the them, and he took it with two trembling hands. He muttered his Latin not from disinterest but from fear of his own inadequacy. He knew he did not belong upon even the lowest step of Sing Sing's chapel altar. Angus now grasped his unworthiness so well that he knew he had not belonged up there even before he had become a thief, before even his first mortal sin. But he also grasped that God needed his presence if God were to be present there later. God wrote straight in crooked lines, and Angus Whitetree hoped that the Deity's number two pencil would write that way with him.

"*Per evangelica dica deleantur nostra delicta*," Father Gelasius responded—"By the words of the Gospel may our sins be blotted out."

Father Gelasius ascended to his modest pulpit. He repeated the Epistle and the Gospel in English. Neither was about hell.

Neither was his sermon.

As was his habit, he awkwardly removed his round, black-rimmed spectacles and placed them before him. In Biblical terms he had spoken from the pulpit seventy-times-seven times, but he had still never become used to sermonizing. No, he didn't mind talking one-on-one to anyone. He relished that. He was, after all, Irish, but preaching from a pulpit to a congregation still somehow made him uncomfortable. Maybe he felt as unworthy as Angus Whitetree felt. In any case, removing his glasses and seeing only blurry, indistinct faces made his task easier. He didn't have to concentrate on whether the face in the third row liked his talk. He only had to worry about whether God liked it.

God was less judgmental.

"You've probably heard St. Paul's comments about love many times," he began, alluding to that morning's Epistle, *1 Corinthians 13*, St. Paul's famous letter on that subject.

"If I speak with the tongues of men, and of angels, and have not charity, I am become as sounding brass, or a tinkling cymbal," repeated Father Gelasius—priests liked to repeat what their parishioners had just heard in both Latin and in English. It ate up time, and it ameliorated omnipresent fears that nobody had paid any attention whatsoever to whatever they had previously heard in either language—"And if I should have prophecy and should know all mysteries, and all knowledge, and if I should have all faith, so that I could remove mountains, and have not love, I am nothing. And if I should distribute all my goods to feed the poor, and if I should deliver my body to be burned, and have not love, it profiteth me nothing. Love is patient, is kind: love envieth not, dealeth not perversely; is not puffed up; is not ambitious, seeketh not her own, is not provoked to anger, thinketh no evil; rejoiceth not in iniquity, but rejoiceth with the truth; beareth all things, believeth all things, hopeth all things, endureth all things. Love never falleth away: whether prophecies shall be made void, or tongues shall cease, or knowledge shall be destroyed."

He paused. He still wasn't sure anyone had really heard or understood what he—or rather St. Paul—had said, though it was powerful stuff.

"St. Paul tells us a great deal about love," he continued in his own words, "and I would hesitate to present myself as knowing more about the Lord or love—or about anything—than Saul of Tarsus, but there are some things about love he does not state. He tells you what it is. He tells you what it isn't. But it doesn't tell you how it stacks up head-to-head against the most powerful and important forces in the universe. Bottom line: love can put any challenger to the canvas. It packs a punch. It is Dempsey and Tunney and Benny Leonard all rolled into one. It is unconquerable. It overcomes everything.

"It overcomes time. Think of all the love of which you have heard or read or seen or even experienced that transcends the decades. Autocars and hand-tailored suits and glistening gold watches go out of fashion in a year or two. A mother or father or lover's love endures through the decades. Lovers age. They go from the beauty and agility of youth to the lines and pains and infirmities of age, from marriage bed to sick bed. Love endures. It conquers the ceaseless advance of the calendar.

"It overcomes distance. Think of the men sent oversees in the Great War and the love felt for them and the prayers offered for them. Think of all the rosaries said in County Claire or Naples or Warsaw or Munich for all the sons and daughters who had set out for a place called America and ended up in places called Hell's Kitchen or East Harlem or the Bowery. Love set all those beads in motion and sent all those Hail Marys across an ocean and through the gates of Heaven itself.

"Love overcomes disease, the most horrendous and debilitating illnesses. Ponder the children with polio, hobbling on crutches, and the parents who love them. It overcomes death. Consider all the tears shed at all the funerals and all the gravesites around the world. Think of the memories of our treasured dead, of the trips to the cemetery each Decoration Day or on any given Sunday afternoon. Death comes. It conquers life. It does not conquer love.

"And love transcends and conquers disgrace. Think of all the mothers and fathers and children and brothers and sisters and friends and neighbors who board the train at Grand Central or at 125th Street and Park and swallow their pride and walk through the steel gate midway down this hillside to sit with men like you for a half an hour.

"Love."

Angus Whitetree sat off to the side. He certainly heard this part. All the men heard that part. Yes, love *could* transcend disgrace.

Father Gelasius continued: "And think of how everyone on the other side of these walls have disgraced themselves. I am not in the business of flattering you men, but I will flatter you now. They who remain out there are little better than you in here. They have disgraced themselves—in greed and sloth and lust and anger and vanity and hatred and malice. But Love Incarnate has, nonetheless, hung upon a Cross for their—and our—redemption.

"Nothing weak can transcend time and distance and sickness and death and disgrace. Nothing but the most powerful force in the universe can overcome such powerful forces—and we see proof each day that love does overcome all of them, that it is indeed so powerful, so irresistible, so *most* powerful—and when we witness the Truth of that phenomenon we should realize—the light should go on—that it can only be omnipotent because it comes from Omnipotence Himself and that Omnipotence Itself is Love Itself—*that God* ***is*** *Love* and Love is Mercy, and that once we comprehend that, we should realize that there is no room in God's universe for despair or for hopelessness.

"But there is room in His universe for all of you—*all you have to do is love Him back.*"

Father Gelasius retrieved his glasses, descended the pulpit, and returned to the middle of the altar.

"*Think I'll leave the sermons on Hell to the Protestants,*" the priest thought as Angus Whitetree fastened the maniple back onto Father's arm and felt a tear stream down his sallow cheek.

No tear rolled Leo Hodges's cheek—until he saw that one rush down Angus Whitetree's—and up went a black-cassocked arm to wipe his own tear away before anyone could see it glisten in the flickering of six high beeswax candles on the Sing Sing altar before them.

"*Credo,*" Father Gelasius began, "*in unum Deum . . .*"

Bad Company

It was 11:35 on a Tuesday night, not among the busier evenings at the Luxor Dance Hall, and that is indeed why what was to occur occurred on that very particular date and time, for, as it transpired, several of Carrie Marek's co-workers had been providing other services to patrons besides dance "instruction."

Carrie now looked far different that she had ever had. Her long black hair was now short and permed. Her wardrobe, though more than a little flashier than good taste required, was, at least, more expensive than any she had ever known. And her manner was distinctly tougher, harder, and more in command than ever.

Had the Luxor's shabby confines been packed with eager, lonely sailors and the ordinary run of neighborhood toughs and lonely hearts as it ordinarily was on any given Friday or Saturday evening, the police raid that transpired might have proven altogether far too messy. At a minimum, a few heads might have required busting. Shots might be exchanged. It was not unknown, after all, for a cop to take some lead in the process of raiding a joint filled with boozed up aggressive males, several of whom might even be avoiding the police for reasons other than they did not relish having their fox trots interrupted.

Carrie Marek saw the invaders enter. Through the house band's raucous and tinny din, she heard an invading army of cops shout "Police! Nobody move!" and, of course, all parties present instantly thought of nothing else *but* moving, of double-timing it toward the nearest exit, of fleeing down the dusty back stairs and through a darkened alley to vanish into the fog-shrouded night.

It was not to be.

"OK, Miss," Sergeant Detective George Tuttle advised, as he placed his powerful grip on Carrie's bare arm and shoved her into the standing-room-only black paddy wagon. "Watch your head," he warned—just before she bumped her forehead anyway upon its rear door jam.

Alongside a dozen other hostesses, she stood for her short but lurching journey to Classon Boulevard's Eighty-Eighth Precinct station house, her head still smarting. *"Even here,"* she mused, *"I have to be on my feet. I can not even sit down when I am arrested."*

Aside from a taxi dancer's headache, the raid had all gone smoothly enough. The Crime Prevention Bureau cops and the somber do-gooder matrons of the Girls Service League had swooped down upon the Luxor, stoutly padlocking it—at least for a few nights. The authorities would hold the dancers and the hostesses in custody until each of their reluctant guests might be sorted out, paying particularly attention to the runaways and the underage girls, looking as well for anyone who might have a record.

Finally, Carrie turn for interrogation arrived. As far as she knew, taxi dancing was still legal, though, she hadn't seen the afternoon papers that day, the day of her arrest—so maybe she *had* missed something. In any case, ignorance of the law was no excuse. A more likely and more-to-be-feared scenario was this: perhaps, just perhaps, the authorities suspected that each and every Luxor dancer—Carrie Marek among them—did *more* than dance. The Women's House of Detention, rumor had it, was not where one wished to summer—or make new friends.

Sure, it would be a frame-up, she thought, but when the coppers were trying to impress the voting public, or just trying to make names for themselves, well . . . it wouldn't be the first time such things had happened. She hadn't missed *every* newspaper article.

"Have a seat, Miss Marek," advised the short-haired, hard-eyed policewoman at the table before her.

Sergeant Louise Harris's fleshy fingers fumbled with a manila folder. She fished a sheet of paper from it, scanned it briefly, and got right to the point.

"Ever been arrested before, Miss Marek?"

"No," Carrie answered almost defiantly, but not so defiantly that she was about to correct Sergeant Harris about actually being *Mrs.* Marek.

"Glad to hear that," came the response, "and you'll be glad to hear that the blood test run on you came back negative. As far as we know, you're disease free."

As far as we know . . . Carrie silently fumed, *What kind of whore do they think I am?* before adding to her thoughts . . . *the same kind of whore I guess everybody else thinks that I am.*

"It would be best for everybody if it stayed that way," Sergeant Harris continued.

Here comes the lecture, thought Carrie.

"If you want to stay in this 'business,' Miss Marek, I'd advise you to remain *only* in this business. Avoid bad company. Get to bed early—and alone. Keep your nose clean, and you'll have nothing to worry your pretty little head about. If you don't, there's a spot waiting just for you and your kind at the Women's House of Detention."

Carrie didn't answer. There really wasn't any answer to give, at least, not out loud. *My kind of woman?* she thought *From what I hear the women there are more* your *kind of woman!*

Sergeant Harris continued: "Of course, you wouldn't be there long, sweetiepie. You'd just be there just long enough to collect your one-way ticket home to Manila."

Deported! Carrie had never *thought* of that. *Was it true? Could they do that to me?*

"Well, that's it," pronounced Sergeant Harris wearily, "You can go."

"Go?"

"Yeah, you're free to go. There's no charges. We haven't got anything on *you* yet. Hit the road, sweetheart! And keep off the street!"

It seemed anti-climactic to just *go* after all that had transpired, but as Carrie shuffled silently past the precinct house's front desk and descended down its weathered front steps, she pondered that tonight no vast difference existed between her and Eddie Marek at all.

Cod Liver Oil

Father Gelasius had carefully avoided being ever alone with Kathryn Beck—not that they possessed an abundance of opportunities for such dangerous moments. On occasion, however, one might reasonably have accompanied the other on his or her way from one dingy prison environ to another. Such instances, however, were filled with clumsy, hastily-contrived excuses on both sides, and, in the end, such innocent, though awkward, walks were remarkably—or, perhaps, not so very remarkably at all—rare. One person advanced ahead. The other remained behind, fidgeting and watching their former lover progress—or headed off in a decidedly new direction, where he or she possessed no real business, pressing or otherwise.

One fog-shrouded April morning, however, Gelasius did no such thing. Unexpectedly—quietly, yet firmly—he insisted upon walking Kathryn across Sing Sing's great yard to the gymnasium. Surprisingly—to him—she did not resist. Something about his manner indicated that if she went one way, he might follow. If she stood her ground, he might stand it with her. She knew that much about him, even now, maybe, particularly, now.

"You seem quite tired of late, Mrs. Beck," he said when they were safely alone. He did not always call her Mrs. Beck, but on these exceptional occasions when they were briefly unchaperoned, he invariably did. It was a signal, not particularly a subtle one, of the boundaries of their relationship.

"Are you well?"

Indeed, Kathryn Beck's expression, speech, and, especially, her movements betrayed unmistakable exhaustion. Her face was drawn, and though she had not gained any appreciable weight, her movements strained as if she had. To watch her exert herself as she climbed stairs was as painful to Gelasius as it seemed to be to her.

Her decline had all progressed slowly, and, for the longest time, nearly imperceptibly—like the darkness stealing the afternoon sky, sunlight fading, shadows waxing. No one minute is perceptibly blacker than the sixty seconds preceding it—until, that is, until that great, final change, when the most immense, most powerful, most vital thing in our universe simply . . . vanishes.

Until that moment, you might not notice the process that had stolen upon you and the earth, or may not have comprehended it until you and all about you were enveloped by shadows. Stewart Beck had also noticed the shadows stealing over his wife, but he was the type of man who never discussed possible illness. A certain paralysis enveloped him upon even the slightest discussion of physical symptoms. On any given visit to Dr. Garrow, on any given query by him, Stewart Beck would blandly aver that he felt fine, absolutely fine, no matter what pain, dull or shooting, or whatever sluggishness he felt. Whatever it was, he told himself it was merely a cold or a flu or a twinge, and it would pass. It always had. For Stewart Beck could deal with executions and cell block riots—and even Superintendent MacFarlane. He could not deal with physical illness.

No, Stewart Beck, was not about to mention what his eyes told him and what his brain and heart denied.

Father Gelasius could—and had.

"I'm fine, fit as a fiddle," Kathryn protested. "I'm not nineteen anymore, you know."

"Nor I thirty. I am neither so young as I used to be, nor so foolish. But I do see what I see, and I am Christian enough to be concerned about it."

"And what do you see?"

"You've worn yourself out. Get some rest. Talk with Dr. Garrow—or whatever doctors women see. Take some cod liver oil!"

Kathryn laughed. Their stroll had degenerated from a feared potential assignation to cod liver oil in slightly under two minutes.

"Yes. Any other words of advice?"

"No, not really." He paused, pondering whether he had said too much or not enough, nonetheless, continuing, "You're a better person than you were at nineteen. You do great work here. Fine work. God's work. More than I do. You're better being better."

"I think that's a compliment."

"High praise."

"Father, do you know the two great differences between Holy Mother Church and the devil?"

"Only two?"

"Well, you force me to admit there may be more than two." The edge returned to her voice.

"Which two did you have in mind?"

"These: When you are tempted to do whatever you may be tempted to do at that moment, Satan tells you to do it. He eggs you on. The Church counsels you not to."

"That's one."

"Then when you've done it, and the devil has you, he sneers that you are dirt, and you can never be forgiven for what you did, so keep doing it, keep wallowing in the muck. *It's too late for you to go back.*"

"Yes."

"And the Church tells you the exact opposite: that you're God's child, and you can be forgiven at any time by your Father. Just ask Him. Just stop what you've been doing. Move forward into the light—and it's over."

"It's over, Father Bryant. We're in the light. Let's stay there."

"Of course. There's no other way . . . Never really was. You put that rather nicely."

"I would think you might find that reasonable. But it's not original. I heard it a long time ago. In a sermon preached from a very high pulpit—preached by you."

They had completed their walk across the relative vastness of Sing Sing's great yard. Before them stood Stewart Beck.

"Cod liver oil?" Kathryn asked.

"Two teaspoons," Father Gelasius responded.

***

In each cell each prisoner—Marek, Strecker, Rossi, and Myers—had long since established according to his own tastes a modest individual décor.

Eddie had small photographs of his wife and mother and half-sister and two postcards of a ship he had served on. It was funny how he now looked upon the Marine Corps with some sense of nostalgia. Sal displayed pictures of his sister Marie and mother Carmella and grandmother Angela—and a small Italian tricolor. Sandy, on the other hand, exhibited tasteful portraits of each of his three wives—all arrayed in their respective wedding gowns, of varying lengths and fashions, depending on the styles in vogue during each nuptial. Eddie thought wives one and three weren't too bad—they were quite attractive, actually. Though he didn't mention it, he wasn't too sure what Sandy was thinking regarding Mrs. Myers number two. Sandy also placed on view pictures of three girlfriends, women he had never presented with rings—at least not wedding rings. Eddie deemed all three girlfriends to be decidedly decent. Nick Strecker—like the others—had a calendar, but only a calendar. It was as though he was not going to set up housekeeping, get settled, or admit he would be there any longer than he needed to be.

One afternoon, as the autumn sun went down upon the Hudson, Eddie and Sandy Myers traversed the "tunnel," the soot-encrusted covered pedestrian bridge that hung suspended over the New York Central tracks connecting Sing Sing's upper and lower yards.

"Sandy, I never hear you talk about your family."

"A man who says he wants to hear about another man's family, usually wants to talk about his own," Myers, a good judge of bad character, answered.

Marek, however, did not answer. Sandy's answer struck him a little too hard. Sensing that, Myers proceeded to do what he had not desired to do: talk about his family.

"I came from good stock. Middle-class. Educated. My father was from Russia, Russian Poland, but he got into trade. A born merchant. Did well. Garments. And then furs. My mother trained in classical piano and three languages four counting English, a language she used primarily to torment my father."

"They sent me to good schools. I attended college. Unfortunately, it had certain standards, and I was asked to leave.

It's remarkable how quickly they ask you to leave . . . if you're Jewish.

"But I digress. My family, you wanted to know about my family—and I presume not about my mama and papa nor brother Harold.

"I married three times. The third time to an actress— vaudeville, some Broadway. Even did a film or three at the Paramount's Astoria studios—and, yes, one for Cosmopolitan, when Hearst had his studio in East Harlem. Bit parts though."

He paused. It was obvious he was still thinking of her.

"Actually, I'm still married."

"I've never heard you say anything about her. She doesn't visit. Does she write you?"

"Well, kid, we're what you might call just technically married at this point, and since my income is quite constrained here, she has no great reason to waste the stamps. That's it. Life."

"Isn't three wives at your age a bit many, Sandy?"

Myers pondered that. "Marek, here's how it goes. A man like me is in the selling business. I peddle stocks, bonds, property —some of it above sea level, a startlingly large percentage not. But above all, I sell myself. I work on people's dreams, but people don't trust their dreams. What they end up trusting when they plunk their money down is the man standing in front of them. I sell myself everyday. To you. To Strecker. To the guards. I don't bother selling myself to Rossi—he's not buying."

"And I sell myself to women. So, after a while you get tired of your last sale and keep selling, putting your merchandise on the table. Sometimes you get married. Most of the time you don't—but that's OK too . . . if you catch my drift.

"Now, kid, do you want to talk about your family?"

"Nah, Sandy, think I'll pass. Besides it's mostly no sale, anyway."

"Suit yourself kid."

***

Two days later the four cons loitered in the gym, half watching a pick-up basketball game. Rossi and Strecker had placed a bet on the outcome—two cigarettes, Camels, not Lucky Strikes.

"I've got it this time," Strecker advanced.

"What?" Marek wanted to know, but not very badly, "The crabs?"

"The main chance."

Marek knew exactly what Strecker meant—escape—because escape and food were all Strecker thought about, for, regardless of his faults, Nick Strecker was a social being and he missed the ramshackle hustle of the Bowery and the neon bustle of Times Square and the hum of all the great thoroughfares and side streets of his city, every pool hall and every grimy back alley. The contrast with Sing Sing was all too stark, too much to bear. Sing Sing meant toil but not progress, indolence but not rest, crowds but not humanity, emptiness but not privacy, silence but not peace—and each twenty-four hours of radiance elsewhere and darkness there cut and bled Nick Strecker just a little bit more.

"Sure, Nick, sure."

"No. It's real, Marek. So real I can taste it."

"You're going to eat your way out?"

"Look, do you guys want in—or not?"

"I'm always game," said Rossi, and, indeed, he usually was for anything Nick concocted.

Myers never was. "Such an offer," was all he had to say, and Marek repeated the phrase, trying to sound like a New York Jew but sounding like a Scranton Polack trying to sound like a New York Jew. Realizing how bad he sounded, he laughed—at himself.

Strecker wasn't sure who Eddie was laughing at but feared it might be him. He remained a firm defender of his own dignity and of the sanctity of his escape plans. "Look, pal," he scolded Marek with more than a tinge of anger, "It's not like you're on the way out. If you're lucky you're out in six at the best. If you're not lucky—if you make just one wrong move, you can be here fourteen more. Think about it."

"I'm thinking," Eddie Marek responded, and, indeed, he was. He had his reasons.

When Marek returned to his cell that night he re-read his reason. He fished an envelope from his shirt pocket, opened it, and read the contents. He had read them earlier that day and read them the day before.

The envelope, postmarked Brooklyn, bore no return address. Its handwritten message read:

> Dear Edward,
>
> I should have possessed the courage to say the following to you in person, but I do not have that courage, and, in any case, even the bravest person would have trouble saying what I am about to say to you in the visitor's room.
>
> There comes a time when people must part, and you and I have reached that time. The fault is not yours. I want you to know that. I think I have caused you as much trouble as any human being can cause another. I did not mean to but I did. It would be better if when you are released you find someone new.
>
> I want you to know that I wish you all the best and hope that you are well and can do well after leaving Sing Sing.
>
> Sincerely,
> Carissa

Some letters can burn a hole in a human heart, and to Eddie Marek this was one of them. He knew things had not been going well. He could have seen it coming. But one is never fully prepared for news such as this. He sat down, tried to collect his smoldering thoughts and composed his own letter, begging Carrie to visit one more time, explaining that he really loved her and needed her, and that her accusations against herself made no sense, that he was the con in prison. It was he who had bought a gun with Foxy Renard and committed the robberies. He had disgraced her and ruined her life. He sealed his own letter in an envelope, waited for it to be picked up, and, as he had never done so before, prayed.

It rained torrents the next day, a steady, soaking, hard downpour, and even the old version of Percy Graham wouldn't have worked a crew in such weather—and he certainly was not about to send his roses and his peonies out either. He remained dry within his quarters, bundled in his cardigan, sipping tea, munching upon his private stock of Lorna Doones, and, most particularly, examining plans for ever more landscaping and construction. He schemed to fashion not merely gardens but an ornate aviary as the centerpiece of his design. He had discussed his plans with Beck. All he required was more money, more men, and more material. In other words, nothing at all beyond the reach of the great Percy Graham.

He heard a knock. He expected one.

It was Marek, looking more dejected than gray weather might require.

"You wanted to see me?"

"Yes, have a seat."

"Excuse me," Graham apologized as he reached for two small red-and-white capsules on his desk and then for his tea, "I've got a proposition for you."

"Yes, Mr. Graham?"

"First off," he said, wiping his mouth, "you've done OK work here, but you're not indispensable."

Marek flushed. Gripping his chair, he managed to control himself. What sort of demon was this Graham? First he builds you up, gives you a pep talk, than slaps you in the face.

"*Psia krew!* Eddie muttered—*bitch's blood!*—for when he was really mad, he reverted to swearing in Polish. It was, all in all, not such a bad habit to have, for outside of Greenpoint, no matter how angry you were, no one actually knew what you really meant.

"The warden asked my advice on something," Graham continued without pause, merely thinking that Eddie had stifled a small sneeze, "The padre's short-handed at the chapel. They need a sacristan, or whatever they call it. Someone to keep the

place clean, whatever they do in there. Keep the vestments neat
and in order. Make sure they don't run out of candles and
incense. Maybe run errands for him. I don't know what they do.
But whatever, it is, I thought I was over-qualified. In any case,
I'm busy. But I figured I could spare you. You're released on
waivers."

Marek caught Graham's drift. The old man was masking
new beneficence in old sarcasm. Marek looked at Graham and
beamed.

"Look. It's not going to be the Vatican, you fish-eater.
You're basically going to be the janitor. *Are you interested? Can you
speak?*"

"Well, sure!"

"Now get the hell out of here. The warden's expecting
you!"

***

Some days later, Marek chanced upon Kathryn Beck. He
regarded the meeting as fortuitous for he had some information
to convey.

"Mrs. Beck?"

"Yes, Eddie?"

He spoke hesitantly: "You see, there's a deaf mute in B
Block. I know you've helped Lemuel a lot, and I thought . . ."

"I don't know sign language, Eddie."

But before Marek could respond, she added, "Take me to
him."

***

Father Gelasius Bryant, violet silk stole upon his starched white
surplice, sat hunched inside his darkened Sing Sing chapel
confessional. He slid open the wooden grate that separated him
from his next penitent, eased it open ever so slightly.

From the other side of that screen, a heavily-accented voice
began with the inevitable formula, "Bless me Father, for I have
sinned . . ."

And out poured a listing of sins, near occasions of sins, of faults and habits, of things done and not done and not even attempted. It was not so much amazing what sins could be committed within the confines of metal and steel, but what sins emanated from the confines of the human heart.

And while Father Gelasius heard what he heard, his mind wandered, as it often did, to a thought, some might have said, was best left unthought, let alone unsaid.

They want forgiveness—from me. Or rather from God through me. They expect it, but if they knew what I have done, would they in turn forgive me? Do they ever forgive any priest? Of anything? Of any of the impatience or haughtiness we exhibit on a daily human basis—let alone what I have done. They expect us to be perfect on the day of our ordination and to improve every day following it. And if we fail, as we always do, do they ever forgive us our sins?

Father Gelasius feared he knew the answer to that question, though he also knew it wasn't *their* forgiveness that mattered.

"Well, that's about it, Father," rasped the voice from across the grate.

The same sins over and over again, thought Gelasius, *They come here and without any improvement at all expect to be forgiven. And they would rip me apart if they had any inkling of what I had done years ago . . .*

And then through his booth's dark shadows, his eye caught the outlines of the tiny crucifix that hung above him upon the confessional wall—and the corpus affixed to it.

"*Indulgentiam,*" Father Gelasius began, "*absolutionem, et remissionem peccatorum tuorum tribuat tibi omnipotens et misericors Dominus.*"

And he actually meant it.

"Thank you, Father," answered the disembodied voice, after Father Gelasius had finished his absolution and prescribed three Hail Marys and three Our Fathers worth of penance.

And he actually meant that too.

***

Percy Graham had not entirely foregone one of his favorite hobbies: torturing those near him.

Today's target was Father Gelasius, and as Graham, walked alongside both Gelasius and Kathryn Beck on their way to the administration building, he started in. The topic was not Gelasius' new sacristan.

"I wish your plaster saints, your pasteboard holy people, were somewhat more convincing Father."

"What do you mean Percy?"

"Well, they are clear products of the imagination—the imagination of somebody in Rome or of the holy card printing industry. Too goody two-shoes. No drama. If anyone wrote about them in my paper they would have a damn sight more interesting. It's all one great immaculate deception."

Gelasius wanted to clock him one, but figured he would offer up his anger and having to deal with this ignorant, malevolent old man, and that he would try educating—and maybe even converting—him. Not that he had succeeded in any of his previous attempts, that is.

"There are no plaster saints, Percy. They are all flesh-and-blood, all possessing free will, all touched by Original Sin. Why even you must believe in Original Sin, Percy? There's enough evidence of it here to overwhelm even the most hardened skeptic?"

"Well, they look like plaster!"

"St. Augustine was quite the carouser, you know. He didn't name his memoirs "The Confessions" for nothing. And so was St. Francis of Assisi before he heard the call. And I think we've all heard of Mary Magdalene and of the Good Thief."

"Yes," said Kathryn, barely audibly to either Gelasius or Graham, "Mary Magdalene."

"Of course, I know all that," said Graham, "but that was *before* they heard the call. Then they don their roman collar or habit or mantilla or whatever, and—presto—a life of non-stop, boring sanctity. No drama. No story line. The plot flattens out in the second act. Unless we get a martyrdom in the third act, the audience might as well go home early!"

Gelasius removed his homburg and slapped it across his thigh. "Percy, do you know anything about saints? That saints are saints because they practice heroic virtue. There's nothing heroic unless you're under fire. There's no heroism in the corridors of the War Department—only in the trenches or on a submarine. The heroism comes from struggle. For the saints, as for the rest of us, is the struggle against temptation. And the devil often turns his mightiest firepower on those with the most potential for holiness, those most capable of harming his infernal kingdom."

Here, certain thoughts of what he was saying struck uncomfortably close to home. He, nonetheless, kept talking. Kathryn remained painfully silent.

"You claim to be an educated man. You've run a city room, overseen a library. Have you never heard the expression 'The Dark Night of the Soul'? A night of doubt. Of temptation. Of a great howling loneliness. 'The Dark Night of the Soul.' That was a book written by St. John of the Cross. Do you think he wrote from abstraction? An abstract darkness or a real darkness? A darkness, a void, he overcame. St. Thérèse of Lisieux experienced the very same thing. So did St. Paul of the Cross. You fall, you sin, you doubt, and God gives you the grace to rise again.

"Heroic virtue, Mr. Graham! Heroic virtue!"

A new train of thought interrupted his current musings. "I'm supposed to meet a prisoner in the chapel! A convert! A Presbyterian! See you!"

He reversed course and dashed off, the thought of winning another soul energizing him even more than his jousting with Percy Graham. "Heroic virtue!" Graham muttered to Kathryn, "Gibberish! Easy for him to say. I'll bet he's never had a temptation or a doubt in his life!"

"Yes, Mr. Graham," she echoed quietly and wearily, "easy for him to say."

***

Nick Strecker's path would also occasionally intersect that of Mrs. Stewart Beck. Those brief and passing encounters, however, failed to prompt Nick to any thoughts of deaf mutes or lip-reading or Braille or to prison charity of any sort. Usually, Nick pondered his festering, ill-conceived idea to kidnap her, to employ her as his ticket home—or to wherever escapees blissfully reside in their dreams.

Sometimes, though, Strecker had other thoughts. For in some vague, mawkish way Kathryn reminded Nick of his own mother—not his real mother though she should have, for neither woman enjoyed anything near true good health—but of Ethel Larrabee, the crone in a tattered black, always black, always tattered, dress, across the Ludlow Street hallway who had taken him in when Alma Strecker had died. Few things moved Nick Strecker, but the memory of Ma Larrabee remained among them.

Strangely, Nick even held kindly thoughts toward Mr. Larrabee—that old drunk. Ed Larrabee may have beaten and kicked little Nick, swore at him, ordered him between curses and insults into Paddy Doyle's corner saloon for growlers of ale, and even pitched the boy down the tenement stairs when he dared steal a foamy swig on the trip home, but Nick no longer held any of that against him. For all he knew, that was how Yer Old Man was *supposed* to act.

Nick figured if *he* had kids, that's how *he'd* act.

In any case, Ma Larrabee never let Old Man Larrabee slam Nick *too* hard, and Nick never forgot that, creating for Nick fond memories of a boyhood that most psychologists and settlement workers—and children themselves—would regard as a Dickensian nightmare. However placid Nick's memories were, and no matter how strongly Kathryn Beck conjured up treasured reminisces of maternal love, none of those thoughts did much to block thoughts of kidnapping her. For, if truth be told, if it had proven to be in his interest, it was entirely possible that Nick Strecker would have pressed a knife close to Ma Larrabee's wrinkled flesh and kidnapped her too.

***

"For you chum," said a sallow faced prisoner as he handed Eddie Marek a letter.

It was not addressed to Eddie. It was, instead, addressed to "Mrs. Edward Marek, 74 Freeman Street, Brooklyn, New York" but it also contained an official Post Office stamp that read, "RETURN TO SENDER, ADDRESS UNKNOWN, NO FORWARDING ADDRESS."

"Hey kid," Strecker badgered, his face pressed unusually close against his cell bars, "Whatcha get? Anything good? Hey, come on . . . don't hold out on me . . ."

Marek didn't answer.

"Hey . . . kid."

No answer.

"Ah, the hell with ya!"

"Yeah," fumed Marek, "the hell with me—and to hell with *her.*"

***

There must have been something in the air—something extraordinally toxic. Percy Graham had accomplished a great deal with his roses and shrubs and peonies and fountains and had more planned. And then . . .

The bottom fell out. The Prisons Department contracted for a new Sing Sing drainage system. The winning bidder's steam shovels and backhoes invaded the yard—destroying everything in their path, everything Graham and Marek and all the men had worked so hard to create—gardens and fountains and roses and peonies. Even Beck remained powerless against the vandalism. Superintendent MacFarlane didn't lift a finger to help.

Graham never recovered. He was seventy-two and too old to pick up the pieces—particularly the pieces of himself.

Your Eminence

"We shall be having a visitor, Father!"

Sing Sing, it seemed, was always receiving visitors. It regularly greeted long-term guests, of course, but there was, additionally, no dearth of those engaged in mere day visits. The alternately comforting, alternately horrifying, emotions of drawing pleasure from seeing one's fellow creatures brought low and the gnawing unease that a similar fate might eventually befall oneself drew morbidly curious humankind like a magnet drawn to gold-plated slag. And the greater one's fame, the greater the pull.

Of course, the more pronounced your fame, the more Stewart Beck would accommodate you.

"And who might that be, Warden?" Father Gelasius answered, hoping it might be a famous ball player, or, if not that, at least, a presentable Irish tenor.

"That . . .," said Stewart Beck, "is for me to know—and for you to discover soon enough. It is my little surprise."

***

And so, forty-eight hours later, at ten-thirty, on a still mist-shrouded Thursday morning, Father Gelasius Bryant found himself summoned to a hastily-scheduled meeting at the Warden's office, topic unknown.

"Good morning, Father, I believe you may have met our guest."

Yes.

He certainly had.

Standing not ten feet before Father Gelasius Bryant, bookended and dwarfed by a beefy, bespectacled, balding priest he had never before laid eyes upon and by Principal Keeper Joseph Patrick McKaig, was a wizened but, nevertheless, steely-eyed cleric, his own finely tailored-and-pressed, black garb accented by a glistening gold chain worn across his chest—a bishop, but no ordinary bishop—the Archbishop of New York,

Patrick Cardinal Cronin. Father Gelasius had indeed met Cronin previously. Cronin, an old Five Points orphan, was a man not easily fooled or trifled with—particularly in Father Gelasius Bryant's case.

It was Patrick Cronin, as a significantly less-wizened auxiliary bishop, who had dispatched Gelasius to Sing Sing.

"Yes, Warden," said Gelasius, his right hand clenched in the tightest, tensest fist, "I believe we have met."

Gelasius nervously advanced toward his superior, genuflected on his left knee and silently kissed the gold ring presented personally to Cronin by Pius XI.

Cardinal Cronin smiled wanly, his face betraying scant emotion. Five Points orphans do not master the world of chancery and Vatican machinations by giving any game away too easily—if they give any away game at all. What Patrick Cardinal Cronin thought—what he remembered—remained an excruciating mystery to Father Bryant.

"Hello, Kathryn," said Stewart Beck.

Excruciating mystery yielded to outright terror. Behind his warden, his former lover—and the most powerful human being cognizant of his decades-old sin. Yes, Cardinal Cronin, would know that. But there remained no great reason that he might know, or even surmise, that the middle-aged woman entering the room, had long before been the mother of Father Gelasius's stillborn child.

"Your Eminence. This is my wife, Kathryn Sumner Beck."

Fear exploded within Father Bryant. It filled both his brain and his body and then seemed to fill the room itself, before surging out to envelope every corner of Sing Sing, its cellblocks and towers and yards, even the Dance Hall itself. And suddenly, instantly, it receded and evaporated, leaving behind nothing in its wake, leaving Father Bryant empty and hallow and so utterly exhausted and defenseless—knowing not what to expect next nor able to react to any new horror that might follow

"Pleased to meet you, Mrs. Beck," the Cardinal smiled, not a wan smile, but a great, toothy Gaelic one.

"Did these aged ears hear your maiden name was Sumner?" The Cardinal's ears were not only aged but quite large, and combined with his rather long, pointed nose, bestowing upon him at the right—or, perhaps, the wrong—moment, the look of an ecclesiastical Nosferatu.

"Yes, Your Eminence." Kathryn answered.

"Do you hail from Auburn like your husband? I sense a bit of the City in your voice."

"No, Your Eminence," she responded guardedly, as vaguely as she dared, her heart racing, her tiny left hand balled tensely into the tightest fist, "I'm from Manhattan."

"Murray Hill!" her husband brightly and blissfully ignorantly interjected, as scant yards way, two bodies stiffened, two souls stopped breathing, and one Cardinal's eyes grew suddenly larger.

"I see," Cardinal Cronin responded.

" . . . I see."

***

And what *had* Patrick Cardinal Cronin seen? And what had he remembered before he visited Sing Sing? And what did he recall upon departing? Were his faculties still so nimble and his memory so powerful as to summon up not merely the circumstances of a young Murray Hill assistant pastor suddenly exiled to Sing Sing—oh, there was no way he would forget that—but the name of the young parishioner involved?

"I see," Patrick Cardinal Cronin had said.

***

Cardinal Cronin indeed saw quite a bit that day—and knew quite a bit as well. He remembered very well his last meeting with Father Bryant and the reasons for it. He did not know, however, that a warden's wife might possess such a significant and disconcerting history. Now, he did.

But he did know more about Kathryn than either she or Gelasius might have suspected. For, as Cardinal Cronin often observed, it was not such a bad thing for a bishop to have very large ears and an even longer nose. In the course of his vocation, he heard many things and sniffed out even more. And, once long ago, in his own private ways, he had surmised the identity of a young priest's lover and to where she had so mysteriously vanished. It was in such a fashion that two mysterious envelopes had reached a certain pregnant young lady in Auburn, New York, each envelope unidentified as to its sender and each containing one hundred dollars in crisp twenty-dollar notes. Kathryn never knew from whence they came and would indeed have been surprised to learn they had originated from an auxiliary bishop's private savings account. And, in the same mysterious way in which they arrived, following the loss of her child, they never again appeared.

The ways of Patrick Cronin were very mysterious indeed. And whether his ways included leaving things well enough alone remained to be seen.

***

"Are you feeling all right?" Stewart Beck asked as his wife changed for bed that evening.

There was no answer.

"Kathryn, are you all right?"

"Yes . . . yes . . . of course. I think I might be coming down with a cold. You know, that achy feeling you get, just as one's coming on. Maybe it'll pass."

She thought of saying more, but could not get beyond what she would say once she said it, and how saying it would send everything in everyone's world spinning out of control. Nonetheless, she began.

"Stewart . . ."

"Yes?"

"Stewart . . ."

She paused yet again.

". . . I love you."

"I love you too, dear," he said, "But tomorrow I want you to see Dr. Garrow about that cold."

Which was more than Kathryn Beck or Father Gelasius, then, or ever, said about what had transpired. For them, it was a day of fear that, mercifully, Stewart Beck might never know—if, that is, he did not know it already.

Spring

A new spring came. Eddie Marek moved aimlessly though the recreation building. A bluff and beefy senior guard named Matthew Harding called out, "Hey, Marek, I want to talk with you!"

It was, as ever, more a command than a request, and a gruff command at that. It jangled Marek's nerves. You never knew when you might be back in the laundry or heading toward some sort of shakedown devised by George Tannahill, but Eddie Marek had little choice and walked grudgingly forward.

"I saw you playing ball in pickup games last summer."

Marek looked back blankly, noncommittally. He wasn't in the mood to sign autographs—nor was he interested in what he knew Harding had in mind.

"You got talent," the guard continued, spitting out his words, not waiting for an answer, "You could use more power, but you can run, field, throw, and hit for average. Why not go out for the official prison team, the Zebras?

"I'm coaching."

Harding coaching was not a selling point.

"Oh, I don't know. I'm no ballplayer. That's for the other guys."

"That's total crap. What are you afraid of Marek? You want to be a hard-head Polack loser all your life, good at nothing except getting caught?"

It was one thing for Graham to call him a Polack, but to hear it from this low-rent, state-issue joker, was beyond the pale. "You're damn right, *sir*. I'm a loser, but I could play all nine positions on my head, whistling Dixie out my behind and playing a bass drum, and that wouldn't get me out of here a minute sooner."

It was Harding's turn: "Let me tell *you* about minutes. I ain't getting out of here any sooner either. I got no education, no connections. There's a damn Depression going on out there—*if you haven't noticed*. I got a wife and six kids, and I'm trapped here as much as you are. My minutes here last sixty seconds—just like yours, not one second more or less. The question is not how many minutes you have. Nobody knows that! Albert Einstein don't know that! It's what you do with those minutes—one at a time. A man's built up one minute at a time—and torn down the same way—if not faster. You can either leave this prison torn down five or ten years worth of minutes—or built up the same way. Which is it?"

Marek and Harding stood staring at each other, both too angry to even yell at one another, let allow reason with the other.

Kathryn Beck walked by.

"Good day, gentlemen," she said, seemingly oblivious to what preceded her, but those who really knew her, knew she missed very little of what preceded or followed her. She was merely very careful to acknowledge what she knew and what she thought about it. Stewart Beck was not the only politician in the family.

"Beautiful day isn't it?" she continued, directing her remark to Eddie, "Days like this make you think spring is around the corner. Spring. Baseball. Life begins again each year."

She departed.

"Easy for her to say," Marek muttered when she was out of earshot.

Harding wanted to haul off and pound Marek into the ground. Not wanting to play ball was one thing. That was stupid enough, but to utter anything disrespecting Mrs. Beck, that was too much.

Harding glared at Eddie Marek one last time, not caring if Marek ever played baseball again in this life or he ever coached it. He turned on his heel, storming off so feverishly he was lucky not to walk straight into the Hudson River.

***

The Sing Sing barbershop bore a reasonable resemblance to its tonsorial cousins in the outside world. True, its furnishings were Spartan, its windows more industrial than commercial, its customers all arrayed in melancholy prison gray rather than bold silks and gabardine, but when you ensconced yourself in its long row of chrome-and-green leather swivel chairs, closed your eyes and settled in for a trim you could almost smell the talcum powder and feel the hot towels layered upon your face and imagine yourself back home with the boys at that elegant little shop on the third floor of the Paramount Building. Ah, the good life.

In one of those swivel chairs, the one at the end near the coat rack—at Sing Sing, not on Times Square—Nick Strecker sat, reminiscing. He thought good thoughts. Oh, sure, every so often the coppers had put the collar on him, and, if they were lucky, they might make something stick. But most of the time he had gotten away with it. Whether it was burglaries or muggings or stick-ups, old Nick had outsmarted 'em nine times out of ten—actually *a lot* more than nine times out of ten.

"It's a shame you could never talk about your successes," he mused, "It wasn't just a question of modesty; it was a question of survival, smarts. Take that stick-up that made all the papers. The fancy French joint over on West Fifteenth Street, Chez Madalon. Me. Al Murray, Mike Donnelly, and "Crusher" Bowman walked in there one night and you should have seen the expression on those swells in their fancy tuxedos and their starched shirts and their gowns.

"'Hand it over! C'mon hand it over! Faster! Faster! Don't count it! Just hand it over! C'mon! The jewels too!'

"Fat wallets. Gold watches. Brooches. Diamond rings. Woulda gone like clockwork if it wasn't for that one crazy guy. I don't know what his problem was, but he had to be a hero. Big newspaper writer—for all the papers. Author. Hero! He comes lunging at me. What was the point of that? So I had to let him have it. Hit him three times—missed once—but hit him three times, once right in the lung. They thought he was going to die, but he didn't. Good thing, but it wasn't my fault. He shoulda cooperated.

"Anyway, we got away with some stuff. Not everything we could have, but it wasn't a bad night's work. In fact, it was one of the better ones. And the geniuses down on Centre Street, down at headquarters, they thought bootleggers did. Well, that was fine with me. They ain't so smart.

"No, they ain't so smart at all.

"The funny thing is that two weeks later, Murray is crossing Twenty-third Street, minding his own business, when a fire truck roars down Lexington, takes a hellacious wide turn and runs right over him. I think they kept right on going to the fire, but *that* was the end of Al Murray.

"Shame. Good man."

"And the funniest thing was how the very next day, I got picked up for the Stillwell Coal Yard job. That was one bad week. One bad week"

"Hey," a husky voice interrupted Strecker's reverie, "Haircut's over. Out of the chair!"

"Aw, stick it, pal!" Nick responded to the angular black con who had trimmed his locks to the requisite level of imperceptible stubble, "You're not going anywhere" before concluding *soto voce*, ". . . *but I am.*"

***

Among Kathryn Beck's many works of mercy was her collecting of books for Sing Sing's prison library, where demand for material invariably outstripped supply. She was dropping off cartons of new acquisitions, collected from Westchester County matrons, literary societies, and garage sales.

Assigned to help her transport them was Eddie Marek.

"You're a tough customer," she told him.

"Sorry, ma'am. I'm no real ballplayer."

"You're wrong. You don't know how good you are."

Marek shrugged.

"But I've got something more important to tell you."

"Yes?"

"Mr. Graham took sick last night. Very sick. Looks like pneumonia. He's in the hospital. Ward B."

"Shame," was all Marek could muster. He felt more but didn't know if he could show it. Deep down he cared—and he was worried.

"He never had a lot of friends," Kathryn continued.

"No, he . . ."

". . . but he likes you. I think you ought to see him."

A male nurse pushed a wobbly, metal chair next to Graham's bed. Marek delicately settled in. The man in the bed wasn't the man he knew. Could the old tyrant have gone downhill this fast? Percy could barely raise his head. He stared toward Marek with a mix of puzzlement and embarrassment.

But when he spoke—albeit ever so weakly—Marek knew this was indeed Percy Graham.

"You're still a dumb Polack."

"I didn't come here to be insulted, Mr. Graham," Marek responded, although, under the circumstances, he really didn't mind.

"Where do you usually go?"

Yes, Percy Graham had once been in vaudeville.

"I'm no diplomat," he continued, "I apologize for that. But there's something I've got to tell you. Come closer."

Marek leaned in.

"Play baseball, you dumb Polack."

"You been talking to someone?"

"Reporters don't give up their sources."

And Percy Graham never did.

He lingered. Eddie visited when he could, though he did not like hospitals, did not like the sights and sounds, nor their smells, that sinister hospital admixture of disinfectants and decay. He found it a lot like visiting his grandfather when he was sick, though grandpa was imprisoned only by his own body and longevity—stronger bars, really, than any man might devise. Sometimes Graham seemed marginally stronger, but those days—hours, actually—were mere detours on the path all creation must take. One afternoon, Eddie sat down and asked, "Do you want anything, Mr. Graham?"

"I want to die," he responded, with more strength and force than he had displayed in some time. Perhaps, it was the shaft of bright, warm sunlight streaming through a nearby window, warming his failing body that gave him the strength not to go on. "I want to get it over with." He fell back upon pillows filled with feathers from the most uncomfortable birds, struggling to point a wizened finger at Eddie.

"There is one more thing. Tell Mrs. Beck I wish to see her."

***

"Another death row visit, eh?" Percy Graham wheezed as Kathryn Beck slowly approached his sick bed, gasping desperately to summon what breath he might.

"Still the charmer, aren't you?"

"Yes—to the end," Graham forced himself upright upon his bed, so clearly preparing to unleash one last barb. His manner was that obvious—and odious.

He inhaled before commencing. "You know Mrs. Beck, you have always struck me as someone too marvelously good to be true—and when something's too good to be true, well, it usually *is not*—is not by a mile." He coughed heavily before resuming: "You know it. Everybody knows it."

"Do tell."

"Tell! No one acts without a reason. No one acts as you continue to do without a compelling reason."

"*Do tell.*"

"You're a woman of conscience. That's so obvious." He seemed to gain strength as his message gained force. "Yours bothers you. It haunts you even as you hide behind this mantle of holiness and goodness—as you trundle from cell block to cellblock, from rapist to swindler to penny-ante stick-up artist to murderer. You hear their stories. Their fears. Their hopes. Fetch them food and medicine. You listen to them. You care. You *force* yourself to care—or, at least, you let them think you care. Your expiation is great because your transgression, your sin, is so great."

"Yes, I listen even to murderers, Mr. Graham." She had by now grown more fearful than resentful of this man who slaughtered souls with words far more easily and skillfully than with a gun. "All our sins are very great."

"I wouldn't know!" Graham laughed—his fiendish chortle quickly interrupted by more coughing, wracking his shrunken frame for what seemed forever.

"What could this sin be?" he continued, "I'm a great judge of human character. Of mannerisms. Of movements. Of men. Of women. Of things said. And not said. I'm a man of great intuition—intuition that transcends the normal bounds of deduction. *I think I know.*"

"Tell me—what you *think you know.*" Her heart raced.

"Dead men . . . ," he answered, his raspy voice now almost placid and shrinking to a whisper, before he added, "*tell no tales.*"

And with that, Percy Graham slowly folded his hands together, as if in city editor's prayer, and said, ". . . and *that* is my farewell gift to you—and yours."

***

And that night, alone in his little bed, under a cheap prison blanket, an hour and yet an eternity away from Manhattan's newspaper offices and hotel suites and rich uncles, scoops and fired reporters and hundred point type, an old man got his wish.

Some said Percy Graham died of bronchial pneumonia. Some said he died because an army of bulldozers had ripped apart his precious gardens. For whatever reason, Percy Graham was dead, to be buried, as he specified, in a cheap casket, next to the wife he had murdered in her sleep a baker's dozen years before.

When they carried Graham's remains to the hearse to at last free him from Sing Sing, not many cried, but Eddie Marek—one of his six pallbearers—did.

And he was not ashamed.

***

Eddie Marek stood pensively in center field—this time not in a prison gray undershirt but in the almost-grand uniform of the Sing Sing Zebras—shielding his eyes from the late afternoon sun.

He had reconsidered.

It wasn't anything Harding had told him. What did Harding mean to him? Matt Harding was just another guard. No better or no worse, though maybe a tad stupider, than the others. But if other folks believed that playing for Matt Harding—and for Sing Sing—meant something, well maybe somehow it did.

And if it didn't, so what? Sure, maybe he'd fall flat on his face. Not be able to hit a decent curve ball. Look like a fool, like some trained monkey in knickers and a baseball cap. But if people, good, decent people, like Mrs. Beck and people who weren't so good—or any good at all—until you got to know them like Mr. Graham wanted you to do something, well, maybe you should.

Maybe, it wasn't all about what you wanted.

Thus, Marek competed against not the usual assortment of cellblock layabouts, but against a team of reasonably proficient semi-pros from Yonkers. Yonkers may not have been Manhattan, but it was a decent-sized city and the carpet mill down there sponsored a pretty good semi-pro ballclub. At lot of these boys had played pro ball somewhere—or could have, if they wanted to. They were, thought Eddie, once he saw them, tough competition indeed.

By the sixth inning, Marek had gone two-for-three, a bloop single up the middle as well as a hard-hit double down the left field line. His solitary out was a line shot at the third baseman. Now, he stood hands-on-hips in center field. CRACK!! The ball sailed over his head into deep right-center. It was, however, hit fairly high, providing Marek with time to race, race, and then race even more into the gap, stretch out his glove as far as arm and hand could go and snag the ball in its webbing, his momentum propelling him a step-or-three further. With just one out and a runner on third, he knew what he had to do, slamming on the brakes, whirling and throwing, without looking really, toward home.

The ball traveled like a bullet into the Sing Sing catcher's waiting mitt. The runner, a full-faced, blond kid piled into said catcher—our acquaintance from Kahnawake, North Gowanus, and chapel, the burglar Angus Whitetree. The Yonkers runner slammed hard into him, and Whitetree toppled over backwards, kicking up a cloud of dust as he landed.

And dropped the ball.

But that did not change what a magnificent throw Eddie had unleashed.

Matthew Harding had spent a lifetime studying the game. He studied better than he played, but no one was about to pay him to explain why he couldn't hit the curve ball. So, as he witnessed Marek's throw, he marveled not such much at the strength of Eddie's arm, but at the raw instinct that made him whirl and throw toward home—without thinking, just doing what was natural on the ball field. Very few players combined so many talents. Harding, in his younger days, would have known he had to send the ball sailing home like that. Unfortunately, *his* throw would have barely gotten past second base and just dribbled toward the catcher.

Harding leaned against the dugout. Arms folded, he allowed himself only a vague smile. But he could have kissed Marek, right then and there.

Angus Whitetree, however, was another story.

In the stands, Kathryn Beck shouted to Harding, "I told you he could play!"

"If you ever want to start a career, Mrs. Beck, I can recommend you to the Giants as a scout."

"Don't butter up the warden's wife, Matthew. Even Lemuel—oops!" she flustered with embarrassment, remembering that Lemuel Dunbar sat next to her "—*anyone* could see that boy could play baseball."

At inning's end Marek trotted back. Approaching the dugout, he shouted, "Coach?"

"Yeah, busher?"

"That throw?"

"Yeah."

"Pretty good throw."

"Yeah," Harding grunted, not wanting to allow Marek too much self-satisfaction.

"Pretty good minute."

Minutes pass quickly. Glory passes quickly. Make a catch. Hit a home run. Sing a song. Dance a dance.

Walk off the stage, and the applause fades before you hit the pavement. That's the way it is for all performers, and especially for Eddie Marek: walk off the field, eat your grub . . . and spend the night in the palatial Edward Stanley Marek Jr. suite of the Iron Bars Inn.

The Broken Vase

Nick Strecker's scheme centered too much on chance., dependent on where Kathryn Beck chose to go, when she chose to go, who might be around, and who might not. It depended on whether Sal Rossi might be accompanying Nick, for this was a two-man operation, and even whether Sal was in the right mood, for the Italian was hardly entirely comfortable with Nick's idea. Part of Sal thought it reasonable; a bigger portion considered it madness. But the biggest uncertainty involved the shiv. It wasn't as though one might safely retain such an object upon one's person, awaiting wondrous opportunities. No, there were searches and shakedowns, and it was best to keep the damn thing hidden, perhaps squirreled away in your cell, but far better still in some heating vent or cubbyhole. It was, it all seemed, as much a curse as a blessing.

Then, one day, it happened. It all came together: Kathryn Beck, puttering about in an isolated, musty little room adjacent to the prison library, distracted, having discovered an odd box of bric-a-brac, vases and such decorative items, generally rare in Sing Sing's steel-and-stone environs; Strecker, lurking in the adjacent hallway, noticing her alone and unprotected; Rossi in tow; no one else in sight; and, above all, the shiv—on its way from one hiding place to a newer one—now stuffed securely in Nick's right sock.

Yes, it *all* came together.

Strecker looked at Rossi. Rossi, not knowing Nick had the shiv with him, had no idea what Nick's quizzical look meant. He stood there, as blank as a con could look. That didn't stop Nick. He reached down and pulled the shiv from his sock.

Eddie Marek, en route from the yard, appeared behind them. And it was a half moment later that they heard a crash— Kathryn had dropped a vase. It shattered on the hard concrete floor, causing her to exclaim "No!" in reaction.

Edward Stanley Marek was indeed a quick study, as one must always be in Sing Sing. It was not hard to put together. The voice of the warden's wife, the shiv, and, above all, Nick

Strecker, with a look upon his face, as cold and calculating and evil as Eddie had yet seen in stir. Eddie looked Nick straight in the eye.

"Put it back! Put it back!"

Nick only glared in return. If he had to cut Eddie first, if that's what it takes, then so be it. He lunged forward and would have plunged the steel into Eddie's flesh—but for Sal Rossi. He grabbed Nick's arm—"Forget it, Nick! Marek's right."—ripping the shiv from his hand, jamming it into his belt and under his jacket.

It was over in a second, a very long second. "Why don't we help Mrs. Beck clean up inside?" said Marek, looking first at Sal, then at Nick. Three men moved uneasily into the adjacent room, as uneasy with each other, as with the prospect of looking Kathryn in the eye.

"Oh, Eddie!" Kathryn greeted them, "I don't know what I'd do without you!"

"Neither do we, ma'am," said Sal Rossi, "Neither do we."

Show Time

Carrie Marek's mother and father had never learned the truth.
She written home and lied that her husband had re-enlisted in
the Marines Corps and shipped off for Panama or Hawaii or
wherever besides the Philippines Marines ship off to. It hurt to
admit the truth to anyone, and certainly to them. They had never
approved of her choice of suitors. There were enough Filipino
boys around, fine young men. What did she ever want with this
Americano?

She had never asked that question. But she had asked why
he had wanted her at all. And why she was so stupid to have ever
thought about taking a job in a dance hall, and how he had risked
all to keep her from it, and how she had ended up in one dime-a-
dance joint after another anyway. And most of all she asked
herself why she had been so stupid as to write to him that
everything was over between them.

And stupider still, and yet more ashamed, to not write again
and confess that she had made the most horrible mistake of her
life.

***

"Sandy, how come you get stuck with all these crap jobs like we
do?" Marek asked Sandy Myers one afternoon, "Why don't you
ever get one of those office jobs?"

"I don't know, Eddie." In fact, for once, he did not know.

"I think you're the worst con man I ever seen. Either that,
or you really are innocent. Is that it? You trying to convince the
parole board that they've got the wrong guy?"

"Oh . . ." Myers started—and never finished his thought.

What Marek could not know and what even Myers himself
did not realize was that numbered among the unfortunate clients
of the late, lamented Spencer-Philips Holding Company was the
brother-in-law of Prisons Superintendent Charles F. MacFarlane.
Hence, a discrete call had been made requesting that office work
not be made available to Prisoner 62548, Sanford Myers, a.k.a.

Sanford Milstein, Sheldon Myerson, and Stuart Morgan. Stewart Beck never asked why. He figured the Superintendent must have his reasons—and he figured he might need a favor some day.

***

"I heard a story today," Myers started to say as he walked to his cellblock with Marek and Strecker, then he stopped entirely.

He had spoken so solemnly that no one wisecracked, no one bantered, "Tell me a story, Uncle Sandy." He had said "I heard a story today" very solemnly, indeed.

"You know Johnny Brennan?"

There was not much to know.

"Quiet fellow," said Nick, taking a long drag on his smoke, "real quiet. In for two years now. Doing ten for forgery. Works in the Administration Building."

"Correct. His wife never visited, you know. She wrote him like once a week, but never came. Always an excuse. Had to work. Couldn't find anyone to watch the kid. Whatever. But always a reason. He understood. He never got mad.

"Then he gets a letter. She's coming—and she's bringing the kid. The boy's three years old now and can make the trip.

"Johnny's thrilled. He used to be so quiet, like a mouse. Now he's Mr. Cheerful. Laughing. Smiling. Joking. Walking on air."

"Yeah, I think I heard about that," interjected Strecker. Marek, focused on curve balls and hook slides, just kept walking.

"Everybody notices. The cons notice. The guards notice. The guards tell him, 'Johnny, you want extra time? Take more than an hour. We don't mind.'

"He doesn't take more than an hour. He doesn't take even the hour.

"He's back in ten minutes. Ten minutes!

"The guard asks him what's wrong. No answer. He doesn't eat lunch. He just sits there. Doesn't say a thing.

"Finally he talks.

"'Yes,' he tells the guard, 'the wife came and the boy, too. I hardly knew the child. He was so grown up and smart. But he was fidgety, nervous, so I called him, 'Come to your papa.' He looked at me, just stared. I figured he was shy. He didn't remember me. Then he looks up at his mother and said, 'My papa is home!'

"'*My papa is home!*'"

"I don't like that story," Eddie Marek said and walked away.

***

A goodly ration of Nicholas Strecker's escape scenarios involved Sing Sing's loading docks. Things entered the joint, and, more importantly, things left. The inmates manufactured any number of commodities besides license plates—shirts and pants and desks and chairs and coat racks and wastebaskets—and they all exited very smoothly through those docks, in boxes and cartons and bales all packed onto truck after truck, inspected with varying degrees of diligence. It was not unknown that an occasional prisoner also departed, or tried to depart, in one of those boxes or cartons or bales.

Nick Strecker devoted much thought as to how he might be the next one, but as Sing Sing's docks were heavily guarded and he lacked access to them on even a casual basis, his thoughts never progressed much beyond the purely theoretical, pieced together from scraps of information provided from men who had worked on said docks or knew someone who had worked on the docks or had heard a report from some lug who thought he knew someone who had heard something once that sounded like it had promise—or didn't.

Because for all the industries Sing Sing maintained, its rumor mill ran, if not with the most efficiency, with the utmost passion—twenty-four hours a day.

Sometimes, though, Strecker employed the direct approach to escaping. You could walk right through the door of the Administration Building, right from the prison itself, and out the other door—right to the street. It seemed so simple. Of course, no one had ever tried it before. Of course, he'd never been in the Administration Building to case the joint. Of course, they wouldn't let Nick into the Administration Building to begin with. And, most significantly, they would have blown his head off from the guard towers before he got ten feet out into the street.

Nonetheless, you had to admire the simplicity of the scheme.

Other people thought about escape too, but took an even more basic approach. Johnny Brennan had enough. He ripped his prison-issue clothes into secure little strips, fashioned them into a short, little rope with a noose at one end. He shoved his bunk near to the front of his cell, tied the rope to the top slats of his cell door, put the rope around his neck, and jumped from his bed. He struggled for a while, but not a long while.

They buried him up the road—in unconsecrated ground.

                                    ***

"How'd you get started?" Marek inquired of Myers as they walked together near the handball courts on one side of the high stone wall that separated Sing Sing from the New York Central tracks.

"What do you mean?"

"With the cons? The con games? The proverbial 'life of crime'?"

"Oh, that was a long time ago."

"That means beyond the statute of limitations." Marek prodded him.

Sandy still wouldn't bite.

"Unless, of course, a *murder* was involved," Marek continued, emphasizing the word "murder" for dramatic effect.

"Boy, you really want to know, don't you?"

"I might want to go into a new line of work some day."

"Yeah, right!" Myers scoffed. He said nothing for a while before commencing the telling of his tale.

"After I was asked to leave school, I fell in with his some gamblers, and at a poker game on the third floor of the Claridge

Hotel, I met a fellow who would periodically venture into the hinterlands to fleece the rubes. It wasn't one of those snake oil deals, because even the rubes ain't total rubes, but it was close. You see, if you blew into some Podunk with something that could cure baldness, restore vigor, reduce weight, cure psoriasis, and raise the dead, unless you could somehow demonstrate these magic properties, the bumpkins were not about to buy.

"You needed something to show them *right before their very eyes*."

Myers paused, as if though checking if any of his old dissatisfied customers had meandered within earshot. Sufficiently reassured, he continued: "We were peddling soap, liquid soap, but this was not any kind of soap. It was unbelievably concentrated soap. Just a drop, the tiniest drop, would yield an entire wash bucket of suds, so that even though a container of this miraculous cleansing substance cost far more, a lot more, than ordinary soap, it was well worth it, well worth it, because it yielded much, much more."

"That was it? That's all you did. That's a con?"

"It's a con, kid—because the soap we sold them didn't do anything more than anything else they could buy at one-tenth the cost."

Marek gave him a look.

"Here's how it worked. Me or my partner would put a miniscule drop of this stuff into a bucket of water, swirl our hands around in it, and there would be enough suds to wash a herd of Indian pachyderms."

"Yeah?"

"Except, it wasn't the soap. Our hands were coated with a clear layer of even better soap, from the tips of our larcenous fingers to our wrists, and when we swirled them the water, that's what made the suds. What you see—*ain't* what you get.

"Not much of a beginning, is it kid?"

They walked a little way's onward.

"So," Marek asked with a wink, "you started out by literally *soft-soaping* the suckers?"

"Precisely, kid, precisely."

It was relatively safe to talk about things long ago and far away, less safe to reminisce about scams closer in the rear-view mirror of life, where the stakes were higher and where your partners still demanded discretion and your victims might demand much more.

Take, for example, the painting scam. It worked like this. An accomplice of Sandy's operating in Europe would approach a struggling artist and offer him a modest commission, a commission with a singular condition: he must paint over an existing painting. Invariably, these artists asked no questions and submitted something approximating artwork in the requisite timeframe for the requisite price.

The painting would then be shipped to New York, but in the interim customs officials would be tipped off to look out for the painting in question, for under it, they were told, was a far more valuable work. The Customs boys would take their cue, scrape some pigment off the top, then a little more, and voila, a Cezanne or a Renoir would appear. The painting's recipient would be charged a higher import fee for the painting and allowed to proceed upon his way. Sometimes, these agents were even provided with a gratuity for their diligence.

The painting's recipient and the man who alerted Customs were, oddly enough, the same person, Sanford Myers, dealer in paintings, sculptures, and all things not quite what they seemed. Myers now possessed a piece of paper, a very official document, from the United States Government, verifying that the image in question was a valuable *objet d'art* by a recognized master of the trade.

It wasn't. It was a forgery, a decent counterfeit, but a fake, nonetheless, worth nowhere near the price Sanford Myers ultimately fetched for it, though he presented that price as a bargain forced upon him by straightened circumstances, for an old family heirloom he hated parting with, but had to—and at such a low price at that.

It was funny how Sandy's victims always thought they were getting a bargain.

Not all of Sandy Myers's little scams involved suspect stock, soft soap, or bogus art. When things were slow, or when opportunities simply presented themselves, there were more sordid enterprises afoot—badger games, for example.

The concept was simplicity itself. Some poor sap, usually an out-of-towner, say from Hartford or Dubuque, picks up a girl, a gay, vivacious, *friendly* girl—or rather she picks him up. He goes to her room, prepares for an evening of romance, or if not romance, sex, but instead finds himself caught in *flagrante delecto,* surprised either by the flash of photographer's light bulbs or the flash of a patrolman's badge. The flashbulbs were real. The badge usually wasn't. But it didn't matter. The victim, scared out of his wits, was about to be offered a way to avoid embarrassment. A large outlay of cash was required, and nobody—not his wife, nor his family, nor his employer, nor his local Elks Club or Masonic Lodge—need know about anything about anything.

It wasn't something Sandy talked about, but it was something that he had done, and depending on the victim it could pay very well. It was all part of a day's work.

Many people did not talk of many things.

George Tannahill, for example, never talked of his daughter. He might have. He might have even played her for sympathy, but he did not want sympathy.

He wanted her to walk.

Grace Louise Tannahill had been born small, so very small she nearly fit tucked into the palm of his great hand. So small, she nearly died, but she did not. Now, she was eight, still so very tiny for her age, and able to lurch forward only with crutches and with helping hands.

She was one reason George Tannahill stole, not that there ever is a good reason to steal, not that he wouldn't have stolen even if Grace had never been born or if she had not survived. But he told himself his daughter needed to be provided for if anything ever happened to him.

And so, he never spent a dime on himself.

And so, he shook down prisoners like Salvatore Rossi.

And so, George Mowbridge Tannahill, loving father, had become the most hated man in Sing Sing.

Hell, No!

Celebrities flocked to Sing Sing: writers, politicians, royalty, clergy—and athletes. Babe Ruth, Lou Gehrig and the rest of the fearsome New York Yankees had visited. So had John McGraw, the "Little Napoleon," and his New York Giants. Now the Giants were returning.

"I can't say it enough, Mr. Thomas, what it means to have you here playing the Zebras," Warden Beck said to the lanky, tough-as-nails Alabamian before him with the black-and-orange "Giants" emblazoned across his white jersey. First baseman Willard Thomas had replaced John McGraw as manager of the Giants.

Two thousand cons were there to see Thomas's Giants: Carl "The Meal Ticket" Hubbell, "Master Melvin" Ott, "Fat Freddie" Fitzsimmons, Gus "Blackie" Mancuso, "Harry the Horse" Danning, "Lefty" O'Doul, "Jo-Jo" Moore, Travis "Stonewall" Jackson. What players! What nicknames! Were these athletes—or guys who used to hang out at Lindy's?

Thomas spat tobacco juice as he spoke. He played baseball not for love but for money. Sentimentality was not an entry in his drawl-drenched vocabulary.

"Hell, Warden, it's a just a train ride up the Hudson."

"Up the river!" joked Beck, employing that witticism for the approximately ten thousandth instance.

"Yeah, up the river," Thomas laughed, but it was a more distracted laugh than normally greeted the line, "As long as we can go *down* the river that's OK. Say, warden, ya'll gonna play that Marek kid today? I hear he's damn good."

"You playing or scouting Bill?"

"Pretty much playing. *He* playing?"

"He's playing."

The sun was bright, the skies clear, and Willard Thomas put his regular lineup on the field, and it was a good one. His Giants were heading towards a World Series. Sing Sing was good too, winning fifty out of the sixty games, though its schedule, it must be admitted, was somewhat easier. Freddie Fitzsimmons started on the mound—Thomas wanted to give Fat Freddy, one of his regular starters, a tune-up. Marek batted with two out in the bottom of the first. He took a strike. "Not bad," he said to catcher Gus Mancuso.

He took a second pitch—just outside the plate and high—for a ball. "Not good," he informed Mancuso.

"I thought catchers were the one with the patter," said Mancuso.

"I thought big leaguers could put it over the plate."

Fat Freddy's third offering broke sharply down and away from Marek like a snake skittering away from danger. Marek lashed it to left-center. It landed on what passed for outfield grass, took one great, long hop, and continued skipping onward in the left-centerfield gap. Marek rounded first, digging hard for second base. Center fielder Jo-Jo Moore retrieved the ball, pirouetted, and threw hard to second. Marek employed a hook slide, coming in low, his foot aimed at the bag, evading the shortstop's glove.

"Safe!"

Willard Thomas called time. He progressed slowly to the mound.

"That boy hits like a son-of-a-bitch, Bill!" said Fitzsimmons.

"What did you throw him?"

"Another curve."

"Didn't it break?"

"It broke."

Thomas didn't believe him: "Did it break, Gus?"

"Yeah, Skip. It was better than the one he took."

"You think we might sign him?" Fitzsimmons asked.

"Hell no!" Thomas snorted, launching a stream of tobacco juice at the ground, "John McGraw might have. He nearly signed a darky once! You know you got to have some standards in this game. No darkies. No cons. *Them's my standards.*"

Deliverance

Carrie Marek had departed the now-shuttered Luxor Dance Hall. The Strand—and the ghost of Foxy Renard—she still avoided like the plague, so she headed for yet another taxi-dance palace, Myrtle Avenue's distinctly sinister San Souci.

She still hated all such places. She hated their knuckle-dragging managers, hated their clientele, hated the majority of her fellow "nickel hoppers," and, above all, despised herself for being one. For as she now knew so very well, the longer one toiled in these dime-a-dance halls, the less one was fit for anything else.

People had their suspicions about taxi dancers—and sometimes those suspicions were right. Sometimes, dancers did more than dance.

The Strand's Al Brown and the Luxor's Oscar "Oyster" Hoffman had merely dabbled in white slavery. If a girl was willing, they facilitated matters, pocketing their cut, and ensuring that all went well—or at least all went well until the flatfeet decided to raid nearly every dime-a-dance hall in Brooklyn. But they never pressured a girl to hustle.

They didn't have to.

They had enough volunteers.

Managing the San Souci, however, was one Sidney "Fats" Weiss, who preferred a distinctly more pro-active approach to such matters, both in terms of greasing palms to ensure continued operations and in not-so-gentle hints to his staff that they might consider augmenting their income in their off-hours.

Carrie Marek was not exempt from such suggestions nor from Fats Weiss's equally crude threats.

"You know, Chickie, a lot of girls are just dying to work here."

Fats Weiss suffered from a vague lisp and had been known to emit a fine spray of spittle as he spoke. He also, it seemed, called every dancer in the place "Chickie"—most likely, because he could not remember their names. You'd think he'd be able to remember his one Filipina dancer's name.

"Why not?" Carrie answered noncommittally. She did *not*, after all, particularly desire to continue working at the Luxor. There was, she reasoned, a whole other borough across the East River. On its better days, it answered to the name of Manhattan, and it had dance halls too. The more she saw of Fats Weiss, and there was a lot of him to see, the more the idea of commuting appealed to her.

"Well," he continued, cracking his knuckles as he spoke, "some people have a funny way of exhibiting their gratitude. Some dames don't go the extra mile. They're not as accommodating as they should be."

"No, they are not, Mr. Weiss. I guess you could say they are not laying down on the job."

The taxi dance business had a way of toughening a girl up—fast.

"Say, are you wising off to me?" Fats demanded. He stopped cracking his knuckles. He still lisped.

"No, Mr. Weiss. I truly enjoy having a talk with you. I do not get the chance much since I am on the dance floor so often, making so much money for you."

Weiss didn't answer.

"I guess," Carrie continued, "I would say there is no other dancer in the whole, big San Souci that brings in so much *dance* business." She had made sure to drag out the word "dance" into about four full beats.

"You know, Chickie," Fats muttered before he waddled away, "I've never once seen a dancer bring in even a plug nickel on broken gams.

"Don't slip on the ice, Chickie. Be careful to never slip on the ice.'"

And though it was May, Carrie Marek resolved to watch for ice far, far more carefully than she ever had before.

***

Even before arriving at the San Souci, Carrie had met a gentleman at a lunch counter near to her apartment. He was an older man invariably attired in a sharply-pressed blue pin-striped suit. For her part, she tended to dress far more conservatively off-hours than she did at the San Souci. He'd be ordering lunch though while she'd be ordering breakfast. They eventually got to talking, about weather and life, and slowly they grew to looking forward to running into each other. Though she had ceased to wear her wedding band, he wore his and never seemed particularly inclined not to not wear one. They were just two people in a big city making small talk. Nothing more, and some days, substantially less.

***

Times were tough in the taxi-dance profession. Carrie made the rounds, but openings remained few and far between, and the rare establishment still hiring "nickel hoppers" made the San Souci seem like a convent of the Little Sisters of the Poor. Of course, there were other jobs, but except for the Little Sisters of the Poor, they weren't hiring either. There remained, after all, that little thing called the Depression. But beyond that, a new factor had been added to the equation. It was nothing Carrie Marek could quite place her finger on, but somehow as she applied for a clerk or a shopgirl's job, she could very palpably sense something—an iron wall of suspicion and resentment. Somehow, these shopkeepers, office managers, and receptionists all possessed a sixth sense about women like her, or, at least, that is how Carrie Marek felt about it. Perhaps, it was the cut of her wardrobe or the fragrance of her perfume or perhaps the slight edge with which she now carried herself, even when she tried her utmost to project the innocent, pre-Sing Sing, pre-taxi dance Carrie. And the stronger she felt about their reaction, the stronger was their sixth sense. Her interlocutors projected politeness and discretion. But they all said no.

Sometimes, she thought about just going home. She had family in Manila. She was not a stranger there, a foreigner. She could save up enough money and live like a queen when she got back, for a while, anyway. But after that, she'd be what she had been before she had left for the States—a young Filipina with no education, no connections, no great talents, and no future.

Brooklyn had its charms—and indoor plumbing.

***

The stranger perched upon the adjacent lunch counter stool never said much about himself. For her part, Carrie lied about where she worked. She said she waitressed second shift in Manhattan. Otherwise she told him the truth—that she hated working nights and told him of her dream of working again in a department store or maybe even at an office at a big corporation. But—hey!—who was going to hire a Filipina for any of those jobs? He listened—over and over again—and ultimately he advanced that while he couldn't help her out with any department stores or businesses, he did know of a clerk's opening at Borough Hall. "If you go to Room 242, ask for a Mr. Conway," he finally said as he slowly stirred the cream into his coffee, "and mention that Assemblyman Moran sent you, I think they'll at least give you a look-see."

"*Assemblyman* Moran?"

"Eight terms. But assemblyman isn't that big a deal, Carrie."

"It is a big deal to me! How do I thank you?"

"Forget it. My business is helping people—and you look like you deserve a break."

There seemed something not quite right about Carrie Marek to the Honorable Daniel W. Moran. That sentiment he shared with these increasingly prescient shopkeepers, office managers, and receptionists. He didn't believe the waitress line for a second. Neither the perfection of her make-up, nor the expensive cut of her dresses and pumps, or the elegance of her enamel-and-jade-trimmed brocaded bag spoke to him of any waitress he had ever known—even a *Manhattan* waitress. But if her story was not quite right, there was also something her to him seemed in need of being made right. Moran was no social worker, but he knew people better than anyone who sat behind a desk and stamped applications all day. And today he decided to roll the dice, to provide a job not in exchange for votes or future favors, but just because he had looked into a strange foreign woman's deep brown eyes and seen not only what was might not be true, but the deeper truth of character.

If he was wrong, well, the borough president's office could just show her the door—and, if the worst came to worst, he'd just have to find another hash house to eat lunch.

"Do I go there now, Mr. Assemblyman?" Carrie said as she jumped off her stool, excited as if it were a raid. Then she paused, and, as if she were back in Manila and standing before one of her own elders, she bowed slightly and grabbed Daniel Moran's right hand, raised it upward and pressed its back gently to her own forehead.

Then suddenly she was in motion again. Gratitude had its moment. The thought of escaping Fats Weiss and the San Souci possessed its own furious momentum.

"Should I go right now?" she demanded, "What stop is this Borough Hall?"

"It's . . . er . . . Borough Hall, Carrie."

"Right!" she responded, "Yes, of course! Of course. I know that! I know that! Borough Hall. OK, Borough Hall. It is!"

"You could walk it too," Hogan said quietly.

"Yes, yes, of course, Mr. Assemblyman! Of course! OK! I know I could walk! Yes, of course!"

She looked down at the lunch room's dingy flooring, embarrassed at how her emotions had betrayed her. "I guess that I sound very silly, Mr. Hogan," she apologized, "But you know . . ."

"I do know, Carrie. I wasn't born an assemblyman with a suit and a watch," Hogan interrupted, "I needed a job once too. It seems like it wasn't that long ago, but I guess it was."

He leaned over and took a paper napkin from the dispenser and handed it to her. "Wipe the powdered sugar off your face," he advised, "and just remember: If you get the job, show up on time each morning. Do good work. And vote Democratic!"

Carrie did visit Room 242, and she never worked nights again—and she *always* voted Democratic.

Visitors Day

It was never Visitors Day if you didn't have any visitors. Carrie Marek had dropped off the face of the earth. Eddie's mother and the rest of his kin knew where he was now but lived too far away. Foxy Renard was long since out of stir, but, funny, he never came to visit either.

Funny.

Eddie would have to remember that one.

Most guys had visitors—wives or girlfriends or family. Even Lemuel Dunbar had folks nearby—and they visited occasionally. Salvatore Rossi didn't have any mother to see him, of course. And his old man was dead too. But his younger sister visited. Their grandmother took the two of them in following what they delicately called "the fire." Salvatore had turned out to be a thug, mad at the world—and probably mad at the world even before "the fire." People look for excuses for why they're screwed up, and the bigger the excuses, the more earthshaking and historic the better. Marie Rossi, on the other hand, wasn't a bad kid. She played it straight. She had even wanted to be a nun, a Carmelite—the name reminded her of her dead mother—or, at least that's what people thought. Marie washed out of the Carmelites. Nobody knew why, but she did.

Salvatore looked at it like she got paroled.

It wasn't that she wanted to marry some guy. She didn't, and she was still religious. She took work as a seamstress, which she was pretty good at, and kept to herself. On Saturday once or twice each month, she'd board the train at Grand Central to visit. Today, five-feet tall, brown-eyed and serious, dressed in black and white like a Second Order Carmelite, she sat across from her brother.

There might have been friction between the thuggish, irreligious brother and his quiet, goody-two-shoes little sister. There wasn't. Marie didn't reproach Salvatore; she only prayed for him—a lot. It didn't seem to do much good, but she kept at it. That's faith.

She also kept visiting, though that also seemed fruitless. Salvatore Rossi was as big a thug today as the day he had first entered Sing Sing, as the afternoon he had pistol-whipped Jonah Glaser, as the morning he first skipped school and swiped some fruit from the A&P.

But he loved his little sister, and she loved him.

It was indeed a busy visitors day. Sanford Myers received neither wife, nor girlfriend, nor family members, nor certainly not any ex-nuns, but once again the very brave, very brazen Ben Miller. They spoke quietly as did all cons and visitors—save when a visit went terribly, terribly wrong. This one was not going particularly wrong, though Myers wasn't so sure.

"Get a hold of him, Ben! He's expecting you. Look at the papers. Do what you have to do!"

"That's not the tricky part—and don't call me 'Ben!'"

"So, *Mr. Salinger?*" Sandy fidgeted, "Who cares about tricks? We're *in* the trick business!"

"Some of us are better at it than others, Sandy. Don't worry. If I were depending on *you* to help *me*—now, that would be problematical."

Nick Strecker sat nearby. It *was* indeed a *very* busy visitor's day.

Strecker's visitor looked far less distinguished than Sandy Myers's, less sanctified than Salvatore Rossi's. A stocky man, not particularly well dressed, he looked like he had previously been on the other side of such visits—or should have—or would. He conversed with Nick in particularly hushed tones.

"You got it *figured?*"

Nick could not hear him. He asked again.

"I'm gonna walk right out," said Strecker, his hand covering his mouth.

"Why not fly?"

"It will be at night," Strecker continued, his eyes darting about the room, "middle of the night. You leave the car for me, with a change of clothes for me and my pals. You got the sizes."

The man nodded. "Extra guns?" he asked.

Strecker's eyes betrayed panic: "Pipe down!"

"Yeah. Extra. Good thinking.

"When?"

Nick dropped his hand from in front of his mouth. "When? When I *say so*! How the hell do I know? What do I look like? A Ouija Board? When we get re-assigned!"

Salvatore Rossi remained with his sister. "I'm getting sick of this place, kiddo. I'm not going to stick around much longer."

"Don't do anything stupid, Sally."

Rossi looked away.

"For me, Sal, don't do anything stupid."

"Do I look like I'd ever do anything stupid?" Rossi responded, blissfully and remarkably ignorant of the utter irony of his remark.

Everyone returned home: Marie and Ben and the stocky man to the city; Strecker and Rossi and Myers to B Block and the yard. While Strecker's eyes darted around the visitor's room, he noticed both Rossi and Myers. He knew Sal's sister. No story there—unless Sal couldn't keep his mouth shut. But who was this joker with Myers? It was none of his business, but being in prison was like being an old-age pensioner, everything in your neighborhood became your business. Your world got smaller, and everything near you—a truck driving by, a dog barking, the wash on the line next door—got bigger, looming up above you, staring down at you, *owning* you after a while.

Nick spotted Marek on the ballfield. He ambled over, bent down, removed his left shoe and shook a pebble out of it.

"Who was that with Myers today?" he asked with no further introduction.

"Where?" Marek answered, having no particular interest in the specific question or even in being interrogated by Nick Strecker in general. Strecker had long since begun to grate on him. He didn't mind Rossi so much, but Strecker had become something else. There were never any words between them. Marek never mentioned his annoyance—that would be unwise regarding any prisoner—but he no longer sought out Strecker, no longer relished their conversations. Nick Strecker, he had decided, possessed all the charm of the average guard.

"Visitors Room," Nick answered.

"How would I know?" Eddie snapped, hardly disguising his irritation, "Cripes, I ain't had a visitor in over a year!"

"I know."

No visitors was serious stuff. Even Nick Strecker understood that.

"I mean, he talks to you."

"He tells me what he wants to tell me. Not everything fits into that category. I didn't even know he had company."

And, in fact, Eddie Marek did not know what transpired between Sanford Myers and his invariably dapper visitor—which was just swell with him.

"OK," said Strecker, "let it drop. I was wondering. That's all."

Eddie had no visitors to turn to, and, in any case, the Visitors Room was hardly the ideal venue for confidences. And there were some issues he felt awkward talking about with Father Gelasius. How, after all, would Father know about losing a woman you had loved so dearly? So, in his loneliness, he opened his heart to the one person so many cons had turned to— Kathryn Beck. So much bothered Eddie, but one item more than all others: Carrie. Was a love between races never meant to be? Why had something that had seemed so strong, turned so sour and evaporated altogether? He knew Carrie wasn't perfect— neither was he—but to be abandoned by her so completely—it was all too much for him. Sometimes he figured it had been wrong from the start. Love is blind, he told Mrs. Beck—that's why he had misjudged her so.

"Love is never blind," Kathryn answered, "Love sees the good in the other person that the rest of the world never sees. Love sees best of all."

Eddie looked noncommittal. He had no idea why love should see best of all, why it wasn't as blind as everybody said. Sometimes, Mrs. Beck didn't make much sense at all.

"Look, Edward. Say you were at college Princeton—and Albert Einstein was your professor."

"Yeah . . . Princeton."

"*Yeah, me at Princeton*," Eddie thought, "*sure, why not?*"

"Smart man, isn't he?" she interrupted his reverie.

"Who?"

"Dr. Einstein."

"The smartest, I guess."

"And how far through school did your mother finally go?"

"Fourth grade, I suppose. Maybe less. Not sure."

"Is she as smart as Einstein?"

Eddie smiled. She could barely spell.

"Your senior year at Princeton. You've taken every course Einstein offers. You've even been a guest in his house. Gone to dinner with him. Strolled the campus with him. Worked on a new theorem with him. Who would know you better—Einstein or your mother?"

"My mama," Eddie answered. Of course, his mama.

"You know why? Because your mother loves you more, and love sees and hears *everything*. Love pays attention. Love *knows*."

"So maybe it wasn't love?" he countered.

Kathryn Beck stood up.

"If it wasn't—isn't—love, why are we asking all these questions, Edward?"

"Because," said Eddie Marek, "I'm not Einstein, Mrs. Beck."

Mr. Powell

Spring training starts far too early in upstate New York. The calendar *claims* it starts in the spring or thereabouts, in March, but upstate in March is not Florida in March. Hell, it's not New Jersey in March. It's cold, damp, windy. You can't loosen up. Grass doesn't grow, but mud does. You wonder why you're out there—which is why you're *not* there. You're in the gym. Running laps, charging up-and-down, down-and-up, up-and-down the bleacher steps, playing pitch-and-catch. It's boring as hell, so eventually you go outside. It's *still* mud.

Another season. Another chance.

This season offered a bigger chance than any other.

Eddie Marek was nearly used to Sing Sing. He knew its routine—what to avoid and what to seek. He was a star athlete and had a decent job at the chapel. Sometimes he filled in at the library. Life could be worse.

On the other hand, life anywhere else—would be better. Great Depression or not, you wanted to *be* out there. You wanted freedom to come and go as you pleased, to stroll down the hot city pavement or hike in the shady woods, to have a lady friend, to wear something besides gray, maybe to take a long, legal swig of cold beer now that Prohibition was kaput.

Freedom.

Freedom wasn't happening anytime soon, though. Eddie was up for parole, but a parolee needed a job on the outside, and there were too many guys out there already without jobs, too many guys with no jobs—and no record. Not many cons had outside offers—maybe those with skills or a family with a business or even friends to put in a good word for them. But Eddie Marek, stranger in a strange land, possessed none of the above.

***

A graying, lantern-jawed man eased his way down the tricky, metal steps. He'd ridden trains for thirty years and still hadn't gotten used to those damned steps. At least today, he didn't have luggage. Today was a day trip.

He caught a cab.

"Sing Sing please."

George Mowbridge Tannahill eyed the lantern-jawed man. "Got business here?"

"Here to see Warden Beck."

"Name?"

"Sidearm Jack Powell. General Manager, Brooklyn Dodgers Baseball Club."

Sidearm Jack Powell. Tannahill remembered Powell from when he was a kid. *The* Sidearm Jack Powell, the great old time right-hander. Back in the old days, when men were men and starting pitchers were finishing pitchers, Sidearm Jack had once won 35 games in a single season and pitched over 400 innings. Of course, he couldn't lift his arm even to sidearm level until the following March, but Sidearm Jack never complained. Men were men, and starting pitchers were finishing pitchers.

"I wish they'd tell me these people were coming," Tannahill thought, *"Someday, I'm going to end up frisking the King of England."*

"Nature of business?"

"Baseball," Powell answered tersely, none too enthused about his destination—the guard towers, the iron gates, the submachine guns, the shotguns—and, above all, *the prisoners.*

"Is the Warden expecting you?

Powell nodded.

Beck met Powell at the gate. They walked to the diamond.

Sidearm Jack had a very large problem. His team, the Dodgers—the "Bums"—truly were bums. They truly, ferociously stunk. Yes, they had approached the storied heights of mediocrity the previous season, but all realistic observers agreed that their modest success had been a fluke, and wise baseball man that he was, Sidearm Jack Powell realized it too. He wasn't about to kid himself. With outfielders being conked on the head with flyballs and three baserunners ending up on a single base, it was all pretty ugly and growing all the worse. Last season Brooklyn had caught all the breaks. Its shabby personnel had played to the limit of their shabby, daffy ability—and then some. But this season would be different. It would be worse. Luck could not possibly hold. Brooklyn's best players had been sold off. Its remaining talent would quickly slide to its natural putrid level.

Brooklyn was a crap franchise. Its ownership was tangled up in feuds and family lawsuits. Liens piled up on the ballpark itself. Creditors seemed to outnumber customers—at least they generated more noise. Cash to hire ballplayers? Forget it. All Sidearm Jack could hire was discards from other teams, drunks, screwballs, and once-respectable major-leaguers bouncing rapidly down the professional ladder. Fourth place seemed a hundred seasons and twenty wins away.

So Sidearm Jack Powell sought talent where talent normally earned a cent-and-a-half a day. The previous summer his team had traveled to Ossining for an exhibition, and Sidearm Jack' manager brought back with him glowing reports of a kid with a rifle arm who ran like the wind in Sing Sing's outfield. The reports were so glowing Powell could not quite believe them— but he could never quite forget them either.

Today no one recognized Sidearm Jack. It had been a long time since he had last played baseball, and he certainly hadn't played in suit-and-tie. Kathryn Beck awaited him and her husband. Sidearm Jack got down to business. He was, after all, a man of business, and his business was baseball.

"Does Marek know I'm here, Warden?"

"No."

"Good. Keep it that way."

Small talk with Powell was difficult. His eyes scanned Sing Sing's rough diamond, primarily focusing on Marek, but taking everything, everyone, in. You never knew what other talent might turn up, and the Dodgers needed whatever help they could get.

Marek staged a typically fine exhibition—three hits, two runs scored, no assists but some fine catches. Powell, however, wasn't keeping score, he was scouting, cataloging not outs and base hits but skills. Could Marek hit? Hit with power? Run? Throw? Could he *think* on the ballfield? Anticipate plays?

Position himself correctly? Throw to the right base? Give himself up to advance a runner? Bunt?

A million questions, but smart baseball men answer them in a matter of innings, and John Joseph Powell was a smart baseman man. Marek wasn't the best player Powell had ever scouted, but he was by no means the worst. He had skills. He had instincts. He would do. He would do . . . if only . . .

"Did I waste your time?" Beck asked.

"You tell me if this was a trip for biscuits," Powell demanded, rubbing his bony chin, "Sidearm Jack's been in baseball for thirty-five years and can see your kid's good. And, frankly, my team . . . could be better. What Sidearm Jack want to know is this: has Marek got what it takes to play pro ball—or will he always be a con?"

The warden said nothing. If Sidearm Jack Powell were a lesser man, Beck's gaze might have unnerved him. Beck did not speak, though he knew what he had to say. He paused, long and hard. Finally, he spoke: "Marek can play."

***

To some it might appear that all Marek did was play—baseball, football, basketball, track, but he also worked at Father Gelasius's chapel, and one day, while sweeping out the pews, who but the devil—or rather, Nick Strecker—sauntered in.

It was not a social call.

Strecker no longer toiled on the prison grounds. He and Rossi had obtained transfers to the prison hospital. If you didn't mind sick people—or people pretending they were sick—it wasn't a bad job.

"How are things in the hospital today, Dr. Nick?" Marek asked.

"I'm a regular Florence Nightingale of the bed pans. Rossi—he's Dr. Pasteur."

Marek felt like agitating.

"You know what Dr. Pasteur's most famous for, don't you Nick?"

Strecker hesitated. He hated quizzes, particularly without a lawyer present.

"Germs? . . . Milk?"

"Nah."

"Nah?"

"Sufficient sleep."

Strecker looked puzzled.

"Sufficient sleep," Eddie repeated, "Yes. He very scientifically calculated how many hours of shuteye a person needed and just when to retire for the evening."

"Yes, of course."

"Sure, think about it Nick, when mothers across America—and France, too—want their offspring to go to bed, what do they say? They say, 'Pasteur bedtime, little Nicky . . . Pasteur bedtime.'"

Nick wasn't amused.

"Don't tell that one to the Parole Board. They'll send you to the Dance Hall for sure. There's a special provision in the Penal Code for offenses like that, *capital* offenses. They sit there, giving you the once over, like they were the guys on the Dutch Masters cigar box, and then . . ."

A wise man knows when to change the subject.

"That night shift must be a bitch," Marek asked.

"It ain't *all* the time. Just enough. *I* like it."

Nick peered toward the Hudson, through Sing Sing's high iron gates, the river's waves lapping gently against the shore.

"I'm going over. Soon."

Marek was used to Strecker's wild schemes, weary of them. By now they amounted to a tired joke.

But there was something different in the way Strecker now spoke.

"What?"

"You heard."

Marek *had* heard, and it scared him. He said nothing.

"You not interested?"

Now Marek *had* to respond, though he responded by not really responding.

"How you gonna do it?"

"That's *my* secret. You just be ready. You want in?"

Marek had always vaguely been a part of Strecker's plans, ideas so gossamer that it mattered not whether you were in or not. This seemed different. Strecker might indeed have something up his sleeve. And Marek's circumstances were different too. He had a soft berth here, fame—if not fortune—on the diamond and the gridiron, the warden's trust, and was coming very near to his parole date, though he still needed a job on the outside to be able to walk, and he had no idea how to accomplish that.

All, in all, there was no great reason for him to even humor Nick Strecker, save for reasons of comradeship and force of habit, and those were exceedingly poor reasons at best.

"I'm in," he said.

Hell, he thought, *it's all a pipe dream anyway.*

No Mothers in Sing Sing

Kathryn Beck would not have liked hearing Eddie's answer. She needed no further troubles at all, for the weight of charity had worn her down. She was not old, but she was not well. Her blood pressure had normally run high. It now ran higher. She felt ill, weak. Previously, moving about the prison, talking to the men, listening to their problems, providing them with advice, was no problem. She had thrived on such activity. Today she moved slower and less steadily. Her face, ashen, weary, and noticeably aged, betrayed her exhaustion.

***

It was Monday, and Kathryn Beck made her rounds, her first destination being a new A Block resident, in for a heisting a still-shiny 1929 LaSalle from a Hunt's Point street corner. He had asked if she might suggest to her husband his transfer to the garage: after all, he liked cars. She would think about it.

From A Block, Kathryn would travel to the library, to death row and the Dance Hall, and home again. It was at 10:15, alone and unguarded, that she chanced upon Nick Strecker, returning from A Block, on his way to the hospital.

It was the moment Nick had dreamed of. True, he had other schemes well along in the works, more complex, more realistic scenarios, but, above all, Nick Strecker was flexible, and when an opportunity presented itself, a man of vision—or, at least, action—took it.

This morning, Nick resolved to take it.

"Good to say you, Mrs. Beck."

"And to see you."

"Where are you hurrying to?"

An innocent question—that chilled her bones. Nick Strecker was not among her usual conversationalists. Nor did she relish him as one.

Today, almost miraculously, Nick had about his person a shiv. It was not his. He was merely in possession of it for another B Block con who held contrary theories regarding contraband armaments, transporting it for profit, for a pack of Old Golds, ten cigarettes up front, the rest upon certified delivery.

And so it was this morning, that Nick Strecker possessed opportunity in spades.

"A Block," Kathryn answered. As she did, Nick glanced downward, then knelt as if to tie his shoelace.

"I think you're going farther than that," Nick snarled as he pulled his shiv from his sock, springing back to roughly grab her arm and press his weapon upon her fine throat.

But she wasn't going further at all. An exclamation—Oh!—emanated from her lips as an excruciating pain coursed through her chest. She crumpled downward, limply as though dead, through his massive arms, landing upon hard concrete. And the sight of her still form at his feet, so shocked Nick that he turned and fled like a thief in the night. This was, he intuitively knew, not a woman who had merely feinted. This was far, far worse. This woman would be no good to him as a hostage. Or as anything. Had he kept his wits about him, he might have slit her throat and eliminated any chance of her reviving and revealing what had transpired so fleetingly, and, now, so futilely.

Instead, he fled like a thief in the night.

Two colored cons discovered Kathryn lying there a few minutes later, so very still and nearly lifeless. They gently picked her up and carried her to the prison hospital. And no one, save her and Nick Strecker, yet knew the truth of her situation.

And neither she nor Nick was talking.

***

"I heard," Father Gelasius said quietly as he entered Kathryn's hospital room. His lips were pursed. His blue-green eyes danced nervously about as Stewart Beck had never quite seen them dance.

Stewart Beck nodded. A muttered "Thank you" escaped, no, stumbled, into the room's antiseptic atmosphere.

"Is she conscious?"

"No . . . no, she hasn't really been since we found her. Dr. Garrow says it's her heart."

Gelasius advanced gingerly toward her bed, as if it might explode before him, or, as though devils might seize him at any step.

"Let me open my case, Stewart," said the priest, fumbling for something to say, without being either inappropriately optimistic—or worse—pessimistic. He unfastened his small leather bag and placed a simple silk purple stole about his shoulders.

A nurse, a prisoner, seemingly as hard as his starched white uniform, entered. He brought with him not medicine nor intravenous but a boxy wooden, bronze, and mother-of-pearl crucifix. Silently, he set it upon a small metal-and-porcelain table before sliding it apart and removing two candles. The first wick flickered and failed to light. He tried again, hoping to complete his task before flame intersected flesh.

Gelasius stood ready. Beeswax candles flickering, bronze crucifix properly set upright, Nurse Edward Doyle, four years to go on his sentence, might have vanished as wordlessly as he had materialized, to resume his rounds, or to simply sneak out for an Old Gold. Instead, he fished into his pocket to retrieve a brown-and-silver rosary, not to pray Hail Marys upon it, but merely to clutch its beads for clutching's sake as he stood by to witness what was to come.

Gelasius leaned forward. His right thumb gently anointed Kathryn's closed eyelids with *Oleum Infirmorum,* the oil of the sick. He trembled, slightly, but perceptibly, as he began, *"Per istam sanctam Unctiónem et suam piísimam misericórdiam, indúlgeat tibi Dóminus quidquid per visum"*—"By this holy unction and his own most gracious mercy, may the Lord pardon you whatever sin you have committed by sight." And as Gelasius did, something within the unconscious Kathryn sensed not only profane flesh and holy oil upon her own flesh but sensed whose flesh it was, for within the realms of the heart and of the soul, the unseen conveys much more than the seen, and Kathryn *knew,* not merely *sensed*, that her faults and sins and omissions were being finally and completely forgiven. And forgiven not just by the Almighty—for the Father's forgiveness is far easier achieved than our brothers'—but also by someone she not merely had sinned with, but who by her distance, yes, her rightly prudent distance, but her distance, nonetheless, she had also sinned against and for so very long.

Gelasius then dabbed Kathryn's eyelids with a small piece of cotton, removing the oil from her weakened body. Five times more he anointed her—her ears, her nostrils, her lips, her hands, and her feet, each time repeating the form of absolution. No instance was easier than the first. But he got through it—his most important work was done: he had absolved her of her sins. But he still had more rituals to perform and more prayers to say, and when he arrived at the "Our Father" and read "*Et ne nos indúcas in tentatiónem*"—"And lead us not into temptation"—he stopped quite suddenly and eerily dead.

"*Sed libera nos a malo*"—Stewart Beck continued for him.

"But deliver us from evil."

"*Sed libera nos a malo,*" Gelasius resumed, his voice rising. And when he intoned his last "Amen," he said, "I think I'll stay, to hear her confession . . ." he paused, choosing his words carefully, "when she recovers consciousness."

"Yes," said her husband, ". . . yes, *when* . . . Stay Father. We want you to stay."

The next morning, Principal Keeper McKaig's staff talked quietly, almost reverently, among themselves. They had no great reason to whisper, but what they discussed was to them so shocking, that conversing above a certain hushed level seemed merely disrespectful, inappropriate.

"Do the prisoners know?" asked McKaig.

"They know something's wrong, sir," Matt Harding answered, "There's a weird atmosphere down there. Still. Quiet. Eerie. Worse than an execution."

An odd atmosphere hung in the air. Principal Keeper McKaig recognized it even at a distance. The men gathered in the yard in a noticeably subdued manner. There was no quickness of movement, no ordinary gesticulation, no laughing or smiling or bravado among men who laughed at death and sneered at justice.

Nick Strecker was not among them.

What it meant, and what it might soon lead to, neither McKaig nor any of his men knew.

"I'm going down," he announced, though what he might find once he arrived in the yard, he did not know. He was not a man prisoners easily approached. There was his position, second-in-command only to Beck himself. There was his immense height and bulk, and there was, above all, his manner. This was no friendly cop on the beat. This was the power of the State incarnate, six-feet-three of muscle, in a gold badge and brass buttons and a polished Sam Browne belt.

You did not approach—casually or otherwise—Principal Keeper McKaig.

Ever.

McKaig descended. As usual, cons looked upon him but did not speak. This time, they *wanted* to speak to him, *had* to.

They had to because they knew—or *feared* they knew. The news had been transmitted not by shouts but by a thousand whispers and odd, pained furtive glances followed by awkward silences from both the bearers of the terrible news to those who received it. There was, after all, nothing one could say after hearing it.

There never is.

And so, McKaig faced a grief-stricken, silent mass of "old timers." They *knew*.

Kathryn Beck was dead.

Eddie Marek, in syllables barely audible, asked, "Is she gone?"

McKaig nodded, and Marek could not even do that. The gulf between Principal Keeper and inmate had shrunk very small, indeed.

"Where is she?"

"At the Warden's Residence. With him."

McKaig returned to his office. Marek remained, frozen by the news. A great circle of men gathered round him. From a distance, McKaig watched Marek speak with them. He saw them speak among themselves. They remained remarkably quiet, but, finally appeared to reach some sort of agreement. Marek led them in one great, gray phalanx toward the Administration Building. They moved, McKaig thought, with a dignity he had never seen before. Not merely for cons, but for anyone—not for the graduating class of guards, nor the cadets on parade at West Point, not even for the Reilly brothers—who all became not merely priests, but monsignors—serving Mass back at his old parish, St. Brigid's.

Dignity or not, McKaig, nonetheless, reached for the microphone on his desk and broadcast an alarm on the building's intercom, "All guards on alert. All guards on alert. Prisoners moving in a body towards the Administration Building. Take no action. Repeat. No action until further orders. Remain in the building."

McKaig straightened his tie, placed his cap firmly upon his graying head, drew himself up beyond his already formidable height, and marched deliberately down the front hall stairs, out the front door, and into a yard crammed with prisoners as he had never before seen.

He remained unsure of what they wanted, though alternatives coursed through his mind. Worse than ignorance of what *they* wanted was not knowing what *he* wanted or how he might respond. *Everything* was all very different today.

Ordinarily, McKaig would immediately seize command, to control the situation, to notify them he was in charge—he had always *been* in charge; he would *always* be in charge.

This was different. It was no time for authority; it was time for humanity.

"Do you men have a spokesman?"

"I seem to be it, sir." Marek responded, though he had never been a spokesman for anything and had never planned on being one under any circumstances, let alone these.

"Principal Keeper McKaig," Marek began, nonetheless, hoping his words would somehow collect themselves into a coherent whole, surrounded by forces he did not control. If McKaig refused to listen, he would lose face with his fellow cons. If they rioted or erupted in any way, he could—and would—be held responsible.

"Principal Keeper McKaig, I believe you know how all of us men felt about Mrs. Beck. I would assume it would be pretty much as you guards felt."

He paused. His voice rose.

"It's not easy to talk about emotions in prison, and it's damn hard to talk—or, even think, about love, but I think I can state flat out that all of us here loved Mrs. Beck." He stopped as tears rolled down his cheek.

"There are no mothers in Sing Sing and precious few friends, but Mrs. Beck was both to all of us. That's the truth, damn it!"

"None of us are demanding anything. We have no right. But we are asking that if you can find it in your heart, we should like to see her one last time. We do not think that is too much. We think she might have even have wanted that."

McKaig did have a heart, but he was a professional, a professional guard, and professional guards do not allow inmates to see their hearts. McKaig did not let them view his.

"Men! I thank you for your sentiments and the honor you pay to the late Mrs. Beck. Your request will be given consideration." He raised his voice still louder. "You will now return to your proper assignments!"

One-by-one and in little groups, they drifted away until none remained.

They had hoped for the equivalent of a state funeral for their friend—taken from them unexpectedly and pointlessly—that she might be laid out in their chapel, that they might file past, shed a tear, say their prayers

It was not an unreasonable request.

But it would not be granted.

It fell not to McKaig to honor their wish. Funeral arrangements for a warden's wife, a superior's wife, a civilian, stood well beyond his purview. All he might do was to convey their sentiments to the next-of-kin.

"It was Marek?" Beck asked.

McKaig nodded.

Enough thoughts flooded Stewart Beck's mind, without this. He and Kathryn had shared a life for nearly thirty years, from one prison and reformatory to another—from Elmira ultimately to Sing Sing. He was as crushed, as destroyed, as lonely, as confused, as any man had ever been, as all men are in such hours. He did not want to think about their request.

Principal Keeper McKaig knew when to walk away.

Kathryn Beck was not about to lie in state behind prison walls.

The next day, a thousand men from the senior cellblocks stood for general assembly.

Joe McKaig was not normally nervous. Today, he was. "I don't know about this; I just don't know about this," he kept repeating to Matt Harding. "It's just . . ."

Harding didn't know either.

McKaig advanced to Sing Sing's south gate. You would have thought he walked to the chair.

But a thousand men never follow to the chair. They now followed McKaig.

To the front gate . . . which rolled open.

"Forward, march!!" McKaig roared, and a thousand cons, all as buttoned up and presentable as cons could make themselves, followed him through toward the Warden's Residence where Kathryn Beck's embalmed body lay in a solid copper casket surrounded by a thousand pink roses.

The cons would not be allowed to enter the residence. But Beck had allowed them join the procession. Eight pallbearers, twelve cars, and one thousand cons would accompany his wife's body to the brick, country church where she had worshipped.

"Are you sure that is what you want Warden?" McKaig had asked when Beck issued his instructions.

"Yes," he answered simply, not wanting to allow McKaig any advantage with which to dissuade him. He would not be dissuaded.

"But, warden, certainly, men have been released for funerals—but never en masse."

"I think we can trust them."

"Yes . . . most . . . but not so many. I'll have to put on extra guards."

Beck looked at the ceiling.

"No."

"No?"

"No decent person invites mourners to a funeral and insults them. When you tell people you don't trust them to do the right thing, you insult them."

He paused, turned round, his back to McKaig.

"There will only be one guard—at the head of the column. That will be enough. Choose whoever you wish."

McKaig selected . . . himself. He explained to the inmates where they would go, how they would get there . . . that he would be their sole escort. He didn't know what reaction that might generate, but it drew almost none. They looked at him poker-faced, unsure of what they heard. They knew one thing: they weren't going to screw up.

Beck too reflected on his decision. Would she have wanted this? Just one escape, one incident, would mar this day—and everything they both stood for.

McKaig led a thousand somber cons up the hill, four abreast, two hundred and fifty rows deep, an entourage, quiet as death itself, as respectful and disciplined as children at First Communion.

McKaig dared not look back. It was so silent. Were they there? Were *any* of them still there?

Marek walked immediately after him. Lemuel Dunbar occupied the same row. But Marek's three comrades— Strecker and Rossi and Myers—had become separated from him, and marched two-thirds toward the rear. Myers struggled to remember the *Kaddish*, the Jewish prayer for the dead. He had not thought of it in some time, and the words came only haltingly to his mind, but, though Kathryn Beck was neither parent nor sibling nor child nor in-law to Sanford Myers, he recited them silently to himself as best he could.

It was three-quarters of a mile to the Warden's Residence where this great gray procession would rendezvous with the rest of the mourners, the Warden, his family, her family, friends, prison officials—and a lot more guards. If anyone made a break, it would be in this first three-quarters of a mile.

Few thought in those terms. Nick Strecker did. He couldn't help it—and he certainly had more reason than ever to vacate Sing Sing immediately, more than any man ever did, in fact, before or since. Under normal circumstances, he would have picked out a section of woods and run for it. Prisoners wouldn't rat on him. Prisoners wouldn't hold him back.

Today was different. If he, or any other con, dared desecrate *her* day by going over the hill, his fellow cons would rip him to pieces. Principal Keeper McKaig wouldn't be able to find enough of him to mail back to the family.

Nonetheless, Nick Strecker strongly considered it. If Kathryn Beck could not aid his escape alive, she might as well assist it dead. Salvatore Rossi and Sanford Myers sensed at least part of what Nick pondered. They could read him like a badly written book. Nick's plot lines tended to be fairly predictable, though this one included a twist not even they had yet imagined and one Nick dared not share with anyone—not here, not today.

Hence, his eyes and head began shifting ever so slightly as he weighed his opportunities. Myers, *Kaddish* complete, wanted to speak but hesitated to shatter the perfect silence. Besides, part of him *relished* having Strecker's brains being beaten out by fellow cons. Rossi, however, felt the first emotion slightly less and the second not at all.

"Don't even think about it," Rossi muttered, "Move one inch out of this line—and you get killed! Not here! Not now! Are you crazy? What about . . . ?"

"Just a twitch," Strecker whispered.

They reached the Beck residence, and not a single man—not even Nicholas Strecker—had escaped or even tried to escape. Marek attempted conveying a few words on behalf of the men. He didn't do very well.

"Warden, I . . ."

He burst into sobs. Beck grasped his hand. McKaig placed his arm around Marek and moved him away. "Come on, boy," he advised. Turning to Beck, he explained what needed no explanation, "She meant a lot to him."

"To everybody, Mr. Warden, sir." said Lemuel.

They fell in behind the hearse, behind the cars jammed with flowers and the cars loaded with mourners, tramping silently on for another mile. And then they all returned, every single one of them.

The men didn't stop thinking about Kathryn Beck. They thought about the meals she had brought the sick, those doomed men she had visited on death row and in the Dance Hall, those to whom she had taught new skills, and, above all, how she listened. The men did not confide much in themselves. They bottled up their emotions. Sometimes they might confide to a guard or a priest or a minister. They more often confided to her.

Their thoughts often led them to memories of happier times, when their lives were stable, when people cared about them—when *they* had mothers.

"You know why I'm so strong for the unions?" Rossi asked.

"Paid better? You just drifted into it?" Marek answered, not sure what triggered Rossi's question, for it materialized from nowhere, save from the invariably dark and hidden reaches of Sal's mind.

"Nah, not really. I got principles too."

"Principles are good."

"My mother."

"She was in the union?"

"No . . . she was in The Fire."

The Fire. That was before Eddie Marek's time and place. He looked blankly at Rossi, not wanting to appear insensitive—it was always dangerous to look insensitive about a con's mother—but Marek had no idea what he meant.

Rossi sensed that.

"The Triangle Shirtwaist Fire," Rossi answered, sure that would explain everything.

It didn't.

"The big fire down at Washington Square, in the Village, Greenwich Village. The sweatshop fire. Nineteen-eleven. Saturday, March 25, 1911. Ma worked on the ninth floor. It was your usual lousy factory job. She sewed blouses. Eight bucks a week, seventy-two hours every stinking week." Sal Rossi paused, thinking hard about it all. "The place was filled with flammable rags," he continued, "A fire broke out on the eighth floor, and they all ran like hell to get out. They got word to the people on the tenth floor—but they never told nobody on the ninth floor until it was too late. The bosses, they used to lock the workers in, bolt the fire doors. That was illegal. You can't do that, but they did it anyway. They didn't care. The people on nine couldn't get out. They was trapped, you know, like they say, like rats. Only they was people not rats. They ran to the windows. They had no other choice. The women and girls, they ran to the windows and looked out. They didn't want to jump out, but they didn't want to burn up either. They ran to the elevators and pried the doors open, but there was nothing' there but nine stories of shaft. So one by one they jump down that shaft, or they crawl out on the ledges and they jump off. They take their chances, but their chances stink. Fifty-four people jumped, and when they landed . . . they landed. They had to scrape them off the sidewalks with a shovel because there wasn't much left.

"One of them was my mother, Carmella Stradone Rossi. Age twenty-eight.

"I was a kid, just a kid, and I got there just in time to . . ."

Salvatore Rossi didn't finish, and Eddie Marek didn't ask him to.

Nothing to Keep Me Here Now

A week later, Marek, accompanied by Myers, chanced upon Strecker.

Strecker nodded toward the prison gate and the great world beyond it.

"See over there, my boy?"

"I do," said Marek, ". . . Nothing to keep me here now."

Myers did not like what he heard. What was Marek saying? His record was clean. Parole beckoned, and he might depart shortly, more quickly than Sandy anyway. But Sandy also knew something about prisoners. The nearer their hour of deliverance, the queasier they grew.

Their minds raced in frenzied circles. *What if the parole board says no? What if I'm set up by some guard or stoolie? What if I really do get out? I'm just some con out on the streets. No skills. No family. No friends. No chances. There's a Depression out there. I could starve. Here, I got bed and board.*

And Marek thought about Carrie—crazy thoughts—maybe he could break out and find her and . . . and . . .

Crazy thoughts.

It all went round and round, and sometimes it came out, *"Nothing to keep me here now."*

Sandy expected such lop-sided thinking from Sing Sing's more anti-social elements, but not from Eddie. Marek was too level-headed for that, but perhaps he remained disoriented from Kathryn Beck's passing. *Everybody* was a little off, and sometimes Sandy forgot how young Eddie still was. Kids in their twenties do not, after all, possess the wisdom of the ages.

"You were saying?" Marek responded.

"I have a plan," said Nick, "You're part of it."

"The man with the plan." Myers couldn't help but sneer at this nonsense.

"Hey, mind your own damn business!" bellowed Strecker, getting right in Sandy's face, then edging away, leaving Marek behind as well.

"I got an appointment."

Myers waited until Nick was beyond earshot. "That guy couldn't plan his way *in* to prison. Ix-nay, kid. Ix-nay. Don't even think about anything so lame-brained. You'll be out soon enough if you play your cards right."

"The hell I will. To get paroled, I need a job on the outside. Where am I going to get one? I got no contacts. I got no friends. You gonna use your connections to get me a job with some big brokerage house, Sandy? Maybe J. P. Morgan? Huh? I don't think so."

"Nick's pretty good pointing out gates," said Myers, "When's the last time he pointed out the guard towers to you. You know, those funny-shaped things, look like pagodas with machine guns? How far do you think you get past those? Tannahill, for one, I'll bet he's got a bullet with your name inscribed right on it.

"And, as you rightly point out, you got no contacts, no friends on the outside. So who's going to hide you? Nick? You want to be handcuffed to him for the rest of your life. You'll end up dead when some guy behind some crummy liquor store counter pulls out a twelve-gauge shotgun his cousin sold him and blows your head off. Or maybe you'll make it out of that liquor store. Maybe he'll miss, and they'll nab Nick and he'll rat you out—just like Renard or whoever your 'partner' was."

"Play the odds. Smart guys play the odds. *Play the odds with the parole board.* Everything else is a sucker's game."

He whirled around and began walking away again, then turned for one last shot.

"I know all about sucker's games."

That evening, with Marek and Strecker in their respective cells, Strecker's plot accelerated.

"Two weeks from now," Strecker whispered, "I'll tell you what you got to do. Just a little belly ache."

Strecker awaited Marek's response. None followed.

"Two weeks from now," he repeated.

Marek knew he had to respond—though he knew Strecker would not like it.

"You go alone, Nick."

"We go *together*. You. Me. Rossi."

"No."

"Why? You crazy? You been listening to Myers?"

"Nah!"

"Look," Marek continued, "I don't even know what you're up to. You're keeping me in the dark, and I'm supposed to buy into this thing?"

"Trust me, Marek. It's in your best interest not to know. You just follow me when it comes time."

"Even if I knew—*I'm not interested!*"

"How can you *not* be interested? You said you got nothing to keep you here. You're not falling for that Beck rah-rah-sis-boom-bah stuff again are you? How many times do I have to tell you? They're using you, kid."

"There's more than that."

"Then what."

"I don't want a life sentence."

"They're not going to catch us."

"That's it. I'm out fairly soon. I can wait. I escape—I'm on the run for life. Always looking over my shoulder. No percentage in that."

"Percentage?" Strecker scoffed, "The rube's talking like a *New Yawkah.*"

"That's the deal, Nick," Marek told him, hoping to end the conversation, though he feared things were too far down the pike for that.

"Yellow," Strecker muttered through clenched teeth, truly angry, violently angry. "I'll mail you a postcard. I hope you'll still have mail privileges."

You In or Out?

There may be a certain lag between events—a wordless, documentless, rumorless interval—providing no hope or hint of progress, leaving one to believe that because nothing has *visibly* transpired, that nothing has *invisibly* transpired, and that nothing will invisibly or visibly ever come to pass.

Ever.

Thus, Warden Beck had pretty much forgotten about Sidearm Jack Powell's visit and his interest in Eddie Marek. So much had occurred in so short period of time anyway, so much tragedy, such great loss, that Eddie Marek's baseball career, or Eddie Marek himself, no longer occupied a very high station on Stewart Beck's sorrowful list of priorities.

"You're interested in signing Marek?" he spat into the telephone receiver.

"Sidearm Jack is indeed interested, Warden," answered Powell, "I think the kid can handle it." He also thought—actually he knew—though he did not say it, that his team was far, far worse that he had ever imagined. The Dodgers badly required talent and publicity. Edward Stanley Marek Jr. might provide both.

Perhaps, this is something Kathryn might have wanted.

"Well," said Beck, mulling over how this little scenario might play out, "with a job waiting for him I think our parole board can make him available." Widower Stewart Beck needed a distraction even more than John Joseph Powell needed an outfielder.

"Are you sure, Warden?"

"Do I have your word that a job is waiting for him in Brooklyn?"

"Sidearm Jack Powell's word is his bond. You spring him, and Sidearm Jack will play him."

Of such significant information Eddie Marek remained blissfully ignorant. Stewart Beck knew better than to raise a prisoner's hopes unnecessarily. Life in stir was torture enough to require no artificial augmentation. When all the ducks were aligned, one beak following another, a man could be given hope—not a minute before.

Eddie Marek may not have known what Sidearm Jack Powell planned, but Salvatore Rossi knew what Nick Strecker plotted. As did two veterans of the Stillwell Coal Yard job, the Chez Madalon job, and a couple dozen other heists of varying success. Nick Strecker had kept quiet for them—and they were about to repay the favor. Besides, before that hook-and-ladder had careened around the corner of Twenty-Third and Lexington and dispatched Al Murray to kingdom come, Murray had told Nick where he had stashed most of the coal yard cash—cash too hot to have been spent right away. It was several degrees cooler now, and Nick knew where it was. They didn't.

Sentiment aside, it was as simple as that.

Except, it wasn't simple at all. Murray never had told Nick a damned thing. Strecker's whole story was a lie, designed to string his pals along and help spring him from this joint. Al Murray had taken his secret to the grave. What his friends might do to Nick once they found out he didn't have the cash was another story—unless, of course, he did something to them first.

The two gentlemen in question, Michael J. Donnelly and Henry "The Crusher" Bowman, resided two stories above a modest tavern in the Fordham Road section of the Bronx, halfway between the Loew's Paradise on the Grand Concourse and the Italian section on Arthur Avenue. Mike Donnelly, the man who usually visited Nick, was merely vicious. "The Crusher" was fearsome. He made even Nick Strecker think twice. If police had been shadowing Donnelly and Bowman, they would have seen them busily engaged in activities that were hardly suspicious for non-suspicious characters, but which for suspicious characters such as they were, were suspicious indeed.

Night had long fallen, but Donnelly and Bowman had gently placed three bundles into the trunk of a 1932 Ford V-8 Three-Window Coupe, not the flashiest car in the world, but one that could outrun coppers when it had to. Each bundle consisted of a complete male wardrobe—suit, topcoat, shirt, underwear, tie, hat, socks, shoes—in sizes fitting neither Mr. Donnelly nor

Mr. Bowman. Only recently, Messrs. Donnelly and Bowman had substituted different sizes in the third bundle.

Nick's orders.

These packages comprised the trunk's least interesting contents. Neatly tucked underneath them were three Browning nine-millimeter, semi-automatic, thirteen-round pistols and several boxes of cartridges. And beneath a soiled red blanket lay still more firepower: three sixteen-gauge, Winchester Model 1897 shotguns. These weapons were not designed for shooting rabbits and blackbirds. They were killing machines—six-shot-capacity, pump-action guns, with barrels just twenty inches long. Couldn't lay hands on a tommy gun? These babies were the next best thing.

"Ready?" Crusher Bowman asked.

Donnelly slammed the trunk shut. They were headed for Ossining, separately. Donnelly drove the Ford, which was stolen. Bowman took their own car, a dark-blue Chevy truck. It too was stolen. They drove separately because their agreement did not extend to being around if the whole thing exploded in Nick Strecker's face.

Donnelly and Bowman would leave the Ford Coupe in a pre-arranged area, a key tucked behind its front license plate— and, to identify the car in question, a raccoon tail tied to its radio antenna. They were also to leave behind them two painters ladders and a sizable coil of rope nearby. If Nick made it, fine . . . if not, their risks were minimal. It was all they promised Nick, and all they planned on delivering. Maybe John Dillinger enjoyed the jailbreak business. Mike Donnelly and Crusher Bowman didn't.

At Sing Sing's hospital, Nick Strecker remained nervous but hopeful. True, everything was a crapshoot. True, Marek had crapped out on him. But Marek wasn't essential—he could be replaced—and the wisdom of not giving him any details of the break was now exceedingly well proven. Nick felt like a very smart man about that. Plus, something *had* gone well, something unexpected. Sing Sing was at this moment short of screws. Maybe it was vacations or sickness or cutbacks, or God-knows-what, but, for whatever reason, it was. Guards were being called in for extra work. Even experienced screws were assigned to the cellblocks, a job usually reserved for newcomers.

Which is why George Tannahill found himself on Block B, Tier U.

It was well after midnight. Tannahill looked into Marek's cell and saw him asleep. Usually, that's what a guard wanted. This was different.

"Marek! Marek!" he called, trying to wake him, without rousing anyone else, "Wake up! I need you to take Whitetree to the hospital. I don't know what's wrong with him." Five cells down, Angus Whitetree, Nick Strecker's soft touch for smokes and Father Gelasius's altar boy, lay weak, feint, moaning. He had vomited heavily. The first three symptoms were standard con malingering skills, the fourth had been assisted by a contraband dose of ipecac—supplied by Nick Strecker.

Marek responded in silence—silent alarm. Whitetree, thought Marek, was a good guy, not really a crook at all, only some sap who made some wrong choices when the jobs dried up and he needed some dough to pay the rent and the grocery bills. A sap just like him.

Whitetree had been on Tier U for a only few months, but he had become reasonably close to Strecker and Rossi—for some reason he looked up to them—and had only grown closer to them since Eddie had turned Nick down.

Whitetree also thought he wanted to see his wife and two boys again and posited that Nick Strecker offered him the quickest, most direct, way to accomplish that. Before Whitetree had been assigned to B Block, Tier U, he had resided in A Block, Tier J, where another second story man "Stretch" McCracken—who had little use for rival burglars and none for Indians—had tangled with him with both words and fists and had ultimately planted a crude shiv in Whitetree's cell. Angus landed in the hole, and worse, his chances for parole went up in smoke faster than one of the Lucky Strikes Nick Strecker would bum off him. Angus Whitetree was now stuck in Sing Sing for a good long time, away from wife and children and freedom, and when Nick

Strecker informed Whitetree about a way home that didn't involve parole boards—he was in.

Tonight, Strecker and Rossi worked on the hospital night shift. Eddie Marek did not want to be anywhere near the hospital or near Nick Strecker, on any given night, but he wasn't about to entrust what he did know, or what he thought he knew, or what he merely feared, to a man like George Tannahill. Very reluctantly, he placed Angus Whitetree's arm over his shoulder, lifted him up, and helped Whitetree hobble toward the hospital.

The commotion woke Sandy Myers. "Don't take any wooden nickels," he advised Marek, "Don't take any wooden Indians, either."

"What the hell does that mean?" Tannahill demanded.

"Beats the hell out of me!" said Marck. He knew damned well what Myers meant. Sandy was very good at knowing things and nearly as good at guessing things. He had guessed right about this.

Loaded down with buckets and cleaning materials, Nick Strecker and Salvatore Rossi hoped to rendezvous with the little party that had departed Block B. If all went well, they'd converge on a particularly isolated corridor, where their numbers and the element of surprise would prove sufficient to overwhelm George Tannahill and take him hostage, before returning back to the hospital, making their break, and meeting up with a 1932 Ford V-8 Three-Window Coupe.

They turned a corner.

Marek!

What was he doing here? Whatever his reason for being there, Nick didn't like it. Eddie's presence was a wild card he couldn't do anything about, except call the whole thing off. He wasn't about to do that.

"Sir, there's something funny going on here," Nick informed Tannahill, in almost conspiratorial fashion, as if he didn't even want Rossi to hear it. "Down that way."

"What kind of crap are you peddling today?" Tannahill answered, "Can't you see I've got a sick man here?"

"He looks healthy to me, mister guard."

"Mister guard" was Stecker's signal. Whitetree sprung to life, breaking loose from Marek, hurling his powerful arms around Tannahill. Strecker flung a vile of clouded liquid—simple but blinding ammonia—into the guard's face. Tannahill screamed. Rossi produced a knife—a crude but exceedingly sharp instrument he had fashioned a long time ago and since secreted in a myriad of hiding places, waiting, forever waiting, for the right time and place for its use—and pressed it hard against George Tannahill's throat. Strecker stuffed a rag in Tannahill's mouth, blindfolded, and cuffed him.

"What do we do about Eddie?" Whitetree asked.

"Good question, Angus," Strecker answered, "I think two hostages—a screw and the warden's pet—are better than one . . . for now anyway."

Marek was now the captive of three of his block mates. It was, he guessed, true: There was no honor among thieves.

Five men shuffled back toward the hospital, to a guard station manned by Leo Hodges, full time guard and occasional altar boy. Hodges remained securely in a little guard station behind a locked door and an iron gate. Before Strecker and his crew reached sight of Hodges, Nick ordered everyone else to pause. He would go on alone.

"Where's your pal?" Hodges asked.

"Rossi? Oh, this was his night to escape."

"Don't wise off to me, you bastard!"

"I'm not wising off. I said the man escaped. Didn't you hear me? Stand up and put your hands over your head. Very carefully."

"Don't give me that baloney, Strecker."

Rossi appeared with his shiv pressed firmly to Tannahill's throat. Angus Whitetree followed, and the sight of Hodges startled him. He felt ashamed of what he was doing—ashamed, but not enough to go back, nor was there any way for him to go back if he wanted to. Leo Hodges reluctantly raised his hands above his head, walked slowly and awkwardly to the guard station door and unlocked it.

Nick Strecker waltzed in like he owned the joint.

It had all proceeded very discreetly. No screams. No fuss. That's why Tannahill had to be ambushed along the way, off the beaten path, in the silence of the night and made a hostage—so Leo Hodges would surrender . . . without a sound.

Nick Strecker had, indeed, given this some thought.

Keys, however, were vastly more valuable than guards. One con or a bunch of cons could always overpower a guard—or even two. Then what? You didn't want a guard. This wasn't the game. You wanted out. Very few keys meant out. Nick Strecker had figured out which did.

It wasn't any of the keys on Hodges's belt—no, not those. But one of those keys opened a cabinet holding rows and rows of keys, and one of *those* keys led to a steam tunnel, which led to Spring Street in Ossining. Two blocks away sat a 1932 Ford V-8 Coupe.

Nick found the key he wanted. He opened the cabinet warily, terrified that it might be empty. Second from the right, third row down was a smallish key, fastened upon a hook marked "Steam Corridor." Strecker took no chances. He stashed it in his left pants pocket and all the others in his right jacket pocket. Why trust these lousy guards to actually return anything to the right place?

He felt quite proud of himself for being so careful.

Rossi asked, "Did you get the right key?"

"I got 'em all, dammit!"

Sal kept his shiv firmly on Tannahill's jugular and one watchful eye on Marek. Angus Whitetree furiously rummaged through Hodges's guard station. Strecker had instructed him to make quick work of it. He grabbed at one locked cabinet drawer with such violence that it sprung open before him.

"Hey! Look at this!" Angus beamed, displaying a pair of shiny service revolvers for all present to behold, some to their pleasure, some to their dread.

Strecker numbered himself among the genuinely pleased. He had hoped to stumble upon a weapon or two along the way. But his elation had a cost. It distracted him. He did not realize that the key cabinet door was ever so minutely ajar and though he dutifully turned the key, he was not really securing the metal box at all.

That was his first mistake of the evening.

The key in his left trouser pocket provided Nick even more confidence. He relaxed—a little—but still calculated every detail of what might go wrong, had to go right, and what had already changed in his plans. He had already decided on what to do with Eddie Marek. Eddie had crossed him. Nick could not live with that. Eddie Marek would not live with it either.

"Well, Eddie, you in or out?"

"I told you I was out, Nick. This ain't going to work."

"I thought you were gonna say that. But that's where you're wrong—on both counts. It's going to work, and you're going with us. The more hostages the better."

"You taking him along, Nick?" asked Rossi, "Why? Just gag him and dope him and leave him." Angus Whitetree nodded agreement. He had nothing against Eddie, nothing at all.

Strecker just looked at Sal, and that look settled the issue. Marek was coming.

Three escapees and three captives progressed toward the steam tunnel. Strecker's extra precaution wasn't necessary. The correct key had indeed rested upon the correct hook. It opened an unmarked solid steel door to what appeared to be Hades itself, a labyrinthine world of unbearable heat, electrical cables, small pools of water, and, of course, hellishly hot steam ducts, leading to who knew where, though Nick was sure it led to a stolen Ford Coupe.

They dropped Hodges off as soon as they got inside. Strecker swabbed his handkerchief with chloroform, giving the guard a more than generous dose. "Hey, be careful!" Angus Whitetree cautioned, but Nick Strecker had thrown caution out the window a long time ago. Hodges crumpled like a rag doll. The remainder of the party advanced only a few steps before Strecker addressed Marek, "I changed my mind, pal. You're not going any further."

Marek lunged desperately for Strecker's pistol, seizing Strecker's right wrist, but he failed to wrest the gun away. Rossi fixed his attention on the still-groggy Tannahill. Whitetree wasn't sure what to do—yet. Marek was strong, but Strecker was stronger, quickly severing Marek's grip. He had Marek where he wanted him. But before Nick could do anything, Whitetree pistol-whipped Eddie from behind. Strecker kicked the side of Eddie's head and gave him a few shots to the ribs for good measure. Blood oozed from Marek's mouth.

"You know what his problem was?" Strecker asked Whitetree, not bothering to thank him for dispatching Eddie.

"Tell me," answered Angus, quite aware, and quite miffed, that no thanks had been forthcoming.

"We're all sorry we got *caught*. I think the rube was actually *sorry* he *did it*."

"That's quite the eulogy," said Rossi, "Now what do we do with him?"

"Leave him. It's going to work out very well that way."

They treaded their way toward the tunnel's end. It was much slower going than Strecker had counted on. "That's it!" Whitetree shouted, "The door to the street!"

"Yup," Strecker responded, as if he didn't believe it himself.

". . . and we're out?" Angus continued.

"Sort of."

"Sort of! You *are* crazy!"

"Like a fox, Angus. There's a big iron fence around the door, see. But there should also be a ladder shoved through that fence—*two* ladders shoved through that fence. I had my guys case the area. Just remember, *I'm in charge!*"

Strecker checked the door to see if it really opened. It was locked. The first key Nick tried didn't open it, and panic filled the escapees' hearts—but the third key Nick tried from his right pocket did.

Nick Strecker felt very smart.

"OK, Salvatore, you get your wish."

"Hostage time is over, Tannahill," Strecker continued, "all over." He squeezed off two quick shots pointblank into the barely-conscious guard's chest.

"OK, Sal, open the door now."

Angus Whitetree hadn't counted on this at all—not at murder. He stood motionless, afraid to move or breathe or think. And, despite Nick Strecker's words, Sal Rossi hadn't counted on this either. Sure, Sal hated George Tannahill, but his venom only resided in punch-in-the gut or kick-in-the-teeth dosages. That was it. That was enough.

Sal's taste for revenge never reached the cold-blooded-murder range. No, not murder. That was truly nuts. *How many men had Nick Strecker killed previously? Murders he had never talked about. Murders no one ever knew of.*

Exiting the tunnel was exactly like Nick said. The heavy, steel door opened upward to the street. There was an iron fence, but there were also two ladders pushed inside it, each slightly higher than the fence itself. Strands of sturdy rope were attached to both, equal in length to each ladder. One ladder went up in a flash. Rossi and Whitetree steadied it and Strecker scrambled upward, placing the rope over a fence spike and shimmying to freedom. Rossi and Whitetree quickly followed.

"What was that second ladder for?" asked Whitetree.

"Insurance. Besides you always see these ladders in pairs. If they were going to steal one, they might as well steal two."

It had, of course, never occurred to Nick Strecker that his associates might actually *buy* ladders.

"The Village of Ossining, New York," Rossi sighed, lowering his voice before finishing his thoughts, "Land of my dreams."

"Stop dreaming, dago. Look for Central and Water—where the car is."

"Better be," said Rossi in what sounded like a threat.

Another guard had soon ventured by Leo Hodge's station, seeking George Tannahill, who had phoned ahead. He saw no one there, the key cabinet door ajar—the door Nick Strecker had neglected to lock—and the cabinet empty, and sounded a general alarm, its scope instantly expanding in wider and wider concentric circles of guards and cops and patrol cars and guns. Sing Sing exploded into full alert. Troop K of the State Police followed. As did the Westchester County Sheriff's Department.

And most significantly, so did the Ossining Police Department.

Not many Ossining coppers pulled duty at 2 AM, just two, in fact, and both had been through this before. The only difference tonight was they didn't know how many cons had escaped, if hostages were with them, or even if they had gotten beyond Sing Sing's walls.

They also did not know if they were armed—but they planned accordingly.

Strecker, Rossi, and Whitetree nervously proceeded toward where they hoped their getaway car might be. "I sized the whole thing up back there," said Strecker.

"Say what?" Rossi asked.

"How to set up Marek."

"How so?"

"Mr. Big Baseball Hero helped haul Whitetree here off the tier. He's left behind unconscious. They don't know how it happened. I gave Hodges enough chloroform to kill two horses—and I know because I've killed horses. And Tannahill certainly can't tell them. They assume Eddie was part of the break—maybe Tannahill brained him for all they know. When he wakes up, they fry Marek for Tannahill. Mr. Baseball Hero instantly turns into Mr. Jailbreak Goat."

The plot made no sense to Rossi.

"If you want him dead, why didn't *you* just kill him?"

"That's your problem, Rossi—all direct violence, no subtlety. Sometimes subtlety is the best revenge."

Rossi resolved to get escape as well from Strecker as soon as he could. He didn't know where. It wouldn't be near his sister—they'd look for him there, but if Strecker could turn on Eddie like that . . .

But first . . . They had to find their car before anyone found them. Unknown to them, two cops, officers Van Houten and Pratt, patrolled a mere couple of blocks away, alert for anything suspicious. At two in the morning in Ossining, New York, anything moving met their criteria.

Strecker's gang surveyed the murky streetscape before them. It looked like . . . It could be . . . Yes, a car with a raccoon tail tied to its antenna . . . Strecker fished behind the car's rear license plate and found the key. This *was* it. He opened the trunk, shone a flashlight into its recesses, and peered in. Clothes. A blanket. Good. He knew what lay under it.

That was as good as it got. Rossi and Strecker pawed through the trunk. Van Houten and Pratt's squad car turned the corner. Van Houten and Pratt jumped out, their service revolvers at the ready.

"You there! Hands up!"

Strecker whirled.

BANG!! BANG!!

The sound of gunfire filled the empty night air, bouncing off houses and trees and cars, filling five hearts with fear. Strecker's first shot missed everything. His second shot shattered the patrol car's windshield, spraying jagged, broken glass over everything, imbedding those shards into Van Houten's right shoulder and arm and hand and causing him to drop his revolver. Pratt bounded from the car, firing away. Strecker and Angus Whitetree fired back. Pratt's third shot hit Strecker in mid-forehead, as neat a shot as one could have wished for on a police academy firing range, blowing Strecker's body backward toward the getaway car, blowing his brains out of what remained of the back of his skull. Van Houten retrieved his gun, fired twice at Whitetree, and hit him both times in the chest.

Only Rossi remained.

Sal had retrieved a twelve-gauge shotgun from the trunk. BLAM!! He blasted Pratt into oblivion. BLAM!! Van Houten sunk like a brick below his pellet-riddled patrol car door. Rossi thought he had killed both men. But whether or not Van Houten and Pratt now dwelt in cop heaven, Rossi needed to get the hell out of there.

Too bad he couldn't drive.

He fled down Water Street, growing smaller and smaller, but not so small that he was not an inviting target. Officer James

Van Houten painfully steadied himself . . . and squeezed off two shots.

It was all over.

Marek awoke in the prison hospital, not knowing who was alive, who was dead, who had escaped, or who had been captured. He knew very little. He knew what he remembered and what he remembered made no sense, a horrible night of terror and stupidity and betrayal. He knew his head and his ribs hurt like never before. Nothing compared to cons beating the crap out of you in a steam tunnel.

He also knew he was handcuffed to his bed.

Stewart Beck stood beside him. Beck was not pleased.

"Edward," Beck began. He had never called Marek "Edward" before.

"Edward, do you want to tell us what happened?"

Marek related how Tannahill had rapped on his cell to help get Angus Whitetree to the hospital. "Tannahill can tell you that," he added for good measure.

Beck just listened.

Marek told Beck how Strecker and Rossi and Whitetree overcame Tannahill and then Hodges, how everyone entered the steam tunnel, how Strecker drugged Hodges—and, above all, how Strecker wanted him to join the escape, but how he refused and how Strecker threatened to bump him off.

"But he didn't—did he?"

Eddie did not like the sound of that. It was never good when you had to apologize for not being dead.

"Well, no, sir."

"Why not?"

Eddie didn't like where this was going.

"I really don't know, sir. Hodges and Tannahill can back me up on all this."

"Tannahill's dead. They killed him in the tunnel. He left behind a wife and four children."

They're better off without that son of a bitch, Marek couldn't help think, but he also couldn't help but think that Eddie Marek wasn't better off.

"Oh," was all Marek managed, "what about Hodges?"

"They doped him good with the chloroform. An overdose can be fatal, and they gave Leo way too much. We don't know if he'll pull through."

"Where's the boys?"

"Dead. Shoot-out in the village. One cop dead, one badly wounded."

Marek didn't need to be told the rest. He was under suspicion. He knew it.

"You don't believe I was in on this, do you Warden?"

Beck didn't answer. He didn't know what to say, and he didn't know what to believe.

Marek had yet another worry: Myers. Sandy heard Marek say he was "in." He never heard Eddie tell Strecker that he wanted no part of his crazy scheme. Would Sandy rat on him? Marek wished he'd never bought into anything of Nick's, not for a lousy second. He wished he'd never met Nick Strecker.

Marek slowly recovered. Hodges didn't. It looked bad for him, worse than even Warden Beck had revealed. Nobody told Eddie anything officially, but the prison grapevine was a marvelous thing.

Leo Hodges was dead.

Eddie Marek was as good as dead. He was guilty until proven innocent. And now no one was left alive to verify he *wasn't* guilty. His parole was down the toilet. He faced murder charges for Hodges—maybe even for Tannahill.

Beck visited.

"I heard about Hodges," Marek advanced. He figured he didn't have much to lose.

Beck nodded. "Good man," he responded. Marek noted that Beck had never said that about Tannahill.

"I have some news for you."

Marek knew what that news would be: murder charges would be filed against him, though he was surprised Beck would convey such news personally—but then again, maybe he wasn't surprised. He rolled everything around in his head. How would he defend himself? Would a lawyer be assigned to his case?

Where would the trial be held? Westchester County? With a local cop dead too, that wouldn't help.

How long before the execution?

It *all* rolled over.

"Before Hodges died, he briefly regained consciousness a couple times. The last time he told us about the break. We asked him. He said you weren't in on it."

Marek released his breath. He didn't know if that was enough to clear him—and he didn't know if Myers had thrown him in—but it sure was a big improvement over what might have been.

"They'll be unlocking the handcuffs, Marek. We had to take precautions, you know."

The weight fell from Marek and yet left him barely able to say—or think or feel—anything.

"I understand."

Beck walked away.

"Warden," Marek called, "if Hodges has a family, please give them my condolences."

Beck departed, leaving Eddie Marek to think about what responsibility he bore for Leo Hodges's death. Should he have revealed Strecker's scheme to the guards? But what would Marek have said? He didn't know any details. He didn't even know if the break was real or merely another longshot Nick Strecker fantasy.

Marek considered it all over and over and over again. It came down to this: cons don't rat out cons.

But his other questions never did go away.

Freedom in Chains

At Ebbets Field, a jug-eared, pink-faced, thick-around-the-middle man sang as he tossed a scuffed baseball into the air and launched a looping fungo into short right-center field.

Albert Leon Molyneaux sang quite a bit.

He sang on the field. He sang in the locker room. He sang professionally, in vaudeville in the off-season in class joints like the Palace and Brooklyn's Albee Theater, fronting for big bands like Dave Apollon & His Apollonians. OK, so nobody outside of Brooklyn ever heard of Dave Apollon & His Apollonians, but it never hurt to have back-up income in baseball or anywhere else for that matter, most especially if you were Al Molyneaux and you were managing the woeful Brooklyn Dodgers.

Sidearm Jack Powell stood nearby, watching, chewing gum, edgily looking toward the field. His team had by now settled comfortably and deeply into last place. Game time was an hour-and-a-half away, and Ebbets Field wouldn't be much fuller than it was now.

Powell trudged up the grandstand steps to his office. He had decided to make a call, the sooner the better.

He pawed through the pile of papers that littered his battered desk, and found the torn scrap of paper that contained Stewart Beck's phone number scribbled up on it..

Sidearm Jack was not calling at a particularly good time. Beck had lost interest in fostering Eddie Marek's baseball career. He was distracted, unsettled, unsure of himself and of the idea. A lot, after all, had happened to Stewart Beck.

"You said he was eligible for parole."

"He is," Beck indicated without much enthusiasm. Kathryn's death had knocked him loose from his moorings. Nick Strecker's disastrous escape attempt—and the death of two of Beck's guards—plunged him into deeper depression. To parole Marek so soon after his involvement in this fiasco—however tenuous it was, however innocent he might be—seemed foolhardy. Beck had built his career taking chances with cons, but he was worn out, wary of more risk. He had lost his wife. If he lost the warden's job . . .

Through his office window, Sidearm Jack surveyed his players' practice. A pockmarked-faced outfielder muffed an easy fly ball. The sight infuriated Powell. "They call this big league baseball?" he thought "Boy, are we cheating the customers!"

Powell couldn't stand having a team this bad. He wasn't giving up. He needed talent, and he needed a drawing card.

"And he needs to have a job if he's going to be paroled?" he asked Beck, then shot out an answer to his own question, "I've got a job for him!"

A grounder skipped through an infielder's legs. Oh, if Sidearm Jack were just ten years, younger—OK, well, fifteen. OK, twenty.

"I know." Beck responded.

"Well, then what's your issue? What's going on here?"

Beck didn't answer. Instead, he merely peered out his own office window. Two prisoners moved across the yard. One was black, the other, blond and white. Beck saw Marek gently guiding Lemuel Dunbar. The blind man's gnarled left hand rested firmly upon Marek's broad right shoulder. His long, white cane jabbing not at the ground but was held for once above it, as both men progressed toward the Mess Hall.

"Are you still there?" Powell demanded of the silent Beck.

"Yes, of course," Beck answered apologetically.

"Look, is this guy going to be paroled or what?" Powell fumed, "Is he right for Brooklyn or what?"

Beck kept staring at the little scene below him. "He's . . .," he began and then paused. "He's . . .," Beck started and paused again, "just what you're looking for."

"Yeah?" asked Powell warily, "You don't sound like it."

"We just have a little paperwork issue."

***

On Block B, Marek spoke with Sandy Myers. He wasn't sure what to say. He knew Sandy hadn't ratted him out but wasn't sure what to say about the whole mess. Some things were best left unsaid.

Sandy spoke first, cryptically, but first.

"I knew you'd never go through with it."

Marek peered around to see who might be lurking within earshot.

"You're giving me a lot of credit, more than I deserve."

"Who's giving *you* credit, you Pennsylvania asshole? I'm giving *me* credit for talking *you* out of it. You never did give my persuasive powers enough due. *Now*, maybe *you will*."

And Myers never mentioned the matter again.

***

Sidearm Jack Powell finally met Eddie Marek. Sing Sing was playing White Plains, your basic run-of-the-mill semi-pro squad. Powell liked what he saw. After the last out, he and Beck ambled down to the field to say hello, actually a lot more than hello.

Eddie sure enough knew who Sidearm Jack Powell was. Every ball fan knew the great Sidearm Jack.

Powell got to the point. "Sidearm Jack is here for one purpose, to see you, Eddie Marek. Like to see you really play ball—with Brooklyn. Like to give you that chance."

Though Marek had never before heard anyone exclusively refer to himself in the third person, he had similar vague promises of pro baseball contracts. Other teams, mostly semi-pros, had dangled jobs before him. Nobody came through. It might have been a question of talent or of money. It was *probably* a question of something else.

"Others folks told me that, Mr. Powell. Football teams. The House of David. How do I know you're serious? Nobody else is."

Nobody questioned Sidearm Jack's sincerity. He barely contained his urge to storm away, but he needed Marek. "Does Sidearm Jack look serious?" he said, "Sidearm Jack's serious, punk. How serious are you—about baseball—and about straightening out your life? Sidearm Jack Powell and the

Brooklyn Dodgers are willing to take a chance on you. Will you take one on yourself?"

Marek stared long and hard at the grass below him, not looking at either Powell or Beck.

"Let me have the paper."

"Sidearm Jack doesn't walk around with contracts in his suit pocket. That's not how it works in the big leagues, kid," said Powell, "Besides, don't you want to know how much?"

"I should pay you," Eddie blurted out.

"How much *are* you going to pay the boy?" Beck interjected.

"Two hundred a month."

Marek looked to Beck. Beck nodded back, and Marek nodded back to Powell.

That is how agreements between gentlemen are concluded.

The upcoming parole hearing terrified Marek. But his inquisition went surprisingly easy. He had a job on the outside. Beck was in back of him. It remained scary, however, to stand before the board members, answering their questions, questions they had every right to ask and no right to ask at all. But he had the right answers, and before long, he had the big OK:

PAROLE APPROVED.

"Don't lie your way into Hell!"

In his chloroformed death throes, Leo Hodges had never uttered a syllable.

At least, not a syllable about Eddie Marek.

Yet, that is not what Stewart Beck believed because that is not what Father Gelasius had informed him.

Father Gelasius had reported to Warden Beck that Eddie Marek was innocent not because of any words a dying Leo Hodges might have uttered—but because of those he heard from a battered Eddie Marek.

It had all come about as Eddie, still bruised and aching and handcuffed to his own sick bed, made his confession to Gelasius. Gelasius had already heard a sufficient number of Eddie's confessions to take measure of the man and of his words. Eddie did not trim. He did not make excuses. He confessed not only actions but attitudes. His voice rang true, and Father Gelasius had heard enough of lies and excuses over the course of his priesthood to separate not only the true from the false but also the true from the truer. And Eddie Marek's words normally struck him as very true indeed.

In this instance, Eddie's confession comprised the usual sins and near occasions of sin, what he had done and what he had failed to do. And while it significantly did contain Eddie's vague concerns about the morality—or immorality—of not ratting out a fellow convict, even more significantly, it did not include anything about actual participation in the actual break.

"Is that all?" Gelasius snapped as Eddie concluded.

"Do you mean?"

"Were you involved in any way in that escape—beyond what you've told the warden? Don't lie to me, my son! You know where you are! Don't lie your way into Hell!"

"No, Father, I *wasn't* in on it! Yeah, sure, I said "OK" when Nick first asked me about going over— but that's what cons do. You go, "Yeah—Sure—OK, boss." And who knew if that crazy squarehead—pardon me, Father—was going to *really* do anything at all? He was always shooting his trap off about that stuff. But then before anything happened, I gave it to him straight—laid the brush-off on him. Big time! Then Nick clammed up and never told me nothing about what was going on or when he was going over or how or with who. He just looked at me like I was a dead man. He talked to me like I was a dead man. And then, in the end, in that tunnel, he decided I *would* be. Nick didn't set me up because I was in on it. He set me up 'cause I *wasn't!* I'm lucky I wasn't plugged! That's the whole deal, Father! The God's Honest Truth!"

"You're lying to me, Eddie! I ought to just unlock these cuffs and knock your lying mug right to the floor!"

But Eddie's story never changed, nor should it have, for it was true, and, as it was true, and Father Gelasius kept ordering Eddie *not* to lie to him, how, in fact, could it have changed?

True stories don't *have* to change.

Which is why it was Father Gelasius who finally surrendered and extended to Eddie Marek Christ's absolution. And so, as well, the priest now thought he knew something *very* important. In his bones, he now simply *knew* Eddie was innocent. But there was nothing he might say, or even hint, about it. Not a word. Not a gesture.

And it killed him.

He had saved a soul.

He was powerless to save a life.

But if he could not repeat what he heard within the seal of confession—even to save an innocent man's life—he might yet utilize what he *did not* hear from a dying man's lips *outside* the seal of the sacrament to save that innocent man from death.

So, when fate placed the priest alone with Leo Hodges as Leo finally expired, it provided him with a perfect opportunity to concoct a story of Eddie's innocence to convey to Warden Beck.

He did not think Leo Hodges would mind.

So he concocted it.

And though Warden Beck at first looked as though he was not buying it, for Father Gelasius was a very poor liar, he bought it anyway, or, at least he bought it, after further considering that there were but three—*not four*—changes of clothing in the trunk of a certain stolen Ford V-8 Coupe—and that *none* of those three fit Edward Stanley Marek Jr.

And Eddie Marek, though not quite free, was also not quite dead.

Thus, while Father Gelasius had not violated the seal of the confessional, he had obviously violated the eighth commandment, perhaps, one might say—and in this case, the civil authorities would most certainly have said it—in sufficient degree so as to commit a mortal sin.

Accordingly, for priests too must also confess their transgressions, Father Gelasius soon also confessed his, to his own spiritual director, Father Raymond Gardiner, pastor of the same small brick church where he had not that long before offered Kathryn Beck's Requiem Mass. Father Raymond fidgeted silently while Gelasius narrated his story. He maintained that nervous silence for some long seconds afterward, as he pondered what he had heard.

Father Gelasius did not relish that silence.

They had, Father Raymond pondered, not covered this in seminary.

"That is a very serious matter, Gelasius," he finally sighed, his voice betraying what seemed to be weight of a great burden.

Father Gelasius did not relish that sigh.

"A very serious matter," continued Father Raymond, "For your penance, say *four* Hail Marys."

Shinola

Sidearm Jack Powell filed Marek's contract with the National League, ready to broadcast word to the papers: the Dodgers had a new player, or, at least, would have a new player when he got sprung, and his name was Edward Stanley "The Battling Marine" Marek Jr. Powell liked that "Battling Marine" part. It had drawing power—like "The Babe" or "The Iron Horse."

Box office.

Al Molyneaux knew how to make Marek's signing into a bigger story than it normally would be. Showbiz. He would not only feed the story to the regular Ebbets Field beat writers but also to his contacts with the big Broadway columnists. That way the story would get a little extra buzz.

Unfortunately, one Broadway columnist printed it before all the others.

Within the white-tiled confines of the Hotel Ben Franklin barbershop, a hundred miles due southeast of Brooklyn, a dark-haired man sat, scanning the *Philadelphia Herald,* having his cordovan oxfords properly buffed.

Sports was his business. Getting his cordovan oxfords spit-shined was his pleasure.

An item caught his eye in, of all places, Ed Sullivan's syndicated column, "The Toast of the Town":

> Brooklyn GM Sidearm Jack Powell will announce the inking of Sing Sing inmate "Eddie" Marek to play outfield for his floundering NL team upon his June 6 release from the famed New York State lockup . . . Marek, convicted of a Gotham stick up some years back, excelled at baseball, football, and track behind bars, compiling a .500 batting average in the current season.

Pierre DeKay ran the league's Philadelphia Phillies and considering what he had to work with he did a pretty good job at it. He did not, however, enjoy learning National League business in Ed Sullivan's column. That was plain sacrilege. Baseball news belonged in *The Sporting News* or at least the sports pages. Not in some damn fool gossip column. "Son of a bitch!" DeKay exclaimed, as he hurled the *Herald* to the floor, scattering its comic pages in one direction, its stock market returns in another. He stormed off, muttering all the way.

"That son-of-a-bitch Powell is making a mockery of the game!"

"Wait, Mr. DeKay! Wait up!" Tony, the hotel's hunch-backed shoeshine boy, called.

"Cheap publicity stunt!" DeKay shouted, heading for the lobby, his left shoe untouched by even the sparsest application of Shinola.

"There goes my tip," mourned Tony.

DeKay kept storming until—and after—he was back at his Baker Bowl office. He commanded his secretary to dial National League Secretary Harry Garwood at his Cincinnati law office.

"Harry! What's this about some damned con playing ball in Brooklyn for Powell? What the hell kind of pissant stunt is that? And must I have to read about it in Ed Sullivan's column?"

Harry Garwood was not feeling well that day and hadn't for a while. The last thing he needed was Pierre DeKay yelling at him over long distance—even if DeKay was paying for the call. He rolled his eyes. His secretary, a matronly woman in an unmatronly red dress, ducked in to make sure her boss hadn't keeled over.

"Damn it, Pete!" Garwood responded, trying to avoid yelling back at DeKay and sending his heart into overdrive, "I'm only the league secretary. I don't like it either—but I can't do a damn thing about it! You want a contract voided, you call Nathan Lloyd! *He's* the president of the National League—not me!"

Lloyd slammed his phone on its receiver. "Pete DeKay's a fine one to complain about stunts—" he muttered, "probably just teed off he didn't think of it. If Murch was in some Pennsylvania prison that would different!"

DeKay was already back on the phone.

Nathan Lloyd was Nathan Jackson Lloyd, a jowly Virginian who ran the National League, or, at least as much of it as its club owners would let him. He was among other designations, a Presbyterian, a Mason, a Knight of Phythias, and a Woodman of the World. Nathan Lloyd was a politician—and a very good one. You had to be to run the National League.

Pete DeKay proceeded to vent.

"Yes," Lloyd replied so very calmly. Lloyd oozed Southern calmness. "I couldn't agree with you more, Pete. Powell called me a few weeks ago to sound me out on this matter. I advised him that it would be . . . er . . . inadvisable, yes, inadvisable . . . not good at all. He didn't seem to listen though. Well, that's old Sidearm. Headstrong. Shame. You file the complaint, Pete—and we'll take care of it."

Well, considered Mr. DeKay, *that was easier than I thought.*

And it was. Lloyd conferred with his executive committee. They were of like mind with DeKay and with Lloyd. Baseball had been through a rough patch fifteen years before. The Black Sox were crooked—yes, even the great Shoeless Joe Jackson. The World Series was crooked. The game was crooked. Baseball had to be kept clean. There was no room for crooks or gamblers.

Or ex-cons.

Sidearm Jack Powell should have seen it coming. Maybe he did but didn't want to believe it. If all the guys he'd played with or against had gone to the clink for violating the Volstead Act or brawling or whoring and been kept out of the game forever after and a day, then the major leagues would have to bring fans down from the stands to fill each side—or, worse, hire coloreds from those Negro Leagues.

Not, of course, that those guys were any angels either.

Lloyd moved fast—even before Marek exited Sing Sing.

"We are of the opinion," Lloyd wrote, "that the interests of baseball generally and the interests of players of the National League will best be served by not admitting players who have been considered by society to be guilty of a much greater offense than offenses for which our own league permanently disqualify a player.

"The matter creates an unpleasant situation. We all have a natural tendency to help the fellow who is down, but we believe the public would resent the signing of this fellow in organized baseball, and there are other troublesome complications which might arise.

"The question has been put before the executive committee of the league whose members concur in the opinion that the interests of the public, the game and the players in it would not be served by the action which the Brooklyn club has been taken."

Marek was dead.

Powell phoned Beck and gave him the news. Powell was from the old school, a scrapper. Most of his kind were long gone from the game. John "The Little Napoleon" McGraw—dead. Frank "The Peerless Leader" Chance—dead. Miller J. Huggins—dead. Wilbert "Uncle Wilbert" Robinson—dead. George "The Miracle Man" Stallings—dead. Ty Cobb—too mean to die—was clipping his coupons on his big estate somewhere. But Sidearm Jack remained in baseball, even if it was with Brooklyn, even if it was in eighth place. Sidearm Jack Powell wasn't about to surrender without a fight, particularly not to some jackass idiot son-of-a-bitch like Pierre DeKay.

Stewart Beck wanted Marek to hear the real story from him—not from the radio or some scuttlebutt around the prison. He owed him that much.

"Beck wants to see you in his office. They'll let you through."

Marek had no reason for concern, save for the odd little feeling all cons get when they're called into the Warden's office, which is not such a little feeling at all.

"Have a seat, Eddie."

More than a small something in Beck's voice made Marek's odd little malaise turn into an odd medium-sized malaise. He ensconced himself in a heavy, wooden chair near the window.

"You know life isn't all good breaks, Edward."

He was calling Marek "Edward" again.

"I know, sir."

Beck quickly decided he'd better arrive at his unpleasant point. It wasn't going to get any easier. "There's a man named Lloyd—Nathan Jackson Lloyd. He's head of the National League, you know like Judge Landis runs baseball as a whole. There was a complaint—from the Philadelphia ballclub—and he, Lloyd, voided your contract with Brooklyn. You can't play for the Dodgers or for any other National League club. You can guess the reason."

Marek jumped up, ready to fight, though not knowing who.

"I told you to sit," Beck growled.

Marek stepped forward.

"I told you to sit dammit! I'm still the warden. You sit when I tell you!"

Marek sat. The fight left him. The two-by-four of life had just smacked him right between the eyes. He had no job outside baseball. For all he knew, his parole had been flushed away with it. Nick Strecker, wherever he was—and Eddie had a pretty strong theory—must be laughing his ass off.

"Warden . . ." Marek barely whispered.

"Don't go yellow on me Marek. You're still walking out that gate tomorrow morning—your parole is *not* revoked."

Walking out of jail was nothing to sneeze at. "Thank you, warden."

"Got that, Marek? Now, the second thing is this: Powell stands behind you. He's going to appeal. . . . "

"Appeal?"

"Appeal. And *I'm* standing behind you. You're going to play ball yet Marek. Now get out of here!"

In the Mess Hall, they crowded around Marek. They slapped his back and congratulated him on getting out and on his new career. They asked him for autographs and made him promise to leave ballgame tickets at the Ebbets Field box office for them—when *they* got out. Marek didn't have the heart or the nerve to tell them the truth. He put on a brave face. For in truth, every con is frightened of freedom as its hour drew near. Eddie Marek's fear now was even worse. He knew what his fellow prisoners yet didn't know—that his brilliant, wonderful, too-good-to-be-true baseball career had indeed proven not true at all and had plummeted into an inky limbo from which it might never emerge.

His last night in Sing Sing, he lay upon his bunk, staring into the darkness, his eyes open, unable to sleep.

This had not been a very good day at all.

Tomorrow would be better, but it sure didn't feel like it.

But when Eddie awoke, tomorrow *was* much better. He awoke, with nowhere to go but breakfast and freedom.

It was full circle time. Enter Sing Sing and they take everything from you, put it in a box and give it back to you on the way out—unless, of course, like Nick or Mr. Graham, you leave in another box. Marek retrieved his wristwatch, his three dollars and eighty-five cents in cash, and his wedding band. Everything looked vaguely familiar and yet vaguely foreign, particularly the wedding band. He wasn't sure what to do with it. He considered leaving it behind, but, instead, he slipped it into his pocket to keep his three dollars and eighty-five cents company.

Clink.

Marek also had before him a pile of clothes from his check-in years before, but his old suit and shirt and underwear were wrapped up in a neat little bundle. Sing Sing presented you with a new wardrobe on the way out since your old one might not fit anymore and for long-timers might be seriously passé. You didn't want to be dropping your shiny buffalo nickel in the slot of the Third Avenue El dressed in knee breeches.

Marek's new wardrobe included a gray, double-breasted suit, a reddish tie, and shiny black cap-toe oxfords. He kind of wished for a suit color other than gray, but he took what they gave him. He placed a snap-brim hat on his head, at a somewhat jaunty angle, and admired himself in the mirror. He kind of liked what he saw. He had, he thought, potential.

He also had a bit of an audience. Beck and Harding and Father Gelasius being among the onlookers. The press wanted in. Nathan Lloyd's edict had transformed a nice, little story into a far bigger one, but Beck refused comment. The impatient men and women of the Fourth Estate would have to wait.

Marek's mood changed. He thought about Lloyd and what he had inflicted upon him.

"All dressed up," he said to his sartorially-splendid reflection, "but nowhere to go."

Beck, Father Gelasius, Harding, and Marek strode purposely across the crowded prison yard. Eddie spied Sandy Myers. Sandy saluted, with a jaunty little gesture like the salutes pilots extend before going airborne or officers give before charging through barbed wire into no-man's land. Eddie's return wave was a little less brisk, more uncertain and guarded, less like an officer and more like somebody's grandma on the front porch.

Now, everybody was waving. The further Marek proceeded, the better his own waving got. One prisoner didn't wave. Lemuel Dunbar couldn't see Eddie moving through the yard, but Eddie saw him. He asked Beck if he might dart over to say goodbye.

"Lemuel, this is it. I'm going to Green Pastures."

"Oh! Don't say that! Don't go there, yet!"

"No, I don't mean that. You know the pastures are always greener on the other side."

Dunbar turned somber. He reached for Eddie's right hand. Marek held it tightly in both of his calloused hands.

"I'm losing my seeing eye guy. You be careful out there, Eddie. Be careful."

"Don't take any wooden nickels, pop." For the first time that day his words had trouble getting out.

"C'mon," he told Beck, "let's get moving."

Eddie Marek double-timed it to the Administration Building. Father Gelasius barely kept pace. "Last stop on this trolley," said Harding as they entered.

Sidearm Jack Powell waited. He was ready to shepherd his prospect back to New York, but other business remained.

"You're forgetting something, Eddie." Harding interjected.

Marek wasn't sure what he meant. For all he knew they branded you when you left.

"You've got to sign some papers—and we owe you your wages—$5.20."

Marek signed. "The wages of sin," he said, pocketing his windfall.

Stewart Beck watched silently. He was glad for Eddie, certainly, he was, and for every man who ever went free, even for those he *knew* would soon be back. But some days—particularly in the time following Kathryn's death—he envied them. They could leave. It was he, their keeper, who seemed trapped in a life sentence, stuck behind the same high gray walls, with the same incorrigibles, both inmates and guards, trudging to the same Dance Hall and the same electric chair, over and over and over and over again.

But what if Stewart Beck did leave? *Where* might he go?

He did not know.

What would he *do*? *Who* would he care for?

He did not know.

In the end, Beck understood this: it was better to stay, for he knew a secret: the burden of caring for others was far less than of caring only for oneself.

Kathryn had taught him that, and, in quite different ways, so had Percy Graham—and a thousand other men like him.

So he stayed. And Eddie Marek left.

Marek's party exited the Administration Building—Eddie, Beck, and Powell. Marek had never pictured his departure this way. Half a hundred reporters, photographers, and curiosity seekers crowded the building. They crowded Marek. They shot questions at him, making noise all at once. Beck and Powell were used to it. Marek wasn't.

"Back where I come from," Marek ventured, "when there's this much folks waiting for a man coming out of jail, it's usually to lynch him!"

The crowd laughed. Sidearm Jack winced.

The reporters wanted more. They demanded facts, and if Marek and Powell didn't have facts, they wanted Marek and Powell to invent them, and if Marek and Powell didn't, they'd do the job themselves.

"Eddie, what are you going to do about Nathan Lloyd's ruling? Do you think it's fair?"

Powell stepped in, "The Brooklyn club has that under appeal, and the appeal will speak for itself."

"Do you think convicts should be allowed into other professions?"

Powell started to answer, but Eddie interrupted. Powell might be qualified to speak about baseball, but he was qualified to speak about cons.

"Not unless the government has passed some law against it, but I don't think Congress has passed any law against people who have served their time playing centerfield—and from what I hear neither has Baseball."

"Good answer, kid," Powell said under his breath as reporters from the *Mirror* and the *Brooklyn Eagle* and the *World-Telegraph* simultaneously shouted more questions. Marek finally heard one above the din.

"Eddie!" demanded a small, skinny man in a rumpled checked sport jacket, "Jerome Epstein—*The Daily Worker*. What will you do if you can't play ball?"

"I think I'll become a reporter—it beats being a worker!"

The answer might well have alienated the knights of the keyboard before him, a notoriously sensitive lot, but Eddie advanced it with a good-natured grin on his face, that even they burst into laughter. He was rolling.

"Is it true you've received offers to play semi-pro ball?

"Yup."

"Where?"

Marek looked to Powell to see if it was OK to answer. Powell nodded.

"Schenectady. Dayton. Places like that."

"We heard a club in New York, too."

"That's right. More semipros."

"Are you interested?"

"Mr. Powell is sticking with me. I'm sticking with him."

Powell adjourned everything, announcing they had a train to catch. A handful of reporters boarded with them, but Powell had booked a compartment, all the better for a little privacy. A man ought to have a little privacy after all these years without it. It was the least he could do.

Powell could exploit the hell out of Marek *after* they got to Brooklyn.

Which he would.

Four hundred fans, reporters, cameramen, and curiosity seekers awaited Marek at Grand Central—an even louder group that had accumulated outside Sing Sing.

"You still think they want to lynch you?" Powell grunted.

"Hell!" Marek responded, "I think they might want to lynch Lloyd!"

It was all just beginning. Something in the story about the con who couldn't play ball touched a nerve with much of the public, and something made most reporters want to treat Marek as if he was Jean Valjean and Nathan Jackson Lloyd was a latter-day Inspector Javert.

Al Molyneaux had joined Powell and Marek at Grand Central, before rushing to Penn Station, to hop aboard yet another train, this one bound for Philadelphia where the Dodgers were playing Pete DeKay's almighty Phillies. Molyneaux wanted to get to know his newest ballplayer—or, at least, who he hoped would be his newest ballplayer. Who knew? The Lords of Baseball might reverse themselves even as Marek rode along. The kid might play that night. If he couldn't, it was still damned sweet to wave him under DeKay's nose.

Some people saw Marek as basically an ex-con. Al Molyneaux gave him the fish-eye all right, but you could tell the question in his mind was: "Can this kid really *play*?" Molyneaux wasn't about to commit himself based on some Sidearm Jack Powell hearsay, but he was smart enough to know his ballclub had one big-ass story on its hand, the like of which he hadn't personally seen since Game Seven of the World Series back in 1920—yes, those were Al Molyneaux's glory days, and he never tired of recounting them. And certainly a much bigger story than when Wilbert Robinson ran him off the Brooklyn club a few years afterwards—a story Singing Al rarely narrated except at a late hour and after several adult beverages and in a very doleful manner.

The City of Brotherly Love

Eddie's train steamed through Newark and Trenton, over the broad Delaware River, and finally into Philadelphia's Thirtieth Street Station. Powell, Molyneaux, and Marek, three disparate personalities tossed together by time and place, by desperation and fate, hailed a cab north to the ballpark. When they arrived, Powell checked with the umpires. They hadn't heard anything either, but when Powell strode onto the diamond just before game time, the crowd buzzed at the sight of the tall, trim civilian who accompanied him. They knew very well who he was.

Overcast skies made Baker Bowl's late afternoon sky bleak and heavy. Three thousand fans occupied the stands anyway, a bigger crowd than usually found their way to this pigeon-befouled, cigar-butt-littered, outright rotting ballpark. Somehow they knew Marek would be making the trip down from Sing Sing and hoped he might be able to play, and if he couldn't play, that they would at least catch sight of him. Somehow they knew because Pierre DeKay had tipped off the local papers.

A buck, after all, was a buck was a buck.

Brooklyn's players interrupted what they were doing. They formed a tight circle around Eddie, introducing themselves, some, though hardly all, wishing him well. Decrepit Baker Bowl had to be not merely the worst ballpark in the National League, but in both major leagues, and a couple of minor leagues thrown in for good measure. The park's most salient feature, save for its stunning awfulness, was a bizarrely short right field, just 280 feet down the line, surmounted by a wall a full sixty feet running its entire length. Eddie half expected to see guard towers atop it. And covering this immense, but, oh so close, outfield barrier was the biggest billboard Eddie had ever seen, proclaiming "The Phillies Use Lifebuoy," illustrated by a huge cake of the soap itself.

Frustrated Phillies fans, however, invariably proclaimed: "But they still stink."

To Marek, however, grotesquely antiquated Baker Bowl looked just fine. Its grass seemed as green and smooth as a pool table. Three thousand fans looked like thirty thousand.

Reporters from Philadelphia's press corps crowded round, peppering Marek with the usual questions about whether he'd prefer to be playing tonight and whether he might grab any semi-pro offers. "Break it up, you members of the libel squad," Molyneaux said, spitting as he spoke, for it was an National League rule, Section 6 (b) 2 to be exact—right after "Unconditional Release"—that managers had to spit while they spoke, "You'll have plenty of time to ask questions. Nobody's going anywhere for awhile."

Practice ended. The first pitch beckoned. Marek and Powell sat behind the visitors dugout. Pete DeKay, for reasons best known to himself, did not say hello. Perhaps, it was because Marek was a con. Perhaps, it was because he now knew that Marek had once taken a Filipina bride. Miscegenation was not something DeKay took lightly.

Molyneaux delivered his scrawled lineup card to home plate, a document not yet including the words, "Marek, CF." He presented it to the umpire. With hands held high above his head, so as to draw attention to himself, he turned initially toward the first base stands, then toward third base, before planting himself firmly facing the stands behind home plate. He doffed his sky blue Dodgers cap to the crowd, did a little soft-shoe and as he expected—for he knew how to work a crowd—it went wild. Ah, he thought, this was akin to trodding the boards at the very Palace itself. He proceeded via very circuitous route to his dugout, detouring past third base and near to Pete DeKay's box.

"Up yours, Pete!" he said, tipping his cap and flashing DeKay his pearliest vaudeville smile.

Sometimes, it was fun to be Al "The Golden Voiced Tenor" Molyneaux.

Marek remained in the stands until the last out. He had to. Until further notice, he was traveling with the Dodgers. In the visiting locker room, reporters ignored the game itself, a listless 5-1 Philadelphia win, focusing their attention on the newly-minted celebrity in their midst. "Marek stays on the Brooklyn payroll all year, whether Lloyd and company OKs him or not," Powell told them, his face flushing in anger, "even if I have to call him the assistant business manager and suit up and play myself!"

Eddie Marek boarded the train back to New York, fielding yet more questions as his car rattled northward, trying to take in everything as he did. When his team reached Penn Station, he was, however, not yet a Dodger, and did not know if he might ever be.

But he was a free man—and that too counted for something.

St. Stephen's Day

Barely seventy-hours after Eddie Marek departed Sing Sing, Father Gelasius also boarded a southbound train from its station.

Eddie Marek's journey was one of liberation, tinged with fear. Father Gelasius' was one of simple, total, absolute, unknown terror.

Debarking at Grand Central, he silently and nervously walked the nearly half mile up Madison Avenue to the Archbishop's great stone residence, to the rear of St. Patrick's— "The Powerhouse." He had never previously visited "The Powerhouse," not when he was ordained, not when he was first exiled to Sing Sing, and, certainly, never since. He pondered and worried what the nature of his summoning might indeed be and who he might be summoned to meet—and why. All he knew was he was to be there at 10 A.M. sharp.

Had it to do with Kathryn? Had somehow her secret become known, muttered in her intermittent half-consciousness, heard by an aide or by Dr. Garrow—worst of all, by her husband. And then somehow relayed to the hierarchy?

No, of course, it wasn't that. It couldn't have been that. He was *there*. The whole time . . . until . . . no, it couldn't have been that. He felt as though he was unhinging. His imagination spun one scenario upon another, as he huffed block-by-block up Madison Avenue, waited uncomfortably in the paneled "Powerhouse" ante-room, and then, interminably, finally . . .

"His Eminence will see you now."

He entered Patrick Cardinal Cronin's office, genuflected on his left knee and kissed his simple gold ring. Cronin, seemed weak and infirm, not the same man he had last met in Sing Sing—and certainly not the man he had first met so many years before. But Cronin's mind remained sharp, and it was clear he knew who Father Gelasius Bryant was and why he had summoned him. He bade his subordinate sit.

"How are things at Sing Sing, Father?"

Very good, Gelasius informed him.

"I have remembered you."

Gelasius was not sure if that were good or bad.

"I have received many letters about you, Father."

Father Gelasius wondered if he might be transferred to Auburn or Attica or even Dannemora. It was possible. All it would take would be a phone call from The Powerhouse.

Cronin stared blankly at Gelasius, his expression conveying nothing in particular, neither foreboding nor comforting. Not for nothing, was he sometimes termed "Old Stone Face."

"You have done well," the Cardinal finally continued, "You have redeemed souls—perhaps, most happily, your own."

If one could have exhaled a great sigh of relief in the presence of a Cardinal, Father Gelasius would have so breathed, but one did not even breathe in such circumstances, and Gelasius did not breathe. Not even now.

"I was once pastor at St. Stephen's parish, Father Bryant—the one on East Twenty-eighth—not St. Stephen of Hungary uptown. I'd like to assign you there. It remains a very good parish. And it is in need of good priests—and a good pastor. *Pastor* Bryant. *Monsignor* Bryant."

Gelasius had never expected this moment—at least he had not expected it since his first unfortunate previous meeting with Cronin. St. Stephen's was indeed a good parish. Once, it had been the biggest parish in the country. That was decades ago, but still . . .

There was a moment of silence. Gelasius, assuming his most careful and formal means of expression, chose not only his words but his thoughts and gestures and intonations so very, very carefully.

"Your Eminence, if I may comment, you have proffered to me a most generous assignment, but there are many good priests in the archdiocese. Far better than me. Though, I remain grateful for the kindness of your offer, I believe it might still be more appropriate for me to serve among the men of Sing Sing. If His Eminence would not mind, I would wish to continue on there."

Father Gelasius finished. He still did not breathe—or, at least, so it seemed.

"Not many monsignors at Sing Sing, Father."

"I know, Your Eminence."

The silence resumed.

"Yes," Cardinal Cronin said so very softly that Father Gelasius barely heard what he said, "You have redeemed yourself."

Cronin fiddled with the amethyst-and-diamond-encrusted golden pectoral cross that hung round his neck before propping himself up to stand. That was a signal for Gelasius to also stand. The interview was concluded.

"Say hello to Warden Beck for me," said the Cardinal, as Gelasius knelt again and the Cardinal extended his hand and Gelasius kissed his ring, "—and if, in the near future, you can think of anyone appropriate for St. Stephen's, please let the Chancery know."

"God be with you."

And God was.

Demi-Monde

Life went on in Sing Sing. The same frustrations. The same boredom and scheming. The eternal indignities.

A long distance call jangled the phone on Principal Keeper McKaig's desk.

"I don't see why he's being transferred," McKaig protested, though without much passion. He peered at the piles of papers and manila folders before him, all stacked and coded and numbered—much like the inhabitants of B Block. He had too much before him to worry about one con or another.

"It's nothing that Myers has done, Principal Keeper McKaig. It's that Dannemora's cell occupancy rate is a tad too low. We have to start transferring men from other prisons to raise that up. We've already moved ten men from Auburn and three from Attica. Bureaucratic formulas, you know. That crap."

Ah, yes . . . formulas. McKaig knew all about the Prisons Department bureaucracy.

Ah, yes . . . crap.

"But what we want to know, McKaig, is this: have you received his transfer papers?"

"Yes, they're here somewhere," he informed his caller, though with only minimal confidence. His unstated emphasis was on *somewhere*.

"Just wanted to confirm that. He's a very clever man. That's why we're sending *three* men to transport him."

"Don't worry. We transfer people all the time."

***

Elsewhere in Sing Sing, Warden Beck received unpleasant signals. Superintendent MacFarlane continued agitating against him. *Why*, MacFarlane asked, *was Stewart Beck invariably fomenting such controversy?* MacFarlane wanted Beck sacked—or, at least, reined in. *Why was Beck wasting time with ballplaying prisoners and not working harder and more effectively to prevent escapes? Three prisoners and two guards dead. Dead! One Ossining cop dead. Dead! All while Stewart*

Beck played bleeding heart and baseball talent scout. When would it end? How many more men would die?

In Brooklyn, Sidearm Jack Powell treated Eddie respectfully, though not extravagantly. He needed to keep a personal eye on his prize prospect. One mistake, one little item in the papers, and Eddie was finished. Powell wanted Eddie Marek where he could see him—living with Mr. & Mrs. Sidearm Jack right above the Sidearm Jack Powell Sporting Goods Store. It wasn't much of a room, a bed and dresser and tiny nightstand, but it was grander than anything on Tier U, Block B.

One Sunday morning, after an early Mass, Eddie took a walk. His solitary, aimless path propelled him through still largely deserted, almost eerily empty, downtown Brooklyn streets, beyond Borough Hall, down past and Ben's Glat Kosher Deluxe Deli and the shuttered Bernstein's Jewelers. For most folks a stroll downtown was nothing special. For Eddie it remained everything in the world. When Eddie paused before the Hotel St. George, however, he noticed something.

He was being followed.

His shadow was a slight man, fortyish, with wispy black hair and a small, waxed moustache. He was well, though somewhat flashily, dressed. Marek crossed Pineapple Street, heading back toward the direction of Borough Hall. The man with the waxed moustache followed.

A grubby, foul-smelling panhandler blocked Marek's escape. He provided Eddie with a sob story of the Great Depression and the Great War, leaving out Prohibition and his own Great Hangover. Eddie listened respectfully but retained his limited supply of dimes for his own use. Edging away from the bum, he heard a voice call, "Mr. Marek, I have a proposition for you."

It was the man with the small, waxed moustache.

"First, let me introduce myself. I am Mr. Samuel J. Burger, theatrical producer."

Burger extended a ruby-ringed hand.

"Pleased to meet you, Mr. Burger." Marek wasn't sure if he *was* pleased. He didn't know much about theatrical producers but suspected they usually didn't schedule meetings in this fashion or hour—and usually not on Brooklyn Heights sidestreets.

"Mr. Marek, might we adjourn to more amenable surroundings."

"You buying?"

Burger betrayed a slight smile.

"I'm amenable."

Mr. Samuel L. Burger was, in fact, one of the sleaziest operators on Broadway, the self-proclaimed "Entrepreneur of Demi-Monde Attractions." His current clientele included numerous strippers, snake dancers, fan dancers, and distaff prizefighters, which, at least, by his standards, was an exceedingly respectable roster. In truth, he'd book nearly anything reputable agents wouldn't touch. He had previously done good business renting out exotic animals. Monkeys were popular ("People get lonesome and telephone me to send them a monkey to keep them company"), but his most spectacular gig involved supplying a team of racing cockroaches for a society party. Hence, Mr. Samuel Burger's second nickname: "The Cockroach King."

Insects and fan dancers were OK, but Sammy really specialized in criminals—or, rather, since most criminals were usually unavailable for public appearances—the relatives of criminals. He engaged John Dillinger's old man and half of his immediate family. He booked both Legs Diamond's widow *and* his girl friend. He tried, but failed, to engage the entire Lindbergh kidnapping case jury. He'd have sent Percy Graham's peonies on tour if they could fill a theater in Poughkeepsie or Akron.

None of these things, Sammy Burger, however, considered worthy of mentioning to Eddie Marek. He steered Eddie to a decent little breakfast joint a few blocks down the street, handing Eddie his business card. Its elegant raised letters read:

Samuel J. Burger
Ballyhoo Associates
Roseland Dance Hall Building
1658 Broadway—Room 412
New York, New York
Ph: Longacre 3-2797

"Mr. Marek, I have followed your situation with some interest and much sympathy," he said with unusual force. He may have even meant it.

"What Baseball has done to you is unconscionable, totally, reprehensibly, un-American. I can tell you the average man on the street does not feel the same way about you playing baseball as does Mr. Nathan Jackson Lloyd—and I know a great deal about the tastes and artistic preferences of the American people. *I make my living that way.* They want to see you play, even if Mr. Lloyd and his silk shirt, plutocratic friends do not.

"I can arrange for you to play."

"I thought you were a theatrical producer, Mr. Burger."

Burger didn't miss a beat.

"I *am*, but I also promote other entertainment events. I can facilitate the creation of touring teams—barnstormers—to properly showcase your talents, both baseball and football—for two hundred dollars . . ."

He paused for effect and repeated, "for two hundred simoleans . . .

. . . . a week . . .

. . . for *you*."

A week! *Matka Boska!*—Mother of God! Four times what Mr. Powell paid—and for the football season too.

Eddie didn't know what to say.

"I know what you're thinking," Burger continued, "You have a contract with Sidearm Jack Powell. Unfortunately, you *don't*. Lloyd has ruled against you. The Executive Committee has ruled against you—and unanimously. You have two strikes on you. I regret to inform you that your chances do not look very good right now.

"Your chances with Ballyhoo Associates, however, are excellent. We have a proven track record in presenting popular entertainments to receptive American audiences. You do not have to sign with us at this instant, but you will, once you extend our proposition full and rational consideration."

Marek trudged homeward, pondering this strange message from a strange messenger all the way. Lloyd had ruled against him and been supported by his Executive Committee. There was no guarantee Judge Landis would help. Sidearm Jack Powell's warning rang in Eddie's head. It rang true. "Landis," Sidearm Jack had told him, "Yeah, Landis. Hell on wheels, that one, that little pisspot! Threw all the crooks out of Baseball—and then some. I remember that Benny Kauff kid back on Mugsy McGraw's Giants. One winter, I think it was 1919, the cops charged him with boosting cars on the street, and Landis tossed him. Kauff wasn't even convicted. Just indicted. That was enough. Gone! Pffft!!"

Pffft! What chance in hell, thought Eddie, did he have?

And then again . . . there was Sammy Burger's two hundred bucks a week, every seven days, through the summer and into the fall, when the leaves were falling off the trees two C-notes per week.

Eddie informed Sidearm Jack that he had an offer, a pretty good one, excellent money—and no jokers like Nathan Lloyd to rule he couldn't play. "Give me twenty-four hours, kid, before you sign," Powell asked him, "just give me that."

Powell called in Molyneaux, who called in his show business sources: newspapermen and performers and agents and publicists, people who knew The Great White Way forwards and backwards and the sharpies that darkened it. "What ever you do," Powell warned Singing Al, "*do not* ask Ed Sullivan!"

Molyneaux reported back to Powell. Powell talked to Marek. "Dollar for dollar," Powell told him, "Burger's offering you more than anything I can offer, and I cannot guarantee that you will ever put on a uniform, but if you do, you'll be a bona fide ballplayer, a man judged on skills and character. If you sign with Sam Burger you won't be a ballplayer. You'll be part of his freak show, a professional ex-con, rather than a professional ballplayer, a sideshow exhibit in The Cockroach King's latest flea circus. Here kid, take a look at this."

And with that, Sidearm Jack produced a gaudy red-lettered poster advertising the most recent of Ballyhoo Associates enterprises: "Three Nights Only! Samuel L. Burger Presents: Direct from Paris' Left Bank: Lola LaGam, Fan Dancer Extraordinaire!"

"Is this your idea of big league stuff?" Sidearm Jack demanded, "Or maybe you'd like this one better?" And before Marek dared answer, Powell produced another garish broadsheet, this one featuring not the smiling Mademoiselle LaGam and her brace of huge ostrich-feather fans but a brace of menacing mug shots—full-face and side view—proclaiming: "One Day Only! Samuel L. Burger Presents: "Killer McCrery's San Quentin All-Stars: The Gridiron's Deadliest Eleven vs The Original Harlem Hellfighters!"

"Take your pick, kid. What do you want to be? A big leaguer—or a big joke?"

Marek had visualized Burger's teams as something akin to the barnstorming teams that Babe Ruth and Lou Gehrig had assembled. Something vaguely respectable. Maybe a touch of hype but nothing too bad. But this—*this*—might be worse than putting on a fake beard and playing for the House of David. Hell, Marek thought, who was he kidding? He was no Babe Ruth.

But still . . .

"The money's real good, Mr. Powell."

He looked Powell in the eye. He thought long and hard, staring at one poster and then another. His voice rose. "But only cockroaches walk away from their friends, Mr. Powell, and only cockroaches walk away from a fight. I'm no cockroach. I'm in it for the duration. And besides, my mother would have wupped me all they way back to Scranton if I signed with a character like that!"

"I'm with you. Mr. Powell," said Edward Marek, "I'm with you."

Transfer

Three reasonably muscular men waltzed into the Sing Sing Administration Building, plopped down a handful of papers, all duly stamped and signed, before civilian record clerk Mr. Harry Ginsberg, and stood there awaiting his response.

"Everything's in order."

"Good," said the smallest of the three, "It's a long trip up to Dannemora."

Ginsberg had been expecting them. So had Sandy Myers. Within ten minutes Sandy appeared in the clerk's office. No reporters or newsreel men awaited him, but there he was, dressed in street clothes, not the free new suit released prisoners received, but the navy blue suit he brought with him four years before. He was not about to trade Rogers Peet for government-issue.

But his old suit hung slackly upon him. Manual labor will do that for a white-collar criminal, even the trim ones.

Click! They snapped a pair of shiny cuffs upon him and led him away. He did not seem happy to be heading to Dannemora. No one ever was.

"Think you can detour to Brooklyn so I can see my old pal, the celebrity ballplayer, Eddie Marek?"

"We don't think so, pal. Maybe he'll send you an autographed ball."

***

Eddie Marek wrote a lot of letters—and he *received* a lot. They flooded into Ebbets Field. People wished him well. They mailed him good luck charms, rabbit's feet, and cheap metal four-leaf clovers with Lincoln pennies stuck in the middle. They mailed him religious medals—to St. Jude, to St. Sebastian, to St. Barbara.

One category of correspondence, Marek found particularly interesting.

Sidearm Jack Powell entered, carrying a roll of tickets.

"Bill collectors find you, kid?"

"Not exactly."

"Marriage proposals."

The tickets tumbled from Powell's hands and rolled all the way to the wall. Eddie laughed. But then he recalled another marriage proposal made years before, one that prevented him from accepting any of those now tendered him. It was made neither on bended knee nor in a parents' living room, but strolling arm-and-arm up in Manila after a feature at a dark-mahogany local picture palace. It was long enough ago that the movie was silent—"The Kiss" with Greta Garbo. It was a romance, needless to say, and that may have played a part in it all.

Eddie asked the question. Carrie said yes, and Eddie was glad she did.

Yes, even now.

***

Early afternoon in Manhattan, the tail-end of the lunch hour. Four men maneuvered themselves through a revolving door, into a modest office building lobby, trooping past a somnolent guard, into a cramped elevator, its narrow confines reeking of cigarette smoke both fresh and ancient, exiting on the third floor, heading towards a frosted-glass door reading, "New Amsterdam Investments" They strolled in like they owned the place.

The office's lone occupant didn't hear them coming, though he should have. He was occupied, staring out the window, surveying the streetscape. A blonde in a red straw hat walking a small, feisty, ginger-brown Pomeranian—or rather it walking her—caught his particular interest.

It required the sound of his own door opening to break his concentration on the dog-walking blonde—that and three syllables, "Pay 'em, Ben!"

Ben Miller bolted from his brass-studded, green leather chair. He rushed to shake hands with the man in the loose-fitting blue Rogers Peet suit before him.

He gave a wink, reached into his jacket and handed him a platinum cigarette case dented a long time ago by a .22 caliber bullet, and grinned, "You're a very clever man, Sanford Myers, a very clever man."

And, indeed, any man who could mastermind the forging of his own transfer papers from within Sing Sing itself, *was* a very clever man.

***

Eddie Marek, sat alongside one of his prospective teammates, an outfielder named Vern Chapman, within the darkened vastness of downtown Brooklyn's Strand Theater, waiting for a new Cagney picture to flash upon the screen before them. But before tonight's feature commenced and before Jimmy started twitching and slugging dames and blasting away with his tommy gun, it was time for the obligatory coming attractions, cartoons, and newsreel. This week's newsreel commenced with FDR signing some new alphabet agency bill into law and Hitler screaming at some big Nazi goose-step rally. And there it was, bigger than life and not much fun at all: a newsreel about Eddie Marek.

There before Marek and Chapman on the screen was Eddie—the celluloid Eddie—departing Sing Sing, tipping his fedora, as a properly stentorian announcer proclaimed to Strand patrons and to movie goers in several hundred motion picture palaces nationwide:

"The popular outcry continues over the Sing Sing bad boy, Eddie Marek. To play or not to play major league ball? *That* is the question. Philadelphia Phillies President Pierre DeKay thinks not."

Old Pierre himself flashed onscreen. He seemed pretty cocky, though he stood stiff as a board before the camera.

"Edward S. Marek will not play ball in my league. There are too many men in this country with clean records that are unemployed. Ex-cons shouldn't jump ahead of them in the line!"

And neither did Willard Thomas. He was up next on the big screen. "My New York Giants have played against Mr. Edward

Marek," he drawled, "and all I can say is that if he is the best the Brooklyn National League franchise can hope for, they might as well padlock Ebbets Field."

"Psia krew!—Bitch's blood!" thought Eddie, nearly bolting out of his seat. *"The lying snake! He's knows I hit the tar out of his ragarm pitchers! Damn! Damn him all to hell!"*

Sammy Burger no longer shadowed Eddie Marek—he had moved on to newer attractions—but someone else, nevertheless, remained on Eddie's trail. Norman Megley had once worked in the NYPD, but an unfortunate case involving a speakeasy had created enough questions about his professional conduct to dissuade any of his many friends from retaining him in public office. So Norman Megley now toiled as a private detective, gumshoeing wandering husbands and wives and mysteriously prosperous business associates in equally mysteriously failing business partnerships, snooping for people who wanted information and were willing to pay for it.

Nathan Lloyd was willing to pay. He didn't like being embarrassed, and this Marek nonsense had become far more discomfiting than he ever imagined it could be. *Who ever cared what happened in Brooklyn, anyway? Why was everybody in love with convicts all of a sudden?* Lloyd couldn't figure it out, but he did figure that a con was a con and always would be and engaged the aforesaid Norman Megley to survey Eddie Marek's current activities. If Marek wandered into some joint he shouldn't have, engaged in any behavior his sainted mother might frown on, or associated with anyone who might sully the honor of the great game of Baseball, Nathan Lloyd wanted to know about it. And once Nathan Lloyd knew about it . . .

Megley now busied himself, sidling up to Marek's new teammates. He asked questions—discreetly, of course, even circuitously. Above all, he tailed Eddie Marek to see where he went and who he went with. Sometimes Megley posed as a businessman, sometimes a workman, sometimes as a bum or even as an observant Orthodox Jew. Sometimes he wore a fake moustache. Sometimes he walked with a limp, but not one so pronounced as to draw undue attention to himself or to cause him to fall too far behind his quarry. A little variety kept his prey off guard, so unsuspecting that even when Marek occasionally happened upon a grubby, foul-smelling panhandler with a sob story of the Great Depression and the Great War, he did not suspect in the least that anyone besides Samuel L. Burger had ever been tailing him.

While Megley kept snooping, the merry-go-round kept whirling.

***

Carrie Marek plunked down her shiny silver quarter upon the marble counter of Sands Street's Gold's Theater. A middle-aged woman in a flowered print behind the ornate metal grill slid her a ticket reading. "ADMIT ONE," but Carrie had no idea what this tiny scrap of paper would soon admit her to.

She eased into a plush velvet balcony seat, and waited for the feature to begin, taking in the coming attractions, the cartoons, the travelogue, and, yes, Lowell Thomas's newsreel. And, yes, there *he* was, *her husband* exiting Sing Sing, discussing his future, progressing, or *not* progressing, toward a professional baseball career in Brooklyn.

Susmariyosep! Jesus, Mary, and Joseph! It was all too much, completely overwhelming. To see Eddie again, and to see him on that screen, all so large, a celebrity now, and in *Brooklyn.* Why Brooklyn? Of all teams, of all places.

Her head spun.

She wanted to flee the theater, to flee Brooklyn and her very being.

But to where?

She remained, of course. In the balcony. In Brooklyn. Alone with her thoughts and secrets. Afraid to share them with any other soul.

She remained in her seat. Her husband faded from the screen. But not from her confused mind—or heart.

***

The forces opposing Eddie Marek had the power plain and simple. They exercised it with Nathan Lloyd. They thought they could exercise it once more with Judge Kenesaw Landis.

And, why should they not believe they might prevail? Sidearm Jack wasn't the only one who had warned Eddie about Kenesaw Mountain Landis, the Lord Hill Commissioner of Baseball. Or was he its Lord High Executioner? "He's a tough old bird," Marek remembered Al Molyneaux telling him, "Tougher coot than me. I think if he was a pitcher he'd throw right at your head and not think even once, let alone twice, about it. Back when he was a judge in Chicago he tossed the book at the Socialists and the Wobblies—said he was disappointed to give the lot of them only twenty years. Wanted to stand them up against the wall and shoot them himself! Probably, meant it too!"

***

"Have you heard from Landis?" Pete DeKay phoned Nathan Lloyd to ask.

"Hell, no. Once he's got something before him he doesn't say boo—and he doesn't want to be bothered, either. But, I'm confident."

"Why's that?"

"Let's say I heard it from a little bird, Pete. I can't say more."

What Lloyd had heard was this: He had phoned Landis's office to see if the Judge had received the case's paperwork and had caught the Commissioner's confidential secretary, a smart young lawyer named Lawrence O'Byrne, in a rare unguarded moment. O'Byrne was used to being circumspect and used to his boss's profanity-laced tirades, but Landis had just received Lloyd's package, and it contained a few morsels not very favorable to Eddie Marek. The newspaper stories had been building up Eddie with the public and, in the process, had played fast and loose with the facts. Some reporters, after all, never permit a true story get in the way of a sob story. Not content with narrating the simple tale of a young man seeking a second chance, they laid it on thicker and thicker. The *Post* claimed the Amsterdam Avenue holdup was Eddie's first job. It wasn't. The *World-Telegraph* claimed he was a younger man being led astray by a much older accomplice. Not exactly. On the radio, the sob sisters said he had only collected ten bucks in the Daniel Reeves holdup. He got a lot more than that. They had not yet claimed that he had robbed from the rich to give to the poor or that he had been sentenced to Devil's Island for stealing a loaf of bread, but they were coming closer.

They did not, however, reveal the real reason for his crime—nor did they ever know it.

In Chicago, Landis blew sky high regarding the false information that was being manufactured, without his input, and, certainly, not in his behalf. It didn't take much to rattle the Judge's cage. And this development certainly did—and Lawrence O'Byrne had let Nathan Lloyd know about it.

Lloyd accordingly theorized that he was in very good shape.

He had not always been quite so sanguine.

"What do you mean there's nothing?" Nathan Lloyd had very recently fairly screamed into his telephone receiver. It was not so much an angry scream, just a panic-driven one.

"I gumshoe Marek every day," Norman B. Megley answered, "He doesn't go anywhere special. Maybe a movie. A walk around the block. A hot dog and an orange drink. That's it. He doesn't hang out with hardly anybody. Powell keeps him on a very short leash. Between you and me, I don't think Powell is giving the kid any dough to go anywhere with. Cheap bastard."

Now, Lloyd *was* angry: "Damn it, Megley, I don't know what I'm paying you for!"

Megley was all too familiar with clients who couldn't deal with reality. He struggled to re-light his cigarette, while juggling the phone—and with his own smoldering anger.

"If you don't require my services, Mr. Lloyd—"

Lloyd reverted to panic mode.

"No, no, Megley! Keep at it! Follow him wherever he goes. Do whatever you have to do. We can't give up!"

Norman Megley didn't particularly care if he gave up or not, if he shoveled any dirt or not. He had looked into Eddie's eyes that night Sammy "The Cockroach King" Burger had interrupted their conversation, given his prey the once over, and the more he considered matters the more he liked what he saw in that face and in those eyes—even if Eddie *hadn't* given him a dime.

Norman Megley was quietly rooting for Eddie Marek.

***

Sandy Myers thought he was in fine shape too, or at least much finer than before exiting Sing Sing right through the Administration Building—waltzing out like Nick Strecker had once vainly pondered.

Of course, Sandy was a lot smarter than Nick, and regarding this particular caper he had been very intelligent, indeed.

It had occurred to Sandy in a flash. He sat there, right in the Visitors Room, just whispering with Ben Miller, nothing big going on, when Ben dropped a little nugget of information:

"I met this guy at Saratoga. He works in the Prisons Department. A real sucker. Likes the ponies. Likes the ladies. I'll see if he can do you a favor someday."

Now, Ben had no idea of what this bumpkin—Martin T. Walsh—could do for anyone. Mr. Miller was just making conversation, giving his pal Sandy a little hope, as vague as that hope might be.

But the light clicked on for Sandy. It was as if someone had shuffled through a deck of cards, as fast as could be, only it wasn't a blur: you could see all fifty two pasteboards as slowly and as clearly as if they were being laid down one-by-one-by-one for a game of solitaire—and you could memorize each one and where they were in the deck and how they all fit together—all the flushes and straights and full houses and two-of-a-kinds. All the clubs and hearts and diamonds and spades. All the jokers. All the knaves.

Everything—and with perfect clarity.

Yes, that's how it was when Ben told Sandy about this Walsh clown. It all came together. Sandy saw it all, the whole plan, how it could work, how to make it work, how it couldn't miss.

"He married?"

"Yeah, I think so."

"Badger game."

Miller smiled a tiny, guarded smile and nodded. Ben thought he knew where Sandy was going—a bit of blackmail, a little favor here or there. He wasn't even close.

Eventually, Ben's crew introduced Mr. Walsh to a young woman—Good Time Lizzy, they called her—who conducted her trade on Albany's rather, shall we say, disreputable Green Street. She had jet black bangs, an ample figure where ampleness counted for much, a surprisingly ready wit, and, as circumstances would quickly prove, no conscience whatsoever. Lizzy and Marty adjourned to a room on the sixth floor of Albany's Wellington Hotel. They got comfortable—and then the photographer and the men with the fake badges came bursting in.

FLASH! FLASH! FLASH!!

"Sorry, Marty," Good Time Lizzy murmured as she gathered up her unmentionables.

She wasn't.

Martin Walsh begged for mercy. His new acquaintances graciously extended it and asked for nothing in return—at least not yet. But they said they would let him know what they would want and when . . . and if they didn't obtain what they desired, Mrs. Martin T. Walsh and all the little Walshes—and for effect they named them one by one—would in due course receive a package in the mail.

But before anyone got back to Martin Walsh, Ben Miller had a little recruiting to do. He required three men brazen—or crazy—enough to pose as correction officers, saunter into Sing Sing, and saunter back out with Sandy.

Oddly enough, nobody local wanted the job.

Ben called Detroit. No dice. The same with the mugs Miller knew in Cleveland and Montreal and Philly. The boys in Chicago thought about it, but said no—they were busy. But they knew some guys in Kansas City, from the late Johnny Lazia's old outfit, who were looking for work—if the price was right.

It took Ben a while to come up with the dough, because even unemployed goons in Kansas City charge plenty to walk into Sing Sing, but he did. Through a middleman he sent out orders to Walsh: Marty was to supply transfer papers for Sandy, three sets of bogus ID papers and three very real departmental badges for Ben's Kansas City-bred fake corrections officers—plus a little coaching on how to phone Chief Keeper McKaig and what to say, and what not to say, so everything sounded as authentic and routine as could be.

Walsh balked. He cried. He shook. He pled. He said it was crazy. He said he wouldn't do it.

He was informed it was crazier *not* to do it. Not only would certain eight-by-ten glossies be dispatched in the United States mails, but a substantial down payment had already been made on three fake correction officers. If worse came to worse, they'd merely receive a different assignment, a rubout Albany cops would never ever figure out, not in a million years.

Marty Walsh cried. He shook. He pled.

He changed his mind.

Don't worry, Ben's go-between assured Walsh, you'll get your badges back. Nobody will suspect a thing.

Ben was a man of his word. Even before anyone noted Sandy Myers's unexcused absence, Marty Walsh had returned three golden badges to the big, steel safe—just one floor below Superintendent MacFarlane's office—in which they normally and peacefully resided.

And seven years and six months later Marty Walsh retired with a full pension—and a decoration for faithful service.

Sidearm Jack Powell, on the other hand, got a call requesting that he and Eddie appear on the radio, but not just on any old show. This was an invitation for "The Kate Smith Hour."

This was *big*.

They wouldn't have the stage to themselves; primarily they'd share it with James J. Braddock, a light-heavyweight who had become "The Cinderella Man," magically graduating from washed-up palooka to world heavyweight champ.

His pals—and James J. Braddock now had a lot of pals— had staged a swell testimonial for him at the St. Moritz Hotel. All the big hot shots attended. Well, not all. Max Baer, the guy Braddock beat for the championship, didn't show, but that was, shall we say, understandable. Jack Dempsey, Gene Tunney, Mayor Fiorello "The Little Flower" LaGuardia—they all showed. And so did Kate Smith, "The Songbird of the South," along with her radio show—broadcasting the whole shebang.

Granted, some of these guys weren't always *Social Register* material—Braddock, so very recently, on relief, to be most precise, and Jack Dempsey, who married a mining camp hooker and dodged the draft and thus, had not always been the most beloved figure in sports, and Gene Tunney, who had been known to associate a little too closely with little Abe "The Little Hebrew" Attell, the ex-featherweight champ who helped fix the World Series. But they were all respectable now. And if Eddie Marek could associate with them, and with Kate Smith, herself, on America's biggest radio network, well, then maybe Eddie Marek was good and moral enough to lace up spikes at Ebbets Field.

It was all white linen and silver candelabras and black-tuxedoed waiters at the St. Moritz. Swell stuff, indeed. Just like Eddie pictured it, only a lot more so, because it was happening to Eddie Marek, and even if Eddie had never served a day of time, there was no way in hell he should be anywhere near anything like this.

Not even as one of those black-tuxedoed waiters.

Tonight, Eddie's fifteen minutes of fame was more like fifteen seconds. An announcer with a deep baritone voice and mellifluous tones introduced Marek and Powell, who gingerly had assumed their own places behind the great shining microphone. Eddie read his first line. The network guys didn't entrust their careers to the spontaneity of ex-cons.

"Kate Smith! It's an honor to meet you."

"Glad to have you and the great Sidearm Jack Powell here tonight," answered Kate.

That cued Powell's solitary line. That was all he got. Sidearm Jack clearly wasn't the star of tonight's show. He wasn't even some supporting actor like Lionel Barrymore. He was more like some down-on-his-luck guy from the silent pictures who they let hang around the studios, collect a check (a very small check) every so often, and stand in the background while the hero threw a saddle on his mighty white stallion.

"Evening, Miss Smith," Mr. Sidearm Jack Powell enunciated. Three words was Powell's quota. Thirty-six wins in one season—and three words tonight.

"Eddie," Kate boomed into the mike, before Powell might sneak a fourth word in, "do you think you'll be playing big league baseball anytime soon?"

"Well, Miss Smith, the way I see it—with so many good people rooting for me—no matter what happens—I've come out ahead of the game."

The audience applauded properly, and actually, with some enthusiasm, but, applause or not, that marked *finis* for the radio team of Powell and Marek.

Exit stage right. Into the darkness. Into trouble.

For Me to Know

A blue-uniformed St. Moritz bellboy, as diminutive and pockmarked as his garb was resplendent, approached Eddie with a message. He had a phone call.

"Eddie, my old pal!"

"Who is this? . . . Foxy?"

"Yeah, Eddie. It's me! Foxy Renard!"

"You son of a bitch! If I . . ."

"Now, calm down Eddie. I have a proposition for you. And if you know what's good for you and for your baseball career, I think you should relax right now. Simmer down and listen very, very carefully to what old Foxy Renard has to say."

Eddie ditched Powell, rendezvousing with Renard a few blocks away, in the grill room of the New Savoy Hotel. The New Savoy had been new when Sidearm Jack Powell was in his cradle.

"Good to see you again, partner!" Foxy, shot and a beer before him, speech slightly slurred, beamed through the room's smoky darkness. The years had made Renard's smile distinctly shark-like.

Eddie stared at him across the table in the corner booth. He knew no good could come from this session. Not here. Not now.

"Well, OK, maybe you're not so glad to see Foxy Renard. I can understand that. But you had better listen. You seem to have a very promising career ahead of you. And I'm happy for you. But maybe you don't have a career ahead of you at all. Just one more little glitch and every door you thought you could sashay through becomes instantly closed to you. It wouldn't take much, Eddie. Wouldn't take much, at all."

"Get to the point, Renard! I don't have time for games. Not from you."

"Make time, you Polack," Foxy said, dropping even the most gossamer pretense of friendliness. He took a puff of his half-smoked Panatela Deluxe.

Eddie sure as hell wasn't about to take orders from this creep. He bolted up from his chair, almost knocking the brown quart bottle of Schaeffer beer out of the hands of the boozer settling himself into the adjacent table.

"Sit down! If you value what's good for you sit down! I'm only going to say it once."

Eddie sat, nervously grasping the table before.

"Now look, jarhead. Here's the deal. People think they know all about you. But say they don't. Let's just say that you were involved in other heists—and maybe they were so bad people even got killed in them. Then where's your big-shot career?"

"*What are you talking about?*" You know damn well I wasn't involved in anything like that!"

"Keep it down! Yeah, I guess I do know that. And I guess you know that too . . . but . . . ."

"But what? I ain't got time for any of your lousy riddles."

"As I told you before, I guess you don't listen, pal, *make* time."

Marek sat straight back in his chair, almost ready to coil and pounce on Foxy Renard if this bastard kept his games up much longer.

"There's somebody who'll swear on a stack of bibles you were in on such a crime with him."

"Who? You? Come on!"

"Not me. That's foolish. Somebody who's away for life. He's got nothing to lose."

"Who's gonna believe *him?*"

"Well, that's a good question," Foxy said, quickly downing his slug of hootch. "How about the police and the district attorney? They might revoke your parole. They might even indict you. Could even convict."

"They'll never get a conviction!"

"Say they don't. Could put quite the crimp in your baseball season anyway. Might push your own personal opening day right past the World Series . . . that is, of course, if the baseball bigwigs don't decide that my friend's story is just about the last straw— or *say* it's the last straw—and use it as an excuse to do what they want to do anyway, which is to blackball you now and forever. *Now* do you get the picture?"

Eddie did.

"What do you want? How much?"

"I want a certain cut of your baseball income. Only ten percent. Now OK, I know you don't have any mazuma now. But Foxy Renard's a patient man. I'm reasonable. No income. No payment. What could be more reasonable than that? Partners again, pal?"

"Yeah, partners."

A bleached blonde in a tight chintz dress slit well above the knee slinked by their booth.

"Hi, gents, what are two good-looking guys like you doing tonight?"

She sat alongside them. As she sat, her slit rose, higher and higher . . . and higher.

"Beat it, whore!" said Renard, "Nobody's buying nothing tonight. And, certainly, not what you've got for sale!"

"Have it your way sweethearts," she said as she moved on to the next booth, to someone she had already noticed before propositioning Marek and Renard. She was not a woman to waste time—or opportunities.

Renard watched her depart and got back to business: "I'll walk you to the subway. Maybe you'll calm down. It's business, Eddie. Don't take it so personal. Please."

They traveled awkwardly down W. 49th Street together, until . . . until Eddie lurched toward Renard, grabbing him by his shoulders, ignoring his shouts and protests and pushing him deeper and deeper into the littered, darkened alleyway adjacent to the Avalon Burlesque House.

"You BASTARD!" Eddie screamed. He smashed Renard square in the face, sending Renard's Panatela flying. Prison had made Eddie Marek tougher and stronger. His blows rained down on his erstwhile partner—hard to his stomach, harder to his head. One blow upon the other. Blood oozed from Foxy's mouth. His right eye closed shut. He tumbled over backward, clattering loudly into a dented, tin garbage barrel, spilling its rotting contents onto the alley's cobblestones, landing painfully in the muck.

"Lay off! Lay off!! You trying to kill me?"

"Now . . . why . . . would . . . I . . . want to . . . do . . . that?" Eddie answered as he continued pummeling the virtually defenseless Renard. In five holdups, Eddie Marek had never dreamt of physically harming a soul. Now, he was ready, even eager, to *kill* Foxy Renard.

"PUT 'EM UP!! FREEZE!!"

The command sank like an arrow into Eddie Marek's heart, echoing loud and clear off the alleyway's dirty brick walls. He turned. He saw a pistol pointed straight at him.

"That's it. Both of you. Hands up. Back away from each other," said the man behind the gun.

"Boy, am I glad to see you," said Renard, gasping for breath, struggling to get to his feet.

Well, this is it, thought Eddie, *Dream's over. Luck's run out. The newspapers will have a field day tomorrow.*

The man with the gun said nothing. He was sorting everything out, calculating what to do next, and since his finger was on the trigger and Eddie's or Foxy's wasn't, he had all the time in the world.

Relatively speaking.

"Like I said," Renard continued, his wheels turning all the while, "thanks a heap. I ran into my old friend here, and I guess he was harboring a grudge—I don't know why. He just attacked me. Went haywire. Crazy like. Shoved me right into the alley. But hell, you might as well let him go. By-gones are by-gones."

By-gones were, of course, never by-gones with a character like Foxy Renard, but, even with his brains half beat out, he was quick enough to know if the cops busted Eddie Marek for this stunt, Eddie would be headed back to Sing Sing on the noon train, and Foxy's little enterprise would be more than over. Best to let Eddie walk and for Foxy Renard to collect some cash later—*with interest.* Yes, with *compound* interest.

"You think everyone's just going to walk away from a fracas like this," said the man with gun.

"Well . . . ," said Foxy, seeing his fortune sliding away. Eddie saw a lot more than that sliding.

"No, pal . . . " the man said, fixing his revolver not at Eddie but at Renard, "*you're* not just walking away from this."

"Me! Why me? What did I do?"

"Yeah, Mr. Innocent, what did you do? Last time I checked, the Penal Code lists extortion by larceny as a felony. I guess the only question for you is whether it's Class E or Class D. I heard the whole thing, *Foxy.* The *whole* thing."

Foxy Renard didn't know what to think. Neither did Eddie. Who *was* this guy? Where did he come *from*? What was *his* game?

"Now, here's the deal," the man continued, his face hidden in the alley's shadows, "on second thought everybody *is* walking away from this little dustup but not the way you thought everybody would—that you'd just continue your little dime-novel plot. No, that's over, friend. Finished. Ever try that little game again, or anybody else ever tries it, and I come out of the woodwork and blow the whole thing out of the water. Just like now. Just like I could blow your lousy, lying head off with one little squeeze of one little finger. Understand?"

Except for the part of having his head blown off, Foxy Renard didn't understand a single word of it—but he wasn't about to argue either.

"Now get up and get out. Now! Before I change my mind!"

Renard edged out of the Avalon Burlesque alley, leaving Eddie and the stranger alone, face to face.

"Uh, you a copper?"

"That's for me to know, pal, and you to guess."

"What happens to me?"

"Nothing. You go right on your merry way. And if you ever see me again, you don't know me, and I don't know you. Perfect strangers. Got that?"

"What are you the Lone Ranger or something?"

"You ask too many questions for somebody who just got his bacon saved. Now I'm going to walk away. I'm going to hang a right. You wait a minute—and I mean a *full* minute, second seconds, count 'em!—and hang a left. Understand?"

Eddie nodded, and the stranger slowly backed out of the alley and into the street. Remaining behind, as ordered, Eddie could not see him head toward a bleached blonde in a tight slit dress waiting for him under the faltering street light on the corner.

"What happened? What was going on back there, Mr. Megley? I was worried."

"Later, Louise," he said as he turned the corner to hail a cab, "but let's just say Nathan Jackson Lloyd didn't get his money's worth tonight."

Son of a Bitch!

"The Kate Smith Hour" aired at 7:00 P.M., Thursday nights, 6 P.M. in Chicago, where on the city's Gold Coast, Judge Kenesaw Mountain Landis impatiently fiddled with the Zenith twelve-tube console at his Ambassador Hotel apartment.

The Judge didn't like what he was about to hear.

Kenesaw Landis was very good at determining what he liked hearing and what he didn't. He didn't like having cases kicked up to him that should have been settled at a lower level. And though he possessed a flamboyant streak as wide and deep as Lake Michigan, he really didn't care for having controversy forced upon him—he liked forcing it on others. And he certainly didn't enjoy watching a firestorm of public opinion engulf a case before it arrived, making it too hot to handle, on his doorstep.

Kenesaw Mountain Landis did not like the Marek case— and he did not like what he heard on his radio set.

The sportswriters were already pestering him, clomping a path to his North Michigan Avenue office, to the office door he had marked grandly, but not inaccurately, by a single word, "BASEBALL." They peppered him with questions. Would he let Marek play? Should a con be allowed in uniform? How would the Judge respond to Powell's complaint? Would he stand behind Lloyd? The same damned questions dogged him every day. Every day Landis gave the same response.

"The case is under advisement. It being under advisement, it would be *highly*, wildly, inappropriate to comment at this time."

When Landis felt sure his pursuers had departed, he turned to his secretary Lawrence O'Byrne. He remained angry. It wasn't an act.

"That damned fool Lloyd! What has he gotten us into? Fans riled! Radio shows! Petitions! Commentaries! Editorials! Pontificating pontificators! All trouble no matter which way I rule!!"

"Lloyd meant well, Judge."

"The captain of the *Titanic* meant well!"

Landis slammed his fist upon his desk. The sensation of oak upon hand made him realize his emotions needed a tad more control—but only a tad.

"Get me Lloyd! Get him in this office tomorrow! Get him on the next train!"

Kate Smith and an equally sizable segment of the press had fallen in love with the Marek story. Not everyone else had. Walter Winchell, the big Broadway gossip columnist for the tabloid *New York Mirror*, for one. He didn't mind criminals. An awful lot of his best sources—and his best pals—were hoods. Why Frank Costello was even a neighbor at his Central Park West digs—and he wasn't a bad neighbor at all. What he hated was that nobody had fed the Marek item to *him*. What Winchell *really* hated was that Singing Al Molyneaux had supplied the story over to his hated rival Ed Sullivan over at the *Daily News*. *That*, it turned out, meant special trouble for Mr. Edward Stanley Marek Jr.

Winchell's column ran in a hundred papers nationwide. His NBC radio show broadcast featured a high-octane version of his newspaper shtick, with the same likes and dislikes, the same nightclubs and books and shows and movies to plug, the same Winchell vendettas to exploit. Each Sunday evening at 9:30, he'd remove his jacket, tilt but not remove his grey fedora, loosen his tie—even unhitch his belt . . . aaah!—and let 'er rip. "Good evening Mr. and Mrs. America," his staccato voice clattering like a Remington typewriter in midnight chorus with a telegraph key and a four-alarm fire bell: "From border to border and coast to coast and all the ships at sea. Let's go to press."

The sound of his voice generated excitement in thirty million otherwise somnolent Sunday night American homes. Yes, once Winchell decided to tap dance on your reputation and let "Mr. & Mrs. North America and all the ships at sea" know what a dirtbag you were, you were virtually deceased. Hell, after Walter got through with Eddie Marek, he'd be lucky to get his old room back at the Warden Beck Crowbar Arms Hotel.

"FLASH!" Winchell's piercing voice exploded into his microphone, "The inmates running the ass-sy-lum department:

On the beauteous Gowanus, one-time pride of the National Pastime Sidearm Jack Powell, now front office guru for the woeful Brooklyn Dodgers has gone around the bend in the cheap stunt department, bringing discredit to a game that brought him fame and fortune."

Winchell dredged up the details of the Amsterdam Avenue robbery. Worse, he brought the public up-to-date on Nick Strecker's prison break, inserting sufficient innuendo to slime both Eddie and Warden Beck. "What ever happened to crime . . . ," Winchell demanded, "*AND PUNISHMENT?*"

***

Nathan Jackson Lloyd caught the first train to Chicago, riding in a cramped Pullman berth. He hotfooted it to Michigan Avenue.

"But, Judge."

"'But' my ass! You fat moron! I'm going to fix this mess you left me. Now get out of here!"

"But I just got here."

"Get out!"

Lloyd did, wondering what had just happened, and hoping it never happened again.

***

In Greenwich Village, Marie Rossi heard something.

"Miss Rossi?" a man said. She turned warily to see who it was.

He looked vaguely familiar, nattily-dressed, even distinguished, wearing a red silk-ribboned boater of finest stiff Italian straw and cufflinks of gold—real gold, not gold-filled. She had been around enough to tell the difference both in terms of straw—and, more importantly, of gold.

No, she really didn't know this man, though she did possess some sense of seeing him somewhere.

"I'm very sorry to hear about your brother."

"Oh, it was a terrible thing," said Marie. She did not like talking about her brother—and certainly not to strangers. It was not a good thing to have had a brother in prison.

"Did you know Sal?"

"Yes," said Sanford Myers, "from the unions, a long time ago. He was a good man, dedicated to the workingman. He meant well. He fought for justice. He had many good qualities. I wanted to tell you that."

"Thank you," Marie Rossi responded. The whole incident puzzled her.

"I was on my way to light a candle for him."

He reached in his pocket and gave her a half-dollar. "Light one for me, too," he said. Candles at Our Lady of Pompeii on Bleecker Street cost only a nickel, but Marie remained too unsure of everything to raise that point. She figured she'd light ten candles or maybe five big ones. Myers handed her a sealed envelope. It had fifty dollars in it.

Fifty dollars.

"The boys in the union took up a collection. . . . for your grandmother."

"Thank you. Thank them for me."

She, after all, had to accept it if it was for her grandmother.

"Well, goodbye."

"Nice meeting you."

"What was that all about?" Ben Miller asked when Sandy Myers returned across the street to Washington Square.

"Lies," said Myers, "all lies."

Lies.

Sandy hasn't changed much, thought Ben Miller.

***

The question haunted Father Gelasius Bryant. It had always haunted him.

But since her death, it has haunted him yet more.

It kept returning to Father Gelasius at ever shortened intervals, lingering longer and more painfully each time it did: Should he tell Stewart Beck?

"Life is strange," Stewart Beck mused one December evening as he and Father Gelasius walked through Sing Sing's great steel gate into the damp and chilling twilight.

"Life is strange, and God's work is stranger still," he continued, "In my own life I've seen the finest good— Kathryn—come into it as a result of something that wasn't good at all. Not good at all. I won't say what—even to you, Father. Maybe, someday I will. I don't know. Maybe something good can come of her passing."

Gelasius comprehended fully well of what Warden Beck spoke, and, as winter's winds buffeted their faces, grew convinced that Stewart Beck did not fully comprehend of what he spoke—and that if Gelasius Bryant never told him, Stewart Beck never would.

"Maybe, good did not come from evil," said Gelasius, reflecting on how a young Stewart Beck had dared to love and care for a young woman who had carried a child not his own. It was an old story, as old as Joseph and Mary, and Fr. Gelasius hoped that by saying anything at all he had not pushed forward a door that opened into his own personal chasm.

"What do you mean by that, Father? Good certainly did come from it! We were very happy together. I could not have been blessed more."

"I am not saying you were not blessed. I am saying, Stewart, that perhaps the good you two enjoyed resulted from *other* good. Maybe she—or even *you*—did something that fostered the good that followed. Think about it. And, yes, maybe some new good, may yet come to you as a result of what has gone before. Good in *this* life—or the next."

Stewart Beck did think about it, but he could not think of anything special he had done that might have created the life that he and Kathryn had enjoyed. The damned often do not fathom the scope of their evil. The sainted often fail to comprehend fully their good.

And Father Gelasius Bryant decided that letting the dead stay dead would be the most merciful thing of all for the deceased—and, above all, for the living.

***

"I got a tip for you, Mr. Winchell."

"Have a seat," said the great man motioning to the space in the otherwise empty corner booth he now occupied at Lindy's.

"Who's sleeping with who?" Winchell growled. He seemed smaller and greyer in person, but, if anything, the raw energy and force of will he exuded seemed even more powerful in person than on the radio or between little dot-dot-dots.

"Nobody's sleeping with anybody," stammered a very nervous Foxy Renard.

"Than why are you bothering me?"

"I got information on this Eddie Marek you're so interested in."

"Like what? And, hey, just who the hell are you anyway."

"Is this man bothering you Mr. Winchell," asked the waiter who had just placed a cup of coffee on Winchell's table. Walter Winchell drank a lot of coffee.

"Everybody bothers me, Morty—even you," snarled Winchell. "We love you too, Mr. Walter," Morty responded, as he moved away. At Lindy's the waiters were as tough as the Broadway columnists.

"Spit it out," said Winchell.

"I'm John Renard, Mr. Winchell. I was in on those robberies with Marek."

"Then why aren't you in jail, punk?"

"I was."

"But you ain't now," Winchell shot back.

"I got out in a year."

"Paroled?"

"No, that was my sentence."

Winchell mulled that over as he stirred the sugar cubes in his coffee. He was not dumb. He had not gotten to be Walter

Winchell by being either unintelligent or not being able to think two time zones ahead of people trying to feed him information. Behind every tidbit, every piece of gossip, funneled to him, there was a motive either as bold as brass or as labyrinthine as a serpent's lower intestines. And because every column inch in Walter Winchell's *Daily Mirror* offerings was worth its weight in gold, he weighed every motive and every column inch like a pawn shop jeweler, and, regarding the case of the stranger before him, he had already formed the impression that he was dealing with fourteen-carat gold plate.

"I know he was in on some other jobs," Foxy lied—lied through his yellowing teeth—but he figured that even fake information might be worth something on the Great Fake Way.

"You do, do you?" said Winchell, stirring, stirring, stirring.

"Yeah."

"But, let me guess, you had nothing to do with them."

"No, not me, no."

"Then how do know about them?"

Before Foxy could answer, Winchell's staccato cut him short. "How do you *know* about them?" he fairly shouted.

"This guy—"

"This guy, huh," Winchell interrupted again, "Well, let me set you straight before we waste any more of each other's time. Eddie Marek isn't that big a story to me, so I haven't got time to track down any guys brought to me by other guys who get past the front door at Lindy's and who may—or may not—be named Johnny Renard or Johnny Walker or whatever the hell your name might be. And secondly, mister whoever you are who only served a year when your partner got eight-to-eighteen, you can only sell out a partner once in this town—even on Broadway—and, pal, you've cashed your chit in.

"Now, get the hell out of here so I can have Morty fumigate this booth!"

***

A ballplayer who doesn't play doesn't necessarily have more free time than ballplayers who do. Eddie Marek trained with the Dodgers, sat in the stands and watched their games, traveled with them, and suffered through their often painfully inept performances. But he still possessed sufficient time to tramp the Brooklyn streets, to once again absorb their sights, to peer in store windows, stare at pretty and not-so-pretty girls, and envy the families who struggled to make a living but who had each other.

The families.

He really noticed the kids, the little ones, all bright and shiny as a copper penny, exploding with hope and energy and promise—and innocence. Not like their parents, weary from bills and debt and fear—and from experience, not all innocent. Families made Eddie think. He must have been like those kids once. Yeah, he was. He was going to be a Marine. That happened—not quite as he thought it would, but it did. He was going to be a ballplayer—that *could* still happen. He *never* was supposed to be a con. Boy, he was never supposed to be a lot of things . . .

No kid is.

He should have been happier. He wasn't. The uncertainty had worn him down. It was like being before the Parole Board all over again, only with the deck stacked against him. And not every Dodger seemed supportive. Powell did, but he wasn't sure about Molyneaux. Most of the players seemed OK, if not what you might call friendly, at least not hostile. But some guys never had much to say at all. Some conversations ended a little too awkwardly when Eddie passed by.

He got the message.

Freedom, thought Eddie, walking past the Abraham & Strauss Department Store, *No job. No chances. No nothing. First they pump you up, then they tear you down.* He remembered that Carrie had worked at A&S after his sentencing, and thought for a moment of going in and asking if they knew of her. But who would he ask? And why would they know?

Or care?

A patrol car approached. It seemed to move slower and slower as it drew near. Eddie thought the coppers inside were eying him. Maybe they were. Maybe not. Eddie turned a corner and headed in the opposite direction.

Old fears die hard.

Kenesaw Landis had his fears too, fears of making the wrong decision, of wrecking people's lives, of damaging the great game of baseball, of torpedoing his own reputation and power. Where one fear ended and another began, no one knew, not even Landis. They all existed and collided against each other in the jumble of his decision-making process. His surface was all bluster and piss and vinegar. Inside, Kenesaw's emotions churned like any other human's. Being Kenesaw Mountain Landis only made it *look* easier.

He debated every option, ostensibly bouncing ideas off Lawrence O'Byrne, but, in reality, conversing only with Kenesaw Landis. "Call Powell," he ordered O'Byrne, his brow furrowed, his eyes narrowed, "Tell him I want to see this damn Marek so-and-so here. In private. Next Monday morning. Alone. No one is to know of this meeting. No one. If anyone knows about it, this Eddie Marek person will wish he had never been born—and so will Mr. Sidearm Jack Powell."

Can I Sweep Floors?

"He wants to see you."

Eddie Marek had no idea who in hell Sidearm Jack Powell meant by "he." Marek's blank expression betrayed that. He was a master of the blank expression. It came in very handy behind bars—whether you knew what was going on or not—and *particularly* if you knew perfectly well what was going on.

This time he really possessed no clue.

"*Landis* wants to see you."

Cops, truant officers, chief petty officers, the Magistrate's Court of the City of New York, innumerable jail and prison guards, Warden Stewart Beck, one parole board, various reporters—even Kate Smith—had all grilled Eddie Marek.

Nothing scared him as much as the thought of facing Kenesaw Mountain Landis.

Powell informed only Marek—not even Al Molyneaux. He concocted a story about Marek being laid up and too sick to go anywhere. Marek told only his parole officer. He boarded the Broadway Limited not at Penn Station but at Newark, and traveled alone to Chicago. Too many people in the Windy City would have recognized Powell.

Reaching Chicago, his destination was Landis' apartment. Meeting in the little man's Michigan Avenue office was too risky. Eddie walked under leaden skies, from Depression-haunted neighborhoods, past jobless, threadbare men and shuttered storefronts to Gold Coast streets, block-by-block ever more affluent, past chauffeured limousines and finely-coifed women walking similarly immaculately groomed dogs. He entered a white-and-black marble lobby, his tentative footsteps echoing and re-echoing against its gleaming walls. He edged past a stern and wary, gold-braided doorman, and into the oak-paneled elevator.

The darkest, heaviest Negress he had ever seen silently opened apartment 4-04's door. The Judge—Kenesaw, himself—stood behind her. His apartment seemed as high-ceilinged as any courtroom. From chandelier to ashtrays, it had been furnished in

258   Dance Hall: A Novel of Sing Sing

the sleekest, most modern Art Deco. In his mind's eye, the most inaccurate of eyes, Marek had pictured it as being more traditional in style. But, in any case, he wasn't there to file a report on the decor for *Good Housekeeping*. Landis offered Marek his choice of coffee or tea. Eddie feared he'd spill whatever the judge gave him on himself, but thought he'd best be polite. He requested coffee, cream, and sugar, but never took a drop.

"Nobody besides Mr. Powell knows you're here?"

"No, sir. . . . Well, just my parole officer."

"Keep it that way. Take a seat, young man."

Marek sat. These art-deco chairs weren't as comfortable as they looked. Particularly today. Landis strode toward Marek, in patented cross-examination mode, one Eddie Marek knew fairly well. He considered Landis's version particularly dramatic.

"Was the Amsterdam Avenue job on Wednesday night, November 19, 1930 your first offense?"

"No, it was my . . . fifth."

"Five? Fifth?" Landis knew damn well it was Eddie's fifth but wasn't about to forego any opportunity to rattle him.

"Yes, Commissioner, yes."

"Not exactly an innocent were you?"

"No," Eddie murmured.

"No," Landis sneered.

Landis moved a few steps away from Marek, saying nothing, not a word. If Landis's glare unnerved Marek, his silence unsettled him still more.

The silence continued—empty, hostile, tomblike, and calculated. It lasted but a few seconds but had its effect, like a pressure point in jujitsu or water surging through a weakened portion of a dam, ripping though steel-reinforced concrete as though it were mere dime store cardboard. Weeks of uncertainly pushed Marek beyond his limits, loosening his control, shattering the emotionless mask he hoped to hide once more behind into a thousand jagged shards.

"What the hell is this about? You call me here all the way just to slam the door in my face? You bring me here to turn your back on me?"

Landis circled once more, slowly and deliberately, still maintaining his unnerving silence, seemingly inhumanly unaffected by Marek's outburst. His sang-froid unnerved Marek even more. He fairly shouted out his anger and frustration.

"Well, let me ask you something, Your Honor. What the hell am I supposed to do with the rest of my life? I'm not even thirty. Do I get the door slammed on me forever? What *do* I get to do? Can I sweep floors? Dig ditches? Clean toilets? Maybe I can't even be trusted to do that? Why bother to let me out? What am I supposed to do Mr. Landis? What am I supposed to *do*? What do *you* want me to do?"

Landis' eyes scanned the room from right to left, and though his frame of vision moved past Edward Stanley Marek, he seemed to stare quite through him, as they he were not present in the least. Landis paused what seemed an eternity before he spoke.

"Maybe you should have thought of that before you went into the stick-up business."

The Rail

Walter Winchell had not lost all interest in the Eddie Marek story. He just occasionally got very picky about his sources.

And that was why when Eddie picked up a copy of the *Daily Mirror* bulldog edition, midway through Winchell's column he found this little item:

> *Three strikes for Marek? Word out of the Windy City is that Horsehide Honcho K. M. Landis will inform a certain jailbird that he is past tense from the national pastime . . . Once a bum . . . Never a Bum . . .*

So that was the deal. Whatever hopes Eddie Marek had still retained were the dreams of a fool. Nick Strecker had warned him a long time ago. "Sure, kid, sure," he had said peering out from inside his cell, "Believe exactly what you want." Eddie had dared to believe. But now, reading Walter Winchell, he no longer did, and the emptiness inside him where hope had once resided rattled about like the great clanging of bells amidst the world's shortest funeral procession. He too had warned himself not to believe, not to hope, never again to ever really care. But he had.

And it was a mistake.

He entered a Nedick's lunch counter, sliding his nickels down for a hot dog and an orange drink. He bit into his dog and overheard the conversation a few stools away.

"Hey, Winchell here says the Dodgers can't sign Marek!"

"Yeah, so what? Who the hell needs him? Who says he can play? And even if he could, what would you want with a character like him stinking up your roster, anyway?"

"Big loss! What they need is a new general manager! Somebody who won't be hanging around jail yards for talent! If old Sidearm spent less time at Sing Sing and more scouting the Pacific Coast League, Brooklyn might win half of a double-header every now and then!"

"'Battling Marine Marek'! Yeah, I guess we can file that one under 'cheap publicity stunt.' Maybe Mr. Jailbird can get job sitting flagpoles or at Hubert's Flea Circus—if the fleas don't mind him!!"

Everybody laughed. The three men down the counter. The clerk in the white jacket and stiff white paper cap behind it. Everybody laughed but Eddie Marek, who left his unfinished wiener and orange drink where they were and vanished into the darkening night before him.

He roamed the streets, heading nowhere in particular, morosely alone with his thoughts. From a first floor tenement window a radio blared out Walter Winchell's weekly broadcast. More of the same: Kenesaw Landis was ready to write *finis* to Eddie Marek's career. Nothing that wasn't in the papers. It just hurt even more to have it dogging you at every step, stalking you at every lunch counter and every city block.

Eddie Marek lost heart.

A light mist began falling. Marek kept walking anyway. He neared the East River. Block by block, Norman Megley trailed him. At the long, sloping approach to the Brooklyn Bridge Eddie began crossing over to Manhattan. Roughly half way over he halted. The wet summer breeze fell steadily upon his face as he leaned against its rail and stared forlornly across the water. Megley, his right hand gripped firmly on his fedora, both to keep his headgear from blowing out to Governor's Island and to shield his face from Eddie, kept moving past as unobtrusively as he could until he reached another patch of darkness, a point where he thought might stand safely beyond notice. Eddie remained motionless, his silhouette barely visible against the night sky.

Norman Megley put two and two together. He formulated a little theory that he hoped was not true.

Jumper.

Megley had also seen Winchell's column. He knew full well what Eddie must be thinking and knew far better than most the sordid pressures he had been subjected to. Now, Norman Megley also stood and waited on the Brooklyn Bridge, leaning over the same rail, near enough to Eddie Marek to know that he might chose this night to end his troubles, far enough removed to be unable to do anything about it if he did.

And Norman Megley was indeed right. For Eddie Marek the line separating life and death now was drawn exceedingly fine.

A very thin woman, in a long dark dress and of a certain age, coming from the Manhattan side, limped past Megley, eying him carefully as she did. As she approached Eddie, however, her gait grew still slower and more deliberate. She paused ten feet beyond Marek. She stood there silently for the longest time, a black shawl protecting her from the evening mist, looking back toward the megawatt-illuminated Gotham skyline that lay before them.

"Something bothering you, son?" she said, her voice dusky and heavily-accented.

Her question startled Eddie. He saw a woman's eyes boring though him, into his very soul, all the way back past that Nedick's and to Sing Sing and to a robbery on Amsterdam Avenue.

"What's it to you, Lady? Can't a man stand on a bridge in peace?"

"Not if he is not at peace."

"And who says I ain't?"

"You do."

"Like hell I do!"

"Like hell you *do*."

Eddie didn't answer. He peered down at the East River nearly three hundred feet below him, avoiding his interrogator's haunting gaze, simply hoping she would go away.

"What is it? A woman? Money? Your job? Are you not in good health?"

"You got a million questions, don't you Lady? But listen, you seem to know all about me—so you tell me!"

"Actually, I do not know you at all. I just know you look like you are not here only to see the view."

"Yeah, well, you're right," Eddie said, still avoiding looking at her, "Mostly it's a job. But there was a woman too. It's life. That's all. It's just life!"

"It isn't life you're here for."

An empty silence filled the evening air, a silence that spoke more than words.

"You have a mother? A father?"

"Yeah. My mother's still alive."

"What would she think—being left behind?"

Eddie pondered that. He looked up at her. "I ought to pitch *you* overboard!" he said, advancing toward her.

"Go ahead."

Her calm only startled Eddie more. "Look, leave me alone! What am I to you? To anybody? What do you care? What are you doing here anyway?"

"Do you really want to know?"

"Yeah, I do! I'm all ears tonight. You'd be surprised at how good my hearing is."

"Two years again last month, my youngest daughter—a beautiful girl—walked across this bridge just like you have. She had lost her job and could not find another one. And she stopped here just as you have. They found her the next afternoon, and I do not know why she no think no one cared because everybody did. Or that there was no any hope. Because there is always hope once you walk off the bridge. Now I walk here every night and I eye everybody on this rail, and most nights I keep on walking. But sometimes I see something, and sometimes I stop. And tonight I stop."

"Oh . . . Oh."

A minute later Eddie Marek walked back toward Brooklyn.

Norman Megley followed. The woman at the rail watched until both had vanished into the darkness at the Brooklyn end of the bridge.

"Believe exactly what you want," is the voice from the grave that mocked Eddie Marek as he had walked on to that bridge not long before—just a mere lifetime ago.

He now heard a different voice, as he set shoe leather once more upon cracked Brooklyn concrete. It was Percy Graham's.

"There's more people in life willing to help you then you ever know."

And right now, baseball player or not, Eddie Marek thought it might be true.

Verdict

The next morning, amid the noisy din of the *Chicago Tribune* newsroom, from inside his disorganized glass-paneled office, reporter George MacDonald's editor shouted for him.

"Get your sorry carcass over to Landis's office! He's ruling on Marek at 10:30!"

"Ah!" MacDonald responded, "The great American sports story!"

"The great American *letdown*," said Frank Arsenault, who like all editors fancied himself both cynical and omniscient, "Landis is lowering the boom on young Mr. Marek. The party's over. Write '30' to this one."

In Brooklyn, Eddie Marek awaited judgment. He knew a bit more than George MacDonald did, but only a bit. He knew about his secret conference with Landis. He knew about the Commissioner's glowers and his silences, his biting questions. He knew what was said—and *not* said. Left most significantly unspoken was the Judge's verdict.

Reporters jammed Kenesaw Landis's office, standing room only.

"We all know why we're here, gentlemen. Let's get to it. Mr. Edward Stanley Marek Jr."

"Is . . ." Harold Derbyshire of Hearst's *Chicago American* began.

"No questions," Landis cut him off, "This is my statement. You can listen and get a copy when I'm over—or you can read about it in your competition."

And so, Judge Kenesaw Mountain Landis began.

"President Lloyd of the National League has made his decision. The Brooklyn club has properly filed its appeal. I have reviewed that appeal. In the course of the considerable publicity in this case, there have been created erroneous impressions which require correction."

Landis's tone assumed a sarcastic sing-song.

"It has been represented that the offense committed, the basis of the ruling, grew out of an 'escapade' wherein Marek, 'drunk' and 'hungry,' was misled into accompanying 'an older man'—or 'a tough guy'—"

Arsenault was right. Marek was sunk. George MacDonald bit his unlit stogie so hard he feared he might sever it.

Landis continued.

". . . into a store, only to discover that his companion's purpose was robbery, which the companion accomplished by using a gun, while Marek, unarmed and merely obeying his companions orders, took '$5 or $10' from the cash register; that this was the only offense in which Marek ever was involved; and that Marek pleaded guilty out of consideration for his companion's wife and children and to lessen his companion's punishment by 'taking the rap' for him."

He paused and added an aside: "That's crap. There wasn't even any Mrs. Renard, let alone any little Renards? Who writes this stuff? What sentimental BILGE!"

He reflected on what he had said.

"Don't print that last remark!"

The *Herald-Examiner*'s Ray Hutcheson, a whimsical little bastard, ostentatiously pretended to cross it out of his notes. "Marek is finished," Derbyshire of the *American* whispered.

"The official record certifies that Marek and Renard entered the store together, held up the clerk with their loaded revolvers, and took $76.25 from the cash register."

McDonald gave Derbyshire a brief nod. Yup, game over.

"The amount is not important—it depended upon what was in the cash register—but $5 or $10 is more consistent with the 'drunk' and 'hungry' representations. Marek was very fortunate he was not compelled to plead guilty to robbery in the first degree, with a mandatory twenty-year sentence. President Lloyd's ruling is essentially correct."

"This case originally presented only a general question involving the hiring of felons, which was decided properly."

"Hooey!" McDonald thought but only to himself. He wasn't about to risk more judicial ire.

Kenesaw droned on: "Since then a new situation has arisen. Conditions have been created as to the destructive effect, upon

Marek's rehabilitation, of not permitting him to enter baseball employment."

What did he say? thought MacDonald. *A new situation?*

"This was not contemplated by the ruling of the National League," Landis continued, "Reputable people have expressed to me their belief that there has been a complete reformation in Marek's character and their confidence in his earnest intent to regain an honorable position in society. Solely for these reasons, Marek *will be allowed to play.*"

That was it. The reporters dropped their pretenses of impartiality. They let out a cheer. Harold Derbyshire slapped MacDonald hard upon the back. MacDonald's cheroot tumbled out of his mouth—on to the Judge's carpet.

"Edward S. Marek can play baseball," Landis concluded, "However, we will not make a mockery of the game—or exploit this young man for cheap publicity purpose."

"Mr. Marek can play regular season National League games for the Brooklyn Dodgers. He will not be allowed to play in any exhibition games, save for spring training, for the Dodgers or otherwise."

"OK," he added, "Get your copies from O'Byrne and get the hell out. And MacDonald—PICK UP THAT CIGAR BEFORE YOU GO! This is *not* the city room of the *Tribune!*"

With that, Kenesaw Landis launched a wad of chewing tobacco-soaked spit at the dented brass spittoon he kept at the side of his desk. It hit its mark.

"Haven't missed yet," he winked at O'Byrne, "Haven't missed yet."

***

George MacDonald picked up a half-smoked cigar. Sidearm Powell picked up his receiver. He listened and nodded. He did not smile. He looked toward the anxious, very anxious, Marek. Breaking into a broad grin, he uttered but a single word . . . "Yes."

Eddie Marek knew what he meant.

"When do I play, Mr. Powell?"

"Saturday. Here. Against Philadelphia."

The announcement crackled out over the Sing Sing loudspeaker system. Every cellblock and shop and office cheered so loudly, it was difficult to hear the voice on the other end of Principal Keeper McKaig's phone—a call of such urgency he took it in A Block.

"What?" McKaig shouted.

"I'll say it again," said the voice on the other end of the line, its volume also rising.

McKaig listened intently. His caller repeated what he had to say, only slower and louder. McKaig blanched. He hung up. Matthew Harding stood nearby. He'd never seen such an expression on his superior.

McKaig looked up.

"Myers . . . He forged his own release papers!"

Which was all Stewart Beck needed.

***

Ebbets Field's 32,000 seats usually sat nearly all pristinely empty.

The Dodgers' home field lay on Flatbush's Sullivan Place, barely three miles from Eddie's old Williamsburg stomping grounds. It was no Baker Bowl, but years of bad teams and worse attendance had taken their toll. A coat or two of Sherwin-Williams wouldn't have hurt the place, but Sidearm Jack Powell didn't quite have enough nickels to spare for paint, let alone for painters.

So Ebbets Field obviously wasn't Yankee Stadium or even the Polo Grounds. But neither was it like hardscrabble Sing Sing, with every bounce an adventure and every slide capable of tearing open the flannel of your uniform or the flesh of your leg.

How different it was for Eddie to stand on its diamond— how magical, with its manicured turf and finely-raked basepaths, real dugouts, genuine—if somewhat pungent—locker rooms, real everything, but most wonderfully of all, after the game . . . you could leave.

Marek's presence on the Dodgers served to demonstrate how fleeting fame was. All the reporters, all the cameras, buzzed around Eddie. He was it. The big cheese. The star. The sudden center of public attention.

He hadn't done anything except serve time; he had not played an inning. But there he now existed, like an R-K-O movie star waltzing down the red carpet at Grauman's Chinese Theater, grinning for his adoring fans, squinting at the volleys of exploding flashbulbs. And yet, on his new team, the threadbare Dodgers, there was a real celebrity, a celebrity everybody now ignored.

"Who's the little guy?" Marek had asked Sidearm Jack Powell upon his arrival with the team, nodding toward a red-faced human beer barrel wearing sweat-stained Brooklyn flannels. The little guy lurched toward them. With each step, Marek's realization grew: *This palooka is shit-faced. He reeked of gin. Wow! Is this what they call professional baseball?*

The little man wobbled forward, cloaked in his own alcoholic daze.

"Jocko," said Sidearm Jack Powell, "I'd like you to meet Mr. Edward Marek, 'The Battling Marine' Marek. Eddie, I'd like you to meet Jocko Mulrow."

Jocko Mulrow.

Jeez, mused Marek, *this is the great Jocko Mulrow, holder of the major league record for RBIs in a season, holder of the National League record for homers in a season? This? And I'm not respectable enough to play?*

"Pleased to meet you Mr. Mulrow."

Mr. Mulrow was, however, not pleased to meet Mr. Marek. Mr. Mulrow, an outfielder by trade, wasn't soliciting any more competition, thank you. Life was tough enough hitting .263 with three homers.

Fame was indeed fleeting. Being washed-up was forever.

"Pleased to meet you, Eddie," Jocko Mulrow, nonetheless, mumbled and lurched off.

Time neared to clear a spot on the Dodgers roster for Eddie Marek.

"Jocko!" yelled Al Molyneaux, "Sidearm Jack wants to see you."

Jocko's spikes clomped up to Sidearm Jack's office.

"You wanted to see me, Mr. Powell?"

"Sidearm Jack's got good news for you, Jocko. We've sold your contract to the Browns."

No, it wasn't good news at all.

Not even for the Browns.

Debut

The trolley cars to Ebbets Field were crammed to capacity that Saturday afternoon. Usually, they possessed seats to spare. But today, the day of Eddie Marek's debut, each car was jammed, a miracle of sorts and doubly so with leaden skies threatening.

Fans pushed through the turnstiles, milling about inside the park's once-grand rotunda, genuinely and pleasantly surprised to see so many of each other present, though diehard customers who usually enjoyed their choice of any seats in the place, now kvetched at no longer being quite so privileged. On the field and in the clubhouses, reporters demanded interviews. Newsreel and still photographers jockeyed for position.

Pierre DeKay sat scowling behind his team's dugout. He wasn't about to pretend he enjoyed losing—though as owner of the Phillies he certainly had enough opportunity. Sidearm Jack Powell, Father Gelasius Bryant, and Matt Harding sat behind Brooklyn's. They weren't about to pretend they *didn't* enjoy this day. Stewart Beck, however, was prominent by his absence, having to content himself with the afternoon's static-filled radio broadcast from far-off Philadelphia. All Superintendent MacFarlane needed was for Stewart to take a day off from Sing Sing for a ball game in Brooklyn—even if it were a Saturday—to launch another tirade. Nervous regarding failed—as well as successful—escapes, Beck feared his next misstep might prove professionally fatal.

Eddie wished that Warden Beck might be there. He wished that Kathryn and Mr. Graham and Lemuel could have been there as well. Above all, he wanted Carrie there.

But she, and they, could not be—or were not—there.

Norman Megley, however, was, a half-eaten box of crackerjack in his left hand, ensconced in a fine box seat—on his own dime, no longer on Nathan Lloyd's National League payroll.

"You know, I've never known you to take in a ball game, Mr. Megley," said his blond companion.

"I've developed quite the antipathy towards the Philadelphia Phillies, Louise," said Megley.

"Come to think of it, Mr. Megley, so have I."

"That's why I work with you Louise—you've always had character."

There were, however, those fans of less character or, at least, possessing less charitable attitudes toward the Brooklyn club's latest acquisition. Parading through Ebbets Fields' narrow aisles were four young men from Manhattan—Giant fans— costumed in two-inch wide black-and-white stripes, bound together by mock oversized prison chains. As they marched, they serenaded the crowd—and Eddie—with lyrics that went something like this:

> *Ed-die Mar-ek*
> *Ed-die Mar-ek*
> *Sing Sing's Best*
> *Will Fail the Test!*
> *Ed-die Mar-ek*
> *Ed-die Mar-ek*
> *He's Guilty*
> *Of Strike Three!*
> *Ed-die Mar-ek*
> *Ed-die Mar-ek!*

Sidearm Jack Powell had, meanwhile, provided his paying customers with entertainment of a more positive sort—a twenty-one-gun salute from Battery B of the 105th Field Artillery, the brass band from the grand Moorish-domed Kismet Shriners' temple he belonged to over on Herkimer Street, a color guard from the Legion post down at Sheepshead Bay, and a reasonably talented, reasonably attractive, Norwegian girl from Bay Ridge attempting the national anthem. It was all very grand, and, maybe, just maybe, Sidearm Jack reasoned, if the customers liked what they saw, they'd return when Eddie Marek was no longer a novelty, even if the team around him still stunk.

Sidearm Jack had everything under control—save for the weather.

On the very last note of Miss Sigrid Knutsen's rendition of the national anthem, the "brave" of "the home of the brave," the first splat of rain landed, a huge raindrop that preceded by scant moments great torrents of water, drenching the diamond, soaking anyone sheltered under the grandstand.

This downpour ended in fifteen to twenty minutes. It left in its wake, however, a field so waterlogged that under normal circumstances the umpires would have merely waited the requisite interval and ordered whoever remained home.

Not this time.

Fifteen-thousand-seven hundred paying customers, some damper than others, sat huddled in the stands, Brooklyn's biggest crowd since Opening Day. No, this game was going to be played. Sidearm Jack Powell had bills to pay.

Men sloshed two-gallon tins of Tydol Flying A gasoline onto the sodden infield. Then—WOOOOSH!!!!—Ebbets Field's infield became a fiery diamond, spewing brackish smoke into the grandstand and the surrounding neighborhood, the afternoon's damp air now reeking of gasoline. The grounds crew took up hoses and buckets, and watched everything very, very carefully. The fires died, and though the outfield still resembled the Everglades, the infield was deemed playable.

The Dodgers trotted to their respective positions, Marek among them, or, at least, he planned to be among them, but Al Molyneaux halted him on the dugout steps.

Eight Dodgers assumed their places, solitary sentries at attention on some vast rain-soaked parade ground. Centerfield, however, remained vacant. Molyneaux patted Eddie on the behind and said, "OK, pally." Lusty cheers erupted from the grandstands, quickly merging into one great, solid roar. Eddie's first instinct was to sprint toward center, but he soon realized the occasion demanded not speed, but a stately trot, not too fast, not too slow.

Dignity.

Pacing.

He reached centerfield in due time, bent down, placing his hands upon his knees and peering toward home plate. The crowd, and most had remained, cheered lustily. But some booed, not as many as cheered, but enough did to chill Eddie Marek's spirit.

Walter Winchell had done his work all too well.

The delay had only increased the nervousness of the Dodgers starting pitcher, a fidgety, little lefty named Herman Ross. Rain delays never benefit any starting pitcher, and Ross walked the first Philadelphia batter on four pitches—none of which came particularly close to the mud-streaked plate. He fell behind the next man but still induced him to line out, then surrendered a single to left before settling down to escape the inning unscathed. Marek sloshed in from center field. He had no time to worry about his first at bat. Al Molyneaux was batting him leadoff.

In the on-deck circle Eddie Marek swung a couple of leaded bats to get loose and carefully spied the Philadelphia starter's warm-ups. Twenty-eight year old right-hander "Crooning Mike" Baia was, strangely enough, not only baseball's second best tenor, able to go note for note with Al Molyneaux, he was the Phillies's ace. Last season he had injured his elbow and pitched so poorly that Pierre DeKay had slashed his salary a full thirty percent, but right now, Mike Baia's right elbow felt much better, thank you. He ranked a respectable fourth in the league in E.R.A. and swore to prove DeKay wrong and recoup his lost bankroll. Baia wasn't about to be let some ex-con get in his way.

Eddie flung down his leaded bats. He planted his spikes in the dirt near the very edge of the batter's box, making him vulnerable to pitches on the outside part of the plate. Six photographers formed a ragged row along the muddy first base line, furiously snapping away. Not far behind the third base dugout, Father Gelasius discreetly made the sign of the cross in Eddie's direction. Methodist Matt Harding noticed but wasn't about to protest—Crooning Mike Baia looked mighty tough out there.

Flashbulbs kept popping. A stubble-faced, raspy-voiced fan bellowed to the photographers, "Get out of there; let him hit."

The crowd followed his lead, echoing his command. The cameramen slunk back toward the tarpaulins.

"Play ball!" home plate umpire Dick Neeley, a veteran of fourteen years in the league, bellowed.

Toward the rear of the third base grandstand, one individual grew unusually impatient. He had waited too long already. He wanted to see Eddie bat and then to be on his way, toward the Hudson River piers and then on to Havana, in fact, to be as far from folks like Father Gelasius as possible. Sandy Myers, now sporting a freshly grown moustache and eyewear of the finest window glass, was more sentimental than most people suspected, but he also was no fool.

He wanted to get out of Ebbets Field as fast as possible.

Philadelphia catcher Elmer "Doc" Leggett flashed two fingers to Baia—a curve. Baia, however, wanted a fastball, a quick strike to get ahead on the count. Then, he could get cute.

Baia got his way. He delivered a fastball, high and hard, just off the plate. Marek swung anyway. He missed by a good two inches.

"Stee-rike one!"

"Ya bum! Ya blind bum!" Norman Megley's blond associate screamed like a banshee as she jumped from her seat.

"Uh, Louise, he *swung*," Megley reminded his assistant as he jerked her back down.

"I get excited, Mr. Megley."

Baia too had noticed Eddie swing Marek had betrayed his anxiousness. He could be fooled, and that was a good thing to know.

Leggett again flashed two fingers. Curve. Baia nodded approvingly. Marek coiled. A roundhouse breaking ball landed outside. Marek coiled his bat, ready to swing. This time he kept his cool and held up. The ball snapped into Doc Leggett's mitt.

"Ball!"

Baia went back to his fastball. Marek grunted and swung hard. His bat ripped through the air above home plate like a Damascus steel blade. WHACK!! He connected, but his timing remained slightly off. The ball sailed into the stands above the

Philadelphia dugout, coming tantalizingly close to beaning DeKay, though not as close as Marek would have liked—that would have been right between the eyes—but close enough.

"Stee-riii-eke two!" Neeley blared. He tossed Baia a new ball.

Marek's bat had cracked. He retreated to the dugout to select a new one. "Guard the plate, pally," said Molyneaux.

Sage advise, Marek thought, those ex-pitchers really know their hitting.

Baia tucked his glove under his arm, rubbed up the ball, and looked in. Again, he shook off Doc Leggett. These guys were *not* on the same wavelength. Finally, Crooning Mike saw a signal he liked—changeup. He nodded, went into his windup, kicked high, and threw.

Marek coiled and swung.

Foul tip. Leggett couldn't snag it. It skittered like a top into the dirt. Marek remained alive—barely.

"One-and-two!"

"A hundred bucks if you strike him out!" Pete DeKay screamed. Crooning Mike would have done it for free.

Baia's next offering veered high and inside towards Marek's head—a purpose pitch. Some might theorize the purpose being to separate Marek's head from his shoulders. It wasn't. Baia merely meant to back Eddie off the plate, to cause him to hesitate, to teach him fear. His control, however, remained suspect, and his pitch came far nearer to Marek than he would have liked.

Eddie tumbled backwards into the soggy, gasoline-seared ground. He got up and brushed himself off.

"Guess it got away from him, kid," Doc Leggett apologized. Marek said nothing. He was clearly pissed off.

Baia, his back to the plate, took extra time rubbing up the ball. No warnings on the next pitch. No curves. No cute stuff. The count was two-and-two. His next pitch would be a fastball.

Marek swung, his bat tracing a compact, measured, but blindingly fast, arc. WHAP!! The ball rocketed toward right center. Philadelphia's center and right fielders raced after it.

Centerfielder Joe Fleming was closest. He accelerated, drawing nearer and nearer and nearer, but the ball kept tailing away and away and away. He dove. S-P-L-A-T!!! The ball dropped safely a good five feet in front of him. Ball and fielder both lay there in the sodden indignity of the wet Ebbets Field grass.

Louise jumped from her seat, bouncing up and down on her Cuban heels. Norman Begley jumped with her. Matt Harding slapped Father Gelasius hard on the back—before sheepishly thinking better of it. In Ossining, Stewart Beck's radio had long since lost the battle of the static—and he had no idea of what was transpiring.

Pierre DeKay bit his lip, sat, and stared.

Save for the rain, the ball would have rolled toward the right center fence. The Phillies rightfielder, a guy named Stanley Schine, sloshed over, retrieved it, steadied himself for a split second and launched a throw toward second base. Marek had exited the batter's box like a rabbit, tearing headlong for first base, knowing if the ball got anywhere near the fence he was going for third. Schine, however, had retrieved the ball far quicker than Eddie would have liked. He'd be lucky to make second.

And he now knew it.

Stan Schine could run like hell—even through swampland —and threw like hell too. His throw this afternoon wasn't merely good. It was a rifle shot—straight as a string, headed for the Philadelphia shortstop's glove. The ball would be waiting for Eddie Marek, making him look like a damned fool, less than a busher—for trying, and *failing*, to stretch a single into a double.

Eddie had two choices—getting cute with a hook slide or going in slashing, spikes first, and slicing the horsehide right out of the shortstop's hands.

Eddie Marek selected option two. Now was no time in his life for subtlety.

Besides, who expected subtlety from an ex-con?

Eddie gritted his teeth and slid hard . . . and knocked the ball loose. Jarred from the shortstop's well-worn glove, it lay there, obviously, *beautifully*, on the ground.

"SAFE!!!"

Eddie Marek popped back up.

Sanford Myers elbowed his way past a row of still cheering fans, politely past a blue-jacketed cop or two, out to Sullivan Place, where he flagged a passing Yellow Cab.

"Where to, pal?"

"Pier 87, and make it fast. I'm behind schedule."

Lutz's Ritz Garden

Ebbets Field's dank locker rooms were no more or less aromatic than any other, their pale green walls no less chipped or peeling. Suffice it to say that anyone even but moderately familiar with New York's penal system might have felt right at home among it crude cubicles and splintered benches. But tonight, the Dodgers home locker room contained not merely mud-caked, sweat-stained flannel uniforms, aching biceps, and water-logged spikes, but distinctly mixed emotions. The Bums had once more lost. Mike Baia had simply proved too much for them. But Baia—and pro ball itself—had not overwhelmed Eddie Marek. He had doubled his first time up. He slashed two sharp singles in his remaining three appearances; and while the infield was too sodden for base stealing, his aggressive base-running so goaded Mike Baia that, attempting a hurried pick-off attempt to second base, that he fired his throw into the dirt. It skittered into shallow center field, and Eddie scampered to third base, coming home on a sacrifice fly to deep right a few pitches later.

And so, Brooklyn's dismal squad finally held in its not always dependable fingers reasonable cause for celebration—a cause named Edward Stanley Marek.

"Hey, we gotta take Eddie out tonight," boomed Eddie's closest pal on the roster, outfielder Vern Chapman. The North Carolinian Chapman required little reason to howl, as several major league managers had found, if not to their surprise, to their displeasure.

"You take him out," responded John Hayes, a catcher who could squeeze a nickel until the buffalo defecated. Spenders like Hayes were keeping this Depression going. Teammates like Hayes made Marek fear he remained not entirely welcome.

Chapman wouldn't take no for an answer. "Ah, you guys are pikers! C'mon who's in?"

Only two players joined them—third baseman Hap Kellert, an older guy from Minnesota, and a Jersey City kid named Stan "Stonefingers" Koski. As his nickname hinted, Koski was not long for the National League. They decided on a joint Chapman liked, Lutz's Ritz Garden on Lafayette Avenue. Good fun, good—and loud, danceable—music, and even good food, proclaimed Chapman. "Luxury," he added, "even Bums like us can afford."

Even Sidearm Jack Powell thought his star prospect deserved a night out with the boys. What harm could it do? Time to blow off steam.

It started to pour again. But even with this new torrent ruining his once highly-shined shoes, Eddie Marek, slopping and splashing toward Lutz's, couldn't help but feel and—look—like a million bucks. With three base hits to his credit in tomorrow's *Daily Mirror* box score, Eddie felt more like Adolphe Menjou or Cary Grant attired in a $150 tailor-made tuxedo—tuxedo, hell, white-tie-and-tails—than some jamoke in a $7.50 prison-issue gray suit. He wasn't sloshing into some shot-and-a-beer parlor Vern Chapman had dredged up but was waltzing into the very Stork Club itself, under its great green canopy and past its solid twenty-four-carat gold chain, with flashbulbs popping and brass-buttoned doormen and perky hat-check girls and red-jacketed waiters and white-jacketed bartenders all scraping and fawning after him. *And look over there*, Marek continued fantasizing, *there's Walter Winchell himself at Table 50. He's coming over. He's introducing himself. He wants to apologize. Well, Mr. Winchell, forgive or forget, that's what I say, but, if you don't mind, my caviar's getting cold—or warm—or whatever caviar gets.*

Eddie Marek, slightly damp, very hungry, strode into Lutz's Ritz Garden.

The first whiffs of stale beer and fresh cigarette smoke hit him like a fastball aimed at his jaw. He wasn't in the Stork Club or "21" or any place like that—just some neighborhood joint with fake oil paintings on the walls, a mechanical bowling machine, and a dozen cheesecloth-covered tables. This wasn't where the action was. The action resided in the room next door, where for one week only, the Harvey Gould Orchestra threatened on any given riff to blow the roof off the joint.

"Sit yourself wherever you find space, boys," a stocky middle-aged waiter instructed them, swooping past with a tray of chicken scaloppini.

They sat, parking their curiosity regarding the boisterous next room. Hunger invariably takes precedence over art.

"Four spaghettis. Two with sausage. Two with meatballs. Four salads—nah, to hell with the rabbit food—meatballs *and* sausages for everybody! And four beers. Not in that order, please."

They ate. Not bad, thought Eddie, even considering how small the meatballs were and what a remarkably infinitesimal quotient of meat they contained. No one dared ponder what the sausages contained. They requested more bread—it was free—and more beer—it wasn't. The longer they listened to Mr. Harvey Gould and his boys, the more they like it. It was a sound Eddie could get used to.

Meal finished, pilsner glasses firmly in hand, Marek, Koski, Chapman, and Kellert edged curiously from barroom to dance hall, from diners to dancers, from seconds-on-the-bread gourmands to threadbare boulevardiers.

Stan Koski dropped his glass.

Before Eddie lay a room lined with darkly-varnished wooden booths. Couples danced cheek-to-cheek. Long-time couples. Couples not yet couples but hoping to be couples—or, at least, hoping, nobody would step on anyone's feet.

The Harvey Gould Orchestra sure packed them in.

"Hey, Babe Ruth! How's it going?"

Eddie recognized neither voice nor face. It had taken awhile for him to realize this was what fame was about. They didn't know you, but they thought they did, and a few of them thought they owned you, or at least, part of you. They bought their way into Ebbets Field's cheap seats, saw you on the newsreel at the Paramount or Loew's Messerole, read about you in the *Daily News* or the *Brooklyn Eagle*—or Walter Winchell's column. They knew all about you.

Marek's new friend looked like he'd departed Ebbets Field for the Ritz Garden somewhere about the third inning, caught all the lights, and put his time to bad use since.

Eddie was a little rusty dealing with rummies and a rookie at dealing with drunken fans—unless one counted a couple of the writers covering him. He figured he'd play along. Why be unfriendly?

"Just fine. How you?" he responded with all the beneficence and forbearance the very slightly tipsy display toward the truly inebriated.

"Learning how to hit that curve ball?"

"Curveballs. Screwballs. Knuckleballs. Learning 'em all!"

"How about high balls?" his new friend winked.

"I'll stick with the stuff on tap," Marek winked back, ". . . in training, you know."

"Yeah, training . . .," Mr. High Ball pondered. An idea germinated.

"Beer is the hard stuff with training wheels on!" he confided and trundled off.

"Words to live by, mate," Chapman nudged Marek.

Eddie leaned against the wall. Nursing his Schaeffer's, he listened to the orchestra, carefully observing the swirling mass of humanity before him—but paying more attention to the swirling mass of femininity before him. Maybe he'd even take a turn on the hardwood dance floor. If not tonight, some other night. Plenty of time. No hurry.

All the time in the world.

Something caught his eye. A flash of platinum blonde—that strange Jean Harlow shade that flowed not merely from a bottle but from a frightfully toxic bottle. That coiffure bobbed like a silvery cork adrift upon on a sea of blue serge and pink chiffon. Even Mr. High Ball couldn't have missed it.

The platinum kept moving around the floor, but soon something else—or rather, someone else—soon caught his eye, oddly enough, always with her face turned away from him or obscured by her partner or someone else in the crowd. And her partner . . . yes . . . her partner looked all too familiar to Eddie Marek.

Yes, there was no mistaking *him*.

But her—he couldn't escape puzzling about her.

"You dancing or watching tonight, Eddie?" Chapman interrupted.

"Watching."

And then he saw her, just a bit, then more, and then a bit more, and with each bit the realization grew and with that realization the desire that it not be so.

Her hair wasn't that short.

She was thinner.

She wasn't as hard.

She was younger.

Of course, she was younger . . . when . . . when they knew each other, when they danced together . . .

When *they* were together.

She didn't seem to see him. That was good.

"It's a small world, boys. It's the smallest damn world I've even seen," Eddie muttered.

"What'd you say?" Stonefingers Koski inquired.

Marek didn't answer. He wasn't ignoring Koski. He didn't hear him for all the noise, not the sound of the Harvey Gould Orchestra or the tumult of the Ritz Garden patrons or the tinkling of glasses or the rattle of waitresses and waiters toting their round metal beer trays, but for the noise flooding his head and making it swim round and round. He didn't know where to turn—toward her or out the door and into the rain and back to anywhere but here—or to just stand frozen, praying the whole thing would pass, would somehow disappear.

The dance ended. She and her partner walked off for a breather, to sit one out, to grab another drink.

Marek's head spun faster. What was *she* doing here, *now*? Had she preceded him here? Had she just arrived? Had fate made *him* follow *her* here?

But first, the basic question:

Was it her? Was it *really* her?

And *him*? Was it for *him* that she abandoned him?

A million questions. Only one answer: Yes, it was *her*.

It was about this time, that she too answered a question.

Yes, it was *him*.

Carrie Marek had indeed seen Eddie and had his advantage. She knew he was now free. She knew he was a ballplayer. She knew, *dammit*, that he was in Brooklyn. You couldn't miss it. Everybody knew it.

And he was *here*.

And so, quite by chance—evil, evil chance—was *Foxy Renard*. Carrie had never graced Lutz's previously, her presence this evening stemming from a girl friend, a Miss Bea Levi, having read a tiny display ad on the movie page of yesterday's *Brooklyn Eagle* promoting the band's appearance. Had Carrie ever previously graced Lutz's Ritz Garden she might have learned that it was among Mr. Renard's preferred Brooklyn hangouts—and might never have visited there again.

Miss Levi and Mrs. Marek had further committed the mistake of standing too near the packed dance floor and far too proximate to the path of Mr. Renard, who remembering Carrie from the good old days and her husband from recent, not-so-good days, convinced himself that he must take this rare opportunity to renew former acquaintances. Reeking of good booze and bad cigars, he fairly hijacked Carrie on to the dance floor. "There but for the grace of God go I," thought the otherwise quite secular Bea Levi.

As they danced—Foxy more lustfully than skillfully; Carrie feeling all too much like she was back at the Strand and not being paid for it—Foxy Renard had not noticed old comrade Edward Marek's presence, nor had he noticed Carrie Marek's growing awareness of it, for Foxy's drinking had commenced long before his arrival at Lutz's Ritz Garden. Had he been cognizant, however, of either of these occurrences, however, he would not have been pleased.

Renard was not the biggest of men, but neither was he numbered among the smallest, and he was highly physical, both with the ladies and anyone smaller than him and most particularly in protecting what he thought to be rightfully his. Right now he considered Carrie Marek in the latter category— calculating that he had earned her, or at least a dance with her, while he lay sprawled among the garbage of the Avalon Burlesque House alley. The orchestra commenced another number, and Renard was ready for another whirl. He liked to dance, after all, nearly as much as he liked to drink or rob. Carrie resisted. He gripped her hand. She acquiesced, reasoning that she might as easily well hide from Eddie in the cheek-to-cheek anonymity of a crowded dance floor as anywhere else in these fearful precincts, and perhaps, if she were lucky, to slink off to an exit from another corner of them.

It was not a sound strategy. Eddie Marek saw them return, and Vern Chapman saw him staring. Vern couldn't help but notice Eddie's eyes narrowing and his jaw tightening. His whole countenance had changed, hardened and shaken, all at the same time, as Vern had never before witnessed. Chapman did not like what he saw. Eddie Marek staring at his Carrie—*in the arms of Foxy Renard.*

"You dancing or watching tonight, Eddie?"

"Dancing!"

Marek bulled his way through the rhythm-crazed welter toward Carrie and Renard. Carrie sensed his approach. Foxy Renard did not.

"Mind if I cut in?" Eddie Marek demanded, roughly tapping his wife on the shoulder.

"Why . . . No."

She freed herself from the exceedingly startled Renard's grasp, glad of her release from Foxy's greasy hands, yet fearful of what might yet come on this night on which surprise following surprise, old acquaintance followed one upon the other, and new fears beckoned yet dangerously faster. And as for John "Foxy" Renard, unsure of what was happening, remembering with more than some unease their last encounter, he backed ever so warily away from Eddie Marek, toward the edge of the room's clamorous dance floor.

Marek and Carrie danced as they had at Coney Island years ago. They looked at each other, as if neither could believe the other still existed, let alone that they now floated in each other's arms. It seemed neither might ever speak.

What could they say?

"It is a small world," Carrie Marek said, her eyes cast downward, in this great din, nearly whispering her response.

And yet Marek heard her. He nodded his agreement.

Carrie thought of telling him that she now knew—and had known for some time—the true reason for the guns and the holdups, the truth of where she had worked, the truth of why she had written to him that horrible farewell and then, though she had wished to erase every jot of what she had written, she never felt that the person who had written it or the person who had caused Eddie his troubles would ever again prove worthy of him. She started to speak, barely knowing what her first halting syllable might be, let alone what she might finally say. She thought first of explaining why she was in the arms of Foxy Renard.

"I . . ."

Eddie Marek looked through her brown eyes and into her soul. To Carrie it seemed like he knew what she was about to say, that he somehow knew all that had transpired and no longer cared. He stared down at her, and Carrie Marek could say no more.

"I always sort of thought I'd run into you sometime, Carrie. But I didn't think it was going to be tonight."

"Well, I did not . . ."

Something in her voice set him off, suddenly and violently. Eddie Marek was a finely wound spring, and the force of this day of one horrible pressure piled upon another, and finally capped by this unimaginable surprise, had finally set him off. "Did not what? Never hoped you'd see me again? Never, thought I'd see you with Renard! Well, look again, sister! I'm here now. And maybe this is the night I square everything!" In Marek's boiling swirl of conflicting emotions, anger, fear—and resentment—had quickly bubbled to the top, exploding, overwhelming what he really felt and what he really wanted to say. His rage frightened Carrie. She had never seen him like this, never seen him like this in so many ways. She pulled away, but her body—and her heart—overruled her head.

She made no further move.

"No, Eddie, it is not that. You are wrong. You are so wrong."

And another something in her voice calmed him. "I . . . I'm sorry . . . I'm such a fool . . . . ." Eddie apologized, "I missed you so much, and now I finally get the chance to see you, and I act like this. I belong in a cage. I really do. I'm sorry."

He held her ever tighter in his arms and could not believe that his flesh—if even for this minute—now once again held hers. Carrie peered deep into his eyes, as intensely as she had ever looked at anyone in her entire life. Still, she had trouble saying much of anything. She felt no desire to pull away from him, nor he from her, though, neither would or could she imagine what the next sentence of their dialog might be, in what direction it might advance, or how it could go in any direction at all. Everything had been so long ago, so much had happened since, so much that was wrong, so much that made them different from the all-too-young people that once-upon-a-time had met, courted, married—and abandoned—each other.

"Eddie, do not say anything."

And Eddie knew he didn't have to.

Foxy Renard watched across a short, crowded, noisy distance. Were he of a more prudent nature he might have already departed Lutz's Ritz Garden, but he was not, and a different certainty now enveloped him. Tonight might be the night Foxy Renard settled everything.

Foxy weaved purposely forward, fixing his narrowed eyes upon Carrie and Eddie the whole time. Interrupting their awkward reverie, he roughly grabbed Carrie's shoulder, yanking her from Marek.

Nobody did that to Marek's wife—no matter what had come between them.

"Hey, that's no way to treat a lady, Jack!"

"Name's not Jack, pal."

When Foxy Renard went dancing, it was not without precautions. Sometimes, those precautions included a Colt Double-Action .22 caliber revolver. Tonight, said weaponry sat outside the Ritz Garden, hidden beneath the front seat of a recently ill-gotten Auburn Speedster. But in Foxy's trouser pocket was another precaution, an Italian-made, eight-inch lever lock rosewood switchblade, an elegant little implement that required no permit, just a flick of the switch to flip its blade open.

And that is exactly what he did.

It happened in a second. Renard's hand darted into his pocket for his switchblade. He flicked its switch, and plunged it deep into Eddie's shoulder. Eddie barely knew what happened. He saw Renard quickly retracting a bloody knife and felt his own gushing blood. He tumbled downward. Foxy Renard had cut something good. Something that when you hit it . . .

All the while—this brief instant—the orchestra continued playing. The crowd continued dancing. Only when Carrie screamed—a great, horrified, awful, piercing scream—did everyone and everything freeze.

Another second—another immense second—of silence followed. The crowd surged toward the scream and to a stranger lying in an ever-widening crimson pool.

Foxy Renard saw the blood. He saw his own life taking a horrible wrong turn. As the throng moved toward Marek, Renard frantically pushed back through it, fleeing from Eddie and Carrie and his own violent handiwork, shoving against a stunned mass of curious and frightened dancers, diners, and drunks. None bothered stopping him.

"Get a doctor!"

"Call the police!!"

"Stand back!"

"Don't look!!!"

Carrie Marek shouted none of those things. She cradled her bleeding husband in her arms, the crimson spreading from his suit jacket onto her satin dress.

Eddie looked upward, into her eyes.

"Can't a man dance with his wife?"

His words came slowly.

Carrie wept. His teammates struggled to keep the crowd at bay, but it swarmed forward anyway, too close and too tight. Carrie ignored them all. For all she knew, she and Eddie were alone in the world and had never been separated, by arguments, or prisons, or years.

"I am sorry. I am sorry."

"That's all right," Eddie struggled to comfort her.

"No!" she protested.

"I never was much of a husband," said Eddie, losing strength by the second, life draining from him, "I . . . disgraced . . . you. Just . . . a . . . jailbird . . ."

She shook her head. Tears cascaded down her cheeks.

"That is all right. That is done, Eddie. What is done is over." She pondered whether or not to reveal any of what *she* had done. Maybe she would someday, but not tonight, not now, with his very blood forming an ever-widening horribly red circle upon her forest green frock.

"I, ah, I . . . play . . . ball . . . now . . ."

"I know. You couldn't not miss that news."

"Think you might . . . come and see . . . me play some day?"

Carrie, tears streaming, nodded yes. Eddie Marek looked up and, in his agony, seemed finally . . . pleased.

That Room's Closed

It being a Sunday night, twenty-four hours after a dance and a knifing, and an hour from midnight, no bands played at Lutz's Ritz Garden. No couples danced. Few patrons drank at its long, dark oaken bar, and those that did imbibed listlessly. Nearby tables lay vacant. Nothing stirred across the way on the darkened, empty dance floor. At the bar one woman drank alone. She arose and moved toward the ink-black void across the threshold—into the dance hall.

The barkeep, a stout man with grayish hair combed straight back and thick rubber bands round his starched white shirtsleeves, knew her story.

"That room's closed, Miss."

She kept walking.

He knew her tale, not because she had ever shared it with him, though people always burdened him with their stories, but because he had been a part of it. He heard her scream. He answered questions from the cops. He saw the big, white ambulance drive up and drive away. He would never forget that and never forget her. It was her eyes. When the police led her away, Carrie Marek's dark brown eyes, blank and doleful, bore half the sorrows of the world. He saw those same eyes again sooner than he had ever thought he would. He saw those eyes again tonight.

"Do you want the light on?"

She didn't answer. He flipped the switch anyway.

She knew she must be somewhere, to mark the evening some way. This was appropriate a spot as any, the only place since Sing Sing they had ever shared. She sat in a booth decorated by a single wilting yellow rose. From her purse, she removed a small velvet pouch and grasped it tight.

And felt two golden bands within.

Dance Hall

The midday sun shone brilliantly at Sing Sing, transforming gray stone to blinding, almost glowing, white, glimmering upon the Hudson, reflecting off its whitecaps, like the luminous morning shafts that poured into Grand Central more than half-a-hundred months ago.

That light, so bright in early afternoon, slipped away, to a night far darker than usual.

Stewart Beck dined with Father Gelasius. This meal, in its solitude and its seriousness, seemed particularly grim.

This night was an execution night.

All executions seemed different and all the same, but this one was more unsettling than most, though Beck possessed no particular sympathy for the accused.

The condemned himself exhibited particular nervousness. Some men await their fate with resignation and dignity, a few with odd anticipation.

Foxy Renard did not.

He was not popular, though popularity had never been an essential on death row. No death room inmates rubbed elbows with the general population. None were there very long by prison standards—or would be.

Neither would Foxy Renard.

In fact, he had already departed—into the Dance Hall.

Men had the opportunity to think in the Dance Hall, though not for long. Renard pondered how unfair it all was, the cruel prank fate had played upon him by sending Eddie Marek—and Foxy Renard—into the Ritz Garden that evening. *Why had Marek cut in like that? Foxy's life could have continued uninterrupted—the gin joints, the dances, the rackets, the women. Everybody's life could have continued. Damn that Polack. Damn that two-bit whore.*

Stewart Beck and Father Gelasius silently traversed the ghostly shadows that enveloped the great, empty moonlit—and searchlight-lit—expanse between the Main Gate and the Death House. With each step they took, great white snowflakes drifted downward, settling one upon the other on their severe wide-brimmed hats and heavy woolen overcoats, and providing a promise of a white Christmas, that some would enjoy and one man would not enjoy, in the days to come.

"Evening Warden. Evening Father."

"Good Evening, Eddie."

Edward Stanley Marek Jr. had not bled to death on the scuffed dance floor of Lutz's Ritz Garden.

Foxy Renard had not murdered him.

He had murdered someone else.

That evening, a cop, having vaguely remembered hearing something about a stolen Auburn Speedster with Queens plates, had pulled Renard over as he sped away from the Ritz Garden. Renard retrieved his Colt Double-Action revolver, and when Patrolman James Corcoran, approached his car, Renard, nervous as a cat, aimed his gun through the rolled-down window, jerked the trigger, and shot Corcoran stone cold dead—a .22 caliber slug in the face, a widow, three children, and a police pension, left behind.

Renard's switchblade had done its work too. It had cut deep enough into blood to nearly kill Marek and deep enough into muscle to sap Eddie's batting of its power and turn his once powerful throwing arm into one that simply wasn't good enough for professional baseball. Eddie's career—nine innings long—was over.

Stewart Beck had found a spot for him—as Sing Sing's athletic director. It was an unusual hire, a con working inside a prison, but Eddie had been an unusual con, and Stewart Beck remained, as ever, was a most unorthodox warden.

No crowds would now cheer Eddie Marek. No chance of glory at Ebbets Field or even Baker Bowl awaited him. He would teach and guide cons like himself—some who wanted to better themselves and some who never would.

He had been granted a remarkable opportunity, but one not so extraordinary as what now transpired, to pass in the December night before two men dispatched to execute the man who had betrayed him each step along the way and who on that final step had shoved eight inches of sharpened steel into his flesh, to send blood mingled with dreams oozing out onto dancehall hardwood. Eddie Marek, freezing hands jammed into his greatcoat, grim eyes semi-obscured by snow falling ever heavier, mutely peered at Beck and Gelasius's taut and mute faces. So many thoughts filled his soul, of pain and betrayal, and the actions he must take, of what he must do, if not for others than for himself. But no thoughts translated themselves into actions or even words—at least none he might now safely reveal. He nodded, merely stammering some indefinable greeting—or was it some farewell?—before broodingly padding off into competing realms of darkness and light, between the jet black sky and the alabaster whiteness of immense searchlight-illuminated snowflakes, between hungering for vengeance and hungering for peace.

Foxy Renard, for his part, had not requested Father Gelasius's presence. In fact, he had bluntly told him his attendance wasn't needed. Priests were for old women and suckers, and Foxy Renard had figured out their game long ago. But Gelasius had a job to do, and it didn't just involve saving the souls of punks like Foxy Renard. It had to do with being there for his friend Stewart Beck.

Beck and Gelasius knew what to say to Renard—the same script they had followed with a hundred other of the condemned.

Foxy Renard also knew what to say to them.

"You understand, he should never have cut in on me."

"But what about the cop?" Beck asked.

"Oh, yeah, the cop, well . . . "

"Have you anything to confess, my son?" asked Father Gelasius. He hoped the answer he received wasn't the one he was expecting. Renard, surprised by the question, shook his head. He thought he had already told Gelasius that. Didn't the man listen? Priests—and confessions—were for suckers.

Foxy Renard was no sucker.

Gelasius took a new tack.

"John, do you remember the parable of the harvest?"

"No," said Renard, his eyes narrowing with aggrieved annoyance.

"You know you do—the one where the workers who are hired at the end of the day are paid the same as those who started at the dawn."

"Yeah," said Renard. It *did* sound sort of sort familiar.

Gelasius had an idea. If he wasn't going to get perfect contrition from this weasel, he'd at least take a shot at a highly imperfect contrition.

"The workers who have been breaking their backs all day," he continued, "feel like suckers because the fellows who join up right at the end—fellows like you—receive the same pay from the master. You can receive the same payoff, the very same reward, Foxy. The Lord is a generous, forgiving master. It's not too late.

"The same deal John. Remember the deal you cut on the Amsterdam Avenue job? It's never too late to come to work on the harvest. You'd be surprised at the people who come to the harvest far later than they should have—and have been forgiven for it."

Here, Gelasius paused, realizing that he wasn't just talking about some death row convict—or about any mumbling, stammering penitent on the other side of his confessional screen. No, he wasn't really speaking about them at all.

"Cut a deal, John. It's a smart proposition."

Renard looking like that might be sinking in—but maybe it wasn't. Who knew what he thought. Gelasius reached back. He kept pitching: "Surely, you recall another parable, that of the Prodigal Son—the same moral. Most people just remember the fatted calf and how the son is forgiven. But remember how cheesed off his older brother was? The Lord keeps making the same point over and over again because He means it. The deal's always on the table—for the late comer as well as for anyone. And if anybody else doesn't care for it—tough beans! But He wants a little something from you. A deal's a two-way street after all, John. Make the deal!"

Renard mulled that over. He liked the thought of putting something over on all the Holy Joes who'd been hauling their carcasses out of bed for 6:00 A.M. Mass every Sunday and Holy

Day of Obligation and choking on mackerel bones every Friday. They'd been keeping their noses clean and, now, those same clean noses would be out of joint at the idea of St. Foxy of Greenpoint. Hah! That's the ticket, he thought, and then he thought again.

"Nah . . . Father . . . nah. . . . That's not for Foxy Renard."

Why do I try? thought Gelasius, *Why do I try?*

He heard a voice from behind.

"Warden . . . Father . . ."

Was it?

"Marek!" Stewart Beck bellowed, "What are you doing here? Nobody's allowed in here without my permission—particularly *you*!"

"I . . . ," Marek, now standing just beyond Renard's open cell door, began uncertainly, "I have something to say to Foxy."

No steel bars separated Renard and Marek.

Only life.

Only death.

"Spit it out," sneered Renard before Beck could respond, "You haven't got long."

"I just wanted to say, Foxy, that there's no hard feelings about anything—the knifing or nothing. No, what's done is done.

"I forgive you. And I will pray for you."

"You forgive me!" Foxy shot back.

Eddie didn't say anything, nor did Warden Beck or Father Gelasius. But Principal Keeper McKaig thought this little scene had already gone on long enough and looked toward Beck, anticipating an OK to shut it all down and usher Eddie out of the Dance Hall. Beck, with the slightest motion of his eyes, indicated otherwise.

"You forgive me for knifing you?" asked Foxy, suddenly much quieter.

"Yes."

"And for that little conversation we had at the New Savoy?"

"Yes."

"Why?"

"Why not, Foxy? Hating never did anybody any good."

"Even with your career down the crapper?"

"Even that."

"Ah, get this guy out of here, Warden!" snapped Renard, "I've got business to take care of."

"OK, Marek! You heard him," thundered Beck, "I'll take that as a last request. Scram!" His words were tough, but not very deep down within he was proud of what Eddie Marek had done.

When Eddie was out of sight and out of earshot, Renard turned to Gelasius.

"That deal you offered me, Father, is it still good?"

"It's always good, my son."

Tears welled up within Foxy's eyes.

"If you don't mind, gentlemen . . ." Gelasius asked Beck and McKaig, and when Renard had finished his confession, he said, "Father, can I ask you a favor?"

"Of course, John."

"Tell that Polack I forgive him too."

A guard placed a sponge soaked with salt water upon Renard's head. He fit a metal skullcap over it. He blindfolded him, fastened solid leather straps across his chest, then slit his pants legs to attach electrodes to patches of shaved skin on his legs. He used a special cream—ElectroCream—to affix the electrodes, to make things go smoothly—for the soon-to-be deceased and the uncomfortable onlookers.

And as Sing Sing's power supply strained and shuddered and cracked as 2,450 volts sizzled through Foxy Renard's body, it created a brief chalice of prison-wide darkness, before flashing back on and silhouetting its cramped cellblocks and deadly guard towers and crumbling brick walls in a luminosity Eddie had never before witnessed as he walked toward Sing Sing's broad main gate.

For so many nights, that gate's immense steel arms had seemed—and were—so completely impenetrable, but now they swung open and granted safe passage to Eddie Marek, no longer in gray hickory but in Prison Department blue, as he passed freely through them and returned home for the evening.

Walking in another door, this one of white-painted wood and lace-trimmed glass.

Home for the evening.

Magic words.

Home, the most ordinary and magical place of all creation.

Home.

To Carrie.

"May I . . ." he asked as he walked through that white wooden door, ". . . may I have this dance, Miss?"

"Yes, corporal, yes, you may."

ABOUT THE AUTHOR

David Pietrusza is the award-winning author of *1920: The Year of the Six Presidents; 1948: Harry Truman's Improbable Victory and the Year that Transformed America; 1960—LBJ vs. JFK vs. Nixon: The Epic Campaign That Forged Three Presidencies,* and *Silent Cal's Almanack: The Homespun Wit & Wisdom of Vermont's Calvin Coolidge.*

Pietrusza's biography of Arnold Rothstein, entitled *Rothstein: The Life, Times & Murder of the Criminal Genius Who Fixed the 1919 World Series,* was an Edgar Award finalist. *Rothstein's* audio version captured an AUDIOFILE Earphones Award.

His *Judge and Jury,* a biography of baseball's first commissioner, Judge Kenesaw Mountain Landis, received the CASEY Award and was also a finalist for the Seymour Medal and nominated for the NASSH Book Award.

Pietrusza has been featured on The Fox News Network, NPR, C-SPAN BookTV, C-SPAN American History TV, MSNBC, The History Channel, ESPN, and The Voice of America. He has served as a regular panelist on FoxNews.com.

He is the former national president of the Society for American Baseball Research (SABR) and the former co-editor of *Total Baseball: The Official Encyclopedia of Major League Baseball.*

He is the Recipient of the 2011 Excellence in Arts & Letters Award of the Alumni Association of the University at Albany.

Printed in Great Britain
by Amazon.co.uk, Ltd.,
Marston Gate.